THE
FIRST CASUALTY

MIKE MOSCOE

ACE BOOKS, NEW YORK

THE FIRST CASUALTY

An Ace Book / published by arrangement with
the author

PRINTING HISTORY
Ace mass-market edition / January 1999

The Penguin Putnam Inc. World Wide Web site address is
http://www.penguinputnam.com

ISBN: 0-441-00593-4

ACE®
Ace Books are published
by The Berkley Publishing Group,
a member of Penguin Putnam Inc.,
375 Hudson Street, New York, New York 10014.
ACE and the "A" design are trademarks
belonging to Charter Communications, Inc.

PRINTED IN THE UNITED STATES OF AMERICA

10 9 8 7 6 5 4 3 2 1

Ace Books by Mike Moscoe

FIRST DAWN
SECOND FIRE
LOST DAYS
THE FIRST CASUALTY

Dedicated to
Lieutenant Robert A. Heinlein, USN, deceased,
who showed us how it was done

To
Lieutenant Commander Loren J. Moscoe, USN Ret.,
who taught me what it meant,
and made me mad enough to learn a hell of a lot

To
Lieutenant Commander Michael J. Brennan, USN Ret.,
and the crew at work who kept this book honest,
as much as they could

And to
Ellen
who keeps all the different parts of me together.

THE
FIRST CASUALTY

ONE

EVERY ALARM IN Sergeant Mary Rodrigo's space suit went off at once. Red lights flashed on her eyeball as her heads-up display demanded her attention. She ignored them.

Mary had five moles laying a minefield for her. Mines were tricky beasts. Laying a field from underground was a tight bitch, not to be left to unsupervised remotes. Twitching her right hand, she froze them in place.

Mary twisted her right wrist and blinked twice, cycling her heads-up display to the screen her alarms were so hot on. The newly deployed infrared sensors were screaming about hot targets. *But there weren't supposed to be any—yet!*

She chinned her mike to a new channel. "Lek, we got a problem. Either our sensors are spooked, or the colonials got here without you knowing."

"Not bloody likely," the old guy said with a chuckle. "Check the angles from the two outer sensors, girl. We've picked up the Colly attack fleet coming around Elmo Four!"

"Acid crap," Mary swore. "They're that sensitive!"

"Bet they made a fuel scoop and got their balloon heat shields out," Dumont said beside her, "What a ride for real, not just a vid-game," the young man from the streets said wistfully.

"I better pass this to the LT," Mary growled. "Let's get back to the mines." In the end, even Dumont and his street kids had voted her for sergeant, but that didn't mean he couldn't give her plenty of lip before he did what she said. Today, without a word, Dumont went back to putting in mines. On the other side of Mary, reliable Cassie had never quit work on the minefield.

Mary switched to the command channel. "Lieutenant, we got targets."

"Sergeant, where the hell have you been? What?" His voice died in mid-question as Mary passed through the visual. "What . . . Where . . . How . . . ?" he stammered.

"This is Major Henderson at battalion. What have you got for me?" So the battalion CO was lurking on their command channel, or had an alert on it. Considering all the lurking and alerts Lek had rigged through the brigade's net, Mary had no complaint.

She shut up; let the young officer talk to the man. Only when the wait stretched and started to bend did she speak. "Our infrared sensors have picked up the colonials coming around Elmo Four. We don't have an ETA on them," she said, though she suspected Lek did by now. No need telling management what they didn't want to hear from dumb worker bees.

"Brigade finally risked a radar sweep about the time the bandits went behind the gas giant," battalion drawled. "I'll pass this report along. Colonials are right on schedule."

Which was not what the command net had been saying for the last fifteen hours. Lek had warned Mary not to believe the official word from HQ. She'd learned long ago not to trust what a foreman said. The old electronic wizard had been passing along to Mary and the rest of the unemployed miners the straight dope.

Battalion signed off; the young LT found his voice.

"Sergeant, what the hell is going on here? We've got to talk."

What the sergeant had going on here was her own usual go at making everyone happy, to give the LT what he wanted, and the rest of the platoon what they wanted. What Mary wanted was to be light-years away from all this with a beer in one hand and a warm hunk on her shoulder. But today, nobody was getting what they wanted. With a sigh, Mary got ready for a long talk.

Captain Anderson, commander, 97th Defense Brigade, frowned at his screen. "Since when does a leg infantry platoon have infrared sensors that good? Not that I'm complaining, but . . ."

His XO, Commander Inez Umboto, grinned at the display, showing no sign of surprise. "Half the troops of that platoon are out-of-work miners. Remember the complaints you fielded from several mine administrators about missing equipment, even a jet cart?"

"God, those things are expensive. Even the Navy can't afford 'em. Though I'd love to have one."

Inez's grin dripped admiration for the culprits. "You may. Each company of the First of the Eighty-eighth has one platoon heavy with miners. All three weighed in heavy at boarding but not enough to complain about." She paused for a moment. "You remember how tickled Comm was to get all those extra channels. It was an old miner, pulling boards from a 'damaged parts' box, that got them for us."

Captain Anderson raised an eyebrow. "You didn't tell me."

"Sir, a good exec doesn't bother her boss with the details."

"What else haven't you bothered me with, Izzy?"

"I wish I knew. There's a shitpot of stuff out there, and I've only scratched the surface. Despite the rumors, I am only human and rarely can be in more than three places at once."

Anderson ignored the humor; today he needed an exec who could be in a dozen places at once. Scowling down at his command display, he shook his head. He'd fought the coming battle hundreds of times in his forty-year career—on the computer display.

Now he was fighting it for real, and it was going wrong in ways even the craziest umpire would not have thrown at him in a war game. Why had a picketboat been waiting for them the moment they jumped into this worthless system? Why was a major colonial force reacting in only seventy-two hours?

He'd expected problems on his side. Lasers were missing parts; power plants were missing cables; crates were miscoded, misplaced, or just plain missing. Most of his grunts were ransacking containers, chasing the critical parts he needed to get the central defenses up. Without them, the colonials could land smack dab in the middle of his base crater. He'd expected time to work all this out. Only one platoon from each company had been shoved forward to block the three cracks in the crater wall.

Everything had gone too fast or too wrong. Maybe, just maybe, the sensors from that platoon would let him give the colonials a surprise or two.

Mary took a deep breath and tried to give the lieutenant an answer he'd like. "I set up the sensors you ordered, sir." She keyed up the different coverages she'd deployed: video, thermal, radar, electromagnetic. She ignored the Navy issue crap—they were too big and too noisy to be anything but targets.

"We don't have all that gear, Sergeant. How'd you do it?"

That was two questions. Mary chose to answer the easy one. With a flick of her wrist, she called up the schematic of the crater rim and the array she'd dug through it. "I used diggers from the mines to set this up. I got the place covered."

She activated the laser designators one by one, let them

sweep the broken ground in front of the pass the platoon was ordered to hold at all cost.

"By God, you do have it covered." The LT whistled. "But how? The engineers are still at brigade. How'd you do this?"

Mary let her breath out slowly. How do you explain to a kid that never wanted to be anything but a toy soldier what it's like to spend twenty years of your life in the astcroid mines, to never want to be anything but a miner? And to get your pink slip and draft notice in the same envelope. "Our last shift at the mine, we figured if something might save our life, and it wasn't welded to the deck, we might as well borrow it. Boss men had just installed a lot of new equipment." Which was why they could afford to let half their workforce go—the senior half. They'd gotten all kind of media plaudits . . . and ignored the seniority clause of their labor contract.

Mary shrugged, or tried to. Armored space suits didn't allow much body language. "Who knows what was gonna be surplus, anyway?" Mary knew damn well the old equipment had already been sold off. She and the other members of her investment club had wanted to buy it. They were close, so close to setting up their own mine, having their own place, being their own people. But the gear went without an auction. And Mary and her friends got themselves a war.

So Mary had walked off her last shift with a jet cart.

"We're about done with the minefield," Mary finished.

"Hurry up and get back here," the LT answered.

Now Mary did fidget. "Sir, remember our deal."

"What part of it?" The LT's voice was cautious.

The first time Mary was elected sergeant had been a joke, a setup by a tough drill instructor to break his ex-civilians of their easygoing ways. The miners voted for her; Dumont's kids voted for him, but there were more miners. Mary was supposed to fall flat on her face. Instead, she'd found what it took to pull this angry bunch of people together. Sometimes begging, sometimes cajoling, sometimes threatening, they'd coalesced into a team for her. Maybe not the team the DI had in mind, but a team that pulled together when they had to.

The lieutenant had shadowed the platoon the last few days of boot camp, long enough to see how things were. Then he'd taken Mary aside. "You know how to work this bunch," he'd said.

"Seems that way," she'd answered cautiously.

"I know how to fight. You know how to make them work. Together, we can get them out of this war alive. If anybody can. You game to work with me?"

He'd been the first to even mention survival; she'd taken his offered hand. For the last two months they'd been a team. Now, she'd find out just how far she could stretch it.

"Lieutenant, I can't leave this network I've built. In the mines, you get too far away from the work, something goes wrong and you can't fix it. From here I can fix anything."

"Sergeant, I've told you a dozen times, your job is to tell other people what to do. Assign somebody to stay out there."

"Can't sir. If it's too dangerous for me, it's too dangerous for anyone." She had a long wait for his answer.

"You dug in good?" he asked.

Mary glanced around the cavern she and Cassie had turned into an observation post—maybe a tomb. Once the servos swung the half-meter-thick stone back, it would be well closed. A billion years ago when the crater was made, a pinnacle had slid from the still molten rock. It sheltered her outpost from observation from across the plain where the attack would come. "Dug in as good as time allows, sir."

There was a long pause. "Okay, Mary, you win this one. Why didn't you tell me what you had in mind?"

"Sir, you said you didn't want anyone on this side of the rim, just a few sensors. In the mines, when management makes up its mind, they don't want more talk."

"What I meant, Sergeant, was I wanted all of the platoon

behind the rim, where their artillery couldn't wipe us out. Maybe I didn't say it as well as I should have. When this is over, we've got to talk about how to talk."

"Yes, sir." Mary said. Talking was what she had in mind. She checked the one digger. Her best, it was halfway across the plain, towing one of Lek's fiber-optic patch lines behind it. If it did its job, even secure communications wouldn't keep Mary and the rest of the miners from having a talk with the colonials before anybody got killed.

"Captain Anderson, sensors here. My witches have something we think you'll like."

"Did she say bitches?" Umboto grinned.

"Down, Commander, we've got a fight coming, and that college professor is on our side."

"Oh, right, I keep forgetting," the commander mumbled.

The captain tapped the comm portion of his board. "Commander Miller, what have you got for me?"

Immediately his board changed to display the gas giant and their moon. Three red lines inched from the giant toward them. "The colonial ships are right on schedule. I expect the vanguard in sixteen minutes. The main body is ninety seconds behind them, led by a pair of superheavy cruisers. *Jane's Fighting Ships* says they have an even dozen nine-point-two-inch laser cannons." Only three months from college lecture halls, Miller did slip easily into lecture mode. Commander Umboto hated it. Captain Anderson put up with it. "There are two more heavy cruisers with eight-inchers. Rest are light cruisers with six-inchers. They're in three lines abreast."

"Probably plan to flatten us in one pass," the XO observed.

"I agree with Commander Umboto," Miller said.

That had to be the first time the two women had agreed on anything. Anderson wished they'd picked a better subject. "I concur," he said. And if they flattened the 97th, the only defenses left to Pitt's Hope would be those in the Pitt system. A major industrial and population center like Pitt's Hope had to be defended here, at least one system out, where the collateral damage from rockets and lasers wouldn't kill a million people. The problem was how to defend this worthless bit of rock. "XO, how's my Crossbow Project coming?"

The commander's smile was all teeth as she snapped to and gave him a drill field salute. "Ancient as you are, sir, but ready at your command."

"I just hope they're as good. Sensors, I need fast and accurate altitude information."

"Not going to be as easy as I'd hoped," Miller answered. "They just dumped their scoop balloon shields and fell off the infrared scanners."

Inez and the captain exchanged nods; that was a critical requirement. No commander willingly took a big, hot flag into a fight, but if he didn't have spare shields, an admiral might have to. This one had dumped his, and was shooting right into Anderson's trap. *Assuming I haven't set a fox trap for a bear.*

Unaware of the silent communication between the captain and his XO, Miller continued. "That infantry platoon has some damn fine sensors. We've hyped up the gain on the video and are tracking the Unity fleet, but, Captain, these bastards are coming on fast. They're not going to make any sudden changes."

Anderson nodded. "At my age, predictable is nice. Even dull would be fine. But let's not assume anything, keep the reports coming." He turned to Inez. "I need you at Crossbow."

"That's where I'm headed."

What Anderson really needed was a battle squadron riding top cover for him. "Where is my damn Navy?" he muttered.

Captain Mattim Abeeb needed for nothing. He had a beer, a quiet corner in a relaxed bar . . . and three active readers. Everything he needed for another long evening studying what the Navy thought a drafted skipper needed to know.

Then Buck Ramsey stormed through the barroom door.

"Damn the Navy. Damn them all to hell. First they commandeer my ship. Then they blow it to hell."

A dozen other merchant officers, also cramming for the Navy commissions they'd been impressed into, glanced up, but Buck locked eyes with Mattim. "I've pushed that ship through space for ten years without a scratch. They have her three months and she's gone." He stumbled toward Mattim.

Mattim put down his beer, pushed his readers aside, and made ready to give Buck his full attention. If the Navy so much as dented his *Maggie D* during the overhaul they were giving her, Mattim would not stop at a bar. He'd head for Navy headquarters with a bomb in his hip pocket.

"What happened?" he asked as Buck plopped into his booth.

"That damn power plant, Matt. They're strapping half of a gigawatt dirtside power plant onto our ships."

"Certainly your engineer . . ."

"Daisy quit over Navy guff. They gave me one of theirs to replace her. 'Top of the line,' they told me. 'Knows everything there is about power plants.' Well, he's learning how to dodge pitchforks now, 'cause he blew the whole stern of my ship to hell. Every one of my engineers . . . except Daisy."

Buck was running out of steam; in a moment the full meaning of his words would slam into him. A waitress showed up dressed in a smile and not much else. Her lack of attire was lost on Mattim and Buck. Anger was crumbling into grief as it hit the captain just how many of his old crew were dead. Mattim spoke without taking his eyes off his friend. "Whiskey. Irish whiskey. Your best."

"The bottle," Buck added. "Dear God, Matt, all of them."

Mattim watched helpless as tears rolled down his fellow captain's cheeks. On the vid above the bar, it was halftime at the zero-g lacrosse game. A grinning announcer told them the evening news had first vids of the marine landing in the next star system out. "An impregnable defense that will keep any rim crazies from getting close to Pitt's Hope."

"Bloody damn hope so, 'cause there's no fucking Navy," a civvy at the bar mumbled . . . loud enough that the officers in training had no trouble hearing.

Mattim got an arm around Buck's shoulders just fast enough to keep his friend in his seat. Still, Matt had to agree with the dirtbag. Until the Navy quit wasting time teaching merchant captains what they'd learned twenty years ago. Until the Navy turned loose the engineers like his own Ivan who knew the power plant of his ship better than his wife's body, the Navy was going to get junk, not the made-over warships they wanted.

And the marines would be on their own.

The bottle arrived. He and Buck began the long, slow process of getting the pain out.

Sergeant Mary Rodrigo edged her mole a fraction higher, checking the echo carefully. There was still two centimeters of dirt between it and the surface of the pass. She backed it out and had it shove the mine back where it had been. To any surface scan, the gap was as virgin as it had been a billion years ago when the cooling rock of the rim cracked and split open.

Good.

"Old lady, what we gonna do?" Dumont was the coolest of the kids, which was why they followed him. Now he was one of Mary's corporals and had listened in on the channel Lek used to pass along what was really happening. He knew the colonials were due any time now, and the rest of the company was a long way out. "I mean, some of those Colly troops were killing people before us street kids were hatched. They gonna stomp right over us and not even slow down. We got to get gone from here."

If they ran, they'd die. "Du," Mary cajoled, "we've dug you good solid holes with the mining gears. Hunker down. If we hang together, we can make it through together." How many times had Mary said that? In the mines it worked. Would it work on a battlefield?

"You old folks always got something up your sleeves. What you dreamed up this time?"

Mary never lied to Cassie, Lek, or other miners who'd saved her ass too often to count. The same didn't apply to Dumont and his kids. Still, she'd rather distract him than lie to him. "You seen the minefield. You know the sensors I've put up. Your girls got us the extra rockets."

"Yeah, some of the girls traded real nice for that shit. But none of us gonna die for that joking green flag." Dumont shook his head; most of the movement was lost in the suit.

Mary hadn't asked how Dumont's girls got the extra gear, especially the big rockets. She was willing to do anything to see her team come out of this alive; they were too. Maybe Dumont deserved the whole truth; Mary checked to make sure she was on one of Lek's very private channels. "Maybe we can talk to the colonials before the shooting starts. Maybe we don't have to kill each other."

"You think so?" Dumont didn't sound nearly as happy about the prospect as Mary had expected. "Them Colly goons don't stop to ask no questions. They just roll up to you and over."

"I heard that too. We'll try to catch them early. And we got enough here to slow them down. Maybe to talk to them. If not, to stop them. Trust me, Du, we're gonna get through this."

"I'm thinking maybe we just might," the kid said softly.

"I'm thinking the last mine's in and we ought to get back." Cassie broke from her concentration, her right hand the only part of her moving as she supervised her moles. She stretched tall, then wide. "Sure you don't want company?" Cassie offered. "It's gonna get lonesome out here."

Mary owed her life to Cassie too many times to count, and she'd returned the favor often enough. It would be good to have someone here, someone to talk to when the time got slow, someone to share the burden with when it got through to Mary what she was doing, really doing. "Thanks, Cassie. You're good, but I got to do this one myself. No sharing."

"God go with you," Cassie whispered as she gave Mary a hug, battle armor to battle armor, and ducked out the hole and onto the jet cart.

Dumont clapped Mary on the shoulder. "Suit looks good. Take care, Sergeant," and he was gone.

As Mary ordered the jacks to swivel the massive stone door closed and settle it solidly in place, it dawned on her. That was the first time Dumont had ever called her "Sergeant" when the lieutenant wasn't listening. "He picked a hell of a time to get respectful," she muttered through a grin.

Mary cycled her heads-up display through the sensor coverage of the gap and both sides of the crater rim. Her diggers were charged; if she had to juggle something, she was ready. Thanks to the jet cart, there were no footprints on this side of the rim. She switched to a view of the platoon. Using the excavator from the mine, everyone was dug in solid. The LT had planned to use the rill for cover. Half the platoon was still dug in there, but two squads now were scattered behind it. Good.

But sensors showed an awful lot of tracks pointing to where the fire teams had gone to ground. Mary wasn't the only one checking. "Sergeant, you on line yet?"

"Yes, Lieutenant."

"We need to dust this place. Make footprints disappear."

"Yes, sir. Nan, use the cart and all the nitrogen we got left. Blow away the footprints and cool down any hot spots. I'll pass you the sensor picture."

"Will do, boss."

On Mary's screen, Nan was out, gliding over the ground in the cart, blowing compressed nitrogen. The lieutenant was also up, walking toward the crest of the gap.

"Lieutenant?"

"Sergeant, I'd like to see the other side, too. You can't

have all the fun." This was the kid's first battle; she'd heard the longing in his voice as he talked about it. She'd needed the same chance to taste the ground, get the feel of how the battle would unfold. The kid was green as slime, but not dumb.

"Aye, aye, Lieutenant. I've turned the mines off."

"Lek showed me your plan. You've set up a good attrition field, Sergeant. Thin them down before we hit them. You dug in deep?" The video showed him standing at the crest, slowly turning his suit to take in the scene before him.

"Pretty deep, sir, in a cavern with a half-meter-thick stone covering the entrance."

"Skunks, five minutes out," the command circuit interrupted. "Everyone to cover."

"Well, everything's done." The Lieutenant turned and started a low-gravity hop down the gap. "Now we do our duty. See you when we're done, Sergeant."

"Yes, sir," Mary said. One way or the other, she would.

Major Ray Longknife sat, his back ramrod straight. From the spare seat on the bridge of the Unity attack transport *Friendship* he had a good view—of the red Unity banner with its yellow lightning bolt painted on the ship's nose, and the blinking displays that made his hands clench into fists. *The Navy was screwing the ground-pounders—again!*

The admiral had promised a cakewalk when he'd ordered the 2nd Guard Assault Brigade aboard ship on an hour's notice. "We'll blow those Earthie scum away with relativity bombs, and seize Pitt's Hope before they know what hit them."

Well, the relativity bombs hadn't hit a damn thing. He'd known they were in trouble when Rita—correction, Senior Pilot Nuu—lowered her beautiful eyes at the admiral's bloody optimism. She'd explained during the three-day run out here that the jump point they'd be using was horribly unstable. She'd been right.

Every ship exited the jump point on a different heading. Each captain followed his orders and launched bombs as soon as he was through and before slowing. None hit even close to where ever so slight hints suggested his enemy was. *Damn!*

The jump had one benefit. Scattered and low on fuel, the fleet had made a scoop pass on the gas giant. That at least slowed the damn Navy down. The cruisers' lasers might actually hit something on their firing pass.

"Quixote." Ray snarled the code word. On that order, the admiral would drop the 2nd right in the crater the Earthies were using for their defense. Did he really expect grunts to tilt with windmills and win? There was a second code word, Rosebud, to land the transports outside the crater. One site would even save them a low pass across the Earth defenses. Ray and Senior Pilot Nuu both voted for Rosebud One. Quixote and Rosebud. Computer-generated code names; Ray doubted the admiral even knew who Don Quixote was. He also doubted the admiral had any idea what he was sending the 2nd Guard up against.

Then again, neither did Ray. That was the problem. Wait until you know more, and you'd face more. Boot the Earth hirelings before they dug in, and he might get the easy win the admiral wanted. The 2nd was a proud outfit; it had never lost a battle. Ray would not be its first CO to break that record.

Carefully, Mary settled into an almost comfortable slouch. Whoever designed battle suits had made them great for running, leaping, killing. They hadn't put much thought into "hurry up and wait." The status lights of the gear around her provided the only light in the cavern. Mary waited; it couldn't be long now.

As the now stretched into a private eternity, Mary found herself with time on her hands and the first time to think in way too long. *What are you doing here, girl?*

Mary scowled at herself. *I'm no girl, and the question has too many answers.*

She was here because she had no choice. A couple of kids from Dumont's gang ran after they got their boot camp "haircut." Their bodies were found the next day, throats slit, decorated with little green flags and a note from the "Patriots for Humanity."

Nobody'd been arrested for the murders.

That night, the platoon talked it out after lights out. Dumont and the other kids wanted to go over the wall, head for the hills until the war was over. When Cassie asked them if any of 'em had ever hunted or eaten roots, they got quiet and sullen.

Some of the miners wanted to strike. Lek asked them to read their labor contract, then unfolded his enlistment papers. "Nothin' in here about a labor rep, but it do say we got to obey the orders of our superior officers. I checked. They can shoot us if we don't."

"They can't shoot all of us," someone in back whined.

"Two kids ran, two kids dead. How many of you got wives that will raise a stink?" Lek asked. "Got family that have any say at the Commissioner's Office?"

About that time it had dawned on Mary. Slowly she'd stood. "We got nobody," she said, looking around the room. "Nobody out there." She jerked a thumb at the rest of the world. "But we do got somebody. We got each other." She opened her arms like some kind of corner preacher—only she felt it. "We got to look out for each other, 'cause sure as pay's gonna be shorted, nobody else gonna look out for us. We can't get out of this. But we can get through it. We can if we do it together."

Which had probably been her first step on the way to being the platoon's sergeant. Cassie told her, after the vote, "We need a ma. You're the closest some of us will ever come to one." That had to be a laugh; Mary had never known her own ma or pa.

So, to keep her friends alive, Mary was here, getting ready to kill a lot of people in a war that didn't mean a damn. And when it was over, the only jobs open would probably be farther out in what was now enemy space. Why not do the job-hunting as prisoners of war? Mary checked; the digger burrowing under the plain was about four klicks out, halfway to the escarpment. "Hurry up, little mole. If they ain't using radios, your little wire patch may be the only way we can get a word in edgewise."

TWO

SENIOR PILOT RITA Nuu liked having Major Ray Longknife on her bridge. It hadn't always been so. He'd done a good imitation of a horse's rear end the first time he crossed her bridge coaming. As the senior woman in Wardhaven's attack transport squadron, she was used to male disapproval. It had taken her a while to realize that his attitude had nothing to do with her and everything to do with his beloved brigade. Once that was straightened out, she discovered she actually liked the guy. Love came later.

They had discovered, both on and off ship, that working together was far more fun than fussing. At the moment, Rita was putting the major's position to good use for her squadron. As usual, the admiral didn't think the transports needed to know boo. However, Longknife's access to the command net was displayed on her heads-up. It helped to know what the hell was happening.

To Rita's right, Junior Pilot Cadow had the conn; his hands showed white knuckles on the stick. Technician Hesper did double duty behind Rita, running the electronic countermeasures stations and communications. Ray rode the jump seat behind Cadow, his portable battle station linked with the *Friendship*'s.

"The destroyers in the van are going in," the major reported. "The *Dry Lightning* is low. The *Stormy Night* is high. Should have visuals and sensors sixty seconds before the cruisers start dusting down the crater." Again Rita wished they had a cruiser attached to the transports. Setting down in that crater five minutes after the cruisers shot it up and two hours before they'd be back was not her idea of smart.

Rita eyed two data screens. One showed strung-out lights representing the gun line. The other waited for sensor data on their target.

The rocket was old, and the dumbest of the dumb. In its nose was a tiny proximity fuse to tell it to blow up a few meters above the ground, scattering its plastic flechettes in a deadly cloud to puncture battle suits or thin-skinned vehicles. Today, the proximity fuse was disabled.

Today, it simply waited for the backup timer to tick away the seconds as its motors blasted at full power. The tiny brain did face a challenge, though. The weight distribution of the rocket was off. The simpleminded CPU had to adjust the rocket nozzles again and again until the missile took on a slight spin. The dumb control unit had not intended the spin, but it did make its job simpler.

The source of the rocket's problem, if it had been wise enough to seek out and solve problems, was a collar that had been added around its payload section. A thick cylinder of sand, barely held together by glue, covered the entire warhead.

Two of the rockets shed their dusty mantles. Three more could not solve the problems created by them and wandered off on their own track. None of them heard Commander Umboto's proud shout. "Crossbows away, Captain. Thirty-one running hot, straight and normal."

"What's that?" Rita and Ray asked at the same moment.

Hesper worked her board with quick, deft fingers. "Stealthy something, not well guided. They'll miss the destroyers by a wide margin. Doubt if the cans'll waste a shot on them."

"Hope all their defenses are as shabby," Rita prayed.

The first sensor reports came in—video of the crater. A couple of piles of ice stood out, but they looked like ship armor that had been dumped there for later processing. "Give me some other scans," the major breathed. "Infrared, electromagnetic. We can't go in there on visual alone."

A new scan started working its way down the screen. "Electromagnetic. Good," the major smiled.

The picture went fuzzy, then turned to static.

"Hesper, get that back," Rita ordered.

"No signal," ECM answered.

"Fix it."

"Can't, Skipper. It's not us. We got a beam from the flag, but it's just noise."

"Is the *Dry Lightning* gone?" Cadow choked on the question.

Rita glanced at her display. "Everybody's still squawking."

"Hesper, can you get me the flag's command net?" Longknife asked softly.

"Lurk on it regularly, sir."

"Please put it on speaker," the major requested. He *never* gave an order on Rita's bridge. If he wanted something, he went through her. Rita didn't begrudge him today's directness.

"Comm," the admiral shouted from the speaker, "get me through to those tin cans."

"No can do, sir, we got a brick wall ahead of us. No comm to or from them."

"Sensors, what kind of brick wall?"

"Damned if I know. Those missiles that missed started exploding and suddenly we got dust and something else all over the place."

"Gun squadron, begin acceleration at three gees. Now." My, but the admiral was sounding a tad hysterical. "Transports." Ah, the admiral finally remembered them. "Execute . . ."

"What?" Cadow yelped.

"Signal lost," Hesper reported.

"Can we accelerate?" Ray asked.

"We're in landing mode," Rita answered. "Even if we go to three gees, we'll float over their base like target balloons."

The major pursed his lips. "Set us down at Rosebud One."

"Once grounded," Rita nodded, "we can always launch out into the opposite orbit."

Ray considered it for a moment, then shook his head. "Political officer would have my head on a platter."

Rita snorted.

"And these folks *have* just landed. It must be a mess down there. I've got seven hundred combat veterans. What have they got? A mob that's never had a shot fired at them."

"That's what the jollies tell us." Rita spat the epitaph for political officers.

"We got to find out sooner or later who's right. If he is, I damn sure want to find out sooner. Land us at Rosebud One."

"I've got the conn," Rita snapped, taking the sticks back from Cadow. "Just once, Ray, I wish you'd let somebody else find out if the buzzsaw is unplugged. Just once."

"Where can you set us down?"

"How close you want to be, grunt?"

"About thirty klicks from the pass," Ray ordered. "It'll make for a short approach march. Put the transports safely out of range, and you can keep the rockets warm if we come running back and need a quick ride out of here."

"Just make sure you come back."

Mary jumped when the infrared signals started screaming again. Six ships, rockets pointed her way, sunk over the horizon. "Landing force arriving," she announced, ready to get to work. To do, as she had done every day of her working life, the job she was paid for.

She checked the digger; still not to the escarpment. They had to get a chance to talk to the colonials! But what do you say? They sure as hell hadn't included that in boot camp. She glanced at her board; she was ready to fight. That they'd taught her well. How do you not fight in a war when everybody else is?

Grandpa always told Ray a soldier expects problems, and problems were staring Ray in the face the second he disembarked. His largest transport, the *Loyal,* stood at an angle, one landing gear in a crater. The right edge of the roll-off ramp was down—the rest hung in space. Engineering platoon was rigging a derrick to offload the artillery the hard way.

The light assault teams of Companies B and C bounced buggies off their transports and went about preparing for as fast a start as Ray would have done when he commanded a company. Good people.

"Santiago." Ray called up his exec. "Use A company for site security and to help the engineers. I'll move out with the vanguard. Get the heavies in D and E company moving as quickly as possible. I'll need artillery as soon as possible."

"Right, sir" was all the answer Ray needed.

Ten minutes later, the light companies were mounted up and impatient to lead the charge. "Santiago, how soon can you give me artillery?"

"How about two rocket launchers right now?"

"You're a miracle man. Good luck."

"Good luck yourself, and Godspeed. Give 'em hell. See you for supper tonight in one of the Earthies' luxury chow halls."

"With real steaks and fresh potatoes."

Longknife swung aboard C company's command rig as it passed and plugged himself into the brigade network. Security was guaranteed by the communication filament trailing out from the carrier to the command post back here. His orders would not be intercepted or garbled. Second Guard was experienced and ready. He couldn't help pitying the poor bastards up ahead.

Mary followed the descending ships, handing them off to battalion, who in turn bucked them to brigade. As Mary lurked in the background, they ended up talking to a very angry Navy type, a Commander Umboto, who was pissed as hell that nobody had any long-range rockets ready to go.

"Miller, you store those coordinates and I'll go kick butt. If we can't get some rockets off the ground, my boot will damn sure get some lieutenants flying in that direction."

The comm link went dead with a loud click, as if the commander had bitten off her mike. Damn, there were some real hard cases here. Mary wondered if they were tough enough to win. She checked her digger . . . almost to the escarpment. What would happen to Umboto if their platoon cut its own peace? She'd probably live through it. They all would. *Come on, digger.*

Mary called up her squad leaders: Lek, Cassie, Thu, Dumont, and Berra. "What's it look like?"

Cassie and Dumont were Mary's backup, neither willing to say who was primary. After a long pause, Dumont spoke first. The kid was subdued. "We're dug in. I guess we're ready."

There was a beep. Mary focused on her heads-up. "Lieutenant, we got rolligons headed our way."

"Thanks, Sergeant, I make out a dozen."

Lek coughed gently to make himself known on net. If the LT was surprised to find a lurker, he said nothing. "Computer makes out ten wheeled vehicles spread out in the lead. Two columns with another ten coming up behind them. A tracked vehicle is pulling up the rear of both columns. Looks like another pair of columns about five klicks behind the first."

"Corporal, put that through to my and the sergeant's heads-ups immediately."

"Yessir," Lek answered.

"Sergeant, looks like we got two companies coming our

way. The tracks are probably artillery of some sort. Damn, I wish we had rockets with longer reach than ten klicks."

The regular issue was short-ranged. The LT knew nothing of what Dumont's girls had gotten them. Just now, Mary wasn't ready to let him know what she had up her sleeve. He'd just want to start whopping the enemy sooner. Mary wanted to keep her hole cards back for a bit. Maybe, if nobody was hurt, nobody would have to be hurt. She checked the mole she'd sent across. It was at the escarpment, but making slow headway.

Mary adjusted a few of her sensors. When next she looked up, the enemy was at the escarpment, eight klicks away, rolligons scattered loosely. One man had dismounted and stared her way, taking in the gap and the rim around it. A gleam came off the fiber-optic cable streaming from his suit.

"Whatcha gonna do, man?" she whispered, hoping he wouldn't do anything until her mole could find his comm wire.

Major Longknife studied the ground before him. Unlike the flat plain they'd just crossed, this was rolling and broken by boulders from the time of the creation of the huge crater, and small craters since. He'd walked similar terrain with grandfather, examining his defense of Goundo Pass Three on Yama-8. Grandpa had earned his colonelcy there. He'd also stopped just the kind of attack Ray was about to make.

Eyeing the ground with twenty years of training and experience, he liked what he saw. The plain, rim, and pass looked untouched since creation. He maxed the zoom on his suit binoculars. At the crown of the pass were footsteps. One set.

"So you had to see for yourself." The man facing him was curious, or just needed to get personal with his battlefield, get past the vid and heads-up.

Good man. Longknife would use that against him.

The major called up his deployment on his heads-up. Two companies here. One coming up, heavier with artillery. Santiago was holding the last company back. He'd send them forward with the last of the heavy stuff. For a moment, Longknife cursed not having his command van with its full sensor suite. The XO had taken him at his order, artillery first. Still, it would have been better to have slipped the van in somewhere in the middle. Weight of salvo was good, but intelligence would be nice directing that salvo.

"Should have thought of that when I was giving the order." Usually Santiago used his head better in reinterpreting his orders. Not today. Well, C company had recon assets.

"Tran, talk to me about that rim."

"Sensors show standard-issue snoops and not much else. Well, we got something that might be a whiff of nitrogen, but it only showed for a second and we can't get it back. No hot spots. No dust. It's clean. We are picking up something underfoot. We've turned lose a counterminer to hunt it down."

"You got anything to send over there?" Longknife asked.

"One Dervish Mod Three is up, other two are busted. We couldn't fix them on the way out here . . ."

"Not much a tech can do in three gees," the major said to absolve the support staff. "If you will, Captain, launch what you can."

"Yes, sir. Tech Sergeant Callahan, boot that mother."

The Dervish was away in a blink.

"What the hell?" Mary yelped. Coming at her in a crazy dance, now up, now down, now right, now left—way too fast to track—was something.

"It's a scout," the LT observed. "A Dervish, I think. Laser, up and ready," he ordered. "Sergeant, feed us a track."

One of Dumont's kids had tested fastest on the one laser rifle the platoon rated. Despite Lek's best scrounging efforts, one was all they had. Nobody would trade anything for what few antimissile weapons they had. Dumont had his fire team sleeping with theirs. Only 12 millimeters, it was small compared to the big Navy guns. Still, it was *their* laser.

Mary passed numbers and hoped the team was as good at

the real thing as they'd been with the vid-game they trained on. The scout reached the base of the rim, dodged right, rose, then jinked left. At the top of the rim, it went right, then left, and slipped over the crest. If Mary hadn't had her sensors covering every square inch of the place, she'd have lost it.

"Dumont, it's yours," she said.

Even as she did the handover, the laser rifle spat a bolt.

First shot missed clean as the scout went right. Next shot was closer, but the damn thing jumped five meters. It jinked to the left—directly into a bolt.

Whether the kid guessed right, or just missed in the right direction, he'd done it. Chunks of wreckage shot out in a dozen directions and began to fall slowly.

"We did it, we did it!" the youngsters screamed as one.

But had we done it soon enough? Mary turned her attention back to the wheels on the plain. Some were already negotiating their way through low places in the escarpment.

"Here they come," she announced on wide net, then gave full attention to her far digger. It had to find that cable.

Longknife zoomed the picture on his heads-up display and scowled. None were completed before the Dervish was popped. Infrared showed hot spots everywhere but a dust down around the rill. Had the idiot deployed his people in there? That was either stupid or a desperate move by an unprepared force. The electromagnetic scan that would show him the location of every racing heartbeat was . . . *jammed!*

In theory that was possible, but he'd never had it done to him before. The major blinked hard. What was he up against here? Someone had downed his Dervish fast. Good shooter or dumb luck? He wasn't supposed to be facing good troops, just hasty conscripts who'd break at the first tap. "Was the dust down for real," Longknife mused, "or just to confuse me?"

"Major, we're ready to move out."

Longknife smiled. It was time to commit, and there was

nowhere near enough to go on. For twenty years he'd faced this, just like Dad and Grandpa before him. *Let's kick over this anthill and see what happens.* Which was all there was to do.

"Companies advance, C on the right, B on the left. Keep your intervals loose. Your objective is the rim wall. Keep your heads up, use what cover you can. Until things develop, hang loose and keep ready for anything. Good luck and Godspeed. Now let's show 'em Second Guard's the best there is."

The fire teams answered with a shout as the carriers moved out. Ten rifles to a carrier and two carriers to a platoon. The Earthies still used the fifty-man platoon. In a few minutes, they'd learn what the twenty troopers in a Unity platoon could do. One hundred to a company, two hundred rode by his command. D company was four klicks out with three more launchers and a pair of tube artillery. If he used his two launchers now, they'd be reloaded before the troops reached the crater.

"Rockets, pop their sensors on the rim. Use the rest of your load to lay down a salvo on the other side. Standard long box pattern. Use the rill as your center line."

"Roger. Salvo on the way." The tracks had leveled themselves on jacks as soon as they halted. Rockets began budding from their launchers as the words echoed in his ears.

Three meters from Ray, the ground erupted. He smiled; the counterminer had bagged its bug, too. The Earthies were losing all their sensors. Hot damn!

"Damn," Mary groaned as the digger across the plain went dead. Mining diggers weren't rigged with sensors; still, Mary had picked up readings through the rock. With something digging ahead of her, she'd pushed her digger to the max, hoping to get a fast patch into the Collies' comm net. The digger was gone, and with it their one chance to settle this nice and easy.

Her heads-up went wild.

"Rockets, incoming," Mary shouted. Pair after pair of missiles appeared on her display.

"Expect sixteen if they're the large ones, sixty-four if they're pelting us with the little stuff." The lieutenant again provided the military analysis. "Those dinky things can't touch us in our holes, so stay low men and hug your boots."

Dumont didn't need the LT to tell him to stay low. He and Tina crouched as deep in their hole as they could, holding each other tighter than when they made love.

"We got 'em." Blacky's voice rang in Dumont's ears.

"Got what?" he asked, like they were back on the Pitt, cruising for rags.

"The rockets. Watch me pop 'em."

Dumont blinked his heads-up to life. It overwrote his eyeball, mottling Tina's pale complexion with the tracks of fast-moving missiles. Mary had promised that what she could see, she'd show them all. *And what Blacky saw, he shot at.*

"Damn it, Blacky, those things'll home on you." Around Tina's nose a second and third dot winked out.

"Not while I got 'em in my sights," Blacky crowed.

A fourth disappeared.

"Private, get that rifle in your hole," the lieutenant shouted, his voice cracking. "Your ammo won't hold out. You're only making yourself a target." Two more dots just below Tina's eyes vanished. But her forehead looked like a bad case of acne. And they were changing direction, arrowing straight for Blacky.

"Can't you do something?" Tina whispered.

"Run over to Blacky's hole just in time to get blown to jelly with him." Dumont wasn't about to do that, even if a corporal was supposed to. And nobody had told him a corporal was. Two more dots disappeared.

"Damn, it's not shooting anymore," Blacky screamed. "Amy, switch me to another juice bag."

"Not enough time," Mary yelled. "Pull it in and get down!"

"I'm going. I'm going," Blacky hollered.

Dumont wanted to look, see if Blacky had finally done what someone told him to. He kept his head down. *Don't make yourself a target.* He could check on Blacky when the barrage was over. Check on what was left of him. On Dumont's display, the dots were flocking to Tina's lips. He wanted to kiss her. Damn suit. Some of the dots farther back, around her eyes, were still spread out. Dumont held his breath and Tina tight. The explosions began. He pissed in his suit and his bowels let go. Tina screamed as he was thrown against her. He gripped the walls of their hole, trying to hold himself, not smash against her again.

The explosions went on—forever.

"Report casualties," the lieutenant ordered on net as soon as the last rocket was down. On her screen, Mary could see him out of his hole, bounding for third squad.

No one else was moving.

The lieutenant came to a halt at the edge of a torn and pocked area. Here, the rill was gone, broadened into a ten-meter hole made up of a lot of little ones. "Third squad, you've lost two men and the laser rifle." Mary knew it was a man and a woman, two kids who'd played one too many vid-games.

"Lieutenant," Mary said, her voice even, "I've got traffic moving in front of us."

"How much?"

"Twenty wheeled vehicles."

"Pick two, wide apart, and give 'em each a rocket." The LT's words were bitter cold. She'd never heard anyone talk quite that way. But then, Mary'd never been around when murder was decided upon.

She selected two rigs, a bit out in front of the rest. By triangulating her vid, she got a good range and position on them without using a laser to range-find. She felt nothing. "Fire in hole twelve," she called . . . just another day at the mine.

"Clear," the lieutenant shot back.

Cold as death, Mary watched the two missiles process as dots across her display. She didn't switch on the laser designator until the missiles were over the rim. She only highlighted the vehicles when they were halfway there. For a moment the missiles did not respond; then they changed direction. Mary grinned as the projected courses intersected the rigs.

Alarms must have gone off in the vehicles when the designators hit them. Plums of dust shot out as they accelerated and turned. They popped chaff—too late. Several battle-suited figures tumbled out of the rigs. A laser bolt shot up—missed.

The missiles hit. Parts of rig and bodies cartwheeled in slow arcs. Mary zoomed a video in on both scenes, passed them along. Let everybody see the payback. There were cheers on net. Mary studied the picture, imprinting it solid. How many times in the mines had she swallowed whatever the owners handed out? She'd stood, clinch jawed, and taken it. *Well, I'm not taking it anymore. You got two of us. We got a lot more of you. Keep coming and there's more where that came from.*

"Lieutenant, can I have a couple more missiles?"

"Yeah." Her request was seconded by others on net.

"We've made our point, Sergeant. We'll need what we got in an hour or so." As the lieutenant headed back to his hole, Mary turned to the enemy. They'd gone to ground, rigs hiding in the cover of rocks, infantry scattered.

"Okay, you bastards. Let's see how you take to getting your own nose bloodied."

"Where the hell did that come from?" The newly arrived commander of D company joined his brigade commander at the escarpment's edge, surveying the wreckage.

"I'd like to know." Longknife could feel the blood lust rising. They'd played him for a sucker—and he'd taken the bait. He wanted them dead. The question was how to do it without throwing troopers away. "Company commanders, report."

"Tran here."

"Lieutenant Cohen, B company commander."

"Where's . . ." Right, there'd been a laser cannon on one of the carriers—a company commander's rig. B company had a new commander. Longknife took a deep breath. "Slight change of plan. Send me back your carriers. Keep the infantry heading for the rim, but advance on foot, leapfrog, use fire and movement."

"Who do we fire at?" the lieutenant squeaked.

"Nobody, unless you see something. Just don't put too many people out in the open until we know what we're up against."

"Sorry, sir."

"No stupid questions, only stupid answers." And how stupid am I being? I'm not ready to put my tail between my legs and run, that's for sure. Of course, it would be nice if those bastards in the pass just disappeared. "Move out, fellows, and keep your heads down. You got an hour to reach the rim."

"Roger" came back to him. He went to the next item on his agenda. "Senior Pilot Nuu, when's the *Revenge* due back for a second shooting pass?"

"Don't know, Major. Whatever they ran into fried every sensor and antenna on the boats. Even lost a nine-inch gun. Some eager turret commander ran his laser out early. Got something in its eye. *Revenge* and company will be low when they go past here. You running into trouble?"

"Nothing we can't handle, but I wouldn't mind the Navy slagging this pass from orbit."

"Sorry, hon."

"I'm having a busy day at the office. Call you later, friend." Ray clicked off. There might have been a whispered kiss just before the line went dead. He stowed it away somewhere behind his heart for later. Right now, he had a battle to win.

What the hell am I facing? The political officer had his own official party opinion. Of course, Jolly had stayed behind to make sure Santiago pushed the rest of the troops forward.

But what was he facing? Really. "Major, artillery here, we got tube artillery dialed in on the laser designators that got our two carriers. Mind if we take them out?"

"Do it." That took no thought.

The gun carriages behind him bucked. The tubes puffed fire silently. A moment later two chunks of the crater rim blew out. A ragged cheer came over the artillery net.

"Artillery, what's your ammo situation?"

"We got five units of fire on the transports, but only loaded out half of one. Sure could use those carriers you just called back to bring up more ammo."

"They're yours. Now, I need some time to think. Don't bother me unless the devil himself shows up."

"No problem."

Major Longknife stood, legs apart, arms folded over his chest, eyes staring at the pass.

What have I got in front of me?

Damned if I know.

What do I know?

They had a damn good laser gunner who kept me from knowing more about them—who was no longer among the living. Gutsy—but knew damn little about his weapon. Only a green gunner would take on a sixty-four-rocket salvo with no backup.

Are all the troops facing us that green? Would be nice. The deployment along that rill line was something only a green second louie would come up with. Are they there, or was he only supposed to think they were? The rockets had homed in on the laser gun, and they'd homed right in on the rill. Could all that be a setup to sucker him in? The response to that salvo had been quick. Whoever coordinated it had delayed illuminating his targets until the last second. Smart move. Why two missiles? Did they have an ammunition problem, or had the salvo killed two troopers? Only real green troops would let battlefield deaths spark their response.

Everything pointed to green troops, but with surprises up their sleeves. *Wonder if they are green enough to surrender. Should have made an offer.* Longknife glanced at the wreckage of two carriers—too late now. "Santiago, I want my van up here fast. I need sensors pronto."

"It's moving now, Sir. Some artillery with it."

"Tell my driver to put pedal to the metal. He'll love that order. I need analysis more than he needs an escort."

"Yes sir."

Major Longknife squinted at the pass. *Who are you? Have I pegged you right yet? How do I get you out of my way?*

Mary studied the situation in front of her. She'd been dumb not to move those designators as soon as she'd used them. She'd reprogrammed the videos to order the lasers to scoot back into their tunnels as soon as their targets were destroyed.

What else am I forgetting?

To surrender. But that was out of the question now. The two blasted rigs and the bodies around them had closed that door. She zoomed in on the solitary figure still standing, legs spread, arms folded across his chest. Mary couldn't make her own suit do that. *Wonder if that means their suits are better or worse than ours? Wonder if I offed that one, would they all go home?* She doubted it. "Lieutenant, they're still coming but hopping. Should we toss a few more rockets at them?"

"Spread out, we wouldn't get many. We don't have enough to trade one rocket for three or four men. No, Sergeant, we wait for them to bunch up again. Then we'll cut 'em down."

Mary didn't like what she was hearing, but she couldn't fault his logic. She switched channels. "Lek, when are those reinforcements gonna get here?"

"They haven't left. Oh, they've pulled A company out of rummaging through luggage, but the transports are spread to hell and gone."

"What happened to that crazy lady who was going to put rockets down on the transports?"

Lek snorted. "She's got her rockets and got her command unit to program them, but the fire control computers don't have any power cables."

"Lek, don't tell me they need a special cable."

"Okay, I won't tell you."

"These apes could never run a mine."

"Ever move a mine halfway across human space, offload it three times at busy stations, shuffle the shipping containers and then try to get it put back together in two days? Mary, they're doing the best they can."

"Lek, we got guys hopping toward us who intend to kill us. Even your mild disposition has got to take offense at that."

"Ain't no use getting the dander up over what you can't do nothing about. Now you stay cool, young lady."

Only Lek would think of her as young or a lady. Mary again checked the situation before her. Nothing had changed, except the guys with guns were closer. No, there were more rigs on the plain, just their side of the escarpment. "Lieutenant, have you noticed the new stuff showing up back there?"

"Yes, Sergeant. A full battery of six rocket launchers, six tube artillery and what looks like a command van. I watched them come up. I think the troop carriers they sent back are headed this way, probably loaded with more rockets and shells."

"How can you sound so damn calm?" Mary snapped. "They're gonna flatten us."

"'Cause I got no rockets with the range." He answered her like she might speak to a newbie in the mines. "All we can do is hit them where we can and take what they throw at us."

"We can hit them." Mary whispered the secret.

"With what?"

"We've got four SS-12's. They've got a range of fifteen klicks, don't they?"

"You bunch of pot-bellied, sticky-fingered jokers walked off with four SS-12's." The lieutenant sounded almost giddy.

"Well, we had to have something up our sleeves, lieutenant."

The kid was laughing. "I love you crazy bunch of military disasters. Where're the Twelves set up?"

"In the rill, with the rest of the rockets."

"That makes it ten klicks to the escarpment, another one or two to the targets. I'd been thinking of wheeling a couple of Threes into the gap to see if they could do something. Now, we got four that can really do the job."

"Shall I lay in coordinates and launch them?"

There was a long pause. Mary wondered if the young man had heard her. "Lieutenant, should I . . ." she started slowly.

"No, Mary. Let me think for a minute." He was really letting his hair down, what little his buzz cut left him. He'd even called her Mary. "You've been a miner all your life, Mary. You ever find an ore vein and have to wait to flush it out? Is there any mineral that has to be aged in place?"

"No, sir." The LT knew nothing about mining.

"My instructors said timing was everything. Now I think I understand. If we blast their artillery now, they can adjust their battle plan for what's left. No, Mary, we wait until they commit. Wait until there's a lot of junk in the air and they won't know what to hit with a laser bolt. No battle plan survives contact with the enemy. Let's wait and make that poor bastard's plan go to hell in a handbasket."

Mary grinned; the kid did know how to fight. She went back to her display. The advancing infantry were moving faster, made bold by the lack of attention. She focused on the guy who'd spent such a long time staring her way. He was moving toward a big, boxy rig with a garden of antennas on its top and side. The lieutenant said a command van had arrived. She could spot only one of those boxy bad-hair-day things. That made it the command van, and that fellow the guy giving the orders to kill them. *You're management. You die first.*

• • •

Now, how do I fight this damn battle?

Major Longknife stepped into his command van. His four staff officers were busy bringing their boards up to date. Most of what the boards showed he'd watched with his own eyes. Here, it was displayed by platoons and with rate of advance precisely calculated. His troops would be at the rim in ten minutes.

Longknife rested a hand on his sensor coordinator. "Tanaka, there's something out there I can't figure out."

"Yeah, I watched that attack from the artillery net. They got this place wired, but they're either load limited or low on expendables. I would have targeted every troop carrier out there. Why just two buggies?"

"I've been asking myself that for the last hour. Haven't got an answer yet. You?"

"No, Sir."

"What I can do is adapt, scatter the troops until they're not worth a rocket, and next time we go in, make sure their laser illuminators aren't worth a damn." The major chinned his mike. "Artillery, what's your smoke situation?"

"Maybe not as good as I thought it was. We biased the unit of fire for the real thing. I've got WP, but maybe not as much as we could use."

"Tell base camp to load extra smoke on the resupply run."

"Santiago's already got the troop carriers headed back."

"Tell him he's too damn fast. Turn the last carrier around and have it reloaded with white phosphorus."

"Yes, Sir."

"Okay, folks, here's what we're gonna do." And together, the major and his team started putting together the familiar pieces that had won the 2nd so many battles before.

Mary was kicking herself. She'd concentrated so much on defending the platoon's position, she hadn't put that much thinking into defending herself. Most of the riflemen headed her way would hit the rim on the other side of the gap or damn close to it on this side. Still about forty would wash up on the other side of her and walk by her place on their way to the gap.

What are the chances they won't notice my hidey-hole?

Damn slim, with a centimeter gap on both sides of the door. Mary called up the map of the rim's innards. There were other chambers; quickly she sent the moles digging. She needed a bolt-hole. Things were getting complicated.

Captain Santiago scowled at the returning troop carrier that now was an ammunition carrier. The driver had to be crazy to race a carrier, overloaded with explosives, but this one was. It made a hard left turn and slid to a rocking halt not two meters from the loading dock. The driver was out of it in a flash.

"Major wants smoke," the excited driver shouted, forgetting his comm link carried a whisper just as well. "He's got enough high explosive. You got to reload me quick with Willy Peter."

Santiago threw open the rear door to the carrier. Forty shells in their plastic cradles were crammed on the floor. Every shell was stamped with WP/V, white phosphorus modified for vacuum, or Willy Peter, if you preferred. Each round was laced with crystals to dazzle lasers and heat to blind infrared sensors. A perfect screen for a man to hide behind on a battlefield. "Damn it. You *are* loaded with Willy Peter."

The driver looked over the captain's shoulder. "Nobody told me what I was carrying, sir. Artillery just said come back."

Santiago gritted his teeth; artillery wouldn't know any better. There'd been no time to inventory the load out to each carrier. He'd assumed artillery wanted it fast. To hell with the paperwork. It had worked—except for this load.

"Soldier, now you know what you got. You are a bat out of hell, so drive like one and get this chaff up the line."

The trooper whirled and bounced off the carrier as he overshot his 180-degree turn. He took two running steps that didn't sit well with the moon's lower gravity and snagged the door to the driver's station before he fell flat on his face. Pulling himself into the seat, he got the rig moving before the door closed.

Captain Santiago chinned his mike. "Artillery, I got a load of WP headed your way just slightly below light speed. I'll have a couple of more loads waiting for you as soon as you get me some rigs to put them in."

"We'll unload them fast on this end. Thanks for the quick turnaround. I figured you for another five minutes."

"Don't thank me, thank the driver. Assuming the kid doesn't nosedive into a crater. Santiago out." No use telling him he could've had the WP ten minutes sooner if he hadn't sent the kid in circles. In the eons of time and space, ten minutes wouldn't matter. Santiago tasted the lie. He'd been under fire; he knew how long a minute could be.

Mary checked the outside situation. In the last five minutes they'd gotten closer. Here and there, pairs of soldiers had reached the rim and waited. Inside, the moles had found a place that might save her life—if they had enough time to do their thing. They were chomping away happily on rocks, leaving Mary to wonder if she'd finally given away too much, taken too little. Cassie was always telling her she couldn't make everyone happy. Mary swallowed hard and checked outside.

Troops were bunching up as they reached the rim. That promoted them to targets, but not easy ones. Mary had a mole redrill a hole at an extreme downward slant and sent a designator into it. A one-second light-up was all she risked before sending it scuttling back deep into the rock. The Unity artillery still had time to get a fix; a shell smashed where it had been ten seconds ago.

The designator squealed as it shook. Still, it reported available when things settled down. Mary was none too happy with the test; the targeting beam had still been ten meters out from the foot of the rim. Well, rockets needed a place to explode and scatter flechettes. That would have to do. She got six moles moving to redeploy lasers. More and more hostiles were at the rim, staying fairly spread out, but still worth a rocket.

"Lieutenant, I think I'm going to need a few missiles in a minute or two."

"We'll have to do this quick. Their artillery has a hair trigger." As if she hadn't noticed. "Sergeant, you also have company."

"Yes, sir," Mary growled. "If you give me a half dozen rockets, I can send one my way without making a spectacle of myself."

"The rockets are yours. Good shooting."

This shoot would have to be timed to the split second. "Lek, I need six missiles programmed for a quick U turn as they come out of the canisters. Can you do it?"

"Piece of cake, miner. I can hold them to a one-klick pop-up. They'll go a few klicks out, then turn back. How do you think the Unies will take to getting rockets in their backside?"

"Maybe they'll bitch to whoever's running those guns and give them a good case of 'Did I do that?'" Mary managed a chuckle. While Lek finished his programming, the moles dug her hiding place.

"They're yours." Lek came back on. "Use two on the rifles at your doorstep."

So the others knew her predicament. Moisture rimmed Mary's eyes. Hadn't been many in her life who cared, certainly not when the missile that saved her life might be the one that wasn't there to save his. Blinking the water away, Mary got back to business. "Three to each side of the crater, and only one on my doorstep. Don't want to hang a welcome mat out."

"You got a fallback position, Mary?" Lek asked.

"Working on one now."

"Take care."

"If I was careful, I wouldn't be here," Mary breathed as she switched off. She did one more check. Lasers were warm, but not in place. She edged them forward. Holding her breath, she punched six missiles out.

• • •

"Rockets incoming," sensors shouted.

Major Longknife twisted around to face the sensor station. "Any laser designators?"

"None pointing. I got strange electromagnetic emissions, but they don't match anything in the Earthies' inventory."

"Artillery." Longknife kept his voice even. "I want WP out there. Air burst at a hundred meters."

"On the way."

"Any laser rifles in range?"

"Two LR's at maximum range."

"Not much help. Artillery, as soon as the lasers light up, I want them smashed."

"We got twelve rounds of Willy Peter out there," artillery reported, "and we're reloading with high explosive. Few problems can't be solved with a round of HE."

"Good." Longknife settled back. It would be a battle between their measures and his countermeasures. He glanced at the sensors board; the rockets stayed low. A laser missed. Its target was turning back. "They're aimed at the rim. Of course."

Mary waited for the missiles to start their turn back to the rim before she lit off the designators. One by one the six red dots on her heads-up display turned to green. *Target acquired.*

Then all hell broke lose.

The infrared sensors lit up like a fire. The lasers chirped in protest as the missiles' dots turned black. *Targets not acquired.* Quickly, Mary changed to vid. Giant puffs of white stuff blossomed along the rim, blocking the lasers.

"Willy Peter, Mary." The LT's voice filled her helmet. "They've blanketing you with white phosphorus. Thick to stop lasers, hot to stop infrared. It'll settle, but in low grav not very fast. The missiles should home on where they were targeted, I hope. Douse your lasers and get them out of there."

Right. Mary had read about WP as a countermeasure for

lasers. Damn, why hadn't she thought about it? Quickly she ordered her lasers to scoot back. On second thought, she ordered everything to scoot. Rocks around her shook. Her missiles were hitting something. Then the chamber really shuddered. Mary danced around like an upped hopper, wishing she had the drugs in her that gave the hoppers the energy as well as the oblivion.

Major Longknife scowled. "Check fire, check fire. Flying rocks are doing their job for 'em."

"Roger." The artillery barrage ceased. The rain of rocks and boulders on his troops stopped. *Wonder how many sensors we killed? How many of our own troops?* Damn war.

The incoming rockets had been bad enough. A laser rifle had gotten only one. Some ballsy assault rifle had clipped another. It hadn't done much good; inertia kept the pieces going in loose formation. Most troops had taken off hopping as soon as it was clear where a rocket was heading. Still, flechettes had gotten too many, and the rockets' flight had been short. Unspent solid fuel, still flaming, had speckled others. Plasti-armor that could stop a flechette burned if heated enough. The computer took the injured off net, but not before the first horrible screams. *War never got easy.*

"Artillery, you got any empty carriers?"

"Some. Was about to head them back for more smoke and HE."

"Hang red crosses, stars, and crescents on 'em and send them out there."

"You don't think they'll shoot 'em?"

"Won't know what kind of war these folks came to fight until we see, will we?"

"Right, sir, I'll ask for life-saver volunteers."

"Get 'em out there, and get your gunners ready. I'm gonna start the show any time now."

The ambulances were a mercy—and a mission. Buddies were caring for buddies. So long as first aid was the priority, combat was a distant second. But once their mates were turned over to the medics, the blood lust would come flooding back to the survivors. The major glanced around. His artillery was ready. D and E companies were ready to roll. Get the wounded off the field, and it would be time. Longknife gave himself ten minutes.

Mary risked two vids. The scene they showed was horrible.

Two hundred people had been huddled under the rim when the missiles came. There were still two hundred battle suits out there, but a lot of them weren't people anymore.

She'd never considered unspent rocket fuel a weapon. Burning figures withered on the ground, trying to put out fire that carried its own oxidizer. The lucky ones sluffed the fuel off as they rolled in the dust. No, the lucky were the ones just lying there, dead and burning.

"God, what have I done?"

A red light flashed, drawing her attention to the top of the picture. Wheeled vehicles were making their way down the escarpment. They were going slower than she'd expect for an attack rush, but Mary no longer trusted anything in battle to be reasonable. "Lieutenant, we got wheels headed our way."

"Show me."

Happy to get away from the close-in picture, Mary zoomed in on a pair of the approaching rigs.

"No shooting this time, Mary. Those carriers have red crosses on 'em. They're ambulances, come for the wounded. We don't shoot at red crosses."

No way would Mary shoot at something come to take those wretched pictures out of her vision. She shuddered; it would take more than ambulances to get them out of her memory. She'd burned and slashed and killed them. And they'd do the same to her if they got a chance. "Lieutenant, mind taking over the big picture for a while? I got house-keeping chores to do."

"Dig deep, Mary. We've got a truce while the ambulances are on the field. I'll mind the store."

Mary started looking for places to hide.

•   •   •

"They're leaving the ambulances alone," sensors whispered as if even a strong word might disturb the delicate peace.

"Might as well. They know we know how to cover vehicles now," artillery butted in.

"Let's credit virtue where it's due," Ray muttered. "Artillery, your crew ready?"

"Just say the word."

"Enough of the right stuff?"

"I'd like more WP, but you know where my ammo carriers are."

"Yeah."

"Sir," whispered sensors, "shouldn't we go now? The more time we give them, the better dug in they'll be."

"Yes, son, but B and C companies are out of it. Their officers and noncoms need time to put them back into fighting order. D and E are our reserves, but only E's got armored carriers. I don't want to send them forward until B and C are in solid contact. And I got a flag of truce on the field. They're honoring it, and I don't intend to make this war any viler than it has to be. We will honor our own flag of truce."

"Yes, sir."

"But that doesn't mean we don't think for the next ten minutes. We've tapped them. They've tapped us. To hell with love taps. I want a knockout next. So far, I don't even know what I'm up against."

"Sir, I think I've got something," said sensors slowly.

"I'm listening."

"I told you the background electromagnetic noise from the rim didn't match any stuff in the Earthies' inventory."

"Right."

"I think I got a picture of what these folks are using." Ray's heads-up changed to an up-close picture of the rim. Shells had gouged it; something dangled from the rock.

"What's that?" artillery asked.

"It's not military issue," sensors answered. "It took a major search of the database to find. It's the latest commercial infrared sensor. They use it in mines. It cost a fortune."

"We're facing mining equipment?" Artillery wasn't persuaded.

"It looks like that to me." Sensors stood his ground.

"That might explain a lot," Longknife said slowly. "They've dug in faster than I expected. They've got a few savvy types and a lot of dumb ones. And all of them are green. Okay, crew. What do we do with that assumption? We got ten minutes before I want to kick this off. Talk to me."

Ten minutes can go quickly when experts at organized mayhem put their minds to it.

The seconds ticked by, each one an hour long and not nearly long enough. Mary had nothing to do while the moles did their thing. Into that time-twisted void crept visions of the hell Mary had created. She didn't turn on the vid. She didn't have to. All her life, Mary had been . . . well, if not a good girl, at least a woman who kept out of trouble. Go to work. Give the man his time. Don't talk back. And cover your mouth when you laugh at the boss man or brown-noser as they get theirs.

Mary got what she deserved. A few beers with friends. A few parties. Here and there a night worth remembering. That was life, thank you very much. Now she had killed. Good God, how she had killed. Now she could pray. Pray that there was no God to see what she'd done. Outside were people, buddies of the ones she'd killed. All she had to do was open the door. They'd find her. One shot from a needle rifle and she wouldn't have to worry about forgetting the pictures. One shot, hell. They'd probably empty their magazines into her. She wouldn't feel a thing.

Mary fingered the door. The jacks would swivel it. They'd do the rest. Through her trembling fingertips, Mary felt movement on the other side. They were coming for her.

"Sergeant, take a look at this."

"Private, get a move on. We're wanted at the pass."

"Nothin's gonna happen 'til the ambulances are out of here. Take a look, Sergeant. There's a hole in the rock."

"There's holes all over this damn rock."

"Yeah, but not in a straight line."

"Straight line?" The sergeant had gone outside the rock outcropping. The private had taken the inside. Two other privates had joined him by the time the sergeant got back.

"Shit, look." The second private fingered the gap in the rocky wall. "It's straight, and as wide as my little finger."

"You mean prick," put in the third private.

"You're just jealous, honey. I got one and you don't." He leaned against the rock. "Doesn't move."

"Honey, you never could make the earth move. Now me, baby cakes, I can make it shake, rattle, and roll." She patted her hips, or more precisely, the satchel of explosives hanging there. "Move out of my way, boy, and I'll show you how a woman does it."

"Hold your horses, Roz," the sergeant put in as he joined them. "We got ambulances on the field. Nobody blows nothing while we're under the red crescent."

"Course, Roz, if you got your heart set on blowing something, I'm available."

"Go blow yourself, before I use some C-20 to do it for you. Sergeant, somebody's had us under observation since we started. That somebody's caused us a lot of grief. If that somebody's behind this rock, I want his ass."

"Okay, Roz, I'll call it up, but close that satchel. Nobody does nothin' til I get the word. Understood?"

"Yes, Sergeant," three privates echoed like four-year-olds.

Mary waited for the door to blow in, crush her under its stony weight. "Mary," Cassie's voice whispered in her helmet, "you've been off net for a long time. You okay?"

"Yes," Mary sniffled. "No problem here."

"Doesn't sound like no problem to me."

"Okay, you want a problem. How do you blow your nose in one of these damn ape suits?"

"You got me. Don't think they made them with crying in mind. Want me to ask the lieutenant?"

"For God's sake, no!"

"Want to talk about it, Mary?"

She sniffed hard, trying to get control of all the drips. Then she sneezed, splattering phlegm all over the inside of her faceplate. Most of it ran down in thin streaks. The faceplate was supposed to be streak-free. It almost was. The suit already stank of fear and sweat.

"I just killed a lot of people," Mary finally said.

"So? That's what they sent us here to do."

"No, *I* just *killed* a *lot* of *people*. I saw them. Lying out there burning."

"I know," Cassie whispered. "I saw the vid, too."

"But I'm the one that killed them."

"Yeah, I know. You laid out the sensors all by yourself. Emplaced the rockets, programmed them. Did it all yourself. Good going, girl."

"I'm sorry."

"No you're not, Mary. If *we* hadn't blasted those two rigs, if *we* hadn't stomped them at the rim, they'd have rolled right over us a half hour ago. How many of us would be dead? Me, Lek, Nan, Dumont, definitely the lieutenant. How many, Mary?"

"I don't know."

"Neither do I. But you saved our asses, Mary, and we're kind of glad for it. Now, you go take care of yourself, girl."

"Thanks, Cassie. It's good to know someone cares. I owe you a beer."

"Then you definitely take care of yourself. I need all the free beer I can get at my age."

"Cassie, I got a few things to do. Call you back in a couple of minutes."

"If you don't, I'll call you. We need you, girl. Dig in good. If anybody knows how, you do."

"Thanks. Mary out." Mary glanced around her cell. Not much bigger than her apartment in the belt. Over there was room for the bed. The cook space was opposite it. The couch would go against the door leaving a whole wall for the vid center. *Where do I hide, under the bed or in the closet?*

The moles must have finished. The jacks skittered away from the original door and headed for a corner. Mary got down on her hands and knees. *Yeah, under the bed sounded good.*

She grabbed her gun and started crawling.

THREE

"B COMPANY, REPORT," Major Longknife ordered.

"Locked and loaded. We want their skulls for hood ornaments."

The major would have expected nothing less. "C company, report."

"In position. There better be enough skulls for us, too. Damned if I'll settle for their guts as antenna streamers again."

"There'll be enough. Where're the ambulances?"

"Last one just cleared the escarpment . . . now."

"Artillery, they're yours. D and E companies, forward at a gallop. B and C, as soon as the smoke thickens, advance and take the pass."

"Roger," "Yes, sir," and "On our way" answered him.

"Lieutenant Cohen." The major called the new commander of B company. "Your folks pretty sure they've found the skunk that's been calling down all those rockets?"

"Yes, sir."

"Well, you don't have to wait for smoke to go after that one. That's a skull I want, personally."

"It's yours, sir." The young voice held no doubt.

• • •

Mary felt the pressure of the explosion even through vacuum. She checked her heads-up display one last time before she doused it, and the hint of light it brought to the cavern. It was all red, hot, and ready. *Damn. The mines!* She'd safetied them for the LT's walk. With a flick of her wrist, she reactivated them. *Then* she doused the heads-up.

Mary eyed her old space through the slit she'd left open to her new quarters. The stone slab lay half in, half out of the doorway. Three grenades sailed through the hole. Mary ducked. Through the stone, she felt the explosions and shrapnel bouncing off walls. Something slammed into her helmet. Carefully, she fingered a bit of jagged metal sticking in the plastic of her faceplate. Bent and twisted, it had ricocheted off the walls before coming to rest, spent, on her helmet. With a glob of safety goo in one hand, she gently pulled the metal out. It had barely dinged the plastic. Mary, never one to take a chance, slapped goo sealant liberally on the ding and risked a look into her old space.

Four infantry, rifles at the ready, entered one after another. Rifles and helmets moving as one, they swept down the entire cavern. Not one square millimeter went unexamined. *So that's how professionals do it.* Three stayed on point and alert. One relaxed his aim, probably a sergeant getting ready to report. Mary didn't want that. She flipped on the laser designator high on the far wall. In its ruddy light, the dust and gases of the explosion still swirled. Like puppets, every gun and eye swiveled to face it.

Mary slipped her needle rifle into the notch left for it below the slit. Her heads-up display back on, it showed the next room. The sights settled on the closest back. Mary squeezed the trigger, gently, like she'd been taught.

The gas vented out the sides of her rifle; she felt no recoil. A three-round burst went into one back. Mary walked her aim to the next closest back. Three more for it, then the next.

That one wasn't a back. She caught him—no, maybe it was a her—turning. Mary stitched three rounds into her side and changed aim for the last one. He was diving for the cover of the stone. Mary had to get him; she couldn't hold

off a siege. His helmet was in her sights. She jerked off three
rounds. Only the first one hit. It was enough.

The faceplate shattered.

Mary lay, rifle in hand, fascinated as the blood flew in
lazy arcs, obedient to the gentle gravity of this moon. She
might have lain there, mesmerized by the deaths she'd
caused, but explosions were seeping into her body.

Her mines were going off.

She ordered a vid to keep an eye on her old space and put
it on motion detection. Switching her heads-up to the outside picture, she nodded. Yep, the minefield was taking a
toll. There was still too much of the WP stuff to use a laser.
It took her a minute to regain the situation. Somewhere in
that minute she was violently ill, but she kept most of the
vomit off her faceplate. Her friends needed her.

Lieutenant Cohen waited for the cloud of Willy Peter to
thicken. After each burst of shell, he'd start counting. When
he got to fifteen without starting over, the swirl of white ob-
scured the end of the pass—and he could believe the artillery net's claim that the barrage was over.

"Follow me, crew," he shouted, and the men and women
of B company lit out after him. He was near the crest of the
ridge when something exploded at his feet. Arms and legs
flailing, he flew up, then smashed into the pass's stone wall
five meters above the ground. Of his feet, he felt nothing.
His ears rang, but not enough to miss the hissing of pressure
fleeing his suit. With his last air, he shouted. "Come on, soldiers, a few mines can't slow the Guard down. Show the
others how it's done. Forward."

Troops double-timed toward him, some shooting up as
explosions blossomed at their feet, others making it through,
rifles up, shooting at what lay ahead. Then darkness took vision from the lieutenant's eyes as his whole body struggled
for breath. It was not a long struggle.

Each shell bounced Cassie around the inside of her dugout.
As best she could, she left space for Joyce to do her own rat-

tling around. Then the lieutenant bellowed on the platoon-wide net. "Infantry in the gap. Heads up. Rifles out. Shoot."

She and Joyce stared at each other. Did that idiot really want them to crawl out of their hole under this artillery barrage? Then again, the place wasn't shaking anymore. Just her knees. Through the faceplate, Cassie could see Joyce's face. Sweat ran down it, vomit speckled the helmet. She was in no shape to stand up, much less shoot. *Wonder what I look like?*

I sure as hell don't feel like standing up and aiming a gun. Cassie was shaking like an unbalanced motor. "I'll fire a round if you will," Cassie said.

"Just one?"

"That's all I got in me."

They came up out of their hole together, slapped their rifles down on the rocky lip, and fired. Cassie didn't try for a sight picture. She just pulled the trigger and held it down, slowly sweeping the barrel over the gap three hundred meters away. Figures in armored space suits poured through the pass. Some flew . . . mines, she remembered. *Good luck, Mary.*

Her rifle quit spitting. For Mary, she popped the spent magazine out and slammed in a new one. Cassie glanced at Joyce. She slumped over her rifle, surprise still showing in her empty eyes. Her faceplate had taken a direct hit. She hadn't suffered. A needle's tiny hole showed between her eyes.

Cassie turned back to the gap, finger on the trigger, gun venting. She wondered why her throat hurt. It wasn't until she slipped the fourth magazine in that she realized she was screaming. She didn't try to stop.

Captain Tran did a belly flop in the dust at the end of the pass. He'd made it! From the looks of things, he might be the only officer who had. Company B was taking a pasting. They'd always been a hard luck unit. Tough luck. The rifle fire on his side of the gap was lighter. "First and second platoon, keep going. Third and fourth, give them fire support.

When they've got the rill, third and fourth will leapfrog over them."

Shouts answered him. A dozen men took off hopping. *Was that all that was left of the forty who jumped off with me at the escarpment?*

Eight made it to the rill. They ducked down and started looking for hidey-holes. "It's like shooting fish in a bowl" came over the net. Tran would give them a minute, then order third and fourth up and forward.

Dumont held Tina. "I can't go out there," she whimpered.

"Don't worry, hon, we ain't going nowhere. No LT's gonna make us."

"They shot her," screamed a voice on the squad net. "They shot her right in our . . ."

"That was . . ." Tina started.

"Yeah," Dumont cut her off. Har had the hole right down from them. Dumont raised his helmet just enough to see. Someone in space armor with the red unity lightning patch was emptying his rifle into that hole. Unthinking, Dumont pulled his gun out, sighted quickly, and blew the gunner away. Someone on the lip of the rill turned toward him. Dumont walked his fire up to blow him off his feet.

Needles stitched the other side of the rill's wall. Dumont ducked before they got him. Needles ricocheted all over the place, but none hit him.

"Du, what is it?"

"Hon, if you want to live, you got to kill 'em. It's us or them time. Tina, can you stand up a bit more and see what's coming up behind me?"

Trembling, she did.

"See anything?"

"No."

"Good girl. Now, something's coming up the rill behind you. Don't turn around. I'm gonna get 'em." He edged his gun out a bit. The vid on it relayed the sight picture to his heads-up. Nothing. He pushed the gun a bit more. There was someone, down a ways, hiding behind a twist in the rill. Not much to aim at. He held the gun with both hands and pulled the trigger. His target fell, kicking and trying to slap his wounds. Dumont put two rounds through his helmet. He didn't move anymore.

Using his gun camera for a sweep, Dumont spotted nothing more at either end of the rill. Lying on his back, he pushed out—hoping the whole time his suit would hook on something and keep him in his hole. Nothing. Crouching, he risked a peek above the wall of the rill. Four dudes hopped forward, firing at the old ladies in the holes behind him. Without thought, Dumont swung his gun over the four, trigger finger locked down. They folded over backward. He felt Tina's hand on his shoulder. "What do you want me to do?"

"Cover my back. I'll take care of our front." One of the four bodies rolled over, grabbing for the gun nearby. Dumont shot him through the soles of his feet.

Captain Tran blinked. First and second platoons were gone. Just gone. He needed artillery before he'd order another assault. He crawled to the crest of the pass to get a line-of-sight on artillery. Climbing up on his knees, he got a signal from the artillery net—and a needle in the back.

It went right through him, leaving a tiny hole that bubbled blood into vacuum. He grabbed for a patch even as he fell. Front hole covered, he wondered how he'd handle the back. Two troopers crawled up behind him. One slapped his back. The pressure in his helmet quit dropping.

"Don't worry, sir, we'll get you back." They grabbed him by the shoulders and hustled him over the crest and down the other side, past blown mines and body parts. He glanced around. There were lots of wounded being helped by one or two friends, all headed back. Here and there a single soldier, no wound visible, no wounded comrade apparent, drifted back. The battle was over for B and C companies. D and E would have to take the pass.

Tran glanced up. D and E were rolling forward, maybe three or four more klicks out. D and E would do it.

• • •

Mary studied her display. The platoon had held against two hundred. Now another two hundred were coming up. It was time to do something—or surrender.

She'd watched Dumont's squad hunker in their holes, trying to make their own separate peace. Half of them were dead for that. Surrender was no option today.

"Lieutenant, Rodrigo here. I want missile release."

"How many, Sergeant?"

"All you got."

There was a pause . . . while the LT thought. No, the background of the pause carried the *ping, ping, ping* of a rifle. He was breathless when he came back on. "They're yours, Mary. We're too busy. Use 'em well."

Mary counted her targets. Twenty carriers, half of them tracked—that meant armored—raised dust plumes as they raced toward her. She had to get them. But there were laser rifles on several of them. These missiles would have to fight their way in. *Okay, flood them, like they flooded us.* Then there was the artillery. She'd heard the platoon whimper under its merciless, impersonal pounding. She'd also heard the screams as they died. Artillery is gonna pay. *And that big square box owes me. Owes me big time.*

The WP stuff was settling. Maybe they'd run out. Mary would not take that chance. She fed solid coordinates into the four SS-12's, offsetting their course so they'd be a deflection shot until the last second. The rigs were different; coming in fast, they kept their intervals. That made them predictable. She assigned the SS-3's areas to search if they lost laser lock.

All the missiles were rigged to one launch button. She shouted, "Fire in the hole!" and pushed it. Behind her, in two salvos, they leaped from their canisters. Twisting into immediate turns, they cleared the ridge by maybe one hundred meters, hungry for targets. Mary lit off every designator she had. This was it. But she didn't just play them on targets. She'd learned; these guys must have some kind of warning system. Those first two had taken off dodging as soon as she'd illuminated them. She programmed the lasers to play around the targets, ten meters to the right or left. Close enough so the missiles would know where to fly. Not so close the rigs didn't keep racing forward—unwarned.

Here and there, a laser bolt shot upward, but the missiles were not coming head-on. Making a deflection shot at this rate of closure, jostling in the speeding carriers, nobody scored.

Ten seconds to impact, Mary had the lasers light up their targets. Rigs began to twist. They were going too fast. Two bolts took missiles head-on, but that close, the wreckage of the missile was just as deadly as an undamaged one.

As a cheer went up on the platoon net, Mary concentrated on the four remaining missiles. The SS-12's reached out to the plain. *Two for rockets, one for guns. One for . . . No, I can't commit one missile to just that command rig. But it looks soft enough. Maybe if I target the gun closest to it?*

Mary grinned and set her designators.

"Major, missiles in the air," sensors shouted.

"Artillery, give me WP now, and plenty of it."

"Don't got any. Carrier just pulled in. We're offloading it straight to a tube. Damn, we needed it ten minutes ago."

"Get it out there." Ray turned back to the battle. Assault rigs still ran arrow straight across the broken terrain. Dumb. "Sensors, did you pass the missile alert to them?"

"Didn't want to juggle their elbow, Major. They've got their own warning system beeping in their ears."

"Don't look like it. Tell 'em for me."

"Yes, sir." There was a pause. When sensors came back, his voice was low, like a man who'd bet his wife and lost. "Sir, the beepers went off as I started talking."

On the plain before him, speeding carriers started to turn. Laser rifles fired. From where Longknife stood he would see the twisty way the missiles came in, making the gunners' job damn near impossible. Carriers started exploding. Here a missile went wide. There a rig dodged. One slid sideways into a boulder. The missile smashed against the rock. Troopers poured out of the demolished carrier, some running, too many crawling. Unable to look away, the major watched in disbelief as sixteen of his troop carriers met the missiles head-on. Nothing survived the collision. *But those carriers each had ten of my troops!*

"Major, Tran here. Request permission to withdraw B and C companies." There was a tremble in the officer's voice. He was hit, or had just watched D and E companies die—or both.

"Permission granted. Get back here any way you can. We'll lay artillery on their positions."

"Thanks, sir."

"I'll try to get some transport out there for you."

"Don't bother, sir. We'd rather walk."

"Major, we got four more missiles incoming," sensors squeaked.

"To where?" The major came heads-up.

"Us!"

Longknife swung himself out of the van. No damn Earth platoon had missiles with that range. What was he facing? Why hadn't they used them sooner? Was this the start of a counterattack? The missiles were above him. Jets of fire pushing them over, plunging them down. No laser bolts rose to meet them. All the rifles went with D and E. *After all, they were going in harm's way. We were sitting back here safe and sound.*

"Duck, you idiot," somebody called.

Whether to the major or some other idiot, Ray didn't know. But Ray hadn't ducked and he was an idiot. He ducked, shouting, "Staff, bail out. Take cover." In the low gravity of this moon, ducking took a while. He was only halfway down when the rockets hit.

Strange how you fall slowly in low gravity, but explosions move just as fast. To his left, a rocket launcher was halfway through reloading when the missile hit. With its own rockets not yet in the armored launch canister, not one but nine rockets blew. Fuel, flechettes, and jagged chunks of wreckage flew, consuming another launcher, stripping a gun mount of its crew. White phosphorus blew in all directions, taking out a second gun.

As if awed by that spectacle, the next two hits were hardly noticeable. One rocket hit one launcher. Another rocket demolished a gun. Then the fourth missile hit. It had the major's name, rank, and serial number on it.

Landing between two guns, its shower of flechettes wiped out half their crews. That covered two-thirds of the perimeter of expanding gas and plastic. The major and the command van took the rest. Pain came from a half dozen pinpricks. Worse, they threw him against the bumper of the van. Something crunched, and he quit hurting. *I don't want to quit hurting.* For the moment, he had no choice.

It seemed like a year before people started hopping around among the fire and debris. Two found him. "You hurt, Major?"

"Mind patching these holes? My arms aren't working and my ears are popping." They pulled goo out of the med pouch on his belt; his air quit getting thinner. As they lifted him off the bumper and settled him on a stretcher, he got a glance at the inside of the van. He'd only caught the low edge of the explosion. His staff, still at their stations, had taken the full force. They were pinned to the front wall like the targets at some fairground knife-throwing show.

The knife-thrower had made a lot of mistakes.

"Can you help my team?"

"Yessir," the private answered. Through his faceplate, Longknife saw the sergeant just shake his head.

Longknife could still chin his mike. "Artillery, I want fire on their position to cover our troops' withdrawal."

No answer.

"Artillery? Is anybody on net? Who's in charge?"

"I guess I am, sir. Second Lieutenant Divoba. I can lay sixty-four missiles on them right now, but we need a minute to get a tube manned."

"Hold your missiles, son. We're not trying to win a battle, we just want to keep their heads down while we walk away.

Use your tube artillery, and back your rockets off ten klicks. Now do it, son."

The pain was coming back.

"You want a shot, sir?"

"Not 'til I'm on ship."

"We can get you on one of the carriers heading out now, sir," the sergeant offered.

"I ride the last one, Sergeant. You want to take an earlier one?"

"Nosir." It was nice to see a sergeant smile the way they did when they found an officer doing what an officer should. Longknife hoped that smile wouldn't cost him his life.

"Private, you want to take an early ride?"

"Nosir." His voice broke, but he got the word out. Poor kid. Stuck with two seniors playing it out by the code. Ray knew he ought to order the kid out, but he might need him to carry him. A cannon shell arched over the major's line of sight. Usually he would have felt the ground shake. *I must be real bad.* The sergeant twisted around to follow the shell for a moment. He got a good view of the troops struggling back from the pass. "Looks pretty bad, sir."

"We've been in some tough ones. We always come through."

Then it got worse.

"Captain Andy," Umboto chortled, "I got six missiles ready to have a go at those transports. I had to teach them their numbers on pencil and paper. I've tucked them in at night and booted them out of bed for the last eternity, but *they* are *ready*! Permission to launch, sir."

"You may launch when ready, Commander."

Captain Anderson glanced around his HQ. It had gone from a morgue to damn near looking like a winning celebration on election night—one of those rare ones where they beat the polls. On his display, the captain watched six dots leave the crater and march slowly toward the enemy's grounded transports. With them gone, the enemy troops would have but two choices: fight on with air getting stale, or surrender.

From the reports he'd been getting back from the first platoon of A company, the colonials were just about fought out.

"Everybody, get your head down," Mary shouted. "We got incoming on the way. The bastards are running like shit downhill, but somebody's tossing artillery our way to keep us out of their way. I vote we let them run, and dig deep."

There were a lot of cheers for that one. Even the lieutenant breathed a hearty "Amen." Then the net squawked again. "First platoon, don't pull your heads out of your holes for this, but if you can look up, those missiles going by are on their way to the transports. Now we got the bastards between a rock and a hard place. Yeehaa."

"Who is that?" one of Dumont's kids asked.

"That crazy woman who was on net a while back," Cassie answered. "I didn't get no name."

"She's Commander Umboto, brigade XO," the lieutenant answered. "And those big missiles sure do look good going over. Mary, can you catch them on a vid?"

"No, sir, not till they come down a bit."

"They sure look pretty."

"Lieutenant, shouldn't you get your head down?"

"It is down, Mary. Don't worry about me."

The barrage was light, but steady. Every minute or so another shell would wander their way. Mary kept up a running commentary—on the enemy running and on the general direction of the next incoming round. Most rounds went right into the gap. Once in a while, one would go long.

"Oh, God, I'm hit!" came the lieutenant's scream. Mary focused a vid where the lieutenant's hole was. A new and bigger one was right next to it. Rocks and debris were still falling.

"Lieutenant, you okay?" Cassie called.

No answer.

Mary took her system out of combat mode and into troop

status. The lieutenant's suit was still on net, but it glowed a yellow-red. "He's alive, but we're losing him."

"Okay, crew, let's dig him out," Lek sighed on net. On the vid, first one, then three, finally six people were out of their holes, headed for the lieutenant's.

"Mary, you call the incoming artillery," Cassie said. "Try to get a good read on where it'll fall."

"Yeah," Dumont muttered. "I ain't never done somethin' this stupid before. Hate to get killed the first time I try it."

More were out of their holes. Mary doubted they'd do any good. "Six is enough. If we need more, I'll call. Don't need anyone standing around watching others dig."

"You bet nobody's gonna watch me dig," Dumont snarled, but the bite was gone. His usual snap drew a laugh. Mary divided her display, half on those digging, half on the artillery. A gun puffed. Mary used her radar sensors for the first time to plot its fall. "Shell's headed for the crest of the gap. No sweat."

The diggers didn't even pause when the shell exploded. Second shot was no worse. "We've found him," Cassie yelped.

Across the plain, the gun carriage bucked. Mary did the numbers. "Oh, shit. You got incoming, and it's gonna be close."

Most of the diggers flattened themselves in the shell crater. Two didn't, huddling together just outside the crater, covering something—someone. Mary forgot to breathe as she counted seconds. "Hail Mary, full of grace" came from one suit. "Our Father, who art in heaven" from another. "Sweet Jesus, help the fuck us" was balanced by someone's prayer mantra.

Mary just counted down: "Four, three, two, one."

A dust plume sprouted twenty meters from the first crater. Again rocks and shell fragments cut their lazy arcs through the vacuum. Mary could only watch as it showered down.

Dumont yelped. "Goddamn it, somebody pull that hot hunk of metal out of my ass." On vid, one of the two figures that had stayed exposed to cover someone else reached over with a gob of goo and started rubbing it on the other's rear.

"Now, does that feel better?" Cassie cooed.

"Yes, Mother. You gonna kiss it, make it well?"

"Only in your dreams, kid. Okay, crew. Give me a hand. Lieutenant's still breathing, but he's out cold. Everybody keep goo handy. I don't know how bad his suit's holed."

"Lek," Mary ordered, "bring the bubble." Mine disasters could hole a suit in too many places for goo—too many places to even find. The bubble could keep you alive for an hour. Longer if they found more air. The next three shells stayed out of the way while they cared for their officer.

"How bad is he?" Mary asked on Lek's private line.

"He don't look none too good. There's a lot broken and we got no way to take a peek at him through all this damn armor."

Mary switched to battalion. "Major Henderson. We got a bad hurt lieutenant here. You don't get us help fast, he's dead."

"Nearest set of wheels is yours." The voice wasn't the major's. Commander Umboto was back on the line. "Load the lieutenant on whatever shows up. We'll have an ambulance with a med team meet them ASAP."

"Thank you, ma'am," Mary answered.

"Thank you, Sergeant. You put up a damn good fight. The Spartans couldn't have done better. No use losing someone who won the battle just before they get it over with. Umboto out."

Mary put a vid on long-distance search. "I think I see a dust cloud coming our way."

"Looks so," Lek agreed.

"Who the Spartans?" Dumont wanted to know. Mary let them talk, but the commander's words had hit her. They had won their battle, but could still die under one of these random shots. It didn't seem fair, to win a battle and get killed before it was over. Miners bitched about owners and their twisted idea of fair. War seemed to have no idea of fair. No idea at all.

• • •

"Major Longknife, Senior Pilot Nuu here, and we've got a problem. The *Hardy, Noble* and *Gallant* are unfit for space. If the Earthies got more where those came from, we're in a world of hurt. Santiago tells me things aren't going well on your end either. I got people who want to lift. What can I do for you?"

"We're in bad shape. Falling back fast as we can. Lighten what ships you got and pile troopers in. Launch them as fast as you fill them."

"How many troopers do we have to load on each ship? You offloaded seven hundred fifty-eight."

"The Second got bled plenty. I don't know what we've got now. The gear's not worth the lift, but the troopers are the brigade. Honey, you got to get them back. With them we can rebuild. Without them, we're all dead."

"Ray, you okay?" The voice went soft, no more the transport commander's.

It was the softness that did it, took the lie from his mouth and let the truth out through clenched teeth. "No, friend."

"I could lift the *Friendship*, drop it down close to you."

"Probably on my head, girl. No, we evacuate by the numbers. You fill up a transport, you launch it away from their damn base. We'll make it," he ordered. "Captain Santiago, you out there?"

"Yes, sir."

"Turn those carriers around as soon as they get back. Pull drivers from A company. Tell them their ticket out is one trip forward. You having any trouble?"

"Nope. Few hotheads want to go up and show the rest of you how it's done, but I got them taking care of the wounded right now. When are you coming back, sir?"

"On the last carrier."

"I'll be driving it."

"And I'll be waiting for you," Rita whispered.

Major Longknife couldn't turn his head anymore. He didn't have to. The vision of a battle bravely started and badly wreaked was etched behind his eyes, never to go away. For two hours he waited as the remnants of the 2nd Guard streamed past. He should have ordered the artillery silent when it was obvious there was no pursuit, but it slipped his pain-wracked mind.

When Santiago loomed over him, he didn't resist the pain spray. The battle was over. He'd lost this one big.

Trevor Hascomb Crossinshield the Ninth stripped naked. He needed to meet the most powerful men on one hundred planets. They were in the sauna; he had exactly five minutes of their time. If he took less, it would be accorded a virtue to him. He could not take more.

Wrapping a towel around himself, he slipped his feet into sandals and padded noisily toward his business appointment. He opened the sauna door only enough to slip in. These men did not suffer cold interruptions. He took the appropriate supplicant's seat on the lowest of the four tiers of cedar shelves, next to the hot stones. When asked, he would ladle water on them for more steam. He would do whatever he was told.

The room was hot. *How can they take the heat?* Not born to this life—or wealth—Trevor doubted he could stand the heat of the highest tier. He would, however, find a place along the middle tiers most comfortable. Searching for the one who had invited him, Trevor risked a quick glance at the upper tier. Steam billowed and drifted there, hiding the men's faces. No, one was a woman. Her towel open, she stretched out languidly along the highest shelf, forcing men to either sit closer together or move to a lower bench. Was she a "companion" on display? The body was sculpted, expensive. Earned or . . .

For a moment, Trevor caught her eyes. There was cold fire there, but nothing for him. He felt like he'd been hacked, the entire contents of his mass storage reviewed and not found worth the effort to format. Trevor snapped his eyes down, locked them on a floor tile and awaited notice. The room was silent; here he would get no dropped scrap of information to sell. *Are my five minutes ticking away?* Desperate, he forced himself to quiet.

"How goes our little war?" a familiar voice spoke from a corner of the highest tier.

"Your war, Henry, not ours," someone in the opposite corner dared to interrupt, and interrupting, to correct—and to challenge. Trevor held his tongue.

"Edward, when all of humanity groans in birth, of course we will be there. We raped her fair and square. The little bastard will fall right into our tender clutches. Of course it is ours." The voice held a chuckle . . . empty of mirth.

"Thank you, Henry. I love your poetry. But let us not forget, the colony planets are throwing their full weight behind their tin dictator. On several fronts their Red Banner fleets advance, spewing their songs of 'One Humanity, United together. The only coin the sweat of the worker. The only just pay what you've made with your own hands.'"

"And I do love your poetry too, Edward, even if it is all secondhand. Yes, they do press us here and there, but they are like any new entrepreneur with a penny vision. They overreach, and just moments before they might have realized a profit, they go bankrupt. That is when we step in with a takeover bid. There is nothing they plant that we cannot reap."

Trevor risked a glance at his patron. Heat swirled around him. Beneath his words were fire, enough to cut down a dozen CEO's of transplanetary corporations. Still he leaned back against the wall, talking coolly, body frozen in a posture of good cheer. Not even a finger twitched.

"You put much at risk."

"Because you were blind, Edward. People seeped out to the frontier like water under a dam. And you ignored them."

"They paid their bills. Living off the interest made you fat, Henry, and left them nothing."

"Nothing, Edward. One moment you speak of fleets pressing in on us. Another moment you call them nothing. You have ignored the frontier worlds too long. It is time to bring them back into the wide river of humanity, to let them grow wealthy and comfortable like Earth and her seven sisters, like Pitt's Hope and the other two score that came after. The colonies must be brought into the family, not by some foot-stamping messiah, but our way. Peacefully, profitably, comfortably. There is no profit in surprises. Left long enough on their own, anyone can dream up a surprise. Edward, we must eliminate surprises."

"And so you play with a war, Henry. Brute force follows no laws, physical or economic. The hounds of war nip at any heel they choose, not just the one you want. You gamble."

"When I gamble, Edward, the fix is already in. Mr. Crossinshield, the fix is in, is it not?"

"Yes, sir." Trevor wasted no time on the gulp he desperately wanted. His button pushed, he spewed his contents in words too rapid to be interrupted. "We have multiple contacts in all major and minor theaters of operations on both the colonial and Earth sides. Information is being received, collated, and analyzed daily. If President Urm's Unity Movement cannot be properly guided, we have subcontractors in place to cancel him."

The woman rolled over, propped herself on one elbow, and crossed her legs. "And there is no one to take his place among the collection of thieves with whom he has surrounded himself." She grinned. There was no humor behind it, no evidence of any feeling at all. "Of course, some of those thieves are our thieves. Very good, Henry."

Trevor's patron opened his lips in an empty smile and went through the motions of a thank-you before turning back to the man across the room. "You see, Edward, this is a restructuring, not war. A growth of franchises that will be handled delicately. Before the next annual reports are due, we will have closed out our wartime contracts profitably and plunged into the next economic expansion fueled by the unmet needs of the colonies on the credit we extend, to managers we select."

"If you are right. If these puppets are truly yours and if they do not slip their strings and discover a life of their own," the questioner growled. His face twisted in a grimace, and he threw up a hand. He knew none of these people of power could hear his words. He had lost.

"I am always right. Thank you, Mr. Crossinshield. It is a pleasure doing business with you. We must talk another time of expanding our relationship."

Trevor stood. "Thank you, sir."

He left. In the cool of the locker room, sweat poured off him that had nothing to do with the sauna. When he could, he walked unsteadily to the shower. Under the cooling spray, he regained himself. *The fix is in. We have agents everywhere. We know what is happening.* It was a comforting mantra.

FOUR

THERE WAS NOTHING worse than being beached. Abeeb men had shunned exile to the land for a thousand years, since the first one set sail in a wooden dhow to cross the blue waters off the east coast of Africa. Well, Uncle Dula had chosen to squat dirtside until this war blew over. Mattim could not. Uncle Dula had seniority and twenty years of good solid profits; he'd be one of the first captains recalled when peace came again. Captain Mattim Abeeb had no such track record.

He'd leaped at the offer: command of his own ship at thirty. He should have looked closer at what he was jumping into. The routes he drew were deep along the rim of human space. He watched prices paid for his cargos plummet as competing bidders were replaced by Unity monopolies—one offer, take it or leave it. And profit was a dirty word, rapidly elevating into a crime. Mattim could only wonder what the storekeepers were paying for his cargos—and who pocketed the difference.

As profits went down, expenses went up. Corporate groused about the Westinghouse fire control he'd bought, but Mattim and crew had been glad for it when they needed it. Maybe that was why his crew, every one of them, had signed with him when the *Maggie D* had been contracted for conversion to a Navy cruiser. They knew as well as he that the Red Flag Line wanted its ships back on routes as soon as the war ended. With luck, Mattim would have the *Maggie* converted back and making money long before Uncle Dula got his recall letter.

Assuming the Navy hadn't messed up the *Maggie* too badly—and they lived through the war. Big assumptions.

Mattim studied his *Maggie D;* staring down past his feet, out through the viewing port imbedded in the floor of the station's corridor to where she lay at Pier 12. She took some getting used to. *Maggie* was not the ship he'd left three months ago.

The blocky freighter he'd commanded for five years was gone. About all that hadn't changed was the thick ice of the dust catcher at her bow. She was now an even five hundred meters long, fifty added to make room for the second reactor. In doubling the engines to twelve, the stern had gone from a rectangle to something like an oval. *Better make sure the engines balance,* he thought to himself.

The hull was the major change. The blocks of thousands of standard containers were replaced by a smooth teardrop, no different from any Navy cruiser. She glistened, metal and ice armor reflecting back the dim light. Amidships, a turret popped up, rotated, then retreated, leaving a smooth hull. Laser guns, ready to boil someone else's armor, were his new business.

Squaring his shoulders, Mattim marched to meet the officers and crew that had breathed this different life into his ship.

"*Sheffield* arriving" blared the moment his foot touched deck plates. He returned the ensign's smart salute, saluted the blue and green flag painted on the aft bulkhead, and turned to find himself being saluted by a three-striper who hadn't been there a second ago. "We've been expecting you, sir. I'm Commander Colin Ding, your exec. Would you like to inspect the ship?"

Without waiting for an answer, his XO turned and

began said tour. He followed the woman of medium height, medium age and medium Asian appearance, wondering if it had all been issued to her. The *Margarita de Silva y Rodriguez Sheffield, Maggie* to him, *Sheffield* to the Navy, was big, one hundred meters at her widest. Plenty of room for fuel tanks and weapons—and redundancies. The Navy was big on redundancy.

And people. He now commanded two doctors. Abdul still ran the galley, though a freckle-faced ensign was in charge. All told, the crew was five hundred strong in dozens of specialties, though four hundred were green as hydroponic goo. The balance was an equal number of old hands from the *Maggie* and Navy types.

Yes, the XO showed him a lot. Fuel storage, food storage, people quarters—everything about running a ship. Nothing about running a warship. *Interesting.*

"Let's drop down to engineering," Mattim suggested.

"It's about time to knock off for chow, sir."

"Ivan was never first in line. Let's see."

Reluctantly, the exec led off. The power plants for the merchant cruisers were still a fleetwide problem. Until somebody figured it out, the converted cruisers were more of a danger to themselves than the colonials—and Mattim commanded nothing but an oversize hotel hitched to a space station.

As Mattim expected, Ivan was at his commsole. From the rumpled state of his uniform, he might have been there all night. "There." Ivan stabbed at his board. "There. That's what killed Ramsey's *Pride of Tulsa.* A damn spike. These dirtside generators throw spikes!"

"Then how come we're still here?" the exec asked as if every day she was greeted with the announcement she should be dead.

"'Cause I'm keeping that piece of shit on its own circuits. The *Maggie*'s power plant can generate enough to handle both plasma containment bottles. The juice from that mud-ball power plant can feed the guns. They got those huge capacitors anyway. A spike or two won't faze them."

Ding rubbed her chin. "Staff want the plants crossfed so damage to one won't bring down any system," she said slowly.

Ivan shook his head violently and tapped his board. "That's the last telemetry out of the *Tulsa*'s engine room. That's what I just got from our own plant. Dirtside, they hitch four or eight reactors together. They can swallow a spike and not lose their magnetic fields around the plasma. With just two here, the hit's too hard. The field comes down and the demon's out of the bottle. How many *Tulsas* do those idiots want? Just 'cause General Fusion's got a war contract for a couple of thousand of 'em is no reason for me and mine to get blown to bits."

The exec looked at Mattim. "I can pass it along to squadron staff, sir. In a month we may get something back."

"In the meantime, those poor damn marines keep getting pulverized," Ivan rumbled.

"Let's talk with the chief of gunnery over dinner."

"The other engineers wanted to know how my tests went." Ivan grinned. "I've been passing them my results live. Bet this talk happens on a lot of ships."

A gray-haired wisp of a commander with Howard on his name tag entered the wardroom as they did. "Afternoon, Captain," he said, extending his hand. "I'm Guns."

"Got a question for you," and the XO launched into Ivan's idea. Ivan hovered, listening, nodding his agreement. His wife Sandy, Mattim's Jump Master from the old *Maggie*, joined them.

Guns stared at the ceiling as Ding finished. It was a long minute before he nodded. "I like redundancy, but I can see why you don't want to crossfeed the second power plant into the containment loop. No power is better than wild plasma. If you set up a feed from the first plant to my guns, I'd be happy."

"Let's think about this before we pass it along to the admiral's staff." Mattim concluded the discussion. "I want to make sure you're all one hundred percent behind it."

"Speaking of staff," the XO put in, "we have an invitation to dinner from the chief of intelligence to go over the 'big picture.' You, Captain, me, anyone you want to bring along."

Mattim mulled the thought. Information was power; that he'd learned at his mother's knee. Since getting tied in with the Navy, he'd yet to get any briefing that was better than a five-minute browse of the news channels. Supper would be a good place to take this guy's measure. Mattim raised an eyebrow at Guns.

"No, thank you, sir. This evening I want to go over Ivan's report. Make sure that second plant's output is within limits. I expect they will be. We design our guns to be forgiving."

Mattim glanced at Ivan and Sandy. He was shaking his head; she was nodding firmly in agreement. "He's been living in that damn engine room. A night out is just what he needs. Let me run him through the shower and he'll even be presentable." Ivan growled, but went when his wife pushed him toward their quarters.

Mattim laughed, as he often did with those two. "Tell . . ."

"Captain Whitebred," Ding supplied.

"There will be four of us for dinner."

Colin Ding nervously brushed a hand down her black dress. In her thirty years growing up Navy and serving in the same, she'd never been to an "O" Club as classy as this one. Or been in the company of a man as impressive as Captain Whitebred.

"The admiral wanted a proper club for the squadron's senior officers. I knew if we left it to the accountants we'd have some run-down slop joint. So I told the admiral to leave it to me. With a bit of private negotiating, I cut a deal with the proprietor. With a war on, he knew which way to jump." Horacio . . . he'd asked her to call him Horacio . . . guided her into the club as he spoke, his hand gently on her elbow, his fingers occasionally brushing her breast.

The Monaco was spectacular. He'd described his negotiations at length the evening he'd entertained all the XO's of the converted cruisers. It had been quite a night. Captain Whitebred held her chair as she sat. Ivan did the same for his wife Sandy; Colin had to wonder at an organization that allowed people to marry and stay on the same ship. She'd heard a lot about how merchies ran ships. Damn loose. Captain Abeeb settled into his chair with a familiarity that brought a remark from Captain Whitebred.

"You've been to the Monaco before?"

"A few times on other people's expense accounts."

"I assure you, service has improved and there will be no gouging of poor sailors." Colin wondered when the last "poor sailor" had passed through the door of this place.

Sandy gave a tight smile. "In war, one must make do."

"A wise woman," Whitebred laughed. "Just what a merchant ship would need in accounting."

"I do the jump navigation, Captain." Sandy hid her scowl behind a sip from the crystal water goblet before her.

"Well, let us not talk shop tonight." Whitebred's broad smile took in all of them. "As the lady reminds us, there is a war on. Let us seize the moments life affords us and squeeze pleasure from them where we will." Whitebred's smile settled on Colin. The words, smile, and gentle way his fingers caressed her hand sent shivers up her back. Abeeb's tight smile was downright puritanical. *Whitebred is not in my chain of command, and you gave this sailor the night off.*

The meal, ordered by Captain Whitebred beforehand, was scrumptious. Drawn from a dozen planets, including Peking duck from Earth, it was a sensuous delight for the eye and the taste buds. Horacio kept up a running description, most of which she couldn't pronounce, much less follow, though Abeeb traded him line for line. And Horacio's hand always returned to gently stroke her's. His smile was always open, offering her . . . what? What every man offered? Or something more?

Over dessert and brandy, the war came up. Though the two captains orchestrated this part of the conversation just as deftly as the earlier repartee, it was not long before Ivan threw down his napkin. "Why are we fighting? All the frontier wanted was decent prices for its raw materials, reasonable prices for the stuff they brought from the developed planets, and an interest rate on their debt that wasn't just short of usury."

"Usury." Horacio chuckled. "That's a term I haven't heard since college. And what is usury, commander?"

"Charging those poor folks an arm and a leg."

"All that the market will bear, wouldn't you say?" Horacio smiled as he settled his napkin tidily in place.

"Damn right," the engineer almost spat. His wife rested a hand on his arm, patted him as if to soothe.

"Come, come." Horacio leaned forward. "And what would you charge them, Commander? Nothing has a fixed worth. Its value is what the market gives it. They want, need, the products of the developed planets so they can develop themselves. The raw materials they provide are nice, but hardly worth the value they think, what with transport costs. Every developed system has mines that are hardly played out. We buy from the frontier as a kindness. If we didn't, there would be no way they could pay for the machinery and goods they need from us."

Ivan snorted. "You can't believe that. What kind of kindness drives people to war? And a costly one. For the war taxes we're paying, you could lower a lot of interest rates, forgive a lot of debts."

Horacio shrugged. "If you pay the Danegeld, you always get the Dane back. Right, Colin?"

"That's what my dad taught me. The Navy's here to keep bandits honest."

"That's what I told my friends in the corporate world when I asked for an appointment to the Navy. Rough times call for the tough to get going. And what we do in these harsh times *will* be remembered." He patted her hand and winked.

As the engineer opened his mouth, Captain Abeeb pushed his chair back. "It's been a delightful meal, and a pleasant conversation, but, Captain, I've got some technical issues I want to talk over with my engineer. If you'll excuse us."

"You won't be taking Sandra with you?" Horacio asked as the Jump Master also stood.

"Sorry, I too must get back to the ship."

"Everyone is deserting me before my dessert is finished. You won't be fleeing, my dear Colin?"

Colin had spent the last three months getting that tub in as good a shape as possible. Didn't she deserve a night off?

"Have you given much thought to what you will do after this war?" Horacio whispered.

"No."

"You've benefited from the flood of war promotions."

"Yes," she scowled. It didn't take a history book to tell her what the usual reward was for a victorious officer.

Horacio moved his chair closer, dessert forgotten. "The Navy isn't the only world. There will be vast opportunities once this"—he dismissed the war with a flick of his finger—"is done. Let me tell you of some of them."

Colin's career counseling had started at her father's knee. She recognized this for just such a session, even if Horacio's fingers roving her arm, flicking by her breast, made it quite different. She leaned forward, not totally ignoring the lingering glance Horacio gave what the scoopneck of her dress revealed. "What opportunities will there be in the corporate world once we've made the galaxy safe for business?"

He grinned. "There is much to share."

At 0600 the next morning, Mattim took breakfast in the wardroom; he used it for a quick staff meeting. Ding sat at his right. She'd been two hours later returning from dinner—and what she did with the time was her own damn business. Guns was at his left. Ivan and Sandy sat farther down the table. The ship's damage control officer, Tina Gandhi, and communications officer, Sparky Sanchez, filled up the table.

"I want the *Sheffield* at underway watches even if we are alongside the pier. Let's get the crew familiar with their jobs." That drew nods. "Guns, any problem with the power from the new plant?"

"Looks okay. I'll check it out today."

"Good. I'd like to spend the morning with your folks."

"Glad to have you, sir."

"The admiral's called for a teleconference at oh-nine hundred," Ding put in. "I suspect it has something to do with engineering modifications made recently."

"Ivan?"

The chief engineer chuckled. "Got calls this morning. Every ship's adopted the layout. We all worked together on it. I just tested it first."

"I don't think Smiley's gonna like it," Guns drawled.

"Smiley?" Mattim echoed.

"Wait until you meet the man." Guns ducked the question.

"I want everyone in my day cabin for the conference." Breakfast was served and eaten quickly. Mattim went with Guns when they finished. The tour of the weapons department added flesh to the lectures Mattim had sat through. Nine turrets were split fore, aft, and amidships and distributed around the center line at different points so two-thirds of them could pour laser fire at any angle. Gravity-focused, they were theoretically lethal out to twenty-five thousand kilometers. "I'd hold my first salvo 'til fifteen thousand K's if I could," Guns suggested. "Heat's a gun's enemy. Don't let the textbooks fool you. Even with a gravity lens for the primary focus, heat buildup on the mirrors adds to the scatter. And the capacitors get hot. By the fourth salvo, it takes longer to recharge and we're getting less energy. Choosing your timing and your range. That's what a battle's about."

"There's a lot I need to learn." Mattim was taking a risk, but after time with Howard, it looked like a good one. Guns had answered a lot of Mattim's unspoken questions . . . and not a few answers had gone against the book Mattim's brief course insisted be followed. Was this the reason this man never made captain? Mattim knew he was a student again. He knew how to manage a ship. Learning how to fight one was his new job.

"Be glad to help, Skipper. Man and boy, I've studied these guns for forty years. It'll be good to have someone new to listen to my space stories." The old man laughed.

"So why do you call him Smiley?" Mattim asked.

Guns glanced at his watch. "About time you find out."

Mattim's day cabin was more proof of the space in the *Sheffield*. A VP at corporate didn't have an office this size, though Mattim's was pie-shaped and lacked a window. The wider end held a table with over a dozen chairs. The middle area was a comfortable conversation area with couch and overstuffed chairs around a low table. His desk filled the narrow end; it was still fairly clear of paperwork.

Behind Mattim, the wall came to life. The admiral held the center block of the screen. Tables like the one Mattim sat at filled the periphery sections—all seven cruisers were present, even the ravaged *Sendai*. The admiral began without preamble.

"Every captain is responsible for his ship's combat availability. These ships were in a sad state of repair when the Navy took them over. I have filed several complaints with the comptroller concerning discrepancies between what was claimed by the shipping lines and what my staff found. The executive officers have attempted to make whole these problems." The man smiled directly into the camera. There was no humor. Beside Mattim, Ding's face was a frozen mask; he suspected she found no comfort in the admiral's faint praise.

"As merchant captains you are no doubt aware you hold primary responsibility for your ship." The smile grew wider. "That no longer includes making a profit. Now it solely consists of making it battle-ready. All nonregulation equipment will be landed to save weight. Some execs have fumbled this, unwilling or unable to make longtime merchant officers follow Navy policy. You captains will correct this."

Mattim glanced at Sandy. He'd invested heavily in sensors as well as that fire control computer. Her determined scowl as much as Ding's shrug told him they were still aboard. Good!

"I am also advised . . ." the admiral went on, his grin growing even wider. How could a man's facial expression be so out of touch with his words? Unease grew in Mattim's belly. ". . . that unauthorized modifications have been made to the power plants. These will be corrected. My staff will visit each ship and assure themselves personally that every ship is in conformity with proper ship configuration."

There was a commotion behind the admiral. A message was handed to him. At the same time, Mattim's communication officer tapped the display before him on the table. "Sir," he whispered, "we just got a message from the Marines in the next system."

"Put in on speaker," Mattim ordered, knowing full well it would be carried over the conference link. A desperate voice came from several sources; Mattim wasn't the only one listening to the admiral's mail. "Ninety-seventh Planetary Defense Brigade to Commander, Cruiser Squadron Fifty-three. Enemy is one jump away. We will be under attack in forty-eight hours. Request assistance. For God's sake, don't let them pound us again. Captain Anderson sends."

The admiral was no longer smiling. He ignored the repeating of this communication as he tapped the message flimsy. "Pringle, can you get the *Significant* underway?"

Pringle was the only other regular Navy captain and his

ship the only other regular cruiser. "We are ready now, sir."

"Unfortunately, the *Reply* and the *Significant* are the *only* ships ready to get under way. We can not engage an enemy force of unknown composition alone. Regrettably, that will have to be my answer." He did not seem broken-hearted.

Mattim was damned if he'd sit here and be an excuse for this man, not after all Ivan had done. He glanced at his engineer and got the barest nod to the unasked question. "Admiral, the *Sheffield* can get under way in four hours."

"Your ship has not been cleared by the yard supervisor."

"Yes, sir, but the ship has checked out in preliminary tests, and I expect we can finish up the loose ends in four hours."

"Your engines," the admiral began.

"Have been tested at full power." Ivan nodded forcefully. "We are ready to get under way"—Mattim now eyed Guns—"and we are fully combat ready." Guns grinned and gave him a thumbs up.

"Well, maybe the captain of the *Sheffield* thinks he can come aboard one day and leave for battle the next, but . . ."

"The *Aurora*'s ready too, sir," Captain Buzz Burka said, never one to pass up a barroom brawl. In a moment, all the rest had piled in.

Smiley was not smiling as he jumped to his feet. "We will see. No ship sorties without yard certification. No ship jumps out of this system until it's demonstrated combat availability."

The center screen went blank. "Sparks," Mattim barked, "get me the yard superintendent. Who's running it?"

"Trong Thon," Ding answered.

"Torchy! Good."

In a minute the answer "Trong here" came back.

"Torchy, Matt here. I need to get under way in three hours. Can you get a team over here to cover loose ends?"

"Matt, my board's lit up like a fireworks display on landing day. Everybody heading out at once?"

"Yeah, Torchy, there's a war on."

"We'll be spread thin, but I'll get you a team if I have to pull my daughter out of grade school."

"Thanks, Torchy, I knew I could count on you."

"Hey, man, with all of you going out at once, there won't be any staff weenies looking over our shoulders. We can get the job done. Thanks. See you in thirty minutes."

All around the table there were smiles, and sighs of relief. Mattim eyed Ivan and Sandy. "What gives? You two have been against this war from day one. Now you want to go fight?"

Ivan shrugged. "Matt, you've never been here for a staff inspection. Smiley's staff don't know much about engines, but they can bury you in paperwork." He glanced at Guns.

"Every blue suiter knows the story behind Smiley. He's commanded a destroyer, cruiser, and battleship . . . while they were in the yard. After he damn near ran his destroyer into an asteroid, they didn't even let him take the cruiser out of dock. As soon as we're operational, another admiral gets to take over."

Sandy shrugged as she took over from Guns. "Given a choice between spending the war dockside with Smiley or going out, the colonials got to be easier."

"That remains to be seen. Let's get this ship tested and out of here." Mattim stood.

Major Ray Longknife struggled upward to consciousness, fighting past corpses and exploding guns. He knew who he was and what he'd done. Because of that, he kept his eyes closed.

He'd awakened before. On the transport, surrounded by the moans of the other wounded. He'd wanted to tell them he was sorry, search in their eyes and words for the forgiveness he'd never allow himself. He'd awakened other times, screaming in agony as lancing fire shot through him. President Urm's reward for defeated commanders was a bullet. Ray hadn't heard they'd added torture. It didn't surprise him.

His body demanded a deep sigh; Ray controlled the urge. He wanted neither the pain nor the bullet. If these were his last moments, he would enjoy them. Memories crowded his mind, most of death and destruction. He pushed them aside, focused on Rita. The proud commander the first time he saw her on her bridge. The dancer he couldn't keep his eyes off as her whole body flowed to the music. In that sundress, proudly showing him around the garden at her parents' home. God, she'd been beautiful. If he had to have a last memory, he'd hold tight to that one.

Warm fingers roved the palm of his hand, circling slowly, then moving out to caress his thumb and fingers. His breath caught in his throat; he opened his eyes. Rita sat beside his bed. It was her fingers playing with his hand. She wore the sundress. She leaned forward, eyes wide, cheeks tear-stained. Her breasts didn't quite fall out of the dress. Not quite.

He found himself stirring, responding to her. He tried to move. His legs weren't there; at least the important stuff was. She reached for him. He opened his arms. They could damn well wait for a few minutes to shoot him.

The executioner didn't show up for quite some time. The hug grew to a kiss. It might have gone further, but Ray discovered his body encased in something a lot less flexible than armor.

"What the hell?" Startled, Rita stood, giving him room to grab the sheets covering him and throw them back. From his chest down, he was encased in white. Well, not entirely. "What the hell is this?"

"A very nice hard-on," Rita said with a grin, "and I am very glad to see it."

"Thank you very much, woman, but what is the rest of this?"

"A body cast. You've got to hold your back rigid. Notice the traction. It's helping you while your nerves regenerate."

"A damn lot of expense just so I can stand up to be shot."

"Nobody's going to shoot you, Ray. You're a hero."

Ray looked Rita square in the eye. "Some kind of hero. Second Guard never ran 'til I took it to that damn rock. God, all the good people killed." He let the anguish flood him, bleed into his voice. "I wish to God they would shoot me."

Rita was back, holding him. He wanted to weep. The commander of the toughest bunch of bastards Wardhaven ever spawned did not cry. He pulled it back in, damned up the pain. Rita was crying; he would not. But that didn't stop the question. "How could they beat us? How?"

"I was at the hearing. Dad demanded it be open. I testified why we chose Rosebud One. Santiago laid out the problems at the landing site and how the battle developed. Even your political officer was praising you. 'Major Longknife took the risk in the best tradition of the Guard. He could not have known he faced a full company, reinforced with engineers and heavy support.' The admiral wanted you for the scapegoat. He didn't get you. I hear he's out for a third sweep. He better come back with a victory, or there's a bullet waiting."

Ray leaned back on his pillow, tried to let it soak in. "I can't think of a man more in need of a new job. But a bullet?"

Rita glanced at the ceiling. "You fail the will of the people, you owe them your blood." She repeated the official line.

"Yes," he mumbled for the hidden mike, then threw off the dark mood. "Enough. Senior Pilot Nuu, what are you doing here?"

She drew herself up, a junior officer answering a senior, but did not release his hand. "The transports have stood down until naval superiority is achieved. While the *Friendship* is in for maintenance, I am on a well-deserved leave. I'm also fishing for a new assignment." The officer vanished; she finished as lover. "Ray, I thought I'd lost you. Enough. Where you are, I am. While you're recovering on Wardhaven, I'm not budging."

"If it pleases God and politicians," he breathed.

FIVE

FOUR HOURS LATER, Torchy stood beside Mattim. As test reports from throughout the ship flowed to his handheld board, it slowly turned from red to green. At 1430, it was all green.

"You got one good ship here," the superintendent crowed. "I'm yours to the jump point. I'll ride the target tugs back."

Mattim glanced around; the bridge was four times larger than what he was used to, and most of the people were strangers. Sandy was at navigation and Thor Jagel now wore lieutenant stripes as he sat in his usual place at the helm. Mattim turned to his exec.

"What does the ship's company say?"

"Our boards have been green for a month, sir."

"Ivan." Mattim tapped his comm link. "One last time. Is the power plant safe?"

"As safe as a babe in his mother's arms."

"Comm, send to the flag. *Sheffield* ready to get under way."

Thirty minutes later they got their orders. The *Reply* and *Significant* had cast off two hours earlier. They now trailed the station in orbit by five hundred kilometers. The five new cruisers were to sortie as a group. To maintain separation, odd ships were to duck below the station, even ships above.

Nothing said whether this was based on the newly painted hull numbers or their order along the station. Mattim raised an eyebrow to the XO. "What's the Navy way for this?"

"Captain, I've never been on the bridge for a multiship departure. All the ship handling manual says is follow the admiral's instructions." She paused, then added softly. "Smiley may be trying to make you merchant skippers feel like, uh, feel dumb."

"He's succeeding. Now what?"

Ding pursed her lips. "Whenever navigation orders are unclear, you have the right and obligation to ask for clarification. But don't expect a thank-you for telling the admiral he doesn't know how to write orders, sir."

"Right. Helms, keep us tied up. Comm, send to flag. *Sheffield* requests clarification. How do we determine which ships are odd? No, make that even, I refuse to feed anyone a straight line." Mattim glanced at the clock. "Wonder how long this will take." Two minutes later, a window opened on the main view screen. Smiley was not smiling.

"For all its claimed eagerness, the *Sheffield* does not seem to know how to get under way. Ships count off, starting with the *Sendai,* and maneuver accordingly. Flag out."

Mattim stuffed his anger away. "I don't think he likes us."

"He did put us last in line," Ding added.

"We'll have to show him we're better than that."

"Without showing him up anymore," Sandy suggested dryly.

"Sir, we're an odd ship," the helm offered.

"Very good." Mattim had taken the *Maggie* out with just himself, Sandy, and Thor. Not today, "XO, you have the conn. Prepare to get under way."

She grinned. "I have the conn. Bos'n, order the crew to underway stations. Announce weightlessness in ten minutes. Quartermaster, initiate the mission clock."

Ten minutes! Mattim usually got the *Maggie* away in two minutes. With ten times the crew and so many green hands, Mattim leaned back in his chair, ready to see how the Navy did it. A chief pulled a bit of gleaming metal from her open collar and leaned close to her mike. After blowing a couple of notes that Mattim had only heard on old vids, she announced. "All hands to underway stations. Weightlessness in ten minutes."

The XO depressed her comm button. "Deck in-port watch, single up the lines. Prepare all attachments for separation. All departments, report readiness to get under way to the Officer of the Deck on the Bridge." A young lieutenant JG who'd been following the XO with attention turned back to his station as a light appeared. Mattim tapped the display on his own commsole, searched through his menus and converted his station to a copy of the JG's—and shook his head. He didn't care about the doc's or supply's readiness. Going back to his main menus, Mattim searched. Yep, Chief Aso was bossing the underway detail. As hatches were secured and attachments cast off, Aso's board went green. This list Mattim watched while Ding prowled the bridge, checking the quartermaster's log, watching the OOD's board, and having him hassle departments that were slow reporting.

When the bos'n reported "Five minutes until weightlessness," the OOD's board was getting green. Three minutes later the XO ordered the last hatches secured. A half minute later, Chief Aso's board was all green. Again, the XO paced the bridge, looking over everyone's shoulders, verifying for herself that reports were accurate and the ship was ready for space. Sitting in his chair, Mattim did the same, flicking his commsole through the stations. He got the same data—and caused his crew a lot less stress.

Satisfied, the exec saluted and reported, "Ship ready to get under way, sir."

He stood to return her salute. "OOD, engage the running lights. Torchy, your gang got anything to say?"

The yard superintendent took a full minute to scroll through his board. It was green from top to bottom. "Quit dilly-dallying, Matt. I want my space pay."

Mattim reached for the brass bar overhead and braced himself for weightlessness. "Announce weightlessness. Mr. Jagel, back us out at five meters per second." The hull rattled as the pier grapples slowly moved the ship backward and kept it from spinning into the next ship to port. As each grapple reached the end of the dock, it released. Thor softly added power, helping the three, now two, now one grapple move them along, keep them parallel to the dock. With a *thunk*, the last grapple let go.

"Increase speed aft to ten meters per second. Sensors, let me know if any of those other cruisers so much as look in our directions. We are not going to ding or be dinged." Much more slowly than normal, they backed clear of the station.

Mattim tapped his comm link. "This is the captain. Police up your stations for drifting gear. We'll get gravity back in a minute or two, and I don't want anyone hurt by falling objects." Behind him, someone got explosively sick. He went on. "There are burp bags under your seats. You were issued motion meds when you came aboard. If yours aren't handy, don't be ashamed to ask. Officers and chiefs were issued extras. That is all."

"Bos'n, I've got some spare meds," he said, turning himself on the overhead rod and pulling several pills from his pocket. He came to a quick halt. The chief bos'n's mate was the one holding a bag over her mouth.

"Sorry, sir, won't happen again," she mumbled around the bag. The chief quartermaster beside her slapped a patch on her neck.

"No problem, chief, too much shore duty will do that to anyone. I took my pill before lunch." He got a weak smile as he turned back to business.

"Helm, bring us around one hundred twenty degrees to port. Tell Ivan to stand by for one-quarter gee acceleration."

"One-two-zero degrees to port. Stand by for point-two-five gees. Aye, aye, sir." That hadn't changed from the *Maggie D*. Mattim would boot any helmsman off his bridge who didn't repeat his orders. Thor swung them about and brought the ship to a deft halt in space. One by one, the other cruisers dropped back toward the flag and took station behind it, the *Sheffield* last. They came around smartly, but not quickly enough to avoid comments from the flag. Mattim shrugged it off and studied the squadron from his unique position at the rear.

The lead cruisers, *Reply* and *Significant,* were regular Navy. Twelve eight-inch guns made them the squadron's real hitting power, reaching out as much as thirty thousand kilometers. The rest, *Topeka, Garibaldi, Aurora, Jeanne d'arc* and *Sheffield* were conversions with six-inch batteries made of off-the-shelf components. Their range was twenty-five thousand klicks, but Mattim doubted they could toast bread out there.

The next six hours held no more than the usual surprises. The new crew went through standard drills and got the standard sprains as they got used to moving in varying gravity.

The first real excitement came when they put a defensive spin on the ship. Given enough time, lasers could cut through any amount of reflector and ice. In battle the ship spun around its long axis. This should spin damaged armor out of the line of fire before burn-through. Spinning a ninety-thousand-ton ship required balance. Now Mattim learned not all of the reaction mass was there for the engines. As they spun up, pumps moved fuel, keeping the ship perfectly balanced.

Right up to 2.6 gees when one pump locked.

The *Sheffield* shook like a belly dancer's hips. In the ten seconds it took to slow down, a commsole popped its bolts and careened into his chair. Mattim got his hand out of the way a split second before he would have lost fingers.

Torchy waited until they were back to 1 gee and no spin before he undid his seat belt and checked his chair. One bolt had snapped. "Matt, you promised me a shakedown cruise. You didn't have to put that much shake in it."

"The *Maggie* always satisfies the paying customer. Damage control, find out what went wrong and fix it."

"Comm here. The flag wants to know if we're returning to dock."

Smiley was offering Mattim an out. If enough of the merchant skippers took him up on his offer, he'd be off the hook. Mattim really did not want to spend tomorrow up to his ears in a space battle. But he wasn't about to give Smiley another chance to smirk down at him from the message screen.

"Advise him we had a minor problem and will be back on station within an hour."

At her station, Sandy shook her head. "Boys."

"Flag says they'll delay gunnery practice until we rejoin."

"Damn." Mattim muttered.

"I'll get my crew on it right away," Torchy said. A half hour later, they met the specs . . . 5 gees and 20 rpm.

They rejoined just in time for the shoot. The lasers powered up in alphabetical order. Turrets A, B, and C forward, D, E, and F amidships, and X, Y, and Z aft. C and Y refused to hold a charge. "I'll get teams on them immediately" was Guns' reaction. "We'll have them on line in five minutes."

"We'll wait until we've powered down the main battery, Guns. Let the yard people tackle them one at a time."

"It's not necessary, sir. The system has baffles to isolate each turret."

"That hasn't been tested live." Mattim cut him off. "Guns, prepare for a seven-gun shoot. Captain out."

Then things got real bad. Tugs twelve thousand klicks off to starboard fired targets, balloons that expanded until they were the size of a ship. Turret A shot first.

"Guns," Mattim snapped, "three shots at this range to hit a target that size?"

"Captain, that's damn good shooting. It would earn an E."

Not from Mattim, but the other ships hadn't done any better, even the flag. Mattim was damned if he'd fight colonials with shooting that bad. "Sandy, is the Westinghouse SG-190 fire control on line?"

"And waiting, sir."

"Feed the numbers to B turret," Mattim ordered.

"What the hell are you sending me?" came from Guns a second later. "There are three firing solutions!"

"And a recommended fourth," Mattim answered. "Use it."

"This isn't regulation," Guns snapped.

Mattim windowed into B turret's gun laying station. It used numbers that must have come from the Navy's standard local fire control—and missed. The second shot used the updated numbers from Sandy—and hit. Guns was back a second later. "You've got a central line control up there?"

"Westinghouse SG-190 series," Mattim answered.

"They never passed mil specs. You can't count on them to take a pounding," Guns shot back.

"This one's still working after our little balance problem."

Guns was silent for a long minute. "Please take the Westinghouse off line until I say so."

Sandy worked her board. "It's on standby," she said.

"Target launched," Guns said. "Bring system on line."

"System on," Sandy answered. "Target acquired. Solution up."

"Fire." Guns shouted. There was a brief pause. "Damn, we got the target before it was a quarter size." There was a longer pause this time. "Captain, I've always wanted to get my hands on an SG-190. Let's finish this shoot, then we have to talk."

All targets expended, the squadron continued its 1-gee acceleration toward the jump point. While Torchy's crew, supplemented by specialists from engineering, worked on the two recalcitrant lasers, Guns paid a visit to the bridge. As Sandy put the SG-190 through its paces, he shook his head. "I been telling HQ for years we needed a central fire control. Something that could take every sensor—laser, gravity, radar, visuals—and refine their results into a single firing solution. What's a merchant doing with one of these?" He changed the subject.

Mattim smiled. "Long before the frontier planets decided humanity needed a redistribution of the wealth, various individuals took it upon themselves to try their hand at it. We only had a four-inch gun, but I wanted it to make hits early and often. That was usually enough to scare unidentified ships away. Chief Aso was on the gun the one time we had to burn our way through a persistent one."

"Aso. He's leading the deck crew," Guns mused. "Good man?"

"Best."

Guns blew out a long breath. "Listen, Captain, this doesn't come easy for a Navy type like me, but it looks to me like we're about thirty-six hours away from a live fire exercise. I want to use your fire control, but I want an experienced gunner on it."

Sandy looked about to come out of her chair. And Mattim was not about to have anyone on sensors but his Jump Master. There had to be a win-win solution to this. The bridge was big enough. "Ding, could you rig a second station beside Sandy's?"

"If the admiral keeps us at one gee, it shouldn't take but a couple of hours."

"Commander Howard, I've wanted someone from gunnery on my bridge. You willing to move your battle station up here?"

Guns laughed. "Saves me from having to beg. XO, you do that. I got some guns to straighten out. At least one of them needs a new turret lead. Chief Aso's crew is under engineering."

Mattim tapped his comm. "Ivan, mind losing chief Aso to gunnery?"

"That's where he belongs, Matt."

"Guns, I think you got yourself a new man."

"Thank you, sir." But Guns did not leave. "When the politicians decided to keep merchant shippers on the converted cruisers, some Navy types were a bit worried." Did his eyes wander toward the XO? "I won't talk for other ships, but we got a damn dinkum good skipper here." Guns' salute was the same Mattim had given his father. Not the day he was commissioned, but after he'd commanded a ship for a year. After he'd learned just how tough the old man's job was.

Mattim returned the salute with the same feelings. Out of the corner of his eye, he saw the bos'n of the watch talk into her comm. What was happening here would be throughout the ship in a matter of minutes. Guns and he had taken a major step into welding the Navy and merchant halves of the boat into a single crew, into turning the collection of bolts, chips, and flesh that rode the *Sheffield* into a living, breathing ship. Good!

The rest of the voyage out was drill and hard work. The *Sheffield* was as ready as any green warship by the time the big jolt came.

"Captain," the exec reported. "We are at the jump point."

"It's not there." Sandy cut her off.

"Of course it's there. That's the buoy," Ding snapped as if Sandy had called her a liar.

"That's the buoy, but I got three atom-laser gyros hunting for the gravity variance of Gamma jump point. It's supposed to be where you see the green dot. None of them are pointing there. The damn thing's wandered."

Mattim hit the comm. "Anything from the flag?"

"Nothing sir, not a peep."

"Sandy, find it for the admiral."

"But, Matt, if Smiley boy can't find the jump, no battle." Mattim didn't back down from his order; Sandy turned back to her board. "With us all dressed up, it would be a shame not to go help those poor marines." Then she grinned. "And to see Smiley's face when a merchie tells him where his jump has wandered to."

"What do you mean, wandered?" Guns asked from his new station at Sandy's elbow.

"This jump point is a category A risk. It's going to swallow one ship out of every thousand through it, maybe more if you don't treat it with respect."

"The Navy hasn't lost a ship in fifty years. Technology has improved so there is no risk to ships." Ding gave a textbook quote, which was all she probably knew. In peacetime, the Navy contracted for Jump Masters.

Today, Sandy wasn't buying a textbook answer. "We haven't had a war in fifty years, and the Navy, like most shipping lines that want reasonable insurance rates, only use G and H jump points, and go through them at a few klicks a second." Sandy raised a questioning eyebrow to Ding. "Right?"

The puzzled look was back on Ding's face. "I guess so."

"And you'd guess right," Sandy assured her. "Even as much as Matt here wants fast voyages, he steers clear of anything higher than an E. Now, this damn war comes along, and we're trying to support marines on the wrong side of an A. Wonder if anybody gave the damn politicians a basic primer on jump point safety." She turned back to her board. "Anyway, low jumps tend to wander, and this baby is a real pilgrim. Didn't anybody record where that help message came from yesterday?"

"That's impossible. It's in orbit around the star." Suddenly Ding stopped and her eyes widened. Sandy grinned, but said nothing. "Which star is it orbiting?" Ding almost whispered. "This one, or the one on the other side?"

"You got it, sister. We didn't make these suckers. We just use what we found. Most dance to the gravity of two stars. This one's got three, plus another ten percent. It's a real gypsy."

"Another ten percent?" Guns asked. Mattim took the moment to check the bridge. The squadron continued decelerating at 1 gee, following the admiral who still hadn't admitted he didn't know where he was going.

"Yeah," Sandy went on. "Add up all the vectors from both stars and you should be able to figure an orbit. G's and H's you almost can. Pick your average E and no matter how hard some college professor does the math, you're missing at least ten percent of the vectors. This SOB is over twenty percent. Damn, I wish we understood these things better."

"In history class, they said we lost one of the first three ships that jumped out from Earth," Ding said. "Is this why?"

"I don't know how they lost that first one. Earth's one jump point is such a docile little H that you'd have to *try* to get lost in it." Sandy tapped her comm. "Ivan, honey, I need your atom laser."

"It's all yours, best friend."

"I'll thank you tonight." She switched off and made a

fourth display appear. "With our broadside to the jump, I need a longitudinal baseline. Ah, there she be." The green dot went red. A new one appeared with numbers next to it. "Five thousand kilometers in just thirty days. Honey, you got to pay your rent. You can't keep toddling around like this." Sandy looked up. "Do we really have to tell our little admiral?"

Mattim glanced around his bridge. Ding and Guns took the question for a joke. Mattim knew Sandy was serious. "Yes."

Sandy took a deep breath and let it out slowly. Then she mashed her comm button. "Comm, send my board to flag, with the captain's compliments."

Sergeant Mary Rodrigo slipped past the hospital's front desk. They were busy, and Lek had told her which room the LT was in; Lek'd even hacked his medical charts. Reading was not the same as seeing, so the platoon had asked her to check up on him. Everyone hoped he was getting better treatment than they were.

The people passing Mary in the halls, whether patients or staff, all wore cloth. Since the hospital was buried fifty meters under the crater's floor, she guessed they were safe. Still, she was in battle armor, helmet under her arm. She'd learned not to take chances.

She also hadn't had a bath since the battle. People passing her tended to speed up, even those hanging onto intravenous packets on rolling stands. Since Mary had a map of the hospital layout, she didn't ask directions. Since the people were nonthreats, Mary ignored them. Crashing relativity bombs and sparkling lasers—those she paid attention to. What could not kill her, she ignored. It was amazing how simple life became.

She paused before a closed door. For a moment she froze. What if the lieutenant had forgotten them, like some in the platoon said? What if they were a part of his life he wanted to forget as quickly as he could? The rest of his life was going to be screwed up. She hesitated, but only for a moment. *You don't read your mail, you never know what's happening.*

She slipped through the wide door.

The LT sat in bed, his nose in a reader. He glanced up. "Mary!" His broadening grin left no doubt she was welcome.

"Hi," she answered, giving him the best salute she could.

"Don't waste that on me." He tossed it off with a wave of his left hand. "Save it for some dumb lieutenant who still thinks it matters. Tell me, what's the platoon up to?"

"Not much, sir. No colonials have tried to take our pass. We're doing what we're told." No need telling him what that was. "What's been happening with you?"

"I got my first lieutenant promotion." He beamed. "And the Navy Cross, or so they tell me." Mary glanced at the sheets covering him; his body under them stopped too far from the foot of the bed. She didn't know what to say; the LT helped her.

"They couldn't save the legs. Too much damage and too long before the docs got me. But I'm getting a new set real soon. In a month they'll insert neural leads in both stumps, then attach prosthetics. I've seen vids. I'll be good as new."

Mary didn't hear much depth in his cheerfulness. "Will you be coming back to the platoon then?" she asked.

"No. Worse luck. It's staff duty for me. Just because a Sthet can run doesn't mean they want you in combat." He scowled and looked away. When he faced her again, he'd found his smile. "So tell me, what's the platoon been up to? They got you and Cassie out telling everyone how it's done. Lek a warrant officer, running battalion communications. Talk to me."

There were too many things Mary couldn't say, so she mumbled. "We're doing okay, sir. Some of us missed you, and they wanted to know how you were doing. I hitched a ride back on a supply run. I got to be getting back or they'll leave me."

As she talked, the lieutenant's eyes went from crinkled smile to hard and angry. "Damn it, woman, don't start treating me like some stranger. You folks were there for me when I was up to my neck in dirt and bleeding to death. I may have been a standard issue shit-for-brains second louie most of the time, but I got my act together that day. So did all of you." His voice ran down. "Don't start treating me like I don't exist." He glanced around, seemed to take in the whole hospital at a glance. "There're enough people doing that. Don't you do it too."

Then he looked her hard in the eye. "Something's wrong."

"Not really wrong, sir. Just everything back to normal, I guess. The whole company's up and we're kind of under-strength what with you gone and others. We got the detail of cleaning up the mess we made, collecting the busted-up rolligons, artillery, that stuff."

"You didn't have to bring in the bodies?" the LT whispered.

"Somebody had to. Captain said we should since the other platoons were on full alert." The first night after the battle had been bad—on Mary and a lot of others. After looking the corpses in the eyes, lugging them to the trucks, Mary wasn't the only one who took herself off net each night. No need to wake everybody when she came awake screaming.

"Mary, let me see the back of your helmet," the lieutenant said softly. She flipped it over; he glanced at it. "You've still got NCO markings on it. I put you in for a battlefield commission. They haven't given my platoon to another LT?"

"No, sir."

"Is Captain Spoda including you in staff meetings?"

"Staff meetings, sir?"

"Okay." The lieutenant glanced away, fixed his eyes on the picture on the wall. Mary stared at it; ocean waves rose up and tumbled onto yellow dust. She'd seen vids of oceans; all that water made her uncomfortable. She looked away. The LT got her attention when he mashed a button beside his bed.

"Yes, sir?" came a cheerful woman's voice.

"Doctor Mardan should be about through his rounds.

Could you ask him to drop by my room? It's a matter of urgency."

"Yes, sir. Uh, your vitals are a bit elevated, but nothing to set off alarms, sir."

"This is a military matter, not medical."

"Yes, sir." The voice clicked off, sounding puzzled.

"Sir, I really have to get back to the supply truck," Mary said, edging toward the door.

"Mary, you and I both know a supply run never arrived back on schedule. And now that I know what you people were scrounging, I'm damn glad of it. Whatcha after this time?"

"Anything we can lay our hands on. Pickings are getting slim, and it's kind of hard to find good trading stock. Dumont always had the best luck when he took a few of the younger girls in the platoon. But lately . . ."

The lieutenant chuckled. "I heard someone ran a ship in here loaded with booze and women and set up shop." He studied Mary for a moment. "Haven't any of you had a shower in the last month?" Mary backed away; she hadn't meant to bother him.

"No, no, you get back here, woman. I spent a week on jungle survival, and boy, did I stink. What is happening to you? The platoon's got a support van assigned to it. You can get a hot meal and a shower. Why aren't you?"

"The captain's got us in reserve. We're back a couple of klicks from the pass. The other two platoons are dug in close. We dug the command and support vans into the rim. They're solid, but ours is sitting out in the open. Ain't nobody getting out of armor, not even Dumont's kids, no matter how horny they get."

The door opened; a gray-haired man with a silver oak leaf on one side of his collar and a medical insignia on the other came in. His nose wrinkled, but in a second it was replaced by a smile. "Morning, Lieutenant. How you feeling?"

"Hanging in. Commander, I'd like you to meet Sergeant Mary Rodrigo, the fightingest marine in the corps and the reason you aren't in a colonial POW camp." Mary turned red, wondered if she should have saluted this doctor-officer. She was starting to when he held out his hand. She shook it.

"Glad to meet you, Sarge. You need anything, it's yours."

"We're fine, sir," she stuttered.

"I disagree with the sergeant," the lieutenant said and quickly filled the doctor in on what he'd extracted from Mary.

The doctor's smile quickly turned into a glower. He shook his head as the LT finished. "I've spent forty years attached to the corps, patching up you boys and girls that refuse to grow up. This is about the most childish stunt I've heard of. You put her in for a commission, you say?".

"Yes, sir. The originals are on the hospital computer in my personal files, along with a recommendation for the Silver Star."

"Mind giving me a hard copy? I'm playing poker tonight. Commander Umboto usually shows up to lose a few bucks. Tomorrow night I'm sharing supper and Shakespeare with Captain Anderson. I think both of them would enjoy hearing about this."

Mary was on the verge of panic. "Sir, I don't want . . . I don't mean . . . The boss man'll . . ."

The doctor didn't seem to understand a word she was saying. The lieutenant waved a hand. "Mary and a lot of her crew had twenty years mining asteroids before they joined the corps."

The doctor nodded. Then the crinkles around his mouth and eyes turned into a smile, warm as the sun and understanding as a proud mother. "I imagine you heard in boot camp that there's the right way, the wrong way, and the Navy way."

"Often, sir."

"Well, you are about to see that applied in spades. Don't worry, Sergeant. I've worn this uniform for forty years and never lost a patient to bureaucratic ineptness."

"Yes, sir." Mary didn't know the Navy or Marine way all that well. She did know basic physics. Shit rolls downhill.

She doubted even a doctor who was a commander could change that.

"I really have to get back." Mary needed away from these people. Nice was something she could only take in small doses, especially from strangers like the doctor . . . and the LT.

As she edged toward the door, the doctor's hand closed on her elbow like a vise. "Even with your suit's biocleaners, if you haven't had a bath in a month, you're a first-rate candidate for skin disease. While you're soaking, we'll get your suit cleaned and liner recharged. It's the least we can do for the people who keep us in business."

SIX

"CAPTAIN, LIVE MESSAGE from the flag," comm said.

"Put it on screen," Mattim ordered.

"Squadron Fifty-three, the marines are in trouble," the man wasn't smiling. "We are going to their aid. Together, we'll show those colonial amateurs how a real Navy fights. Squadron will stay in formation behind me, use only passive sensors. Good luck, men."

The screen went dead.

"Not even a thank-you for us," Sandy pouted.

"Suddenly he's spoiling for a fight," Mattim mused.

Guns shook his head. "His stateroom's full of history books, real ones. Maybe too full."

"General quarters," Mattim ordered. "Today, we find out."

Settled into his captain's chair, Mattim allowed himself a moment's reflection. Guns and Ding were visibly excited, ready to put years of training to the test. Ivan and Sandy hated the war, but they'd followed him. *Followed me where we could all get killed. Am I leading them right?*

His five years skippering the *Maggie* had seen the red Unity flag with its lightning bolt shoot through the sparsely populated colonial worlds. One by one, his ports got new harbormasters; his contacts changed from working folks to

Unity henchmen who bought for monopolies and held their paws out for "donations" and "special considerations." Mattim missed the traders and factory managers who took him home to meet the family. The Unity bullies' idea of a fun evening usually involved someone weak getting hurt.

Mattim suspected that boatload of Economic Reformers they blasted was crewed by Unity punks eager to cut out the middle man. At thirteen, Mattim had shipped out with his dad. This wasn't the same universe.

So now I'm heading into a battle to help people I've never met. Mattim, are you getting a late-blooming case of chivalry or whatever it is that causes a guy to get himself killed at midlife? Getting killed was low on his list of things to do today. Yet he wanted to charge through that jump, guns blazing, and save the poor doggies. This was crazy. *I think they call it war.*

On the flag's orders, the squadron passed through the jump at a few thousand meters per second. It should have been an easy jump, but the ships came out scattered. Despite the flag orders for tight communications, the admiral was quite liberal with irate orders to re-form. Sandy just shook her head. "This jump point is all kinds of flaky."

Mattim had other worries; where were the colonials? Passive sensors drew a blank. "Must be under EMCon," Ding concluded. "Don't use search radars and lasers, and no one can follow your signals back to you."

"Sandy, do a visual search on every inch of space between Alpha jump and the marines. Somewhere are glowing engines."

"They're decelerating engines away from us," Sandy said.

"So maybe it'll reflect off the next ship in line. This armor reflects lasers. Maybe it reflects other things."

"Optimist. Me, I bet they're in echelon toward us, reflecting away from us," Sandy chided him, but went to work.

An hour later, Mattim got his first hint of what lay ahead. "Captain, comm here. We've picked up a message tight-beamed from the Ninety-seventh to the flag. It's probably in response to something from the flag, but we didn't get that."

"I'll take what I can."

His station quickly displayed the answer to the admiral's unknown question. ENEMY FORCE IS ESTIMATED AT 5 DDS AND 6 CCS, GUNS VARY FROM 6" TO 9.2". ETA HERE IS 22 HRS 18 MNTS. THANKS FOR COMING.

"Let me guess, DDs are destroyers, CCs are any kind of cruiser. Right?" Mattim asked Ding.

"Yes, sir."

"So how do they know? Ninety-seventh isn't emitting anything."

"Ship makes a gravitational pulse as it exits a jump. The bigger the ship, the bigger the pulse. In their first action, the Ninety-seventh spotted five DDs, nine CCs and transports. No transports today. They're just here to pound the poor joes."

"Sandy, you got anything?"

"Nothing. They're dark as space."

"Sandy, we know where they came from and where they're going. Find them."

Four hours later, she did. "Matt, I got 'em. Guns and I got those puppies. It's beautiful." Ding was at Mattim's elbow a second later as they hovered over Sandy's shoulder.

"Visuals was a waste. They heard us come in. They knew how to hide. So I gave up on eyeballs," Sandy ran on. "Ships are big, but with that big gasbag's gravity well, I couldn't get shit out of the gravity anomaly detector. So I tried electromagnetic. There the gasbag helped. It's emitting across the spectrum like the biggest radar ever turned on."

"Yes," Ding cut in, "but they'll be operating in stealth mode. You won't get any radar bounces off them to pick up."

"Right." Guns grinned. "That's what Sandy went looking for. Those turkeys are a hole in the radar return."

"Look there." Sandy pointed. "Five holes, then six bigger ones. Five destroyers, six cruisers. You can hide, but you can't hide the hole you're hiding in."

"God damn," Ding breathed slowly. "She's got them."

"Wait 'til the admiral hears this," Sandy crowed.

"We're under radio silence," Ding said.

"They heard us come in," Mattim snarled. "What you want to bet they've been following us visually? Once we flip, we'll be brighter than a star. If the admiral has a battle to plan, he'll want to know this. Comm, get me a tight beam to the flag."

"You got it, Captain."

"*Sheffield* to *Reply.*"

"*Sheffield,* you are under EMCon One. Use of tight beams toward the enemy is not permitted. Cease your transmissions at once."

Mattim went doggedly on. "This is Captain Abeeb."

Again he got the same lecture, only louder; Mattim gritted his teeth. "We have located the enemy electromagnetically."

"You couldn't have" was followed by the same lecture, now at the top of someone's lungs.

Mattim cut his comm. "Guns, I need advice on how this Navy way works. So, what is this shit from flag?" Mattim regretted his loss of control. Still, it felt good at the moment.

"I didn't recognize the voice, but you can assume the admiral approved cutting you off. I expect sensors on the flag is desperately trying to duplicate Sandy's achievement and assuring the admiral since he can't do it, no accountant can."

"No use trying again?" Ding concluded.

"No, ma'am. Late in my Navy career I concluded you can't teach pigs to sing, at least not those sporting more gold braid than you. Do merchant sailors learn a similar lesson?"

Mattim chuckled. "Last few years, it was becoming apparent I should. So far I avoided it."

"Congratulations, sir. You will have to decide for yourself whether to follow my experience or your own lead."

"Tight beam coming in, Captain, from the *Aurora.*"

"That's Buzz's ship. Let me see it."

"Congratulations, Matt. No surprise Sandy did it. I've got

a Navy type on my sensors. She swears it can't be done. I told her if Sandy did it, she can. I owe you all a round. When the boss lets us communicate, tight-beam me the full story. Burka out."

"Captain, we got message traffic from all the reserve cruisers. Do you want to see it?"

"How many of them offer to buy the first round?" Mattim grinned at Sandy. She preened.

"Uh, all of them, I think."

"Boy, Saturday night's gonna be fun," Sandy crowed.

"Enough, Commander O'Mally. Guns, could having the enemy track help the others develop a firing solution?"

"No, Captain, we're hours away from a shoot."

"Then no more communications until it's authorized. Guns, does this tell you anything about what the enemy's up to?"

"Yes, sir. We're in no danger, for the moment."

"And how long will that good fortune follow us?" Mattim got ready for another educational experience.

Guns fingered the display. "They came out of the jump headed for a fast pass on the marines. About the time we jumped in, they sheered away. They're headed around ELM0129-4 and will meet us head-on over the marines. We'll have shoots twice an orbit until one of us breaks for a jump. They've rigged it so they can bug out without us observing them."

Mattim chewed on his lower lip. "They're playing it safe."

"For them, sir. They've got DD's. If they put two in polar orbits, they'll know if we cut. We won't know the same for them."

"That assumes," Ding cut in, "they've got someone as tactical-trained and professional as one of our war college grads. They *are* colonials."

Guns said nothing; Mattim took a deep breath. "XO, they've been fighting among themselves for fifty years. Just because newscasts call it 'childish squabbling' doesn't mean smart folks haven't been learning. I'd expect some pretty canny behavior."

"Yes, sir" came from both the XO and Guns.

There was little behavior of any kind from the flag. Over the next eight hours Mattim rotated his crew to chow and a free hour. The hostiles were just disappearing behind the gasbag when the admiral finally ordered a full sensor sweep.

Mattim ignored the huffy communications between the flag and the 97th. The admiral demanded to know where the "so-called" enemy fleet was. The ground-pounders sarcastically voiced their joy that the admiral could see his way to visit. Mattim passed Sandy's search methods to the other ships. Two had duplicated her find. The others were grateful as well as impressed.

Mattim listened in on the gunnery net as Commander Howard sketched the enemy's probable past and future movements to the other gunnery chiefs, including the *Reply*'s and the *Significant*'s. "We should encounter hostiles in sixty-seven minutes, just as we pull away from the marines. However, note that if the skunks make a fast, fuel scoop orbit, they will arrive over the moon just as we do, in fifty-two minutes. I'm betting on a scoop and shoot." Guns found no takers. And Mattim began to suspect his gunnery officer was more of a jewel than he could have hoped for.

The admiral did nothing that Mattim had hoped for, neither revising his simple orders of "Follow me" nor informing his captains how he proposed to fight the coming battle. It was as if he still didn't believe his enemy was in-system. Or maybe out of sight, out of mind.

Or maybe just out of his mind.

"Ships coming out from behind the gasbag," Sandy reported in a low, controlled voice. "They are low and fast. Guns, I think you won your bet."

"Yes," he said, "skunks are climbing out, using lots of delta V. I suspect they did a fuel scoop. I have three cans and six cruisers, including two *Revenge*-class super heavies."

Guns whistled. "I thought the grunts were just seeing willies under their beds. Other four look like six-inch conversions."

"Thank God for minor favors," Ding breathed.

"Cans look to be falling off to their unengaged side." Guns frowned. "I'll concentrate on the skunks we've got. Sandy, if it wouldn't be inconvenient, could you look around for those other two DDs? They aren't much, but a chance appearance at an inopportune time could be most unpleasant."

"Got you, Guns. I'll keep up the search."

"Thank you, Commander."

"We ready for this?" Mattim asked Ding, hunting for what he'd forgotten . . . what could cost him his ship.

"As ready as we'll ever be, sir." The young woman grinned like some carnivore stalking prey. She was actually excited by the prospects before them. *Well, maybe if I'd spent the last ten years of my life training for this moment, I'd be excited too.*

He hadn't. He wasn't.

"Guns, XO, when do we put spin on the ship?"

Ding deferred to Guns, who pulled a handheld calculator out of his pocket. The Navy seemed to go in for obsolete technology. "We're closing at six-hundred-twenty-thousand klicks an hour. Those nine-point-two-inch monsters could hit you at forty thousand klicks, but I doubt it. I'd start spinning at forty-five thousand, sir."

"Thanks, Guns. Sandy, range to . . . what do they call them . . . skunks?"

"Yes, sir," Ding assured him.

"Just passing fifty thousand, Skipper."

"Bos'n, inform the crew we're putting spin on the ship in five seconds and give them a countdown."

"Yes, sir."

Mattim leaned back in his chair and got ready for the ride of his life. His *Maggie* had been built the way you expected a ship to be built. The screens that showed you what was out there faced *out*. In a Navy ship, the damn screen was on the inside. You went around all day with your back to space. As the ship began to spin, the ship's 2-gee acceleration pulled him "down"; the spin firmly put his back in his chair, cuddled up like a kid in his dad's lap watching a vid. Of course, this vid was about killing people—and it was interactive.

"Crew," the XO reminded the bridge party, "do not lean forward if you can avoid it. You've got a big supply of burp bags. If you have to lose it, don't be bashful. You'll probably see me or the captain use the bags. It's all just part of a battle in space. You'll get used to it."

She sat down beside him. He gave her a smile; she was loosening up with the crew. With a bit of work, she'd fit just fine on the *Maggie*. Then he leaned over, whispering, "You've never been in a fight. How do you know?"

She didn't even blink. "Fleet exercises, sir. They say if you've been in a couple of them, battle holds no surprises. I sure as hell hope so."

"Skunks, forty thousand klicks. Two lead ships opening fire on the flag," Sandy drawled. "One must appreciate their tastes."

"Guns, you mind telling me what's going on? Better yet, you got any problems with this going out to all hands?"

"No, sir." Guns mashed his comm link, "All hands, this is the chief gunnery officer. The skipper asked me to keep you informed as to what's happening. When I get too busy to talk, trust me, you'll be too busy to listen." There was a chuckle on the bridge. Mattim suspected it ran the length of the ship.

"The colonials have opened fire on the flag at extreme range. That's plain stupid. They're wasting energy, heating up their lasers and just helping the flag let off a little steam. Since we're head-on to each other, that means that by the time they pass us, their lasers will be hot and inaccurate. Ours won't be. Gunners, put on the kettle." That got a cheer.

Guns was good. This might become a regular battle drill.

"Range to skunks, thirty-five thousand klicks," Sandy reported.

"The old gunner's mate who taught me my trade," Guns went on, "liked to sucker them into close range, say barroom length. Battery that gets the most energy out has a beer bust on me." Another cheer, this time accompanied with yelps from the crews of the secondary batteries.

"Okay, two beer busts, one for the hottest six-inch turret, the other for the best four-inch crew." The cheers were unanimous again.

"Skunks at thirty thousand klicks . . . now."

"And the flag's opened fire." Guns continued his play-by-play. "The rate of fire from the colonials is slowing. The flag's steaming a bit. That water will pass down the line to us, causing the end of their lasers to bloom. Ours, on the other hand, will be fresh and cut right through it. If your shipmate's fallen asleep, don't bother waking him yet. We got a long minute or so before we'll do anything."

Mattim studied the screen. The two heavy cruisers were applying a slow and deliberate fire to the enemy's two super-heavies. The light cruisers on both sides were out of range.

"Skunks passing twenty-five thousand."

"Well, crew, the *Topeka* has weighed in with her six-inchers. The range is long, but it looks like she's making some hits. The enemy flag is switching fire to the *Topeka.* I imagine our flag's glad of that. By the way, if you've got anybody snoring near you, you might want to wake them up. We're about a minute 'til showtime. Just enough time to wash their face and brush their teeth before things get exciting."

"Oh, I've got a note here from the crew of turret A. They say they've already picked out the bar for their bust and the rest of you can quit worrying. What do you think of that?"

The gunnery circuit was awash with boos.

Mattim checked the live mikes in each turret. While Guns' verbal horseplay might be taking the edge off the raw terror, the crews were going about their duties as they'd been trained, dialing in their gear, verifying that, while the target was available, they had it locked in their sights. They were as ready as ninety days of training and drill could make them.

"Lead skunk is at twenty thousand klicks."

"Folks, at this point we will be signing off. Showtime is in just a few seconds. I hope you enjoyed the preliminary and will stay around for the postgame review. This is your chief of gunnery signing off." Guns shook himself. "Damn, that was fun, I got to do that more often. Tommy, show me your plot."

Around the bridge, the crew was grim but determined. Mattim tightened his seat belt, tightened his gut, and studied the screen, measuring the flow of the battle.

"Sir," the XO put in, "their two big R's are going down the line, switching fire from one ship to the next. I can damn near tell you to the second when they'll take us on. Mind if I jink ship to put them off?"

"XO, you've got the conn. Helm, stand by for orders. Ding, coordinate with Guns. Let's not jink him out of a hit."

"Right, Captain. Guns, I'm going to bounce ship, ten meters per second high for three seconds, then ten meters per second sideways."

"Hold those bounces for five seconds," Gun muttered.

"You're on."

"Fire!" Guns shouted. Lights dimmed as energy poured from the ship. A green arrow on the main screen reached out from the green dot that was his ship to touch the enemy flag. The red triangle glowed yellow in a corner. Was that an actual hit or wishful thinking by the computer? Mattim didn't ask.

"Bounce," the XO said softly, "up . . . right . . . NOW!"

The extra twist did wonders to Mattim's inner ear. He wasn't sure where he was going. A red arrow flashed from the enemy flag to him. He felt nothing.

"We'll cease bouncing for forty seconds, Guns. They're taking forty-five or more to recharge," Ding reported.

"I suggest bouncing in thirty-five. I'll fire the next salvo at thirty."

"You're on."

Mattim listened and did not interrupt. In theory, his ship could get a salvo off every ten seconds. Why was Guns holding back? He'd ask later.

An eternity ticked by, one endless second at a time.

Then the ship's lights dimmed. A second time, a green line reached out for the enemy. Again the triangle turned yellow. Ding ordered a bounce to starboard, and Mattim's inner world twirled. He wondered how the green kids in his crew were taking this. A diminutive guard by the hatch reached for a burp bag.

Ding bounced them two more times before the enemy cruiser lashed out at them. Another miss. But Guns was laying it on heavy now. Every ten seconds, another two-second salvo. Mattim had enough of the overprocessed pablum on the main screen. He tapped up gunnery on his own board, selected the main battery, and found himself staring at the gun pictures of one of his six-inch lasers. It showed nothing but stars twisting by.

A pip at the upper edge drew his eye. In a blink, a streaming comet appeared. Quickly, the pip tracked the ship across the screen. The laser was recharging; nothing happened. Mattim risked a breath as the pip whipped back to the top.

When the comet reappeared, it was already transfixed by spears of light from the other guns. One blinked off just as this gun shot out its own spear. For two eternal seconds, Mattim did not breathe. Light, passing through the gossamer swirls of steam from the ships ahead, shone like a golden road. The comet rode transfixed at the end, more steam boiling off her.

Then beam and comet were gone.

Mattim shook himself; something like this could mesmerize. His job was to fight the ship. "Sandy, where are those tin cans? Now would be a good time for a missile run."

"They've dropped below the enemy gun line, sir. They're just . . . damn! They're coming in, jinking like mad."

"And their missiles are worse." Ding interrupted her own bouncing to add to their problem.

"Secondary batteries, prepare to take the destroyers under fire as soon as they come in range," Mattim ordered. "Hit them hard and hit them often."

"Captain, please belay that order," Guns snapped. "I'm targeting cruiser engines. I need the energy."

"Secondaries, hold your fire. XO, what about our own engines?"

"We're about to do a fleet flip, but the flag hasn't ordered one."

"Flip us. I'm not risking Ivan's engines."

"Aye, aye, sir. Helm, use thrusters to rotate us around our center. Do it . . . now." Hands flying over his board, Thor echoed his orders, a few seconds before he followed them. Mattim's stomach lurched, twisted, and left for points unknown as the spinning ship flipped end over end.

In the process, a lightning bolt passed where their engines would have been.

"Damn good, Colin, Thor." Mattim applauded. "Damn good."

"Forward batteries, fire." As the enemy line passed, the forward batteries had been masked. For the last minute, only the aft and amidships guns had done anything. The forward battery came back with a vengeance. The red triangle glowed yellow on the board again, but Guns was shouting. "We got him up the kilt, we got him up the kilt. Sandy, is he slowing? Tell me, girl."

"There's a crazy wobble in his course, as if he's missing on a few of his engines. I think you got him, Guns." The cheer at that announcement damn near shook the entire ship.

"Those cans are closing," Sandy continued. "Fifteen thousand klicks."

"All power to the secondaries," Guns shouted. "Lay it into them." Now it was the turn of the twenty secondary guns. The crews of the four-inch lasers turned to with a will. Each destroyer had ten missiles, any one of which could vaporize the *Sheffield*.

"Hold course," Ding ordered. "Let's give them our broadside for a while. Slow rotation by half, the big guns are out of range, and we want to be steady for those buggers." The colonial DD's closed to ten thousand klicks, dodging and jinking all the time. Finally, they launched three missiles each and turned away. Four streaked for the retreating line of Society cruisers—two headed for the *Sheffield.*

"The admiral's still headed away," Sandy called.

"But they'll have to start decelerating soon to get into orbit around the gasbag, and those missiles will be waiting for them," Ding warned.

"What about the ones headed straight for us?" Mattim asked.

"That's another matter," Ding muttered. "Guns, can you take care of those little buggers?"

"Trying, XO. They're a bit uncooperative."

"Keep trying. Helm, take the spin off the ship. Now, when I tell you, I want you to turn into those missiles. Countermeasures, you got the icemaker powered up?"

"Yes, ma'am," came the answer.

"Icemaker," Mattim echoed. Had another critical part of his education been glossed over?

"Right now, those missiles are homing in on us, aiming for the middle of this nice long target. 'Course, we're throwing steam off. That messes up their picture, but they're smart enough to accommodate it." Ding stared hard at the main screen. It was expanding, showing only the *Sheffield* and two missiles in ever greater detail.

"In a moment, I'm going to turn close on to their course and spew ice chunks and decoys to port. They should mistake them for us and keep heading for the middle of it. With luck, one of those ice cubes will do a job on their warhead. Guns, in a moment I'm going to need you to check fire."

"Charging the damn missiles. Way to go." Guns didn't look up from his station. "I never did like turning tail. Ready on your order, XO."

"Helm, steer for the missiles, thirty degrees to port of their reciprocal. Guns, check fire, check fire. Countermeasures, Jezebel One, Jezebel Two."

"Yes, ma'am's" echoed from the comm links as an entire ship did the XO's bidding. On screen, the green dot that was the *Sheffield* swerved into the paths of the oncoming missiles. A white shadow grew to one side. The missiles stayed on course.

"Good," Ding breathed softly, the hint of a smile crinkling her lips. Was this the moment a naval officer lived her life for? *Damn, I'd settle for a well-done bargain where we both win.*

What Mattim did was settle into his chair, look unconcerned for the bridge crew, and struggle to keep his heart from racing. The gunfight had been wild and fast and over. This waiting could kill a man. "Sandy, you got any passive sensors on those beasts?" he asked.

"Visual only. They're head-on. Not enough of a shift to notice."

"Let me know the second you get any," Ding whispered, eyes locked on the main screen. For a long moment, there was nothing. No one breathed on the bridge, probably on the whole ship.

"First missile, range opening to port. She's going to miss us to port," Sandy yelped.

"Put missile on visual," Ding ordered. Half the main switched to a live view of space. A missile moved across it, tail now plainly visible—and offset—from the nose. "A miss," she breathed as the missile entered the ice field. A moment later the missile started shredding parts as it hit first one then another bit of ice. At their relative speeds, it didn't take much ice to rip its thin skin to shreds.

"Second missile is close, but it's a miss," Sandy said. It was passing close down their port side, but it was a lot luckier with the ice. Unscathed, it began a skewed U-turn.

"Guns, it's yours," Ding shouted. "Crew, prepare for maximum acceleration. Ivan, your engines good for five gees?"

"Zero to five in twenty seconds, Commander."

The turning target suppressed its jinking program. Eight secondary batteries reached out for it, crisscrossing space around it. And threw it. The missile was suddenly an expanding ball of glowing gas. Then nothing.

"Guns," Mattim breathed, "I think we owe a lot of people a beer bust. Like the entire crew."

"I think you might be right, Skipper."

Whatever the crew thought of the idea, they were too blown to do more than let out the breath they'd been holding. Mattim's knees were shaking; he felt like collapsing. Since he was already sitting, he settled for swallowing hard and tackling a long list of things left to do. "Well done, XO, very well done."

"Thank you, sir." Now that the battle was over, Ding looked pale. She made no effort to rise either. Someone's teeth were chattering. One of the guards. Ding sent him to sick bay.

"Captain has the conn. Thor, get us headed back to station. I imagine the admiral's disappointed that we're out of line. Sparky, any traffic from the flag?"

"We've been getting a steady flow of message traffic, each sharper than the one before. I'm only required to pass messages along to you within ten minutes. Allowance for if you're in the head and stuff like that. The first one was four minutes ago."

"Thanks for not jiggling our elbow. Anything I need to know?"

"No, sir, just get back in formation."

"Pass it to my day cabin. I'll use it for bedtime reading tonight. Captain off." He turned to Ding. "You'd think the bastard has better uses for his time." Mattim shook his head and got back to business. "Sandy, where are the hostiles?"

"Decelerating, sir, pulling back into orbit."

"And our guys?"

"Decelerating, too."

"Helm, put us on course to rejoin the squadron."

The prodigal son was not welcomed back. Mattim suspected the admiral would have relieved him where he sat, but there was no one on board who didn't share in his high crimes and misdemeanors and no way to transfer anyone. The squadron decelerated, facing backward as they accepted ELM0129-4's powerful tether. To Mattim, it looked like the

Sheffield was now the head of the line. He doubted the admiral shared his view.

With things reasonably settled down, Mattim released half the crew for a quick chow. Many needed a change of underwear or to clean up from burp bag overflows. The mechanics of orbits guaranteed them time. Gunners went about lavishing care on their lasers the way few had ever shown a significant other.

While some of the damage control crews carried sandwiches to the gun crews and engineering, the hull and armor team waited for the course to settle in, then sent squat robots out to examine the one large gash in the *Sheffield*'s armor. Insulated lines began showering a mist into the hole, slowly packing it with ice, less dense ice, but armor nevertheless.

Mattim got his team on net. "Guns, great going. The enemy flag will remember us. Engineering, solid performance. Sandy, you were wonderful on sensors. Okay, we done great. We've got an hour before we meet those bastards again. What do we need?"

"Guns is ready" was all Commander Howard had to say.

"Sensors are undamaged. I've got a couple of antennas that have been shaken up a bit by all the jostling, probably hum connectors, but I don't see us fixing them any time soon."

"Skipper"—Ivan's gravel voice had somehow gotten even lower—"we've done a lot of bouncing around, changing acceleration and the like. It's been a major drain on our reaction mass. I also don't think the stuff we last took on has anywhere near the density required by Navy specs."

"How far down are we, Ivan?"

"Forty percent. Normally I wouldn't worry, but if we have a few more hours like the last, we could end up limping back."

"Assuming we were in one piece." Sandy scowled.

"Guns, suggestions?"

"Book says you must refuel at fifty percent, 'barring unavoidable circumstances,' whatever those may be."

"Comm, send to flag, *Sheffield* at sixty percent fuel state.

However, reaction mass is not at required density, request fuel scoop."

"Yes sir, sending."

"If we're all heading for fifty percent, why hasn't Smiley laid on a fuel scoop pass?" Mattim asked.

Once again, his XO seemed reluctant to offer an opinion. "Guns," she said.

"Skipper, data would seem to indicate he's made up his mind, one more firing pass, then we head for the jump."

"Bit obvious, aren't we?" Sandy drawled.

"I fear so," answered Guns. "Possibly to our detriment."

"Comm here, Captain. Flag says maintain station. Fuel state not critical."

"Why am I not surprised? Thanks, comm." Mattim leaned back in his chair. "Any suggestions?"

Heads nodded on the bridge. The net was silent. "Okay. I'm the captain of this ship and ultimately responsible for its safety. I read that somewhere. Helm, captain has the conn. Break from formation and do a fuel scoop pass. Use whatever fuel is necessary to get us down and back in one hundred seventy degrees of orbit."

"Laying in course. We'll need some three gees deceleration, sir."

"Give the crew five minutes warning." Mattim again tapped his comm link. "Comm, flag will be sending us more of the same messages. Pass them to my day cabin . . . uh, unless he threatens to shoot us. Pass that one direct to me."

The fuel pass was smartly done. The flag, while frequently sending its displeasure, stopped short of shooting. As they climbed up, Sandy studied her boards.

"Skipper, I think I've found one missing destroyer."

"Where?"

"She's on a high, elliptical orbit. Active on radar and lasers. She's got us and squawking. What she knows, the rest of those bastards know."

"Pass it along to the flag, if they'll let us get a word in edgewise. Comm, put this on a broad beam. Make sure all the squadron picks this up."

"Yes, sir. Sending."

Mattim leaned back in his chair. "So, they know where we are and we got no idea what's up behind this big ice ball. Ding, Guns, any ideas of what you'd be doing?"

"They put on a lot of acceleration during that firing pass," the XO mused slowly. "They'll be high this time around, probably diving for a scoop run, maybe? Guns?"

"Agree with the high part. Not so sure about the scoop. That would depend on their fuel state. They seemed to be coming up from one last orbit. Unless he's neurotic about fuel, I'd skip it this pass. Captain, sorry we can't be more help. The skunks will be high and either coming down to our orbit or diving for a scoop."

"If they're high, when will Sandy catch them?"

"After the rest of the squadron. Remember, we're low."

"Hate to depend on the flag for anything." Mattim rubbed his jaw. "Comm, send to *Aurora* on tight beam. Mattim to Buzz. We're low, let us know when you topside folks spot something."

"Sending." There was a momentary pause. "Buzz says he'll look sharp." They waited. Damage control reported all repairs made. Even one of Sandy's cable runs was replaced. Things were looking up. "Comm here. *Aurora* sends 'Hostiles in sight,' and passes their sensor picture to us."

"Sandy?"

"Got it. They're high, heading for our level. That's strange. We ought to be getting an angle on their bow at this distance in orbit, but they're keeping straight bow on to us."

"No change in formation. The three cans are a bit further ahead, six cruisers behind in line. One of the cans is radiating. Just what you'd expect," Ding concluded.

"Matt, I'm not so sure," Sandy cut in. "This is all radar returns. Nobody's using gravity sensors."

"How soon until we get a look?" Mattim asked.

"Should acquire the picture in ninety seconds." Sandy answered. They waited. As the enemy line swung into sight, Sandy went active. "I got 'em—radar, visual, and gravity. They may be head-on to the rest, but they ain't to us. The two big bastards are in front acting like destroyers, and they got another cruiser with them! The cans are in rear formation this time!"

Mattim mashed his comm link. "Send our board to the flag."

"Doing it, sir."

"Any reply?"

"No, sir."

For five long minutes the squadron continued in line ahead, the *Sheffield* playing catch-up.

At forty thousand klicks, the enemy's lead ships did nothing—as a destroyer would. The flag's targeting lasers came on, sweeping past the lead ships to concentrate on the six in line. "He doesn't believe us," Sandy muttered. From their perspective they could see the lead cruisers swinging around, keeping their narrow face to the squadron.

At thirty thousand klicks the *Reply* opened up on the lead "cruiser" in line. The two leading colonial "destroyers" were at less than twenty-five thousand klicks when they pinned the *Reply* in their combined beams. Hit, the *Reply* threw water like a fire hose and twisted out of line—toward the enemy.

The other cruisers of the squadron tried to take the new target under fire, but it took time to change firing solutions, especially at maximum range. Thirty seconds later, all three colonial cruisers snapped out at the *Reply*. Again she shed steam. It looked like her wobbling might jink her out of the lasers' paths. It didn't. The *Reply* burned.

"Guns, we in range of a target?" Mattim snarled.

"Not as close as I want to be."

"Get their attention."

"Fire."

Lights dimmed. Arrows reached out from one electronic icon to spear another. Mattim steadied himself for the shock of return fire. The closest enemy was a light cruiser; it did not respond. For the last few seconds, it had been firing at will. Now it fell silent. Mattim checked the chronometer. Thirty seconds since the heavies last fired.

The enemy line lit up. It reached out, pinned the *Reply* in its focus, slammed it with all the power of bitter humanity. The flag expanded, gas shooting off in jets and streams.

Then it blew.

Chunks of hull rode the expanding gas out toward the stars. The explosion turned out and in and then was gone. Where a ship and six hundred people had been—nothing.

"Guns, pour everything we've got, mains and secondaries, into that cruiser. Get her attention. Don't let her do that again."

"Roger, Skipper. Can you get me more power?"

"Ivan, we aren't at high gees. Feed the guns."

"I got backup cables to the midship batteries. I'll feed them off ship's power. Next time they recharge, I'll switch."

"You hear that, Guns?" Mattim checked to make sure.

"Got it. Just a second. Just a second." Light stabbed out from the *Sheffield*, reaching for the other ship as it turned its weapons on the *Significant.*

"Damn, they're going to do it again," Mattim snarled.

"Ivan, give me the juice," Guns shouted.

"On the way."

The four-inch lasers reached out, raking the cruiser, boiling off patches of the surface ice. When next *Sheffield*'s six-inchers spoke, they stabbed at the already warm ice. Slush streamed off into space, leaving fantastic patterns in the cruiser's wake.

"We better start jinking," Ding said.

"Do it. XO has the conn," answered Mattim.

They dodged left as the cruiser fired—at them. Light streamed harmlessly by to port. Mattim hoped Pringle was grateful for the help.

"Good call, Ding." His voice broke. He swallowed hard.

Now the XO danced with the enemy cruiser. She'd hold the *Sheffield* steady on a zig while their battery unloaded energy. Then, as the tenth second since the enemy last fired approached, she'd jink. Three times she dodged the lancing light. Three times the *Sheffield* slashed and cut at the enemy's frozen armor. Some of what streamed behind the cruiser was not steam or ice.

"We've peeled her," Guns shouted. Ding ordered a dodge-up, but no fire came. As she turned to the helm to order a second jink, the enemy battery stretched out to them.

The *Sheffield* shuddered, but held to her spin. By the time Thor started the jink, the fire ceased. "Damn," Ding snapped. "Guns, when's your next volley?"

"Soon as we're charged."

"Hold the one after that for closest approach."

"Will do."

Four long seconds passed. The four-inchers slashed out every two or three seconds. Then the big lasers spat. As soon as the light blinked out, Ding started talking.

"Helm, port thrusters, one one thousand, two one thousand. Low thrusters, one one thousand, two one thousand. Starboard thrusters, one one . . ." The enemy cruiser's lasers passed harmlessly to starboard. Two tried to track in to where the *Sheffield* was, but winked out as they touched ice.

"You did it, Commander."

She didn't seem to hear Mattim's praise. Her eyes were locked on the hostile cruiser as they closed the final distance. They couldn't be more than three thousand kilometers out. "Helm, prepare to rotate ship. Keep nose to hostile."

"Aye, aye, Commander."

"Guns?"

"Ready."

"Helm, rotate now." As they passed, the *Sheffield* spun on her central axis, keeping her armored hull between the enemy and the vulnerable engines. The enemy spun too—a second too late.

One of the four-inchers stabbed into the giant bell of a rocket engine. With power no longer equally applied, the ship wobbled, presenting more of its vulnerable rear. Two six-inchers stabbed into engineering spaces. Out of control, the ship cartwheeled.

"Sweet Lord," Sandy breathed.

"Have mercy," Ding finished.

"Check fire, check fire," Guns shouted. "Recharge and switch fire to the target I designate." The next four-inch laser reached out for the nearest cruiser—the enemy flag.

It was rotating, covering its engines from the one surviving heavy cruiser. A *Sheffield* four-incher nipped an engine, but the resulting spin twisted the flag's fantail away. When the six-inchers spoke, it was to ice and steam. Mattim checked their first target. Its twisting was slowing, as was the defensive spin. It coasted, struggling to put things right before risking power. Its guns were silent.

Our flagship blown to pieces, one enemy light cruiser wrecked. Quite a battle. Now let's get the hell out of here.

That seemed foremost on everyone's mind. All the ships were flipped now, falling backward away from each other. Fire was desultory. Maybe lasers were hot, maybe engineers had chewed their nails enough, watching reactors dip deep into the red. Maybe a lot of things. A breathless peace hung between the ships as they receded out of range.

"Message from the *Significant,* Captain. Assuming command All ships make best speed for Beta jump. *Sheffield,* appreciate taking the pressure off me. You are best fueled, and best shooting. Continue rear guard station. Independent movement authorized. Godspeed and good luck. Pringle sends."

"Gee, thanks," Mattim breathed.

"Should I send that reply?"

"No, comm, send 'Thank you and good luck to all.'" Mattim went quickly on to what had to be done for what lay ahead. "Ding, Guns, Sandy, Ivan, we've done such a good job we get to stay in this hell a bit longer."

"I keep telling you, boss." Sandy was not smiling. "All you get for doing a good job is a worse one."

"Point taken. Captain has the conn. Thor, put us in line behind the squadron. Ivan, Guns, how do things look? Can you join me in my day cabin for a few minutes?"

"Yes, sir," they answered him. Mattim stretched; it felt good to be alive. "How long before we see the colonials again, Sandy?"

"Thirty-five minutes or so."

"Ding, I want coffee and sandwiches in my cabin for us."

"Quartermaster, have a runner lay down to the galley and get us sandwiches and a couple pitchers of coffee."

"Aye, aye, ma'am."

Sergeant Mary Rodrigo had forgotten how good a warm shower felt. By the time she got back to the supply truck, it was loaded. There were hostiles in the system, but their rocks had landed well away from the base, deceived by the noisemakers her platoon had put out. The Navy pukes had finally got the colonial ships off the marines' backsides. It was a good time to sleep . . . so she did.

SEVEN

MATTIM WAS EXHAUSTED, terrified, and damn proud of his crew. They'd taken *Sheffield* to the gates of hell and not only survived but done good. At least one enemy light cruiser would not be nipping at their heels as they bugged out. As the command staff wandered into his day cabin, Mattim was glad to see he wasn't the only one with weak knees. Even Guns was a bit uneven on his feet before he sank into a stuffed chair.

Settled around the coffee table, the Navy types ladled heaping spoonfuls of sugar into their coffee. When Sandy and Ivan followed suit, Mattim broke his usual practice. His tongue found the coffee overly sweet; his body appreciated the jolt. His first sandwich gone, Mattim sat back. "What do we face?"

"A day-long running gunfight," Guns growled, "with them gunning and us running."

"We'll be a couple of hundred thousand klicks away from each other when we break orbit," Sandy observed. "It ought to take most of the trip to close the range."

"Maybe, maybe not," the XO observed. "They know we're running for the jump. They know we want to get there fast, but have to bleed off speed before we pass through. They'll send ships clipping across our sterns, aiming for our engines. We can do a lot of things, but change course is not one of them."

"Skipper," Guns observed, "all bets are off for today. They'll do whatever they can to damage us, cut us off from each other, turn this into a rout where they can pick off strays one at a time. We've got to hold together."

That turned out to be tougher than expected.

The *Significant* ordered the squadron to 3.5 gees acceleration as soon as they left orbit. As the ships accelerated, something big flew off the *Significant*.

"Damn, her armor's caving." Ding scowled.

The new lead ship sidestepped out of the column even as communications buzzed Mattim. "*Significant* unable to accelerate above two gees. The rest of the squadron is to continue at three point five gees. *Significant* will take rear guard. Godspeed and good luck."

"And be cut to pieces," Ding predicted.

Mattim rang up hull and armor. "How solid is that patch you put on us?"

"Readouts say it's clinging tight as my college boyfriend."

"Can she trust her readouts?" Mattim asked Ding.

She winced. "Probably. Navy's done its best to understand ice, but it's still ice—with a mind of its own at times."

"Comm, send to *Significant*. '*Sheffield* will guide on you.'"

"Matt." Sandy turned in her chair. "Is this a good idea?"

The trader in Mattim certainly agreed it wasn't. Another part, the one that came with the star of a Navy line officer on his shoulder boards, said yes. He glanced at Ding. She nodded slowly, her face a mask. "We've got the extra reaction mass. The rest don't. They can't. We can. Therefore, we must."

Comm beeped. "Flag says thanks. Operate as you will."

With a deep breath, Mattim prepared to do just that.

• • •

The opening gambits were simple. A light cruiser and two destroyers shot across their stern, only halfheartedly threatening as they covered for two cruisers that came out of orbit a lot slower and headed for the other jump point. The two cans came on fast and shooting—too fast. Their missiles had trouble adjusting, and most went wild. The *Sheffield* evaded and destroyed her three while helping *Significant* gun down her five. The *Aurora* got clipped by a near-miss explosion. One of her engines had to be taken off line, and a second to keep acceleration balanced.

As the enemy destroyers edged over to join the exiting cruisers, Buzz's cruiser slowly fell behind the others. "Figured I'd join the crippled division," he quipped to Mattim, as he matched *Significant*'s acceleration.

"Gives us a good concentration of fire," Mattim answered with cheer he didn't feel.

"Not bad," Guns drawled. "We mangled two cruisers, and they detached a third and a pair of tin cans to escort them out. Odds are down to two superheavies and a light cruiser to our heavy and two light cruisers."

For the next long hours, the two opposing lines accelerated out and drew inexorably closer. The lead half of the squadron reached flipover a good five hours ahead of the trailing units. The colonials seemed content to let them escape; the three remaining enemy cruisers matched their acceleration to *Sheffield*.

Mattim did not waste the time; he hoped Buzz and Pringle kept their crew as active as he did his. At two gees there were problems, and the inevitable casualties. Still, Mattim made sure his armor was in as good a shape as it could be. He took acceleration down to one gee long enough to mend a few cables, then took the ship up to three gees to verify it could still take it. The *Significant* and *Aurora* slowed to one gee with him. So did the colonials. Who made the best use of the time?

"Folks, I want ideas," Mattim told his bridge crew.

Guns pursed his lips. "Ever play chicken as a kid?"

"Nope," Mattim answered.

"They know where we're going, and about when we'll get there. They got reach on us. We need a surprise."

Sandy looked at her fingers. "We loaded a dozen big rocks."

"Relativity bombs," Guns shook his head. "Throw a rock fast enough and you can get quite a boom when you hit a planet. But the relative velocity between us and the colonials is pretty low, and the odds of a dumb rock hitting aren't that good. We don't have an accelerator on board, anyway."

"If we threw a lot of little rocks, we'd have a better chance. And sand on a laser lens . . ." Sandy shrugged.

"Is not my idea of fun," Guns finished for her.

"We've got plenty of ice," Ding added.

"Ivan, how long to rig a slingshot?" Mattim asked, careful to keep the excitement from his voice. The damn colonial 9.2-inchers had double his range. If he could make their life miserable, he wanted to.

"A few hours. Not quite the rail gun you Navy folks use, but good enough. I'll need one gee to work in."

"I'll go to three point five gees now. Let me know when you're ready. Who can grind me up some rocks?"

"I'll take care of that," Ding said.

"Let's do it," Mattim ordered.

No message came from Buzz or Pringle as they fell away from *Sheffield*. Two hours later, the *Sheffield* went to one gee. In the time it took to rig the magnetic sling, create and load bullets for it, and set everything up for loading at high gee, Mattim caught up with the two ships.

"Glad to have you back," Buzz called.

"Had a few things needed doing," Mattim answered.

The colonials had slowed, falling a bit aft of the *Significant*'s rocket engines. Not a solid up-the-kilt shot, but too damn close. Pringle swung the group a few degrees closer to the enemy and away from the jump point. Now he adjusted course, paralleling the colonial fleet and keeping their fantails angled enough away from the enemy. At five hours to jump, the two columns were forty thousand klicks apart—in range of the 9.2-inchers.

The dance with death was joined.

The enemy light cruiser cut deceleration, sliding to cut across the *Significant*'s rear. Mattim cut deceleration too, surging ahead of his mates. The colonial quickly realized if he held his course, *Sheffield* would be in a place to blast his own vulnerable rear. For several minutes they traded shots; then the colonial edged back toward the others. Mattim held his position.

"Well done," *Significant* sent.

It continued that way, one of the colonial cruisers trying to edge around them, drop behind them, force them into a compromised position. The three Navy ships dodged, zigged, zagged, and otherwise went the way they had to, all the time keeping the jump point their final goal. The 9.2-inchers kept their fire slow and deliberate—every two or three minutes. Most shots went wide. They could afford to bide their time.

At thirty-five thousand klicks, Mattim waited until the heavies fired, then swung his fantail around and tossed out a couple of ice and dust bullets to where the colonial line should be in an hour.

"Sir, isn't it a bit early?" Ding half asked.

"Yes, but the real surprise isn't what we've got. It's what he's willing to do about them." At thirty thousand klicks, Mattim launched another six, then blew the first collection of dust, gravel, and ice into puffy clouds. The next 9.2-inch broadside showed bright yellow as it passed through the thin collection. It got the colonials' attention. Five minutes later, their secondary battery began random firings, hunting for the extent of the crud, trying to sweep it out of the way. They must have missed at least one big fragment. Just before they were due for another broadside, the enemy flag lit up amidships.

Ding grinned. "Looks like a turret hit. With luck they'll be fighting a major electrical fire for a while."

It was ten minutes before the next enemy salvo.

The closer they drew to the jump, the slower time passed.

Waiting for the big lasers to reach out got to be worse than dodging them. Minutes became hours.

"I'm gonna quit jinking after the next shot," Ding muttered. When that salvo missed, she settled the ship on a steady course, eyes glued to the chronometer. Twenty-nine seconds slid by. "Up thrusters," she said a fraction of a second before the colonials broke with their practice and fired as soon as they were loaded.

"Tricked ya." Ding grinned . . . and settled the *Sheffield* on a steady course. She had the computer generate a random series of ones, twos, threes and occasional fours. Still, she chose where in the random numbers to start the sequence, and when to jump around in the order. "With my life, and the ship, I don't trust a computer," she muttered.

Mattim could only agree.

After each colonial salvo, he'd swing the ship around to bring the sling to bear, and toss a few more packets across the enemy course. The angle was carefully chosen. If the enemy kept their deceleration even with Mattim's, or swung away, the chances of a hit would drop. For the next half hour, their secondaries continued to sweep their course, and they continued to close.

"Damn, it's gonna be tight," Ding whispered.

Then everything changed.

The enemy flag wobbled, then cut its deceleration to 1.5 gees. "We nipped another engine," Ding crowed. "The flag's falling ahead. The other two look to be holding their course. We'll be rid of the flag in a half hour, but until then, she'll be getting a better angle on our sterns."

To Mattim, this looked like a hell of a situation, or a golden opportunity. "Guns, you got any suggestions?"

"We got reaction mass. We got the best damn shooting I've ever heard of. I'm getting bloody damn tired of doing it their way. We can sit here on our hands, Skipper, dodging, or we can give them something to send them on their way."

"One for you Navy folks' history book."

"Yessir," Guns grinned.

Mattim glanced around his bridge. Ding was grinning and breathing hard. At the helm, Thor's eyes were fixed on the board, hands on the controls, ready to answer orders. The kids around the bridge looked scared, but ready. Sandy swiveled to face him. If there was any mature judgment left, it was hers. She hated war and all that went with it. "How much maneuvering room do we have at three gees?" he asked. She could squelch any cowboying around with one sentence: We'll miss the jump point.

Sandy reached behind her, tapped her board, and a red dot with an expanding yellow cone appeared on the main viewer. "That assumes the jump point hasn't moved. I'm not in sensor range yet."

Mattim studied the screen, projected the enemy course on it. Weighed his own options, then mashed his comm button. "This is the captain. We've dinged the enemy flagship and she's falling out of line. Still, she can cause our friends trouble in the next few minutes. Alternately, we can cause them a lot of trouble. With a little bit of luck, we can run the other two colonials right out of range of our ships. We got the reaction mass, and our shooting's been hot. Strap down, folks, for the ride of your life." He took his finger off the comm button. "Exec, put us on a course to close with their flag."

It took the colonials five minutes and two salvos at the *Significant* before they realized *Sheffield* was headed for them with a bone in her teeth. The dance turned into a mad cavort. Ding would dodge a salvo then swing around and use full thrust toward the enemy. At twenty-two-thousand klicks, Guns began to reply to the enemy salvos with contemptuous single shots—that scored!

"Now let them wonder when I'll smack 'em with a broadside," Guns chortled.

It was amazing how good it felt to Mattim, knowing he wasn't the only one sweating out the unknown. The long fight was telling on the colonials; their beams were wider. The 9.2-inchers were a meter wide as they flashed through the ice *Sheffield* spewed at every chance—and hid behind when she could.

As expected, the *Significant* and the *Aurora* dropped off the colonial target list; the *Sheffield* was it. Jinking became a constant as the colonials gave up their slow salvo fire. Each cruiser lashed out as quickly as it could recharge. Still, the time between shoots stretched from thirty to forty-five seconds to a full minute. Now Guns shot with everything he had—the forward six guns at the flag, while the aft three kept the other cruisers on their toes. The enemy flag had gathered them in. They made the *Sheffield*'s life tenuous, but rapidly fell out of position, giving the *Significant* and *Aurora* a clean shot for the jump.

"It's working." Mattim grinned.

"I found the jump," Sandy shouted. "It's moved!"

"Where?" Ding and Mattim roared together.

"Refreshing the board," Sandy snapped.

One glance at the screen told Mattim he was in trouble. The red spot had only jumped a few inches on the display. Those represented kilometers—and some hard, unforgiving maneuvering, if they were to catch their ride home. "Ding, change course."

"Already doing it," she breathed.

"Cruiser launching missiles," Guns shouted.

"Only destroyers carry missiles," Ding muttered, not letting this latest distract her from her course change.

"I fear our intelligence may be a tad out of date," Guns drawled. "Launch ice. Secondary battery, stand by."

Lasers snapped at them, missed, or grazed the *Sheffield* when one side outguessed the other. The missiles inched closer.

"XO," Guns said slowly, "the missile spread is aimed toward the old jump location. Most will miss."

"Thank you," Ding said as the ship swayed under her orders, and more lasers flashed through the steam and ice the *Sheffield* streamed, some by intent, some from damage.

"It's gonna be close," Sandy whispered.

"Get ready for four gees," Ding ordered. A laser volley raked them as Ding jinked left. The *Sheffield* shuddered in her spin even as pumps struggled to rebalance the hull. Ding goosed them up to four gees.

"We're going to overshoot," Sandy cried. "I've got to have control of delta V."

"You've got it for ten seconds," Ding shouted. "Put us through the jump or lose it."

"Can you take off the spin?" Sandy yelled back.

"Not if you want to live," Ding answered.

"One missile's still coming," Guns said evenly. "I got all secondaries firing a pattern."

"Here we go," Sandy cried.

"Got the bastard," Guns exulted—as wreckage or evasion drove Mattim sideways in his seat.

The main screen wavered as one set of stars was replaced by another. Ding collapsed on her board. "Captain has the conn," Mattim announced. "Cancel spin. Take us to one gee. Lay in a course for the station."

"He can't," Sandy croaked.

"Why not?" Mattim eyed the screen. He knew the answer even before Sandy spoke again.

" 'Cause Pitt's Hope ain't there."

EIGHT

MARY SLEPT ALL the way back to the platoon. Cassie greeted her as they pulled in. "You see the space battle?"

"Nope. They throw any rocks?"

"A few, but we hardly felt 'em. Captain wants us to head over and replace any noisemakers they broke."

"Hope no more rocks are on the way," Mary muttered. Once the supply truck was unloaded, they used it to run Cassie's squad over to where they'd "built" an HQ, setting up noisemakers to imitate the electromagnetic and heat you'd expect to leak from a base under twenty meters of rock. The place was cratered, but not as bad as the last time. Apparently they were using smaller rocks or tossing them at slower speeds. Mary moved the noisemakers away from the new craters, and dialed them down. Even headquarter weenies would know to dig deeper and be quieter.

Moving the decoys, Mary found an extra one, camouflaged almost good enough to pass for a rock. Still, rocks don't have thin antennas spreading out from them. Mary tossed a real rock at it. It blew up. Gingerly, she collected the pieces. Lek would want a look at it.

"Repeater," he growled. "Given enough distance, even a tight beam gets wide." He fingered different parts of the wreckage. "Stuff here to intercept radios and lasers. Good workmanship. You say it was out where you set up the fake HQ?"

Mary nodded.

"Better pass this along to brigade. If Collies don't intercept anything at your fake, they gonna start dropping these around until they do. Isn't the information war wonderful?"

Mattim rubbed his eyes, driving his palms into them, trying to wash away the fatigue clogging his brain. When he looked again, the stars hadn't changed. How many times had Sandy warned him to respect jump points? So he dives balls-to-the-wall into an A. Instead of being blown to bits, they'd hurled themselves . . . where? "Sandy," he asked softly, "any idea where we are?"

"Leave me alone, Matt, I need time."

Mattim glanced around his bridge crew. "I'm open to suggestions," he said softly.

Guns whispered into his mike. "Tommy, put a save on all the gunnery sensors for the last five minutes."

"Okay, boss."

Thor at the helm coughed softly. "Skipper, I've got a magnification on the star, er, stars."

"On screen," Mattim whispered, not wanting to disturb Sandy.

There were four, and they were beautiful. A giant blue star was high above a brilliant yellow one. Close to the yellow was a red dwarf. Very close to the blue one was a . . .

"It's a neutron star," Guns swiveled around. "I heard about this foursome. They're halfway across the galaxy. What a jump. Quite a few vectors on the boat going in, but at least we got it on tape." Guns spoke matter-of-factly, as if he got hopelessly lost among the stars on a regular basis.

Sandy looked up. "I've located enough pulsars to get a rough fix. You're right, Commander Howard. We've gone about thirty thousand light-years. I'd like to have a look at your data."

At Mattim's side, Ding had caught her breath, but now she was struggling to stop shaking. The rest of the crew would be picking up rumors before too long. It would be better if they heard it from their captain. Mattim keyed his mike.

"This is the captain. We made it out of a hell of a mess and punched a hole for the other ships. With all the shooting going on, we hit the jump in a nonstandard configuration." Sandy rolled her eyes at him; Guns chuckled noiselessly. "We know exactly where we are and exactly where we want to go, so it's only a matter of a few adjustments and we'll be heading back. In the meantime, we'll keep the ship on a low-gee acceleration and concentrate on damage repair. That is all."

Mattim raced into a checklist. "OOD, get a list of all damage. Tell damage control to prioritize and coordinate. Ding, you head up the navigation problem. Let's go over it in my day cabin." He turned to the bos'n. "How about some sandwiches and lots of coffee? Sandy, could you get Ivan up here?"

She was doing that already. "Hon, I've got a bit of a problem, and I'd sure like you handy when I brief Matt."

"Nothing popping down here, love. Be right there."

The fight hadn't left Mattim with much reserves; he doubted anyone aboard had anything to spare. He'd have to order his crew to a night's rest soon. But first, he wanted to look this problem over while it was still fresh in everybody's minds, even if those minds were far from fresh.

"Okay, march soldier." Rita ordered, mean as any drill instructor. Ray hung between two handrails, trying to move his left leg. The mirror beside him showed the knee move up a smidge. He didn't feel anything, but he concentrated harder. The foot came up. He swung it forward.

"That's cheating, Major," the physical therapist snapped—and moved the foot back to where it started. "You've got control of that leg. Use it. You're not some cripple with a busted back who's never going to walk again. Walk."

That stung; Ray wanted to spin around and read the man

out. Except he was right. That agony he'd mistaken for torture had saved, regenerated, and otherwise patched up enough of his spine. He'd seen it on the doctors' view boards. He could move that leg. He could walk. He shook his shoulders, gritted his teeth, and focused on his right knee again. *Move, damn you!*

Slowly, the knee came up. With every muscle in his body tied in sympathy knots, it moved three inches.

"That's the way, honey," Rita crowed. "Now the next one. Show them you can walk and I'll get you checked out of here."

"Checked out?"

She came close. "Yeah. Once you're walking, I can take you home. We've rigged rails for you. You can practice a lot at home. The tech will visit." She leaned close to his ear. "And we better get you away from those damn mikes before you get yourself shot."

He took four steps in the next hour, two with his right, two with his left. The therapist left to fill out the discharge paperwork. Back in his room, Ray found a large envelope on his bed. After Rita helped him from the wheelchair, he ripped it open. A red box fell out. As a soldier, he recognized it; only the contents would be a surprise. He flipped the lid open. The Presidential Cross with Diamonds stared back at him—the highest honor Unity conferred on a fighting man.

He snapped it shut and tossed it to Rita. "See if you can't find a bottom drawer to lose that in."

Rita opened it. "Cross and Diamonds," she whispered, oozing respect and pride—and looking straight at the corner they agreed held the mike. "Dad will be so proud. He'll have it hung in the parlor. He was an early member of the party here on Wardhaven."

She handed it back to him, and bent to kiss his ear. "We've got to get you out of here."

"Yes, love."

After a sponge bath, Rita helped him into undress greens, even draping his medal around his throat under the pretext of bending to kiss him. Like a child whose fussy mother was dressing him for church, he put up with it. The therapist showed up. Yes, he was signed out. Yes, he could leave immediately. "You remember what I told you," he said knowingly to Rita.

She reddened, but nodded a quick reply.

"What was that all about?" Ray growled as she wheeled him down the hall.

"I'll show you later."

What began as a quiet journey broken only by the creaking of a wheel turned into a spectacle as staff and patients paused to watch. Someone clapped. Ray waved, meaning to silence the fool. Others waved back and began clapping too. The applause grew. Neither shushing them, nor rolling his eyes to the ceiling, nor waving them down with both hands did any good.

"Face it." Rita leaned forward to his ear. She almost had to shout to be heard. "You are a hero to them. Act like one."

With a sigh of resignation, Major Ray Longknife, Commander of Wardhaven's 2nd Guard Brigade, accepted the acclaim of the hospital. Most he ignored; others were harder. A cluster of his own men in bathrobes stood to attention and saluted.

Now the major wept.

Mattim ordered the *Sheffield* to a night schedule once he was sure everything that could be done was. It took Ivan physically pulling Sandy to get her out of Mattim's day cabin.

"I'll be back as soon as I put Ivan to bed," she insisted.

"Ivan, you two get eight hours sleep. Either of you touch that terminal in your quarters and so help me, I'll rip it out of the wall." The two went.

The exec held back until after the others. "What kind of watch do you want to set?"

"Make it a skeleton watch tonight. Everyone gets serious sack time. Then work their tails off so they don't have time to think. We took enough damage; let's fix what we can.

Heaven knows, we may jump back just in time for the next shoot."

"Right, sir. I'll have tomorrow's Orders of the Day posted before I hit the rack."

"Which better not be more than a half hour from now."

She just smiled. He raised an eyebrow. "I didn't hear my order properly acknowledged."

She grinned as she said, "Yes, sir."

Mattim walked her as far as the bridge. The four suns were still on the screen. Space did turn up some beautiful oddities. "Thor, what's the system like?"

"Some small gas types, rocks not much bigger than asteroids. Their orbits are as crazy as the suns. No sun orbits another. The big blue and yellow stars do some kind of mutual swing with the little ones near them, then the two pairs do their own swing around a center of gravity between them."

"Lay in a course for the nearest gas type. Hope it's got what we need." Mattim rubbed his eyes to help him focus on the star picture. "Were they hatched like this?"

"Sir, if you'd like, I could run a full workup on the gas types so you could select the better one. I'd love to do one on the stars, too, see if they share the same origin."

The new voice, speaking from the darkness beside the hatch, startled Mattim. "And you are?"

A girl, thick glasses falling over her nose, stepped forward. "Excuse me, sir, Security Striker Second Zappa, sir. But I just got my masters degree in System Engineering before they drafted me. My paper was on the . . ." She paused as if doing a translation in her head. "Something about jump points, sir."

Mattim appreciated the interpretation. "You've got an advanced degree, and we're making you a guard?"

She drew herself up to what couldn't have been one hundred twenty centimeters. "I've got my black belt, sir."

"You misunderstand me." Mattim waved a hand. "We've just launched ourselves on a grand voyage of discovery . . ."

"So I noticed, sir," she interrupted dryly. "We know where we are. We know where we want to be. So we'll make a few minor adjustments, twitch our noses, click our heels together and bingo, we'll be home. That was quite a whopper, sir."

"That obvious, huh?"

"To those of us with any training."

"And how many might that be?"

"There's two of us with Ph.D.'s, nearly a dozen Masters like me, and twenty B.S.'s. Didn't you check the personnel rolls?"

"We were rather busy," Mattim flinched.

"I guess you were. We'd be glad to help." Eager eyes, wide with youthful confidence and innocent folly, stared at him.

And who knows, they might help. And he sure as hell did not need the rest of the crew getting an alternate viewpoint from their own science team of child wonders. Co-opt them before they clobbered him. "I think you have a deal. Can you stand this watch and be ready to form up in a team in the morning?"

"No problem, sir. I've pulled all-nighters and aced the test the next day. We're kids, sir, not old folks."

Mattim headed back to his cabin, not sure who was co-opting whom. A computer search verified what she said. As a businessman, he shuddered at the waste. As the captain of a ship halfway across the galaxy from the nearest port, he was glad. With that, he stumbled to bed. It was exactly one half hour since he'd sent his officers off. When they asked, he could answer that he'd followed his own orders. About the time his head hit the pillow, he was asleep.

Ray sat in the passenger seat as Rita drove them home. They were delayed by several troop convoys, red unity flags flying, packed with recent draftees still in civilian clothes. The new troops looked less than enthusiastic. A red flag bedecked stoplight showed the alternative. Two bodies swung from it. Around one neck was a sign reading "Earthie symp," around the other "Draft Dodger."

Rita scowled. "We only have enough transports to lift one division. Why raise more troops?" Ray had no answer.

Her parents had converted a second parlor on their spacious ground floor into his bedroom. The rails and mirror were there for him to practice on at all hours. A housekeeper and her husband were there to help. Recalling that Rita's father was an early Unity Party member, Ray wondered if he'd just traded a camera watcher for a human eye.

Thrown into close proximity with Rita, even in his present condition, the proprieties became difficult to maintain.

"Mother wants to know when we can announce our engagement. I told her I wanted to announce the wedding date instead."

"And she was properly scandalized," Ray growled.

"No, she agreed. What is a good day for a wedding?"

Ray sighed; the day was too beautiful for this. Clouds floated on a soft breeze. Flowers swayed; trees rustled in full dress greens. It was too good a day to argue. He was sprawled on the grass after another long hour on the bars; Rita had put the wheelchair out of sight. He could almost believe it was last summer. But dreams were one thing, reality another. "Rita, I'm not in any shape to be a husband. No job, no . . . nothing."

Ignoring the verbal slap, she picked up a flower and settled it behind her right ear. She wore the sundress; with the sun behind her, he could almost see through it.

"You look man enough for me," she told him. Her eyes slid from his face to his exercise shorts. He glanced down; the bulge was growing far too obvious. He tried to cross his legs. He couldn't quite manage it yet.

"Let's see." Rita grinned and grabbed for his shorts. If he hadn't been trying to cross his legs, he'd have reacted faster. She had his shorts down before he grabbed for them. By then, she'd yanked them over his sandals. For a moment she whirled them above her head like some trophy. Then, looking down at him and grinning at what she saw, she tossed his shorts away.

"Rita, the house."

"Is blocked by the trees. It is time we *talked* this through, and I think I have you where I can finally *talk* to you."

"Rita, I can't."

"You look ready enough." She fondled him.

"Rita, the plumbing may be willing, but the back is not behind it. I can't." He choked on the words.

"That's not what your physical therapist says."

"You've talked about this with him!"

"And why not? He told me exactly how we can do this." She reached for her dress. In one fluid motion, she swept it up and over her head. It fluttered away on the breeze to land beside his shorts.

"Now, let me show you." She stepped astride him.

"I don't think there's any more of you you could show me."

"Yes." She bent at the knees, slowly lowering herself. One hand balanced her, the other hand guided him in.

Lost forever, he reached for her breasts.

"Oh, yes," she said. "Oh, yes."

Later, she lay beside him. "So, what do I tell Mother?"

"You're going to tell your mother?"

"A date for the wedding. Could we make it soon? They're sending an entire division to Elmo Four-A, and I'd like to go as Senior Pilot Mrs. Longknife."

He reached for her, pulled her halfway on top of him, let her breasts crush against him. "You may tell your mother anything you wish."

"Good, because Father wants to talk to you tonight, and I'd rather he was talking to my fiancé than to some stranger."

"Your father doesn't own a shotgun, does he?"

"Shotgun?"

"An ancient earth appliance often used as a marriage aid."

"I've heard about those things. Maybe once I'm a married lady, I can get someone to sell me one."

Ray measured the distance to his shorts. It was not too late to back out. This woman had been nothing but one star-tling surprise after another since he first saw her on the bridge of her transport. How could anyone go so quickly from efficient spacefarer to beguiling young woman? Marriage to her would be full of surprises. Hopefully less painful than those he'd found commanding the 2nd Guard. But just as he could not think of not commanding the 2nd, he could not think of not loving Rita.

Mattim had breakfast served to his "old folks" tiger team in his day cabin. He wanted to make sure they got one decent meal, even if it was wolfed down. "By the way," he began blandly, "you know you're not the only science team on this problem." He relished the dismay on every face—except Guns.

He snorted. "You found out about my brain trust. How?"

"That little snippet of a guard. She offered last night to run a major workup on the suns. Also told me in very precise details of the whopper I told the crew."

"Ah." Guns grinned. "The Kat who got away."

Mattim glanced down his list. Guns was right; all but two or three were in his department. "How good are they, Guns?"

"Quite good. Of course, there're a few that aren't quite as good as they think they are, but time will educate them."

"We need them now."

"Then I suspect we need to adjourn to a mess deck. The wardroom would be better, if you don't mind turning a bunch of strikers loose in officer's country."

"As a merchant skipper, I've issued midshipman warrants."

"No can do here, Captain," Ding said without hesitation.

Guns gnawed his lower lip. "Of course, sir, you are still a licensed merchant captain. I, for one, think these kids would be a lot easier to deal with if they were not part of my usual chain of command. If you gave them temporary midshipman ranks and assignments, it might avoid a lot of confusion."

"Exec?" Mattim raised an eyebrow at her.

"I think it will be a bloody confusing chain of command

any way you cut it, but I'll go along with you. Somebody once told me if you're going to screw up, screw up big."

"That was my grandmother," Mattim sighed.

The computer accessed the old Red Flag portion of his files, matched the names on his overtrained and underemployed list and printed out merchant midshipman warrants. When ordered, the kids reported to the wardroom, along with a dozen or so officers and chiefs that had been added to the "science" side of the ship for the duration. Mattim handed out the warrants. Ding swore them in. Then they got down to business.

"Any with experience in the theory of jump navigation or something close, join Lieutenant Commander O'Mally's team. If you're good with computers or image enhancement, Guns keeps you. The rest help Lieutenant Jagel analyze this system."

"Are we homesteading?" came from the back of the room.

"No. Commander O'Malley has repeatedly told me that the gravity of the known systems acting on the jump points only accounts for eighty or ninety percent of their movement. I want to know if this system accounts for the missing twenty percent, or if we should be prepared for more. I'm open for other proposals for study. Write them up and hand them into the Exec. Any questions?"

"Do we get new uniforms, sir?"

Mattim studied the questioner, who'd jumped to attention before asking. He glanced at Guns, who rolled his eyes. *So this is one of them who had a bit to learn.* "We've got a damaged ship to repair. We'll see what we can do in our *spare time.*" He took a bite out of the words to show there shouldn't be any.

The questioner wilted back into her seat.

"Good. Let's get organized. I want action plans to me by oh-seven hundred tomorrow." He hunted for Zappa, found her. "Looks like an all-nighter to me. And I'd like a team to run a full set of tests on the gas planets to see if we're headed for the right one. Good day, ladies and gentlemen. Have fun."

Two days after the supply run, the roof fell on Mary.

"Sergeant Rodrigo, report to Company HQ, pronto."

From the look on the captain's face, all Mary's luck was sludge. He stood, glowering at a message flimsy as she reported in her best recruit manner. He left her holding her salute. "Do you have any idea why I'm to report to brigade tomorrow morning with you and a couple of your corporals in tow?"

"Nosir."

He tossed the message on his desk and returned her salute with a sour wave. "You ain't gone crying to your mommas?"

"Nosir."

"Yeah, most of you are too old to have mommas, and the young ones aren't any better than whores' trash anyway. Hear this, woman. You wrecked one officer's career and damn near killed him. You aren't wrecking mine. You bozos may have gotten a few pissant colonials to bug out. Next time they show up, they'll see how real marines do it. You hear me."

"Yessir." Mary heard him loud and clear. She'd kept her platoon alive—most of them—and his ego was all bent and busted. *Fuck you and the tailpipe of what you rode in on.*

"Dismissed, woman. And get cleaned up. Use some lipstick. Have one of those tramps show you if you don't know how. Make sure the rest of those stinking bums get a bath."

The man expected her gone. She didn't budge. "Request permission to use one of the other platoons' facilities vans."

"First platoon has its own."

"Yes, sir, a sitting target for a rock."

"I ordered you to dig it in. I've got a hard copy right here." So it was cover his ass time.

"Yes, sir, but there is no location in the platoon area that provides reasonable protection. Us miners know our rocks, sir."

The red was rising past his neck to his cheeks. Mary prepared for another blow. "Permission granted. Now get the hell out of my sight."

There was some serious celebrating that night. Nobody had the foggiest idea what was up, but that didn't matter. They had the run of second and third platoon's showers—not just Mary and the three who were going with her, but all the platoon. They used the vans' showers until the hot water ran out, and were none too careful about the mess they made.

Later, as Mary settled herself deep into her fighting hole, she remembered the captain's order about lipstick. She'd forgotten. She didn't care either.

Thor brought Mattim the analysis of the system. It was over an inch thick. He looked up at Thor with a lopsided frown. "The top page is the summary. You wouldn't believe some of the programs these kids have on their personal computers. One plugged his into the new antennae the Navy hung on the *Maggie* and damned if he didn't have this in no time. I figured you'd want the full report on hard copy. I got lost in it on the computer."

"We're headed for the right one, I take it."

"Yes, sir."

The watch woke Mary. She and the others gathered beside their holes and waited. At oh-four fourty five, a truck rolled up. "You folks pile in the back," the driver said.

"Is the captain coming?" Mary asked.

"The command car'll get him at oh-six thirty. You wouldn't want an officer to miss out on his beauty rest?" Apparently the captain had done nothing to win a popularity contest among the drivers.

"Thanks for the ride," Mary said. "Sorry about the hour, but a truck is just fine by us. We'll sleep."

"We aim to please the good guys."

By the time Mary climbed in, Lek and Dumont were already flaked out, snoring. Mary took them off net.

"You have any idea what's up?" Cassie asked.

"No," Mary answered. She'd kept a few things back about the talk with the lieutenant. There was no reason to change now. Besides, how do you tell your friends that you may get a medal and a promotion for what they all did together? If it happened, it happened. If it didn't, Mary didn't want to have to eat her words.

They settled on the truck's floor and quickly fell asleep.

"Hey, folks, we're here," the driver hollered, opening the tailgate. "You can take off your helmets. You got air." From the looks of it, they had slept right through the base airlock. Mary glanced at the ceiling—bare rock.

"Looks safe enough," she said, and cracked her helmet. Damn, the air smelled good. The mixture of machine oil, human sweat, and recycled air made her feel right at home.

Beside the driver stood a navy chief in khakis. "I'm Kawalski, Master Chief of the Brigade. I got some spaces reserved so you folks can change into dress uniforms."

Mary let herself down from the truck bed and tried to think. "Uh, sir, we don't have any dress uniforms."

"You can call me Chief, Sergeant. I work for a living just like you." He looked them over; then a sparkle came to his dark eyes. "On the other hand, I can't think of a better uniform for an honest-to-God marine. You'll do just fine."

"Can we see the lieutenant?" Cassie asked.

"Why not? We got half an hour. Don't want the officers to think we enlisted swine don't have anything better to do than wait around on them. Follow me." They found the LT in his hospital room sitting in an unpowered wheelchair. He was in full dress blues and trying to figure out how to place his sword.

"I refuse to hold it in my lap," he said, scowling.

"Let me take a crack at it, sir." The chief measured the sword and the wheelchair with his eyes for only a second before he started loosening the leather harness that held the sword to the lieutenant's belt. At maximum extension, the sword hilt easily reached the handles on the chair. There it rested, clearly his. The chief started to wheel him up to the mirror; Mary stepped in to take over. While the lieutenant checked himself out, Mary could hear the chief doing his own check. "So that's the way it is. It's a damn good officer who can earn a medal and the respect of his sergeant."

The lieutenant glanced up in the mirror. "They had their doubts. Right, Mary? Cassie?"

Mary blushed. "Damn right, sir," Cassie answered.

The chief glanced at his wrist. "'Bout time. Can't keep the elephants waiting."

"Elephants?" Cassie echoed.

"Big earth animal. Huge. 'Bout the size of some officers' egos. Let's get moving, crew." He led the way. Mary followed, pushing the LT. The rest came up the rear; they made quite a parade. And they weren't ignored. It seemed every patient, doctor, and nurse was in the hall to see them on their way.

And they were all saluting.

Mary was trying to figure out how to push the chair one-handed when the chief saved her. "We're working, Sarge. Let the lieutenant salute for all of us."

Sandy and Guns took over a mess deck for their teams and pored over the gun data for the last seconds before the jump. When they reported to Mattim, Sandy was not happy; they had no idea what had gone wrong. "Was it the spin?" Sandy asked the overhead. "That missile near miss added lateral movement at the last moment. Nobody's taken a type A jump point at our velocity, and we were still accelerating." She threw up her hands. "There's so many things. What did it?"

"There was also a wobble on the ship from the damage we'd taken," Guns added. "So many factors to sort through."

"And any one or all of them may be why we're here," Mattim summed up. "Without the right combination, we don't get back."

"Yes, sir." Guns nodded.

Mattim leaned back into his chair as Guns did the same.

Sandy was up and pacing. "Which ones? Which ones? We'll have to isolate each one and test them one at a time."

"Does anybody know how many ships have been lost in these damn holes?" Mattim asked.

"Three hundred and forty-seven," Guns answered right back.

"Three hundred and forty-*seven*?" Mattim echoed.

"One of our middies researched that," Guns said with a chuckle. "She has her paper on her own pet computer, complete with all her research notes. We've got the full benefit on the subject of every file on Pitt's Hope. She got an A on the paper," Guns added with a raised eyebrow.

In the next month, she'd get her real grade, Mattim thought. "Is there any thread running through the losses?"

"She didn't find any then. At the moment, she's reviewing her data with a lot more personal interest."

"Did any of the ships have sensors like ours?" Sandy stopped dead in her pacing to shoot the question.

"There haven't been any losses in fifty years, so we're several generations of equipment up. Also, none were bugging out of a shoot with all gun sensors on. I think we've got a leg up. If we can just find the right leg in all the data."

"Are there any observations of a ship just before its loss?" Mattim asked.

"Only that first one from Earth that didn't make it back," Sandy mused. "Nobody saw anything wrong with the *Santa Maria. Challenger* and *Morning Star* made it through the jump, but she just wasn't there." She shivered. "The *Maria* had problems with one of her directional jets. That's why they always told us to keep a ship perfectly steady into a jump."

"If we'd held the ship steady, we'd have been blown halfway across the galaxy." Guns left no room for doubt.

"Yes. Tough choice," Mattim agreed.

"We'll have to make some test jumps, but we'll find our way home." Guns sounded like a grandfather assuring a child.

"Yes, yes." Sandy was back to pacing. "Assuming there is

a reason and it's not that they've been good little jump points for fifty years and decided it was time to swallow a ship."

"Sandy!" Mattim snorted.

She whirled on him. "Well, it's not like we know what makes the damn things tick. They're just there. We ride them like rivers. We can't make them; we use them, like electricity, but try to get some genius to explain that one." She wound down like a robot on exhausted batteries. Mattim went to her, held her; to hell with Navy regs. He'd seen her exhausted and spun up, tasked by a problem she didn't think she could beat. She always did. She just needed a hug. Guns looked away.

"Sandy," he whispered to her, "maybe you're right and the jump point demon was overdue for a sacrifice and we got tagged. But you and I both know that there're a hell of a lot of good, scientific reasons for this to happen. Let's look them over. See what we see. I bet you the kids are having a ball."

She chuckled through a sniff. "Bloody children don't even know it's impossible."

"Which is probably why they'll do it, and be shocked as hell to discover it was impossible afterwards. Come on, Sandy. You love puzzles. You've got some fun people to chew at it with you. This ship's good for ninety days or more. We've got plenty of time. Let's go have fun."

She sniffled. Guns handed her a box of tissues. "Sorry, Matt, Commander," she said, blowing her nose. "I didn't mean to get all blubbery on you. I didn't sleep well."

"No problem." Guns tossed off the apology. "And you might as well call me Howie. While I may insist Navy regs stretch halfway across the galaxy, I'm not so sure about Navy etiquette. Most of those kids are on a first-name basis, and I doubt I can keep them terrified once they've lectured me a few times about what was 'obvious' to them and I was totally blind to."

Mattim walked them to the door. "Guns, when I came

aboard, I wasn't too sure about how the Navy part of the crew would take me. You're a good man."

"Won't say I didn't have my own doubts, but right now I can't think of anyone I'd rather follow thirty thousand light-years from home with only three months worth of food. You're good, Captain."

"Matt, if you want."

"Captain."

Mattim watched them go. He'd taken care of his two most critical team players, given them the assurance they needed. But who'd take care of him? Mattim returned to his desk and the proposals Ding had passed along.

Mary squared her shoulders. A clock struck two bells as the chief pushed opened the door and led them into the vast space of the command center. Across the low-ceilinged room, computer terminals glowed; people were everywhere, khakied officers and enlisted in whites. They went about their duties, but Mary doubted any missed the little procession.

The company commander stood in the middle of the room, beside the battalion CO. Mary hadn't seen him very often, but the major's bantam rooster stance was unmistakable. The chief led them toward the two marine officers, settled the lieutenant to the major's right and the others to the captain's left.

The captain glowered. "Where's your dress blues?"

"We were never issued any," Mary whispered.

The captain started to say something, but the chief's booming voice interrupted him. "Attention on deck. Captain's mast, meritorious, Captain Anderson commanding."

Mary couldn't see anybody commanding, but she dared not move her head. Still, her eyes roved the center . . . and spotted movement. A tall, balding man in Navy whites wound his way through all the work stations. There were three—no four—stripes on his shoulder boards. So this was the brigade's commander. Beside him was a much shorter but strikingly beautiful woman. There were three stripes on her shoulder boards. As they approached, the chief called, "Hand salute."

The captain returned it. Beside Mary, Cassie breathed a sigh of relief. So far, so good. Then the woman commander looked Mary over, frowned, and turned away.

"You've done it now. Pissed off Commander Umboto," the company commander whispered out of the side of his mouth.

What have we done? Mary wanted to ask, but knew better. The Man made the rules and The Man applied them. She'd find out sooner or later.

"Second Lieutenant David S. Donovan front and center," the brigade commander ordered. This time the chief wheeled the lieutenant up to the Navy officer. Umboto read a commendation that started with him taking charge of raw recruits . . . that must be Mary and company . . . training them and instilling in them the finest traditions of the corps, and ended with him defending their pass against overwhelming odds.

Mary breathed a slow sigh. That was the way it always was. You did the work and The Man patted himself on the back and took the bonus. Did she really expect this bunch to be different?

They finished up by promoting him, taking the gold bars off his collar and replacing them with silver ones. Mary shook her head. She knew these people put silver ahead of gold, but after twenty years of mining, Mary would never understand why. They were crazy.

As the chief wheeled the LT back, she was glad they'd let them come see him get his medal. From the look on his face, there was no question it meant a lot to him. He might be part of a crazy system, but there was no reason to hold that against him.

"Staff Sergeant Mary Rodrigo front and center."

Mary glanced around for this other Mary Rodrigo. She knew she was supposed to be at attention, but she couldn't help it.

Cassie nudged her. "They mean you, hon."

"Move," the company commander growled under his breath, "and act like a marine for a change." That last slap made Mary mad.

She could dance their little dance with the best of them. Cutting every corner, she marched to the Navy captain. "Reporting as ordered, sir," she snapped.

"Very good," the old captain whispered through a smile.

"In the finest tradition of the corps," the commander began, then cut to the battle. "At great personal risk, Staff Sergeant Rodrigo did establish herself in an exposed observation post . . ." Mary had a hard time believing what Commander Umboto was saying. She'd just done what she had to do to save her friends' lives. She'd do it again if she had to; it was nothing.

Umboto finished; the chief opened a blue box. The captain withdrew a beribboned medal. And smiled. There was no way he could pin it to battle armor. Beside him, Umboto cleared her throat, reached in her pocket, and pulled out a roll of tape. "When I saw we had some real marines with us today, I thought you might want to improvise, captain." She grinned.

So they taped the medal, a gleaming Silver Star, on the chest of Mary's armor. While they improvised, Mary struggled with herself. Her eyes had gone moist, and she was blinking a lot. Her medal wasn't as fancy as the lieutenant's, but the brigade CO was handing it out, and Commander Umboto thought enough to hunt up tape so the moment wouldn't be spoiled. She wanted to spin around and give the company commander the finger, but that didn't seem quite right at the moment.

They finished; the medal was at a crazy angle. Mary was at a loss as to what to do next. She glanced at the chief for help, but he was handing the brigade CO a new set of papers. The captain cleared his throat. "Staff Sergeant Rodrigo, I am authorized to offer you a Second Lieutenant's commission in the Society of Humanity's Marine Corps. Do you accept?"

"Ye . . . yes," she stammered, all the time wondering how she could say no.

"Raise your right hand, and repeat after me. I, Mary Rodrigo . . ." So Mary found herself swearing to bear true faith and allegiance to a constitution she'd never read, and to defend it against all foes, both foreign and domestic—and wondering just how much freedom she had to distinguish friend from foe.

Nobody tried pinning the gold bars on her suit, but Umboto had a single length of black electric tape to add to the one black line on the back of Mary's helmet. "Now everyone behind you will know you're leading. Makes you a better target." She grinned.

Now the chief's eyes led Mary through a salute and a march back to place. Cassie and Dumont were next. Bronze Stars for each of them for "courage in combat above and beyond." Lek was last. A Navy Commendation Medal, which had to be the first time a claim jumper got a commendation. Done, the chief brought them to attention and dismissed them, which wasn't really a dismissal at all. Nobody went anywhere. Mary and the corporals hugged each other, and tried to keep the happy squeals down to a decorous level. Umboto joined them and did some squealing of her own . . . and hang the level.

They swamped the lieutenant as soon as the senior marine officers moved off. Between Mary, Cassie, and Dumont they lifted him out of the chair for a solid round of hugs and back-pounding. "Damn, I don't get my legs until next week," he grumbled.

Umboto tapped Mary's back and pointed. The Navy captain was talking to the battalion CO, company CO at his elbow. "I imagine this solves the hole in your officers' slots, Garry," Captain Anderson said.

"Yes, sir, it does," the major answered.

"If I were in your boots, I'd be passing these folks around to the other companies. They came up with some pretty unique approaches to preparing a position."

"Already intended to," the major agreed. "Don't imagine

the captain will mind loaning his command car to the new LT and her team for a week so they can cover the other passes. Do you, Ted?"

"Nosir," the company CO answered without a pause.

"Good." Captain Anderson nodded. "Keep me informed how it goes. We haven't seen any colonial ground-pounders for a while. Don't expect that will last forever."

"Never does," the major and captain answered in unison.

Umboto turned back to the celebration around the lieutenant. "That ought to take a bit of the pressure off you for a while."

"Thank you, sir."

"You folks owe me a bigger thanks than that. You remember those rockets that took out the transports?"

"Yes," five marines answered.

"They were mine. Let me tell you what the rest of us were doing while you were having all the fun." One story led to another. Then there was lunch. Umboto knew where a chief in supply kept a still, and that led to a private celebration. They were late getting to the truck for the ride back. Sprawled out on the truck bed, Mary didn't even try to sleep.

Dumont spoke first. "I'm glad for the medal, but I didn't do nothing special. They were going to kill me if I didn't kill them. I did what I had to do to stay alive."

"Yeah," Cassie mumbled. "I wanted to hide in my hole. Joyce and me, we were just going to stick our heads up long enough to fire a clip. When I started to duck, Joyce was dead." Cassie was crying. "Where's the medal for Joyce?"

"This ain't no different from the mines," Lek drawled slowly. "Sometimes you hit it big. Other times you don't. You never know why. It just happens."

"It just happens." Mary repeated the words. Let them roll off her tongue slowly. She'd said that a lot in her life. *It just happens.* She was getting awful tired of just hanging around to see what happens next. She doubted Umboto did. That was one woman who knew how to kick butt and take names until she got what she wanted. *I'm an officer now. Do I get to be like Umboto?*

It was a pleasant thought to fall asleep on.

• • •

The engagement of Rita Nuu to Major Raymond Longknife was a most indecorous week long, though her mother seemed no less enthusiastic for the date. The honeymoon was a very short week. Then Senior Pilot/bride Rita Longknife reported to her ship for a lift the admiral assured everyone would end resistance on ELM-0129-4A.

A week later they informed Ray he was a widower.

NINE

LIEUTENANT MARY RODRIGO tried to keep an open mind about her new job. She *was* getting away from the captain. Of course, she'd be meeting two more. Still, it was a kick taking off with the captain's command car; Dumont said it was better than stealing wheels. The drive over was like old times after a shift. No beer, but it felt like the freedom you got after long hours in the hole. Maybe they treated her a bit different, but not that much.

At B company, there was a difference. The others headed off to spend time with the sergeants. A runner, stiff as a board, led Mary to the company HQ. She hoped this new captain wouldn't be as big an ass as hers. She passed through the airlock, prepared to report like she'd learned in boot camp. What she saw stopped her dead in her tracks. Not one captain but two were waiting for her. Both sat, feet up on the desk, unlit cigars in their mouths. When she started to salute, the one that seemed to be most behind the desk waved her off. "Damn fine bit of fighting, Lieutenant. Damn fine."

"And even more impressive field preparations," a third man said, standing to shake her hand. "Lieutenant Hampton. They call me Hambone. I'm in charge of the engineering platoon. How the hell did you do all that in the time you had?"

"With the mining gear we . . . uh . . ."

"Stole," the other captain put in. "Call me Hassle. That's the best most folks can do with my name. I've got C company, but I figured I might as well trudge over here so you can brief us together. Our passes are only two hundred klicks apart, so we're right neighborly. Right, Trouble?"

"Tordon, Company B." He reached across the desk to shake Mary's hand. "Tordon to my friends, Trouble to anyone else." Then he shrugged into a sly grin. "Okay, Trouble to everyone."

Hambone got her a chair. She was later to discover, not from him, that he was a first lieutenant, and therefore outranked her. What she did discover was a man very intent on learning everything he could about battlefield preparation. For the next two hours, they listened while she described the deployment and battle. When Mary finished, the engineering lieutenant walked around the desk, examining the map Mary had called up. "Outstanding killing field."

"And holding those SS-12's to the last minute," Trouble said slowly. "Brilliant timing by your lieutenant. And your targeting was just as smart."

"The way you played the laser designators." Hassle looked up from the board and fixed her with a hard eye. "Yours were programmable. I could use a few like that."

Trouble leaned back in his chair. "We got a lot of retraining to do. And a lot of work. We better get cracking."

"I figured on a day to fix you up like us." Mary immediately felt dumb as all three officers shook their heads.

"They've tried straight on with you," Trouble said.

"They'll be indirect on us," Hassle concluded.

"We've got to prepare a lot of rim," the engineer muttered.

Mary kept her mouth shut as they worked their way around a map of their own positions. They didn't expect anyone would be dumb enough to land in the crater. What they did expect was small teams of spotters working their way over the rim and around their positions. "We got to spread out, Mary," Hassle told her. "Your diggers and sensors can cover a lot of territory. With rockets and gunners to back them up, we should be able to cover a big chunk of the eight hundred klicks of rim we got. How long will it take to bust your gear loose from Ted?"

"There's a truck parked next to our rig. It's got everything you'll need." Mary grinned. These guys were nice to be around.

"Woman," Trouble said, "if you could cook, I'd marry you. On second thought, I've eaten so much marine chow my taste'll never recover." He dropped to a knee. "Will you marry me?"

"Better decide quick," Hassle cut in. "He's got a lousy memory, but I must say, his tastes are improving."

"Well . . ." Mary hesitated as if in the throes of indecision. "It is the best offer I've had this week."

Trouble was off his knee, reaching for a helmet behind his desk. "Let's go see what Santa brought us good little girls and boys in her truck."

"Too late, Mary, you've lost him," Hassle sighed.

The *Sheffield*'s tanks were topped off. What battle damage they could fix was repaired. They floated a hundred klicks from the unruly jump point. Mattim took his chair and punched his mike. "All hands, this is the captain. We've got the ship in as good a shape as we're going to, short of a yard period. We've got a good handle on this system. Let's see how these jump points work."

Sandy had done her best with what they knew of this point's wanderings. This system might account for as much as ten percent of the travel, or as little as two percent—depending on how you factored in the inverse square effect. In other words, they were guessing.

"As you've probably already figured out, all we can do is try a few jumps and see what happens. Since we're almost dead in space, we should be able to do them fairly quickly. Strap yourselves in tight. Here goes the first test."

He killed the mike. "Sandy, take us through."

"Thor, activate course Sandy One. Let's see what a spin with a bit of lateral movement gets us. Keep her under one klick per second." Mattim forced himself to breathe normally for the minute and a half it took to reach the jump. *When had ninety seconds been so long? Right, in battle.*

He waited.

The *Maggie* entered the jump without a shudder. One moment the stars were there, twinkling in the unique way the gravity fluctuation in the point made them. Then they were different. Mattim waited for the specialists to tell him how different.

"It's not Pitt's Hope," Thor quickly reported.

Sandy and the three middies around her said nothing.

"Scan the system," Mattim ordered.

"Doing it, sir," Thor answered. "Got a single yellow sun down there. My middies will need a while to check for planets."

"Thanks." Mattim let out a long sigh. He'd have to do better at waiting. He didn't like waiting. He'd better learn.

"I'll need a couple more minutes to refine this," Sandy said a short time later, "but it looks like we're about fifty light-years from our last system."

"Closer or farther from human space?" Mattim asked.

"Neither. We lateraled."

"Sandy, how much of a workup do you want on this system?"

"A pretty full one, Matt, if you don't mind."

"Thor."

"Give us a few hours. My team's pretty excited. That sun's got about the same heat and light as old Sol. If we find a rock in the right place, we might go into the real estate business when we get back."

Or know where to go when we give up, Mattim added to himself. "Guns, any ideas from your team?"

"One of them may have something. We aren't sure.

Could we make the return trip at just a few meters per second?"

"Sandy?"

"It's worth a try."

Time was a blur for Mary. Both companies had half a platoon of miners. Once Mary gave them a chance to shine, they were quick to open their own private stashes. The captains were honest enough to admit they'd goofed, hearing about what Mary'd done and not looking in their own ranks for the same skills. They quickly corrected that, establishing an interim two squads of engineers in each company. Battlefield prep went quickly.

B and C companies spread out until they touched in the middle, then they stretched the other way as far as they could. B company should have touched A company, but Captain Teddy refused any assistance from Mary and her team. Digging in the other two companies turned into an endless task. First they did it as far as they could, as quickly as they could. Then they did it again, better. Finally, they did it a third time, looking for what they'd missed, improving what they had. They were only half done with the third iteration when all hell broke loose.

The *Maggie* drifted toward the jump point at exactly ten meters per second. Mattim had this terrible urge to keep asking "Are we there yet?" He had a moment of dizziness as the stars changed; there was a . . . bump?

"What was that?" Sandy asked even as she started her search to pinpoint their location; four suns were not waiting for them.

"Felt just like when we hit a waterlogged log in the boat back home on the lake," Zappa mused without looking up from her work. "Did we hit something?"

"Damage control," Mattim snapped.

"No alarms, sir. No reports. No visible damage to the hull."

"Guns, did that happen in the jump or around it? Were you expecting something like that?"

"I don't know, and no. We're stumped down here, too, sir."

Mattim put the thump aside for the moment. "Thor, am I right, a new system?"

"Yes, sir."

"Sandy?"

She rubbed her jaw like she'd been hit. "Speed was the only variable. But it's not supposed to have any effect!"

"It looks like it did this time. Flip this ship while we've still got the same motion on it, and put us back through the jump at the same slow speed. Now." Mattim couldn't wait for this new disaster to shoot through the ship. The middies might be having a ball studying new worlds, but the rest of the crew, not to mention the captain, wanted to find their way home.

Thor did the flip. He headed them back at the same terribly slow pace. This time, Mattim still felt dizzy, but there was no thump. And the stars changed back to the last system they'd been in. "We *can* repeat a trip," Mattim breathed in relief.

"But velocity shouldn't have any effect," Sandy mumbled.

"It does now," Mattim concluded. "It does now."

"No bump the second jump," Zappa noted. "Wonder what it was?" Mattim had other questions. That one he'd leave to the kids.

Lek alerted Mary and the captains as soon as the first jump point coughed up activity. The Collies were expected; not thirty minutes later, Pitt's Hope spat out its contribution. Everyone dug in deep and sweated out the eight hours for the relativity bombs to hit. They did a lot of rocking and shaking, but there was no damage. Mary's team sidestepped to the right of B company. They would cover the midpoint between A and B. If the captain didn't want them, at least they wouldn't be too far away if he hollered.

Eight hours later, the scene above Mary was hellish in its beauty. The Navy and the colonials went at each other with no holds barred. Lek showed Mary the situation. There were thirty, forty transports. The Navy wanted at them; the colonials had to keep them away. In the black sky above Mary, ships burned yellow and red. Bright comets swept across the sky, ships holed and bleeding incandescent. Stars, as bright as Mary had ever seen, flared up and disappeared in a blink. She knew this was war and people were dying, but it was beautiful.

Lek kept a running count of the transports destroyed. The marines on net cheered at each he reported gone.

Rita held the *Friendship* in formation, jinking and dodging. The Earthies had not gone for a head-on pass, but had angled over, matched orbits with them. Two were now dogging the formation's right flank, nipping and cutting at any transport that came in range. Rita jinked wrong.

"We're hit. Losing pressure in tank five," Cadow reported.

"Pump it dry," she snapped, and jinked again. Her little transport didn't have the ice to take too many hits. Where were those damn Unity cruisers? Three dropped from the higher orbit, and the Humanity cruisers got busy and then got gone.

She came in fast and low for her landing zone and hit heavy. The troops didn't mind; they piled off in less than ten minutes. Their rigs and a month's supplies added another ten minutes to the *Friendship*'s stay. It was too long.

A rocket landed close; fragments rattled the ship. A second missile took out the *Brotherhood*. Loaded with heavy weapons and ammunition, the ship disintegrated. A thick slab of hull smashed down next to the *Friendship*—and bounced in the other direction.

"That was close," Cadow breathed.

"Too damn close. Hesper, we unloaded?"

No answer. Rita scanned through her video stations. An outside shot showed a supply rig upside down, smashed by a jagged fragment. Hesper's orange suit was half under it. Rita tuned to the vitals from Hesper's suit. The suit was still sending; it just had no vitals to report.

"Prepare to lift ship," Rita ordered.

Mary hated each and every ship that landed. They seemed to be setting up a base in the general direction of C company. Mary was glad to have them over there—then ashamed. Hassle and his crew didn't deserve what was headed their way. "Mary, Trouble here. Can you spread out to cover my right? C's going to catch all hell, and I'm shuffling some teams to cover his right."

"No problem." Mary sent Cassie and Dumont to fill the hole. They'd be covering thirty klicks, but with the sensors and rockets, they should be able to keep any surprises under control.

"Mary," Lek interrupted her, "one, maybe two ships have landed in front of A company."

"If Captain Teddy Boy can't handle two ships with twice the people we had to hold six ships, he's not much of an officer." Lek didn't ask Mary what she honestly thought.

Rita lifted ship fast, but a Society cruiser was swinging by just as she did. With no other target, it devoted itself to her obliteration. Rita jinked and ducked the other way, heading in-system—away from the jump. It got her out of range of that damn cruiser soonest. She was almost clear when a laser sliced through the *Friendship*'s cockpit like it was a ripe grapefruit.

Mary watched as the battle raged, in space and on the ground. Transports didn't hang around this time, but took off fast. Still, Commander Umboto got a couple of long range missiles off at them. *That woman is one bloodthirsty lady.*

Mary didn't feel even a tiny bit guilty twelve hours later when things started to settle down and her sixty klicks had not been tapped. Only a fool looked for a fight.

"Lieutenant Rodrigo, battalion here. Report to A company and assume command."

"Sir?"

"Do I need to repeat myself, Lieutenant?"

"Nosir." She recovered herself. No need to ask over the net for what he didn't want to give her.

"Lieutenant, we're assuming all radio and cables are compromised. There will be a coded situation report waiting for you at A company HQ. Try to straighten up that mess over there."

"Yes, Major."

Mary was quite amazed at what a command rig could do. She made it back to A company in two hours even with stops to return fire. The HQ was a shambles, but casualties were few. The miners and kids had learned how to look out for themselves.

She doubted there were more than two companies attacking, but they'd spread out and come in as infiltrators. The captain had done a poor job of spreading his outposts. When they broke through, he'd led a fire team out to fill the hole—and died.

It took Mary most of the next day to stabilize the situation. Keeping a firm hold on her center, she threw her teams first at her right flank, then at her left. Once the colonials saw they weren't going to take the pass from the rear, they fell back in good order. Mary tried to track them, but they spread out and went to ground. They'd be back.

"A company, battalion here. Could you spare C company a platoon? They're being pushed mighty hard."

"They're on the way, Major."

"Thanks for cleaning up the mess."

Mary refused to say "You're welcome."

She hadn't cleaned up all the mess. She checked in where they had the captain's body. The wound was in the back; it had come at close range. So the miners and kids had done what they had to do to keep their casualties down.

She turned to the medic who'd brought her. "Clean the burn off his armor and patch it. We may need it. Once you peel the body out, make it presentable and send it back to brigade."

"Will do, sir."

Mary wondered what other messes she'd have to clean up.

Out of consideration for his rank, they informed Longknife the day before the casualty list was released. They asked him to invite a vid crew out. He should make a statement, he and industrialist Ernest Nuu. They didn't tell him what he should say, but something along the lines of "It is a joy to die for the Fatherland" was strongly hinted at. Ray told them to go to hell.

Mrs. Nuu's wailing went long into the night. It did not keep Ray awake. He sat in the chair he had been sitting in when they brought him the news. He had sat there ever since. The doctors said he had to move, to circulate blood and avoid skin lesions.

The doctors could go to the same hell as the politicians.

About 0200 hours, Mr. Nuu came to his door to apologize for his wife. Ray invited him in, offered him a seat, and pointed to where an untouched bottle of cognac waited. The man poured two glasses, offered him one, and sat. For a long time, they stared silently out the window, undisturbed by the weeping. "I am sorry I could not protect your daughter, Mr. Nuu. I always thought it was a man's place to die, a woman's place to live."

A wail from upstairs punctuated Ray's sentence. It died out and the night was quiet before Mr. Nuu shook his head. "Since she was twelve, Rita wanted to be a pilot. 'How can I carry a man's child if he has faced death and I am too delicate to stare it in the eye? Let me fight, then see the mother I'll be.'" The man took a long drink. In the dim light, Ray saw his eyes blinking. Ray's did too; it was not easy to keep the tears back.

"She would have been a very good mother," Ray finally said.

"Yes," her father sighed. After a long moment, he muttered, "What a waste." He seemed taken aback by his words. He glanced at Ray, expecting condemnation. Ray was long past any emotions.

"It's all a waste. All of it. This whole war is nothing but a waste. Those who died under you. Your being crippled. My daughter. It is all for nothing."

Ray let the word—nothing—roll around his skull. It was a good word. To feel nothing. To be nothing. A good word. For now, he could do nothing. Say nothing. Begin being nothing, as so many of the men and women under his command had become. Did their mothers still weep? Were their fathers looking at what they had sacrificed their lives for and seeing nothing?

Ray deserved to be nothing with them.

"We had such hopes, such dreams when it all began. Unity would bring us together. United behind one powerful man, there would be nothing we and Urm could not do. Foolish lies by those who said them. Foolish dreams by we who listened. And a foolish old man has killed his only child." Now the man wept, deep, racking sobs that shook his body, yet hardly a noise escaped him.

Ray left him to his silent tears. He had much to contemplate. He had gambled with the lives of so many men and women. They had died, trying to make true the foolish lies he spoke as orders. Rita had said he was forgiven, and in her body he'd found the words could be true. Now she was gone, swept away by a commander's foolish lies. Gone, leaving him alone with hundreds of faces, faces that screamed "murderer" at him, "foolish dreamer" at him, "nothing" at him.

An officer and a gentleman would use a pistol. Yet among all his gear that Rita had brought to her parents' house, neither pistol nor knife were present. He raised his glass in silent salute to the hundreds of eyes accusing him in the dark. "To nothing," he whispered, and drained the glass.

Having successfully repeated one jump, they turned the *Sheffield* into an experiment. If speed mattered and ten meters per second got them to one system, where was the change? Fifty meters, one hundred meters got them to the same system. Somewhere between five hundred meters and one klick per second found them staring at a new sun.

Mattim relaxed only when he was once more gazing at four suns. Or, rather, he returned to that level of tension that had become his norm since the dead admiral ordered him to the tag end of the squadron line. Mattim wondered if he'd ever relax again.

Using both hands to push himself up from his chair, he stood. "All right, crew, we can repeat jumps. Let's knock off, get some rest, and look things over in the morning." There were a few mutters, but most of the bridge watch headed for the hatch, the middies chattering enthusiastically to each other. Tomorrow, he suspected, they'd have a lot to say.

"Guns, have your chiefs make sure those middies get at least eight hours sleep."

Guns was chuckling. "I've already had a few chiefs ask me if I'd back them up. I told them there was a baseball bat behind my stateroom door they were welcome to."

"Exec, set a minimum watch. Keep the middies out of it."

"Will do, sir."

"Sandy, do I need to get Ivan to haul you away?"

"No, I've fought my demons. I'll get a good night's sleep and return a hardheaded rationalist." With a wave, she went.

Mattim treated himself to a long, thoughtful shower. They'd gone where no human had gone—and come back. There was a logic to these damn jump points. Yet, they still didn't understand something. What was it about their original jump?

The question did not keep him awake.

Ray was still in his chair the next morning; he doubted he had slept. The day passed slowly, marked by the ticking of the clock on the fireplace. Ray let the *tick-tock* fill his mind. For a man who had been forever active—thinking, planning, doing—this was the closest to nothing he'd ever been. They offered him food. He ignored it, as he did the pitcher of tea they left.

Night and day and night came again. The cook begged him to eat, to drink. Mr. Nuu pleaded with him. "Even my wife eats something. Drinks a little tea. Please, Major."

He answered them with nothing.

Captain Santiago arrived and sat beside him. The silence between them stretched. They spun it into soft nothing. Occasionally, the captain would add words, more to ornament the silence than break it. First words were about the brigade. It was being rebuilt as a division. Its commander had two stars, though until recently he'd been a party hack. Santiago had wrangled command of a company of old hands.

The quiet grew. Others left them alone. Only then did Santiago weep—and it was not for Rita. His kid sister had shared with her church group how much she didn't want her only son drafted. The police had come for her in the night. The family had been required to pay for the bullet. Only the captain had dared to face the police and collect her ashes.

Paying for the bullet was an old tradition. Santiago had never thought he would serve a government that followed it. Neither had Ray. For this Rita had died?

Ray did not notice when the captain left.

Another night and day passed . . . maybe two. The doctor came; he muttered of dehydration and punctured Ray's arm with a needle, left a pole standing beside his chair with a plastic bag that slowly emptied clear liquid into him. That night Ray removed the needle. They did not put another into him.

Time passed into nothing. A car drove up the tree-lined driveway. Rita raced across the grass. It was not the first time he had seen her. This time, she seemed so happy. Maybe this time she had come for him. He closed his eyes, willed himself to nothing.

The door slammed open. "Ray, Mother, Father. I'm not dead. I'm home." Ray opened his eyes. Rita . . . bedraggled, begrimed, still in a pilot suit that stank of fear and old vomit . . . threw herself at his knees. "I'm alive, and you look like shit."

If he had the moisture to spare, he might have cried.

First Lieutenant Mary Rodrigo stared at the map projected on her eyeball. The damn colonials had landed another ship on her front. Just one. Not more than a company. More people to kill. More people killing her own. With an exhausted sigh, she began moving her forces to meet them.

For the next three hours, they came at her in twos and threes. Nothing bigger. Most of the time, Mary did nothing. Her troops were dug in; sensors out, rockets ready. Colonials died trying to cross her rim, find her people, fix them in place or force them into the open, do anything that would let them kill the pass's defenders, punch a hole through the wall into the crater.

The colonials came, and fought, and died.

And through it all, Mary hardly felt a twitch.

She felt nothing even when she sent Dumont out with a fire team to mop up what was left of half a platoon of colonials. She watched the hostile icons disappear from her map, but felt no relief. There were more behind those. She wasted no time on visuals of the fight. The enemy was colored pixels. Just that, no more. Her forces were different-colored icons. Just that. No more. Friendship was something hardly remembered from a distant, forgotten past. She sent a sergeant here, another there. She tried not to think of the name—Cassie, Dumont, whatever name had been attached to the rank.

In four hours, this battle was over, the wreckage of the colonials slinking back. She let them go; she had nothing to risk in pursuit. She'd held them, and kept them from learning what they could not be allowed to know. Company A was not here.

Mary commanded the remnants of first platoon, puffed up with a few green replacements. Second and third platoons were long gone, gone to reinforce bled and shattered C company. Mary could not remember how many times she'd held the pass. She'd held it again, and would keep holding it until . . .

Hold until relieved, her orders said. She wondered if there would be anything left of them by the time relief came. She shivered, and shook that thought off. She had things to do.

She keyed her mike. "Sergeant, fourth squad. The left needs some shoring up. Can you loan a fire section to first?"

"We're getting a little thin." Cassie answered as the tough sergeant, then softened. "But Dumont looks to be even thinner. They're on their way, Lieutenant."

"Thanks, Sergeant."

"Mary." The voice was soft, full of memories Mary couldn't afford to touch. "When are you going to take some R&R? Everyone's been back to brigade for a couple of hours. Everyone but you. Mary, you can't carry this damn pass forever."

"Thank you for your opinion, Sergeant. I'll take it under consideration. HQ out."

Mary switched off before Cassie could argue with her. Before the soft voice would remind her of another person she no longer could afford to be. "Rest is for the dead," Mary muttered, and checked the ammunition expenditure for the last four hours. Battalion wouldn't like it, but she'd forward the list to them. If she had to look like a company, she had to shoot like one. Supplies and how they got here was a Navy problem. It was her job to see that every round counted.

She'd taken care of her job. Those Navy pukes had better take care of theirs.

Mary glanced at the list of the messages that had backed up during the firefight. One said she was a first lieutenant. The rest were end-of-month reports; she'd be all night. She didn't mind all the reports. She didn't even mind all the colonials. She just wished they'd get their acts together and coordinate.

Rita told her story as she spooned soup into Ray, her mother and father at her elbow, the handyman and cook standing at the door of his parlor. "They knew we were coming. There were Earthie ships all over the place." A spoonful of broth.

"I think our admiral goofed when he killed their last one. This one's a fighter." A spoonful of broth.

"They went straight for us transports. It doesn't take a genius to know that you can dash around in space all you want, but Ray's ground-pounders were the ones who'd give us that damn moon." A spoonful of broth.

"I took hits, but landed in one piece. I had a hundred troopers, and every one of them was alive when they left the *Friendship*." A spoonful of broth.

"We had cargo rigged for a quick drop. I offloaded despite a missile damn near taking the rockets out from under us. The *Brotherhood* wasn't so lucky." A spoonful of broth.

"When we booted out of there, I thought the worst was over, but the Earthies weren't done with us. They hit us hard. Cadow died. Hesper died. We lost most of our comm gear. The main tanks were hit, streaming, making us a target, so I ducked and ran, headed in-system, away from the fight. There were other, smaller, gas planets. I refueled from one."

The bowl of broth was in her hand. Her eyes were

somewhere else. Ray had been there. He was hungry now, but not hungry enough to call her back. He waited.

"We patched her tank as best we could. Comm was lost. We could barely navigate. Once everyone had left, we tried for the jump. More by luck than anything else, we found it. I even made it to the next jump point. There was a tiny picketboat that took us aboard. We aimed the *Friendship* at the sun and left her. I tried to call. They said the battle was under strict secrecy. The Earthies kicked ass, and our brass doesn't want anyone to know. Christ, the Earthies damn well know what they did." She glanced at her father. "The Earthies aren't the ones the brass are keeping secrets from." Her father, her mother, and Ray nodded. The handyman and cook just stared.

"I landed a half hour ago. They said I needed to debrief. I told them where they could go and grabbed the first car I could get my hands on. I'm afraid, Dad, it may be considered stolen."

"William and I will return it. William, you may drive my car. I will drive the borrowed one."

"Yes sir." The handyman looked relieved.

"Oh, Ray, it must have been horrible for you." She threw her arms around his neck. The soup bowl, inconveniently placed and forgotten, spilled its contents. Neither mother nor cook fussed. For a long time, Ray just held Rita as she cried. Now the tears came. She was here, safe in his arms. He would never let her leave.

Mattim joined the wardroom for breakfast. Guns presided like a proud grandfather over a table of chattering middies. At Sandy's table, personal computers took up as much space as trays. The damage control officer, Gandhi, had a table with one vacancy; he headed for it. The officers at her table were watch-standers, leaders of the divisions that kept environmental support going, the ship working while the flashy kids explored stars. They led the young and scared able spacers who held the ship together. They deserved his attention.

They also fell silent as he sat down. Half his plate was empty, this table a quiet island in the sea of stormy, excited conversation, when one JG put his fork down and looked square at him. "Are we going to make it back, sir?" Forks hesitated just short of mouths. Eyes, directly or furtively, were on him. They had a right for a straight answer from their captain.

"We've gone out, and we've come back."

"Yes sir, but we didn't . . ." An ensign fell silent as she was nudged by the officers on either side of her.

"Right, Ensign. We went, but not where we wanted to go. Not yet. The team we've put together here on the *Sheffield* has learned more about the jump points in the last couple of days than the best scientists have learned in the last three hundred years. We've still got some trial and error. I'd like to tell you we'll have it all together for the next jump, but it may be the fifth or the tenth. Still, if I was a betting man, I'd give better than even odds we're home in a month. Six weeks at worst. And you can pass that along to your chiefs, and they can tell the crew. We've got sensors like no other ship before us. The best the Navy has *and* the best my *Maggie* had as a merchant ship going through jumps the Navy would never touch."

"Right," Commander Gandhi agreed. "We got the best of both worlds. And those kids may have been a pain in the ass to lead, but no one ever said they weren't smart."

There were murmurs of agreement around the table. Most plates were empty. A collection of late-rising middies were just exiting the steam tables, plates full. The officers around Mattim excused themselves. He sent them on their way with a smile, hoping he'd made their day better.

Quickly, he found himself surrounded by the kids, talking between themselves. Arguments over the data were settled by dueling computers. Arguments over the significance of the results were settled with rising voices. Following Guns' lead, he let it roll for a while before rapping a glass with a fork. "Let's take it down to a dull roar. Volume does not make truth."

Shamefaced, the two culprits did. A few minutes later, Mattim dismissed himself. His departure did not interrupt a discussion of something he knew nothing about.

The house returned quickly to the bustling, happy place it had been. Rita had Ray on the rails, walking. It took him two days to recover to where he had been; Rita was merciless. She was also loving.

Mr. Nuu watched the news each day. The propagandists were in hyperdrive. The dead were saints; Earthies were devils. Every man, woman, and child along the frontier must avenge the fallen martyrs. More workers were called up, divisions formed. Ray frowned at the reports. Why organize troops you could never use?

Rita discovered she was an unwanted commodity. Less than half the transports had survived, and most needed major time in the body and fender shops. Despite the casualties among the crews that came back, the brass weren't sure they would have a ship for her. She cut the flip-flopping at Personnel by demanding to be seconded to Military Intelligence.

"They knew we were coming. Who's looking for the leak?"

She got her reassignment, but to Threat Assessment, not Internal Security. "At least I can stay close to you," she told him. That was all that now mattered to Ray.

Rita's father was changing. The near death of his daughter had drained something out of the buff, confident industrialist. There were no more references to his early party membership, and the news reports did not go uncommented upon, though never when the cook or handyman was in the same room.

Still it was a surprise when he asked Ray to visit his plant. "I'll go too," Rita jumped in. Ray shrugged; he'd had enough of being the invalid. It was clear, even to him, that he would never command troopers again. He might as well get to know the industrial side. He *had* married the boss's daughter; there had to be something he could do with himself.

The "plant" turned out to be a sprawling complex that they drove through on an electric cart. "This is just the ground side. We've got mines in the asteroids. The dirty work is done there. One of the larger shipyards in orbit is mine, too."

"Dad began with that little shop we started at," Rita said, pride shamelessly dripping from her voice. "When I was just a little girl, I'd go there. I've watched it grow."

"These were good times." Ernest—*yes, they were now Ernest and Major; Ray had been offered and ignored*—shrugged off his daughter's praise, but with a happy smile. "People were looking for work. I gave them jobs. The more work we did, the more opportunities came our way. We grew together, me and the crew."

"Have you been able to keep them together, your workers, what with the draft?"

"Some volunteered. I've promised them jobs when they return." It was kind of him to say "when," not "if." "Out in the mines, I just installed some new equipment, reduced my staffing needs by half. I'd intended to spread the miners out and expand. I'll save that for after the war. Unlike other companies, I've managed to keep the raw materials flowing to the plants. My people are busy, and the draft boards have plenty of idle workers elsewhere." He shrugged. "Some say I'm using my connections with the party. Maybe, but if I did not deliver the ships, war supplies and other gear, they would not remember my low party card number for long."

Ray had been checking out the equipment; jigs, presses, drills in one shop; chip fabrication in another building. "You have a very sophisticated setup. The names on your heavy equipment read like a who's who of the largest corporations in developed space. How could you afford it?"

"It is close to lunchtime." Ernest's face had gone flat.

"We have a picnic basket, and I always keep green around my plants. Let us eat among the trees."

As usual, Mattim's check with Guns and Sandy showed teams hard at it and swapping members back and forth. Thor's teams, done with the present system, had expanded the scope of their study to the galaxy's core. Nobody had ever been this close. Kids at Christmas could not be happier. Mattim wasn't sure how that would get them home, but he wouldn't rain on their parade.

Since nobody had any miracles to report, Mattim did what he usually did when things were slow aboard the *Maggie D*; he took a walk. Starting at the bow, he worked his way down. Any work party got a few moments' pause to observe. Some seemed a bit flustered by the attention, but there were enough hands from the *Maggie* who knew him. After one old chief asked his officer's permission and invited Mattim over to see how they'd patched some battle damage, the rest got the hang and invited him over for proud sessions of show and tell.

The *Sheffield* wasn't just being patched. Imaginative ratings and recruits were changing her, adding improvements, making her stronger. None of these were solo performances; each involved checking with the chiefs and officers. Each mod went into damage control's data file. Here was a captain's job as Mattim had learned it. Observe and praise. Toss in a suggestion here and there. Running a ship, that he understood. Running the galaxy he'd leave to any god who wanted the job.

He enjoyed the day, including lunch and supper on the mess decks with whatever team he happened to be with when they got the word to knock off for chow. The crew looked a lot happier, and even a bit relieved. How bad could it be? The old man had time for us enlisted swine. Things were looking up.

Mattim found himself relaxing, too. He finished his day with a drop by the teams. Guns' and Sandy's teams looked wilted. He shooed them out of the room and threatened to post a guard on it until 0800 tomorrow. Muttering counterthreats of mutiny, rebellion, and a strike, they went.

Thor's stargazers were in just as grubby a state. Mattim considered giving them the same treatment, flipped a coin, and decided no. If somebody wanted to see into the heart of their god, why interfere? He did turn up the air flow.

The industrialist was strangely quiet as he guided the cart among the trees, as if hunting for just the right place for their lunch break. Rita did the final preparations while her father meandered around them, whistling off key and frequently glancing at his watch. "Father, I am working as fast as I can."

"Oh. Sorry, dear. Not you at all. Something else."

"Will someone be meeting us?" Ray asked from where he still sat in the cart."

"I certainly hope not."

Sandwiches prepared to order, Rita settled on the blanket she had spread. Ray took a bite, swallowed, then casually said, "Ernest, how could you afford the plant machinery? The costs and the duties for half of that would beggar a business man. You do not live in poverty."

Ernest laughed, glanced once more at his watch, and shook his head. "No, my family does not live in poverty. My plants were built debt-free. Or at least they were before those crushing war taxes were passed." He pursed his lips, studied his daughter and Ray. "Major, I hope you and my daughter will have a long and happy marriage. I hope to pass all of this along to you"—now his face took on the impish grin Ray saw so often on Rita—"and my grandchildren. I wish you much success growing this business, so let me tell you how my garden grows."

And Ray learned that not all trade between planets went through customs. No surprise; everyone bought wine, whiskey, perfumes, silks, and vids with custom seals that would not stand scrutiny. This was the frontier. Thumbing your nose at Earth's laws was a duty solemnly observed by all. But entire factories!

"It can be done. Best by skipping the usual ports."

"Dad, I'm a jump pilot. You come through a jump hole, you better stop at the nearest station and clear customs."

"If you come through the usual jump points. Others are not so closely watched."

Rita sat back to munch her sandwich. Ray was no longer hungry. "Corporations, like armies, take inventory seriously. I can not lose a rifle or rocket. I can't imagine a corporation that takes no notice when an expensive plant vanishes."

"Not a plant," Ernest agreed, "but scrap metal, ah, that is another matter. Upgrade, improve, replace is the lifeblood of business. If you do not improve productivity, you are out of business. And what do you do with the in-efficient machines?"

"Sell them to someone less efficient," Ray said slowly.

"Yes, Major. If you are great Earth or one of her seven sisters, you sell off to one of the newer forty. But the forty developed planets are the end of the line. We frontier plan-ets do not exist. No, on Pitt's Hope, the end of the line is worthless scrap, worth a few pennies a pound."

"But . . ." Ray kept the door open. Ernest slowly turned around, his eyes on his watch. Ray hadn't heard that an-tilistening devices could be fitted into a watch case. Then again, he was learning a lot today.

Ernest turned back to them, a grin on his face. He tapped the watch. "From a friend on Pitt's Hope. Very ver-satile. If you know the right people, you can get anything. Scrap metal, for example. A check for a few pennies a pound from a legitimate scrap dealer. A second check of equal value on another account to the right person, and look what you have!" His arms stretched out, taking in his domain like a proud king.

"But how do you get it here, Dad?" Rita's sandwich was down.

"Pitt's Hope is easy. Two jumps, one hardly noticed, the other hardly known but to a few smugglers."

Ray and Rita looked at each other. Her eyes were wide.

"Dad, it's seven jumps to Pitt's Hope. It's four even by the shortcut through ELM what's-its-number."

"You don't know all the jump points."

"Dad, I've jumped into ELM. There are *two* jumps. We got one, they got the other."

Ernest glanced at his watch. "There is a third."

And it came to Ray why that hunk of rock was worth all the blood that had been and would be paid for it. It was not the jumping-off point to seize a fully developed planet. Earth had them by the dozen. No, it was the last line of defense between the Earthies and Wardhaven, one of the few planets the frontier had making ships and the heavy equipment war ate so voraciously.

Unity knew this. Had Earth learned yet?

As Mattim left the wardroom, Sandy fell in step with him, a half dozen middies behind her. "We need another test jump."

"What's up?"

"Velocity, sir." One of the middies stepped on Sandy's line just as her mouth opened.

"All right, Chandra, you tell the captain."

"Sorry, ma'am, but look at it. We hit that first jump point racing like a tiger. We went thirty thousand light-years. We tapped the same jump at a walk, and only go fifty light-years. At a crawl, we went even less. The more energy you have, the farther you go. We need some high-energy test jumps to see if it's acceleration or velocity."

Mattim saw the point; testing would eat time. "Sandy?"

"That seems to be what we're learning, Matt. Speed never made a difference, but every jump point has a maximum posted speed. You don't exceed it, and no one makes money going slower. Damn, I wish we knew what we were doing, not just flopping around in the dark. But we ought to try some more test runs."

Five days later, they headed into the jump with the same spin, velocity, and lateral displacement as on the sour jump. The stars looked familiar to Mattim as they exited, but not enough to say anything. While the bridge waited silently for Sandy and her team to do their search, Thor said, "It's a single star system."

Sandy did her numbers, shushed a middie before he said something, then spent five minutes rechecking all the numbers again. "We're about one hundred light-years from Pitt's Hope."

"I've found two, maybe three jump points," a middie chirped in. "Maybe one of them will take us home."

Mattim shook his head. "We know one jump point took us there and will take us back. We are not going to go chasing down every blind alley. Thor, turn us around and head us back."

"Aye, aye, sir."

"Well, at least we know speed or acceleration does have something to do with reach," Sandy sighed.

"Sir, would you please come look at this?" The speaker was Zappa, the guard, now midshipman, who'd started the whole crazy process with her offer to run tests for Mattim.

"The text book says the jump is instantaneous, right?"

"That's the way it's always looked to me," Sandy agreed.

"For proof," Zappa went on, "they offered the behavior of the atom lasers that keep the ship stable and spot jump point gravity fluctuations. They don't show any change, right?"

"Right." Sandy nodded.

"I always wondered. Nobody's done any high-speed data recovery on the gyros recently." Zappa smiled. "Everybody *knows*." Mattim wondered if he'd put up with a boy doing this slow routine on him. Zappa was cute as a button; he kept listening.

"We hitched a computer to one gyro. Next couple of jumps didn't do much; the digital readout kept missing the moment of jump. We changed to analog this jump so we could choose just what point we wanted. Look at this." The film's elapsed time in the corner was measured in nanoseconds. One showed the usual screen. The next showed a wavering. The third was all over the place. By the fifth shot, everything was back to normal.

"Does it usually do that?" Mattim asked.

"No," Sandy answered slowly, pulling on her ear.

"Might be why I felt dizziness on the slow-speed jump."

Zappa reran the five shots. "There's another question, sir, ma'am. Near graduation, what with a war coming on, the profs had us do some practical stuff, things that might help us land a safe job in a wartime economy. I tested explosives. They didn't come out right." Mattim raised an eyebrow.

"Explosives should expand equally in all directions. That's what the manufacturers advertise. Mine didn't. It wasn't mixed properly, so it didn't explode evenly. Did the missile that missed us before we jumped explode evenly, or did its shrapnel hit us unevenly? What did it do to our spin?"

Mattim mashed the comm link at Sandy's station. "Guns, pull up those pictures from just before we jumped. Enhance them all you have to, but tell me exactly what our spin was."

He turned to Thor. "Hold us at a gee and a half. Turn us around fast. We're going back through the jump. This time don't bother with lateral displacement, just spin and velocity."

"Yessir."

Two days later they were back to the four-star system. It took another two days to get turned around. The explosion *had* changed their rotation. The tiny fraction of one percent spin had been a bear to hunt down. Still, it had been there, and they added it as they approached the jump. The stars twinkled, then changed.

"Two suns," Thor shouted.

A moment later Sandy confirmed, "We're home."

"Comm," Mattim ordered, "get me the watch at Ninety-seventh Brigade."

"Got them, sir."

"Ninety-seventh Brigade, this is the *Sheffield*. Are there any colonial warships in system?"

"Hey," came a surprised voice, "we lost the *Sheffield* a couple of battles back. Who are you? Uh, code Delta Alpha, one three seven. Respond."

Mattim looked at Ding. She glanced at the quartermaster of the watch. "We got any answer to that challenge?"

"No, ma'am."

The exec raised an eyebrow. "You're on your own, Captain."

"Ninety-seventh Brigade, this is *Sheffield*. We are not lost, just misplaced. Helm, begin a three-gee deceleration. Ninety-seventh, do you have a science officer of some kind?"

"Commander Miller on sensors was a college professor."

"Please patch me through to him."

"I shouldn't, but the longer you talk, the better targeting fix we get. It's your funeral."

"Commander Miller here," a woman's voice said.

"Commander, this is Captain Abeeb of the cruiser *Sheffield*. We sour-jumped thirty thousand light years. It's taken us this long to get back. We have several new theories about how jumps work. Before we risk a jump to Pitt's Hope, I'd like to download them to you."

"I imagine you would, colonial, but I don't want to crash our system nearly as much as you do."

"Miller, all our codes are a month old. If you'll give us some calls that we can answer, we will."

"And since New Canton was raped two weeks ago, you colonials got plenty of codes to answer with. Still no takers, you Unity bastard."

Mattim glanced at Ding; apparently the war had taken a bitter turn since they left. He took a deep breath. "By now, you know it was Beta jump we used. I can convert our data dump into encapsulated packets. What's in them stays in them. Load them to a stand-alone computer and bring it up with no network attachment. It can't crash what it's not hooked to."

Before any answer could come back, Mattim found Midshipman Zappa at his elbow. "Are you professor Elaine Miller? I studied under Professor Uxbridge at Nuevo Madrid University. He still speaks of you as his best student."

"So how's Gimpy getting around? Does that beer belly still look like he's ten months pregnant?"

Zappa eyed the mike like she might a snake. "He's thin as a rail and jogs. Are you thinking of someone else?"

"Nope, and you do know the old prune. Captain, what is this data you want to send me so much?"

"I'd rather not go too deeply into it on voice. We've put it in our highest code. Is it enough to repeat that we've been halfway across the galaxy and are back?"

"The first ship back from a sour jump" came in awe from the speaker. "Yes. Yes, I do want that data! Send me your first packet. If it causes us any trouble, I swear . . ."

"It won't."

Twelve hours later, the *Sheffield* had killed all its momentum and was heading back for the jump point when Commander Miller came back. "Sweet God, I can't believe it. This worked?"

"We're here."

"Yes. Hey, is there any chance you could come down here? I'd love to go over this data with your specialist. What are you doing with a team of scientists on a combat cruise anyway?"

Mattim explained their brain trust.

"Jesus, this war is a waste. On second thought, when would a bunch of kids get a chance to cut loose and show what they can do in a situation like that? You lucky bunch."

"We weren't so sure of our luck after three bum jumps."

"Well, say hello to the new admiral. She's a real scrapper."

"We got a new admiral?"

"We're on our fourth."

"That bad?"

"Up there and down here both."

The *Sheffield* jumped, ship steady as a rock, and moving at only a few klicks a second. Pitt's Hope never looked so good.

Every jump point has a navigation buoy. It would go through before a ship did, announcing its pending arrival, avoiding a collision in space. Many buoys had a second duty, transferring speed-of-light messages from one side of a hole to the next side.

In wartime, buoys became listening stations.

The buoy at Alpha jump had acquired additional antennas, a faster computer, and more storage. The struggling colonial troops on the rock called it to order supplies. Intercepted messages among the Earthies were passed to it. Only very high-priority messages could cause the buoy to make a trip through the jump before it had filled its storage. The code the Earthie cruiser used raised a flag.

The buoy slipped through the jump, transmitted the contents of its storage to the next buoy, and then returned. The message passed from one buoy to another several times, each time its code raising a flag. Emotional surprise was not registered until a human downloaded the message on Wardhaven. "This must be a beauty. Let's see if any of the codes from New Canton like it."

One did.

The technician knew a lot about communication protocols and a bit about the theory behind the codes he used. The rest of his education stopped at middle school. Still, what he saw made him whistle. "Worlds as numberless as the stars. Hey, Senior Tech, know anyplace I could get my hands on a ship?"

"They're either on guard or in the yard. Why?"

The junior tech explained the message to his senior, who shook his head. "Ain't you heard, kid? There's a war on. If it don't help the party kill Earthie scum, it ain't worth shit."

The junior didn't argue, but he did take special care to send a copy of the package to the folks at Intelligence Assessment. Some of those people used their brains.

TEN

RITA BOUNCED OUT of her car and across the lawn. She looked as excited as a puppy . . . and cuter. Ray smiled, in spite of his own day. First he would listen to whatever made her dance; his news could wait. The front door flew open. "Ray, you won't believe it. Dad, are you home?" she called.

"No, hon," her mother answered from upstairs. "But I expect him home early."

Rita gave Ray a hug where he sat in his chair, then settled down at his feet. "Hon, the most wonderful thing happened. We intercepted a message from a ship that was lost."

"Like we wrote your ship off." Ray leaned forward; a forehead so excited needed a kiss. Rita accepted it demurely, then captured his cheeks with both her hands and kissed him solidly. His wife was excited, and not just about her news.

With her tongue wandering his mouth, Ray could almost forget the letter in his pocket. Rita came up for air. "We will save that for later. First you've got to hear what happened."

Licking his lips slowly, Ray asked, "What happened?"

"The message got shuffled to Technology. There's only three of them, but they knew what they had after a page. One ran down the hall looking for me. 'Mrs. Longknife, you're a pilot. Will you read this?' It's so nice when they call me Mrs. Longknife." She smiled, the tip of her tongue escaping her lips.

Bending quickly for a kiss, Ray asked, "And what was this they wanted you to read, Mrs. Longknife?"

"Ray, a ship came back from a bad jump!"

The blank look on his face was not what Rita expected.

"Ray, ships have been going into jumps and never coming out for centuries. If you make a bad jump, you don't come back."

"And why were we poor passengers never told?" he growled.

"Because we pilots worry about it enough for all of you."

Ray drew back, aware he'd stomped his bride's professional pride. He kept his mouth shut. Excited, her glower was short-lived. "In the early days, they had a lot of bad jumps. For a century they've become rarer and rarer. We haven't had one in fifty years. You know what causes them?" Ray shook his head, not about to risk another misstep.

"Speed! Speed and spin. The faster you go into a jump, the farther you go."

Now Ray was puzzled. "You said you took the jump into that hellhole at twice the speed you would have if the admiral hadn't ordered it?"

"Spin *and* speed," Rita repeated. "Spin the ship up, hit a hole at high speed, and zoom, you're halfway across the galaxy. Think about it, Ray, a whole new bunch of jump lines to survey. Millions of systems to visit. Enough cheap resources and good land for humanity to stretch out in. Ray, we've got to get this damn war stopped so we can get on with the real stuff of life!"

Which brought Ray back to the letter in his pocket. He pulled it out and handed it to her. "It appears that few share your enthusiasm for peace," he said dryly.

Rita glanced at the letter. "You're invited to brief the President on the progress of the war?"

"Please glance at the second page."

It took her a moment to read that letter. Handwritten by an acquaintance of Ray's who was now on the General Staff, it offered him "advice" on how to handle—more like survive—the briefing. *Do not* interrupt the President. *Do* look attentive to everything the President says, no matter how long he speaks. *Do not* correct him. And, most important, *do not* say anything that would cast doubt on the eventual victory of Unity forces.

Rita scowled. "That's not a briefing, that's a . . ."

"Deaf-mute leading the blind," Ray offered.

"I was groping for something truly obscene. But nothing I've heard in my Navy time was bad enough. Ray, people are dying, and the President has his head buried in the sand."

Ray leaned back in his chair, took a deep breath, and let it out slowly. "I'm a soldier, Rita, but sitting here, trying to make this body more than a lump of wasted tissue, I've had time to think. Your father is an interesting source of information. As are you. We need a private talk. I imagine violating any of the general's Dos and Don'ts would be a career-ending decision." Ray glanced down at his legs. "Somehow I suspect I do not have much of a career left. Maybe it wouldn't be a bad thing to go out in a blaze of glory . . ." He hadn't intended to pause, but the words came to glaring life behind his eyeballs before he finished. ". . . telling the President what no one else has the guts to tell him."

Rita paled; the pause had not gone unnoticed. "Father should be home soon. Let me help you to the garden. I think he would like to talk about this among the flowers. Mother, send Dad to the garden when he gets home," she shouted.

"Yes, dear. Dinner will be at seven."

"Thank you, Mother."

Ray managed to make it under his own power to the hidden glade of pleasant memory. Rita was at his elbow, carrying

three light lawn chairs under one arm. They were just settling in when Rita whispered, "Father is coming."

Coat thrown over his shoulders, sleeves rolled up, and
whistling, Mr. Nuu sauntered toward them. "Mother told me
you had something to tell me."

"Yes, Father, I've had a very exciting day." Her voice
didn't sound excited. Ray wished he could turn back the
hour, let Rita once more bubble of doors opening and the
galaxy falling into their hands. Maybe he should not have
mentioned his letter. Being a husband was more difficult
than he'd expected.

"Can you tell us what time it is, Father? Mother was very
specific about dinner."

"Of course." He glanced at his watch, then raised an eyebrow at them. Ray nodded.

Ernest frowned and turned around slowly. "Can't read it
in the sunlight. Just a moment. Ah, yes." He took his chair.
"We are in the clear. What must we talk about?"

Ray nodded to Rita. "Tell him of your discovery."

"It's nothing," she said, but she quickly told her father of
the ship that returned from the lost."

"Sweet Mother of God," he breathed. "Each jump point
leads to a dozen, and we have only made use of one. Oh, my
daughter, what this will mean to you and your grandchildren."

"There may be no children, Father." She handed him
Ray's letter.

He read both pages; finished, his hands collapsed into his
lap. He stared at them, mouth agape, no words coming out.
"I . . . have . . . been hearing things." He shook his head as if
to free himself of a daze. "I have known powerful fools who
like to rewrite history, sometimes events only a week in the
past. But the Unity Party is living in fantasy."

"What can we do, Father, to make them see?" Rita
pleaded.

Slowly, Ernest shook his head. "Maybe it's too late.
Maybe they've gotten away with changing the past for so
long that they no longer fear the future. Major, a friend of

mine sits in the Wardhaven legislature. The night we voted
to join Unity, they suspended the rule barring nonmembers
from the floor of the legislature. Thugs with billy clubs wandered the hall. Thugs!

"But even with clubs, they could not thwart our traditions.
The vote of the members was to join Unity after the people
approved the issue in a referendum. Do you remember that
vote?"

Ray shook his head. "As a soldier, I ignored politics."

"Father, I have not missed a vote since I turned twenty-
one. I don't ever remember hearing of that ballot."

"You and the rest of the planet. I recently had cause to review the law that brought us into Unity. The official one
posted on net has several differences from the one I downloaded the morning after our legislature voted."

"They can do that." Ray left the words hanging. Not a
question, not quite a statement of fact.

"They did it," Ernest answered.

Rita rose from her chair and went to stand behind Ray.
Gently she rubbed his back. "Ray is thinking of using this
invitation into the presence of the President to end his military career in a blaze of glory, telling him what he does not
want to hear. Would words mean anything to him?" Rita
choked on the question.

For a long time, no one said anything. When someone
moved, it was Ernest. Glancing at his watch, humming a patriotic tune, he paced around them. After one circuit, he continued pacing, but talking low, as if to himself. "I have a
friend you two may wish to meet. It might shock you,
daughter, but I know a spy. He may see in the major's sum-
mons opportunities that most people only dream about. Let
us talk again tomorrow afternoon."

He quit studying his watch, looked Ray in the eye with a
gently twisted smile. "Let me help you up, Major. You have
got a lot of walking ahead of you."

•　　•　　•

If Mattim didn't care for the greeting they got from the 97th, he liked Pitt's Hope's even less. Ordered to immediately halt, they hung in space while four heavy cruisers came out to meet them. They were scanned by everything Sandy had ever heard of and a few she hadn't. Only after they'd been boarded were they allowed to head for Beta Station. Even then, security teams spread out over the ship while ten very suspicious types under the direct supervision of Captain Horatio Whitebred kept everyone on the bridge under close scrutiny. The *Sheffield* ended up in dock while Mattim was hustled off to report to the admiral.

The new admiral, or the newest admiral, received him without waiting. "Captain Abeeb, you were mentioned very prominently in Captain Pringle's report of the first battle. Highly flexible approach to fighting, but good instincts."

"I did what I had to do to get us out of that mess. Was the *Significant* badly damaged?"

"No, they patched her up before the next shoot, and lost her with all hands in that one, sorry to say."

It was a kick in the gut. All the risks Mattim had taken to get them out alive only added a few days to their lives. *Damn!* If the admiral noticed his reaction, she only hesitated a moment. "The *Sheffield*'s going to be a while in dock, Captain."

"We made most of her battle damage good," Mattim interrupted. "The crew needed work to keep their minds off being lost. The ship's in good shape."

"I don't doubt that, Mattim, but we've learned a lot in the last six weeks, and your ship is about two mods behind in hardware, three or four in software. What was good enough for fifteen or twenty years of peacetime service gets replaced in two or three weeks now.

"I've been wanting to do something since I took command last week, but didn't have anyone. Now, I think I do. While the *Sheffield* is being updated, I'd like to detach you to the Ninety-seventh. Captain Anderson and Commander Umboto are damn good, but they've spent most of their careers on the defense. The squadron keeps getting clobbered in running gun battles. They keep getting clobbered from space when we're not around. We're each fighting our own separate battles. I want us to fight together."

Mattim liked her point. Still, he hardly saw himself as the man to glue two different Navies together. "You must have someone better at this than me."

"Captain, I came in with the Forty-ninth Cruiser Squadron. Right now every ship, except the *Sheffield*, is battle ready. I know what kind of battle I want to fight. Until Gamma jump starts hollering that colonials are in-system, I intend to spend every minute training the ships I've got to fight just that battle.

"You fought the *Sheffield* pretty independently. I'm game to give you that freedom next battle, too. But for now, I want you with Andy, coming up with ways we can support each other."

What could he say? "Yes, ma'am. When do I leave?"

She returned to her desk, tapped it a few times, and glanced up. "A couple of destroyers were due to make a supply run tomorrow. I just moved them up. They leave in two hours. That enough time to get your kit together?"

Mattim saluted. "On my way."

Next afternoon, Ray and Rita were taking the sun in what had come to be *their* part of the garden, when Mr. Nuu approached, a short, roly-poly man huffing along beside him. Rita offered him her chair, then settled on the grass beside Ray. The two men carried on a running commentary on the trees, flowers, and bushes, while the newcomer produced several gadgets from the pockets of his disheveled suit. He'd glance at each, move it around or hold it up, glance at it again, then make it disappear. Finally satisfied, he leaned forward.

"Ernest tells me you would like the President to see the light, grasp the hopelessness of his policy, and end the war."

Ray nodded; so did Rita.

"You realize that answer is itself a capital offense."

"Already?" Ernest failed to sound surprised.

"The Presidential Proclamation came in yesterday. Anyone found defaming either the President or the glorious war against the Earth scum is to be arrested immediately, hurried before a peoples' court, and executed within twenty-four hours."

"The people of Westhaven won't stand for that," Rita said.

Ray remembered Santiago's sister. What the people would stand for and could survive were not the same anymore.

"Most of Westhaven is in uniform, like you two, and subject to even more draconian measures. You haven't been reading your mail, Senior Pilot." Rita blushed.

"You're saying," Ray mused, "that matters are totally out of hand. They are drafting an army they cannot deploy. But it can enslave the people on the planet it is supposed to defend."

"I am afraid so," the newcomer agreed.

"How did we get ourselves into this mess?" Ernest sighed.

"If I may be to the point," Ray said, leaning forward, "the matter before us is how to get out of this mess. I take it that either no efforts have been made to redeem the situation, or they have all failed."

"Many fine men and women have died trying to strike at the head of this gang that throttles us, but our President only increases his security."

"Then what chance have we?" Rita whispered.

"More than you might think." The fat man pursed his lips. "Major, the tools at our disposal are quite good, but not perfect. Your disability opens doors closed to others. Your mobility is presently limited. For a long journey it would be only natural to fit you for walking assistance. Walkers are very helpful, but the skin must be toughened. I know just the medicine you should use." The spy grinned.

Rita swallowed hard. Her hand clutched at his. "This is not a suicide mission. Ray will survive it, won't he?"

"Of course, Mrs. Longknife," the spy master assured her. "The President needs to see the light. I think Ray has a very sound grasp of the problem."

"Of course, honey. I will do the job, like a soldier." *I might survive.* "There's no defense I can't handle."

She rose up on her knees, looked him hard in the eye, searched his face. He dared not look away. "Good, because I'm going with you. I want to be carrying your child—our child—before you meet the President."

The Destroyer Navy was an interesting place to visit. Mattim would not want to live in a tin can. The officers and crew were young enough to handle four gees with panache, if not without grumbling. For him, they had a full water tank, and he was glad for it when the *John Paul Jones* and the *Yamamoto* dashed for the jump point. They backed through it at a few klicks per second. In-system was a surprise. "Colonials. Looks like a couple of their cans just made a supply run," the skipper told him. "Doubt they'll cause us any trouble."

If the trip was boring, the ending made up for it in stark terror. On final approach, the *Jones* held to two gees and they introduced Mattim to his drop shuttle. The *Jones* would not land. Supplies and the single passenger were cut loose in packing crates with rockets and a tiny navigation control.

"Does this work?" Mattim asked incredulously as they crammed him into a space no bigger than a bed, and a narrow one at that.

"Never had any complaints from the others," the chief supervising his installation assured him.

"Dead men tell no tales," the second class tightening down Mattim's straps muttered.

"Knock it off, Peadée."

"Right, Chief."

Mattim glanced around his tiny cell. "How often do you use this drop system?"

"Whenever we drop replacements to the Ninety-seventh. We only land when we've got casualties to lift out," the chief said.

Mattim glanced at the second class. "We deliver the poor jarheads." He shrugged like a boathand on the River Styx.

With that kind of lead-in, Mattim expected the worse. He was not disappointed. The canister creaked and groaned as it dropped away from the *Jones*. Rockets slammed him into the thin cushion of his seat. Something snapped; Mattim did not like the sound of it, but he had no control over this thing. It began to spin. He had no view out. After twenty years in space, he discovered what claustrophobia was. Gritting his teeth, he concentrated on what he could control—his breathing. And his bowels. Tightening his gut, he waited. The damn suit he'd been loaned didn't even have a chronometer. Mattim wasn't a strong believer in hell; this bucket introduced him to it.

Without warning, he hit with a crunch that jarred him to the bone and sent a spasm of pain through his back. The canister stood for a moment, then slowly collapsed, leaving him dangling from his straps. Someone was supposed to be right along to collect him.

"Hello, Ninety-seventh, this is Captain Mattim Abeeb. Anybody there?"

Dead silence. He glanced at his air supply. The backup canister showed twenty-nine minutes. The main supply showed—nothing. He tapped it. It still showed nothing. He rapped it hard. For a second it showed zero minutes. Then it went back to blank. Then the entire canister went dark.

"Oh, God," he breathed. Mattim wasn't any surer about heaven than he was about hell. At the moment he hoped there was a God watching over him, 'cause the Navy was doing a damn poor job of it. He started to shiver. It wasn't that cold. Yet.

• • •

"Company A, brigade here. We got a stray supply canister in front of your position. Could you collect it?"

Mary had sent her radio operator to the sack after a thirty-two-hour shift. She had managed to catch a two-hour nap during that thirty-two, so she considered herself fresh. "Supplies or replacements?" she asked without thinking.

"Neither. Navy sent a captain down for a little talk-talk with Anderson, then misplaced him. We've got to pick him up. He's got two hours of air and a half hour backup. No big rush."

The miner in Mary took that in, divided them by two, then took the smaller. She gave herself fifteen minutes. "Roger, brigade, we're on it."

She glanced at her boards. Dumont had the reserve squad. "Du, how many rolligons have we got working today?"

"Four. Who wants to take a drive in the country?"

She passed along the situation. "Put a driver and gunner in each, and a driver in my command car. I'll take this one out."

"Good, I can get back to catching up on my beauty rest. Damn, this being in reserve is great."

Mary would bet a month's pay the gunner on the lead rig would be Dumont. Her command rig was slowing as she exited the HQ. She grabbed a handhold, and it accelerated away. She kept the rig open to space, but it could be closed up and pressurized.

Four captured rolligons were already raising dust as they hustled through the pass; she joined the tag end of the column. The colonials had just tried their hand at walking in singles, heavy explosives packed on their backs to leave behind as calling cards. It had been a real snipe hunt, but those that hadn't been chased down had been chased off.

And they were now barreling out into the ground they'd disappeared into. Isn't life in the corps wonderful?

Mary had a rough position for the capsule, and the frequency it should be squawking on. No surprise; it was silent. "Lek, a little rocket ship landed on our front door a few minutes ago. Did our sensors pick up anything?"

"Have them aimed down, looking for man-sized movement, and not finding a hell of a lot. You want me to reprogram them and go over their records? I'll need a good half hour."

"Better do it, Lek. May be a friendly out there trying to breathe vacuum."

"I'm on it. Just a second, Mary. I've got movement six klicks from the pass, forty degrees left."

"Unknown or colonial?"

"One . . . no, three colonials, coming from different directions, closing on something in a deep crater, if I can trust my map."

"Dumont, swing us left."

"Heard, already doing. I'm point. Kip, you keep right. Dag and Zori, swing to my left. Start zigzagging." Dumont's timing couldn't have been better. A rocket lofted from behind a rock, hung in space for a moment, then arrowed straight at the rightmost rig. Kip popped chaff, then ducked right. Chaff went up again; then the rig came to a bouncing halt behind a boulder.

The rocket ignored the first chaff cloud but dove straight for the second, dispensing bomblets as it crashed into its center. A moment later, Kip's rig was at full speed, heading in the general direction the rocket had come from. The rigs dodged two more small rockets, each one from a different location. They ended up with two captives. The third took too long deciding between POW and fighter. She died.

Dumont raced past the crater Lek thought might hold their wayward Navy type. "Something's down there, and it didn't shoot at me. Might be what you're looking for, Mary. Squad, spread out, keep moving, don't make a good target, and don't draw attention to that crater. It's all yours, Mary."

Mary told the driver to slow as they passed the crater. She

grabbed two different emergency kits. She'd made lots of rescues in the mines; this was just a different twist on a familiar job. Of course, Dumont could have missed something, and the crater's contents might be unfriendly. Rifle ready, emergency kits dangling from both elbows, she stepped from the rig and slid down the crater's crumbling walls. A standard, man-rated canister rested on the opposite side of the crater, nose down.

It had the green and blue Society of Humanity emblem. She tried opening the red emergency exit hatch; it didn't budge. Mary tossed her rifle aside and unzipped the first of her kits. Powered rescue gear gleamed. She only got to use three of her new toys before she was in the canister and staring at the cheapest excuse for a space suit she'd ever seen. The helmet was fogged; it didn't take an engineer to know that the two and a half hours of air hadn't been up to specs.

She dragged her second kit over and unzipped it. The oxygen bottle had several attachments. She grabbed the sharp one and slipped it through the soft material at the neck joint of the suit, slapped goo around it and opened the bottle a crack while she twisted the manual override on the suit's vent. Through her gloves, she could feel stale air hissing out, replaced by the good oxygen. Damn suit had no monitors; she guessed at how much, watching the plastic faceplate as it slowly unfogged. The Navy officer's lips were blue, but he was breathing.

"Du, get my rig back here. You got a lifesaver in your squad?"

"Kip's gunner is."

"I'll gun for Kip. Get both rigs back here."

"How's the Navy doing?"

"Not breathing too well. They make a man a captain, then give him a suit I wouldn't wear to a Sunday school picnic."

"Never went to one, myself. No beer. Okay, Kit, you head kind of sly but quick for the crater. Rest, keep your heads up. If anyone's left, they want our hide."

Careful of the oxygen bottle, Mary dragged the uncon-
scious man up the rim of the crater. She left him lying there
as she dropped back to collect her rifle and emergency kits.
She also checked in the capsule. The guy had a briefcase and
clothes bag. She added them to her load and made it easily
out again just as two rigs came to a quick stop beside the officer.

The oxygen must have been helping, because he pulled
himself up on his elbows. Mary patted her mouth and ears
through her helmet, then made a quick slit across her
throat. *You're not sending or receiving, Joe.* He seemed to
nod; then the others were on him, lifting him into the command car, slamming its door shut with the captain and the
lifesaver inside. The driver secured his hatch, and Mary
spotted dust blowing every which way as pressure built up.
Good.

As the command rig took off zigzagging for the pass,
Mary swung herself up into the gunner's slot on Kip's rol-
ligon. "Okay, everybody, we've done this the easy way.
Let's back up careful like and keep this a cakewalk."

"This is fun, old lady," Dumont chortled. "We got to go
out like this more often."

At her feet, a POW was taped like a mummy. Mary
doubted he—no, she—considered today fun. Well, one person's fun was someone else's bad day. *At least you're out of
the shooting, hon.* Then Mary snorted. Once, a long time
ago, all she'd really wanted was to surrender. Who was the
winner here?

Rita drove next morning as they headed into the country-
side. There was a thirty-minute wait at a checkpoint. Though
they were waved through with only a glance at their ID
cards, the wait left them plenty of time to contemplate the
three bodies twisting on red flag waving gallows. "Earthie
Traitors" the sign read.

"Already," Rita whispered as she pulled away.

The hanging bodies stayed with Ray. He was sworn to defend these people. Now his uniform was being used as an

excuse to kill young men. This was not what he and his father and grandfather had bled for. The hangmen, and the President signing their orders, had to be stopped.

Rita found the dirt road that led into the abandoned quarry. They went well past a swimming hole on a rarely driven path. In a blighted opening among the trees, the spy master waited, a briefcase in hand. The fat man showed Ray how to open the case. "We've included a computer with your slide show on it and extra batteries for the computer and your power walker."

"So, I am to bludgeon the President to death with batteries?" Ray observed dryly.

The other closed the briefcase. "Now put in five-nine-three for the combination."

Ray did, and did not open the briefcase. He felt a very slight hum, then nothing.

"It is armed now. Open it, and there will be a very big hole in the ground, and very little of us for forensics to find."

"Let's see its effect."

"We only have three."

"A soldier practices with his weapon. Until you have fired the weapon, you are just reading a book."

"Not an unexpected attitude, Major." The spy master ducked into his car, returning with a strange gizmo. Briefcase under his arm, and whistling a happy aria, he plodded away. At three hundred paces, he stopped, did something, and hastened back to them. He offered Ray a small box. "Would you do the honors?"

The box was a cliché: one red button. Ray pushed it. Across the distance, he could hear the click as the briefcase fasteners were pushed open, a snap as the lid popped up. The explosion was not much louder than the noise the lid made. A small puff of smoke rose from the case.

"I've seen more dangerous firecrackers on Landing Day," Rita snapped.

The spy stared at the quickly dissipating cloud for a moment, then nervously licked his lips. "I would appreciate it if you two left. I have some bomb disposal work to do. I will get in touch with you in a day or two."

They left.

Rita turned on the radio; all stations were blaring marches or patriotic songs. She called up music of her own choosing from the car's memory and headed away from town. "There's a lake I used to love when I was a little girl" was all she said.

Ray leaned back in his seat, took a deep breath of the spring air, and concentrated on Rita beside him. Tomorrow could wait. Rita talked about yesterdays, sharing what it had been like growing up the treasured only child of a father rapidly building an empire and a mother both beautiful and vain. Ray imagined somewhere in there were the roots of the woman he loved. A woman who would insist on piloting her own starship and now very much wanted a child of her own. His child would probably grow up like Rita. Assuming he or she did grow up. Assuming the bomb killed the President and brought down the government. If Ray failed, everyone who ever knew him would be denounced, tortured, and murdered. *I will not fail.*

They left the main road, meandered through trees and dales until Rita took off down a dirt road. A lovely lake came in view, but the trees hid it more often than not. Its waters reflected back the blue of the sky. Its surface was ruffled by the wind, but Ray saw no boats. Then Rita turned down a path that was more a hint than a road. For a few minutes the car fended off tree limbs and brush; then they came to a halt in a grassy area that gently rolled down to the water.

"Mom and Dad used to camp here, long ago, before they bought the summer home where everyone had a summer home. I asked Dad not to sell this patch. He gave it to me." She helped him from the car, settled him on a blanket that just happened to be in the trunk, then began to undress. Slowly, methodically, completely, the clothes came off. "Now, we talk. No more bullshit. No more hiding behind nice words. We talk."

It was uncomfortable, sitting there in uniform, facing his naked wife. But Ray was not willing to so much as loosen his tie. It was not the bare skin that he feared, but the bare soul Rita demanded. That, he most certainly was not prepared for. "Talk about what?" he dodged.

"Oh, God, Ray." She turned away in exasperation. "Somebody jiggered the bomb. Face it, our security is hash. Two to one you're walking into a trap. Even if you get past the guards and searches, how much you want to bet the damn bomb doesn't work?"

That was one question Ray could answer. "The bomb will work. I don't leave here until I'm absolutely sure it will blow the President and everyone in the room to whatever they expect after this life."

She turned back to him, settled to her knees across from him, swallowed hard. "And you too."

"This bomb will kill the President. Other considerations are secondary." There, he'd said it.

Rita shot to her feet, paced around him like a cat stalking a mouse caught in a trap. "God damn you, Ray. No, God bless you. You always were a good soldier." She did not look at him. "And there's no bloody way I can change your mind."

"Is the President killing millions?" he asked her.

She shivered as she had when she saw the hanging bodies. "Yes."

"Does he have to be stopped?"

"Yes."

"Do you know of anyone with a better chance of killing him?"

"Damn it, Ray, how should I? That spy says you're his best bet, but there're a hundred colonial worlds. How many of them have guys like our spy, all trying to kill our Unity idiot?"

"I don't know. I just know I can do it. Rita, I've seen green soldiers freeze, and die for that lost moment. I've been a soldier all my life, and a killer for most of it. There's a lot of things I can't do. This is one I can."

"And you owe it to all those brave soldiers of the Second Guard that followed your orders and died. I watched you break down at the hospital when you faced your men. Do they mean more to you than me?" Tears streamed down Rita's face. Ray wanted to kiss them away. She kept pacing, far beyond his reach.

"Rita, I owe it to the men and women who died at my command. I owe it to your father, and the people working in his factories. Because I can do it, I owe it to every man, woman, and child on a hundred colony worlds and, yes, even Earth." He paused, then played his last card. "And the child of ours that you want so much. You spoke of a million worlds opening to us. What will be left to us if we let this damn war burn humanity down to a husk? Someone has to stop the madness. I can. Would you really expect me not to try? Try with all I am?"

Rita was sobbing now, and tears were coming to his eyes. He let them flow. Rita ceased her pacing and settled beside him, her arms around his neck. It took his left arm to keep him balanced upright. His right arm went around her. For a long time, they cried together, holding each other as best they could.

Then Rita began to undress him. "I know I married a wonderful man. Some women look at a husband and see a man to remake. I looked at you and fell in love with what I saw. Even if I'd known then the price I'd pay for loving you, I couldn't have walked away. I loved the commander of the Second Guard. I knew when I flew you into battle that I might not bring you back. So what is so different about this mission from the others?"

Ray knew the difference. In one he took a soldier's risk.

Canes left behind, she helped him into the water. Free of his own weight, he floated. Rita let the water wash away their tears, the sun warm them. Then she brought out joy and happiness from her vast storehouse and made him laugh.

She started a water fight. In chest-deep water, he found he could stand well enough to splash back. The fight ended with them standing like lovers with four good legs, arms entwined. They explored each other. When Rita drew him into the shallows and made love to him, he had forgotten about tomorrow. She loved him. He loved her back.

Washed clean by the sun and water of both hope and fear, they lost themselves in love. For today, that was enough.

ELEVEN

"LIEUTENANT RODRIGO, HOW long since you've had a break?"

"I take one every day, sir." Every few days battalion would ask that question. Each time she ended up talking to a higher-ranking officer. Mary was up to the battalion CO. Lieutenant Colonel Henderson was on the horn this time.

"Lieutenant, I don't mean the last time you caught a nap. I mean the last time you really kicked back and relaxed for a couple of days. Before they drafted you, right?"

Senior managers were usually idiots. Why did this one have to be different? "Pretty much, sir."

"Lieutenant, you get your ass in here. If you don't report to my HQ before oh-eight hundred tomorrow, I will relieve you and put the greenest LT I can find in command of A company. You hear me?"

"Yessir."

"Mary, I'm not just being a stickler. Troopers who survive their first week on the line get sharp, damn sharp. But stay on the line too long and you get hollow. Start making mistakes. I don't want to lose troops to dumb. If I could, I'd give you a couple of weeks off, but I can't trust the colonials for that long. Couple of days will have to do. Come on, woman, get in here. Get drunk. Get anything else you want. You'll be in a lot better shape when you go back."

Mary gave up. "I'll be there, sir."

"Good. See you soon. Battalion out."

"Damn busybody," Mary growled at the phone. "Don't you got nothing else to do?"

Mary looked up as several throats were cleared. Cassie, Lek, and Dumont filled her doorway. Cassie held a packed kit bag; they were smiling like the canary that ate the Cheshire cat.

"What are you all grinning at?" she tried to snap, but their smiles were contagious.

"At how well you obey orders. Sir." Cassie shot back. "Your kit's all packed for three days."

"Your coach awaits." Dumont bowed and swept a hand outward.

"And since ain't nobody around here gots a glass slipper, we figured you might as well be on your way," Lek finished.

"Somebody's been listening in on my mail," Mary charged.

"A time-honored practice by worker bees who survive the confused misdirections they get from management," Lek retorted.

Which knocked the wind out of Mary. Did they really see her as management?

"Come on, Mary." Dumont came around the desk and, taking her hand, pulled her up. "As the colonel said, we can't have you stupid. And we sure as hell don't want to break in another officer. Two in one war ought to be a limit." Arm gently on her elbow, he urged her toward the door. "Go on, Mary, have fun."

The vote seemed unanimous. Mary collected her helmet, accepted her kit, and two minutes later was in her command rig, the driver going hell for breakfast for the center of the crater. Mary wondered if he had a three-day pass in his pocket, too.

Then she remembered. Except for a few mending in hospital, no one else in A company had R&R just now. For better or worse, she could let her hair down and not worry about someone telling tales to the troops. She wouldn't have to save anyone's bacon. Neither would she have anyone to pull her out of any brawl she started. She could never remember a time when she'd been this free of strings. More surprising, she liked the idea. Nobody to take care of; with a sigh, she spread herself out on the back seat. *What do we want, girl?*

A bath. A bath and a decent meal. After that . . .

She was asleep before she got to whatever might come after.

"We're here, Lieutenant. You can take off your helmet."

Her driver helped her out, made sure she had her gear, then headed back just as fast as he'd come. She really was on her own. Looking ridiculous with her helmet on, she undogged it and gently put it in her kit bag. A corporal gave her directions to battalion HQ. She reported to a sergeant only to find the colonel had left for C company two hours ago.

"He's taking out replacements and trying to come up with some new twists on Hambone's defense," the sergeant told her.

"Well, if the colonel asks, tell him I got my butt in here. Know any place a woman can get a nice long bath and a good meal?"

The sergeant tapped her board, then scowled. "BOQ's full, as usual. You don't want to go near the Sommersby joints. Naomi's Place is good for a bath and a bed. Make sure she knows you're renting by the day . . . and want clean sheets."

Mary wondered how noisy the traffic would be in the hall. She'd slept through worse lately. "And a drink?"

"Officers usually drink at Joe's."

"And honest people?"

This time the sergeant laughed. "Try the Dog Palace. Honest drinks and no more than one fight a night."

"Thanks. Where's a safe place to stow my battle gear?"

"Armory's down the hall. Tell Sergeant Datril you've

been on the line for a while and will be back for it in a couple of days. He'll see that it gets recharged and updated."

"Thanks." Mary hefted her kit and started down the hall.

"Tell Naomi that Beth sent you."

Mary waved without looking back.

An hour later, clad in a sweat-stained suit-liner that was enough for any off-duty miner, Mary went hunting for Naomi's Place. It wasn't hard to find the general direction. A dozen blazing neon storefronts along one underground avenue promised everything a man could dream of—booze, boobs, and all the rest.

It took sharp eyes to find Naomi's small sign. "Baths, Beds, Honest Rates." Mary whistled at the rates. When had highway robbery become honest? Since she hadn't spent a dime of her pay in months, she figured she could survive three days. Mary sauntered into a room that wasted no money on lighting. "Beth told me to ask for Naomi," she told the small oriental woman behind the counter. The woman backed, bowing, through a door, leaving Mary wondering if she'd helped herself . . . or just announced she was a pigeon ready for the plucking.

Moments later, a tall, olive-skinned woman appeared behind the counter. "What may I do for you?" she smiled.

"A bath and a bed for three days. Beth at battalion says to remind you I want clean sheets."

"Of course, Sergeant . . . ?" The woman eyed Mary, as if measuring her for a ball gown or a coffin.

"Does it matter whether I'm NCO, officer or civilian?"

"Not if you do not want it to" came the fluid answer.

"My money's good. Just treat me like a human being."

There was only a brief pause before the woman nodded. "They make the best guests. You may call me Naomi."

"Mary, just Mary." She presented her credit chit. If the woman wanted to know more about Mary, the chit would give it away. Naomi fed the card into a machine and did not glance at the screen while it was processed. When the machine beeped contentedly, she handed it across to Mary, still unread. Mary signed for three deluxe baths and three nights lodging, removed her card, wiped the screen and handed it back.

"Please follow me while I draw your bath. Do you have clothes to wash or mend?"

Mary did a quick mental inventory of her kit bag. She had no intention of wearing the uniforms. And not because they still had sergeant stripes. Everything else in the bag was underwear or toiletries. "Only the clothes on my back."

"May I loan you something? We can't have our guests being mistaken for dirt miners or space riggers."

Or whores, Mary suspected. No, more than likely a lot of her customers were. Then again, the woman was offering to share clothes with Mary that weren't military issue. "I'd be grateful for anything you might lend me that would keep lonely troopers from sniffing around me." When the bath was full, Naomi squirted several bottles into the tub, leaving it smelling like a garden Mary had once visited. Stripping quickly, Mary let herself down into the tub slowly, luxuriating in every delicious moment.

Naomi took her suit-liner and closed the door behind her.

For the next forever, Mary lost herself in the sheer joy of the fragrant liquid. Its warmth soaked through her, taking tensions and unkinking muscles she couldn't remember not hurting. Its buoyance lifted her, and her spirits rode right along. Now she knew what she wanted to be if she survived this war . . . a professional bath taker. To Mary's surprise, when the water cooled, there was more hot water waiting. *Deluxe!*

A soft knock at the door. Naomi entered before Mary could manage a response. "How is the bath?"

"I know what hell's like. Now I've been to heaven."

"If you should ever choose to leave heaven, I believe this dress will be most comfortable." Mary had heard of the simple black dress; this one fit the bill. It said she was a woman. If she said no, the dress wouldn't confuse men. She had no intention of saying yes.

"Thank you. I am truly grateful."

"You are not the first woman I have met who wanted free

of her present for a few days. I am glad to loan you my dress. I have included nylons and a bra. They are disposable. Wear them if you wish something more feminine than the corps gave you."

"Is marine tattooed on my ass?" Mary laughed.

"It was when you came in. I think it has washed off by now." The other woman smiled.

Mary couldn't remember the last time she'd worn fancy underwear. "I'll take it. Add it to my bill." She grinned.

"If you do not wish to look wrinkled as a newborn, you might want to consider ending your bath."

"I never want to get out," Mary groaned.

"I can arrange a full body massage," Naomi offered.

"I've never had one," Mary answered, suddenly unsure what was being offered.

"It can reacquaint you with your skin and make every muscle in your body happy to share that skin with you. If you've never had one, you really should try one." So Mary found herself wrapped in a towel, padding barefoot down the hall to a warm room with a raised bed. Moments after she had settled under the clean sheets, a knock at the door and "Are you ready" came.

What followed proved to Mary that there were two levels of heaven: one for baths, the other for massages. On the line, her battle suit touched her constantly. Now, the delicious caress of fingers worked up and down her arms, legs, and back. Every inch of her skin got a personal moment of attention. Muscles Mary thought had relaxed now turned to water as the masseuse worked them, or just rested her warm hands on them. If Mary had gone limp in the tub, she became a puddle on the table.

A few strokes went long, touching on soft, intimate areas, offering to ignite them. God knows, Mary was hungry. But the emptiness inside her was too vast, too threatening to risk a quick tumble. Mary feared if she ever dared try to fill that void, she'd implode. She edged her legs closer together. The strokes were shorter, but no less relaxing, no less pleasurable.

Her hour done, the masseuse left Mary alone to dress. Getting up enough strength to roll off the table took a small eternity. Mary loved the feel of the bra and panty hose as she drew them across her reawakened skin. Shoes were waiting just outside the door—medium heels she could just manage to balance on. A tiny purse, like a lady might carry, was also there. Mary quickly transferred her ID and credit card, discovered her room was not yet ready, placed her gear in a locker, and left Naomi's Place to look for food and a drink.

The woman leaving was a far cry from the one who went in.

Mattim stared into his beer, wondering if somewhere in the chaotic bubbles he might find his answer. After two long days of talks with Anderson, Umboto, Miller, and company he was no closer than he had been when they started.

The admiral wanted some way the Navy and the marines could work together. It sounded like a good question in her office, but out here, the answer was a bitch. Brigade lasers lacked the range. Kinetic weapons like rockets, rocks, or anything with energy and mass came with a problem. Newton was wrong; what goes up doesn't necessarily come down. That change in the law had damn near killed Mattim. Suspicion was that his capsule had been dinged by a grain of sand left over from the first desperate defense of this rock. No one offered to send a team to retrieve the capsule. Mattim had seen what the marines went through to save his life; damned if he'd order them back out there.

Mattim glanced around the Dog Palace as his brain spun; no familiar faces. Good. The brigade's officers were desperate for news from the outside or just a new joke, and Professor Miller took every chance to squeeze him about their jump data. Tonight, Mattim had ditched the others, switched to casual sweats, and was letting his mind wander. The place slowly filled as more people knocked off for the day. Most came in twos and threes, with group joining group and tables growing full. Except for a woman across the room from him, he was the only one drinking alone.

He leaned back and stared at the ceiling lights. Rock mines sounded great, if you could keep them from becoming equal opportunity enemies. Miller had tracked the orbits used by colonials and the Navy in the six battles so far; no piece of space was not shared. Lofting aimed rockets at the hostiles wasn't likely to get past the four-inch secondary battery. Show them a large enough target and they'd dust it. Even a dust cloud like Anderson had used in the first battle could be partially swept by the four-inchers if they knew what to look for. Dust hadn't worked since that battle.

A few hundred stealthy mines, crammed with passive scanners and the necessary computing power to recognize friend from foe, would change everything, but none were assigned to this sector. Ships that took years to build were under construction in every dock available, but only one plant made the relatively cheap mines. And neither Mattim nor anyone else on this rock could think of a good stand-in for them.

He took a long pull on his drink, then flipped through Miller's analysis once more on his reader. Damn good workup. Damned if he could spot anything she'd missed.

He glanced around the room. It was getting crowded. Friends were holding private conversations at the top of their lungs. Lots of four-chair tables had eight people gathered around them, and not a few gals were holding guys on *their* laps.

He took in a deep breath and let it out slowly. It was relaxing watching people just be people. For once, he had no responsibilities. A man approached the lone woman at the table across the room. A quick shake of her head sent him on his way. Another woman noticed him and sauntered his way, hips swaying. "Want anything, sailor?"

Now it was his turn to shake his head; it had been a long time, but a quick, mindless tumble was hardly worth the effort. She shrugged and moved off. A waitress made a quick walk by. "Never seen a beer last so long," she muttered.

Mattim spent another half hour people-watching, letting his brain idle, waiting for something to jump out and yell

"Surprise!" Nothing did. Then the bartender popped his own surprise. "Youse leaving anytime soon, like right now?"

"No," Mattim shook his head.

"Well, I think youse should. Sees, it's Friday night, and the boss don't like for any empty seats. Youse got an empty seat." He pointed at the other chair at Mattim's table.

"She's got an empty chair." Mattim nodded toward the woman in the black dress across the room from him.

"Well, likes I talks to hers as soon as youse leaves."

"Or I sit in her other chair."

"Suits yourselves."

Mattim watched the woman fend off another approach. Maybe he ought to just cut his losses and run. But staring at the ceiling in his BOQ room was not where his mind cared to wander. Picking up his drink and his reader, he headed across the room. Four people immediately filled his vacant table.

She spotted his approach and pointedly looked away. He stopped in front of her anyway.

"I ain't buying whatever you're selling, sailor," she said in a voice that meant business.

Mattim heard a bit of shop foreman or sergeant in there. Maybe some officer too. Hard to tell. "I'm not selling, but I would appreciate renting your spare chair. It may be to our mutual benefit."

"That's a line I've never heard. You got a lease on that chair for just long enough to show me your follow-through. Like five seconds."

Mattim slipped into the chair. "Miss . . . Ma'am . . . ?" Neither one of them drew a reaction, nor did she offer another handle. He charged on. "The management here likes to fill all its chairs, preferably with two. You now have the only table with an empty chair. Since we both seem to enjoy quiet people-watching, I thought we might ignore each other together and watch the rest. If we don't, I'm afraid that you are next in line to be invited to share your table or leave."

"By who and what army?" she growled.

Black dress or no, Mattim quickly revised his assessment

of the woman, adding sergeant stripes to her bare shoulders. She was too old to be a junior officer, and there was no doubt that she was comfortable in the company of troopers—make that killers of the line variety. If this woman got into a brawl tonight, he would be wise to distance himself very rapidly. Now might be a good time to start. Instead, he found, in his best negotiator's voice, he was still trying to maintain his claim to the chair. "No army'll be needed if we simply twist their rules to our benefit. We both want a quiet corner to watch the human theater. And," he said with a grin, "by us occupying this table, we keep them from loading it with four drink-swilling sponges."

"You a merchant trader?"

"In a previous incarnation I might have tried my hand at it."

"'Cause you could sell refrigeration plants on an ice planet. Prewar, of course."

"Ancient history," Mattim agreed.

"And getting more ancient with every endless second."

Mattim nodded slowly. No question, this one was a fighter like the ones who'd rescued him. He'd met a lot of dangerous people in his life, but never the cold-blooded killer this one looked to be. Once again, the exit sign looked attractive.

"Tell you what I'll do," the woman said, arm sprawled across the table. "You buy the next round, and you've got a lease on that chair until at least midnight. About that time, I'm crawling into a bed with nice clean sheets."

The "clean sheets" clinched it. The Navy took their bunks with them. The combat Joes slept where they could. Her drink looked to be as full as his. "You've got a deal."

A silent half hour later, about the time he ordered the promised round of drinks, she leaned forward. "What's it like, merchant trading, free to go where you please, do what you want?"

Mattim laughed. "For about six minutes if you don't show a twenty percent profit. No excuses accepted."

"Bet you've seen some beautiful sights."

Mattim thought of the four stars he'd recently seen, and how beautiful this wretched system looked when they finally jumped back. "Sister, you don't know the half of it."

"Call me Mary."

"Mary, I'm Mattim," he said, offering his hand.

"Mattim the trader, I'm Mary the miner," she said, giving his hand a quick shake.

They sipped their beers in silence for several minutes. Then Mattim pointed his glass at two tables where a strange swapping of women and men was underway. "I don't know what's going on there, but I'll bet you the next round of beers that there's going to be a fight."

Mary grinned. "I have it on good report that there's rarely more than one fight a night here. That doesn't look hot enough for me, trader."

Mattim raised a shoulder in a shrug. "One fight is one fight. I'm betting on that one."

Mary looked at them for a long minute. "One table's full of line animals, fresh in. The other one is headquarter weenies." She shook her head. "Maybe there'll be a punch or three thrown, but a fight? Naw. It'll be over too fast."

One of the women at the animal table was approached by a man from the other. Mouths moved. He put his hand on her shoulder. She coldcocked him so fast he never saw the punch coming. He fell into the waiting arms of his friends while she turned back to hers, gave someone a quick kiss, and hefted a beer high.

"You owe me a round." Mary laughed.

"Night's young. I think your animals are spoiling for a fight. Your glass is half full. Let's see how things are when it's empty. Time will tell."

Mary said something that was lost in the background roar as she leaned back in her chair.

"What'd you say?" Mattim asked, moving his chair a foot closer around the table.

She leaned forward; the neckline of the dress wasn't so high that he didn't get a pleasant view of well-defined breasts. "Time always tells. Well, trader, what'll you do after the war?"

So, the woman was defining the rules. Before the war and after the war were okay topics. Now was taboo. Without thinking, Mattim nodded agreement and really looked at the woman across from him. The lines of her face and neck were drawn hard. But the hint of a smile and the gleam in the eyes behind the hard lines . . . something was different there. He wouldn't call it soft. "Same thing I did before the war, push freight between the stars." That might not be true, not with what he now knew about jump points. But surveying new jump points was hardly a topic to excite a deadly line beast. "What about you?"

She leaned back in her chair, eyes lost in the dark. "Me and some friends plan to start our own mine." She shifted in her chair. Suddenly she was facing him, aggressive as an army in full advance. "Like you, starman, we just want to go back to where we were. Safe and grateful to be alive."

She paused, looked away. "Stupid, aren't we?"

That was a question Mattim wasn't willing to tackle. He drained his beer. She followed suit. Since no fight had broken out, Mattim ordered the next round, and upped the order to the best Irish cream they had. Mary raised the question with an exquisite eyebrow . . . and let him take the first sip.

Her first taste was more tentative than he'd yet seen Mary. Eyes wide, she smacked her lips. "Good stuff." Two sips later, she was back in form. "Now tell me, starman, after what we've seen, what we've done, do you really think we ought to go quietly back to our corner and keep doing just what the boss man wants?"

Mattim moved his chair closer. If they were going to be philosophers tonight, he did not do philosophy at the top of his lungs. She measured him for a moment. He got ready for a punch that would put him out for the night. Then she relaxed.

"And if you love doing what the boss says?" Mattim said.

"Yes, starman, but what if you don't?"

"Then why do it?"

"How long can you breathe space or eat vacuum?"

"Man does not live by bread alone."

"Speak for yourself. This woman doesn't live without it."

Their shared laughter broke the ice. She moved her chair closer to him the next time he spoke. His arm brushed hers, and she did not draw back. The woman's thoughts were deep, as were her scars. He doubted her education had gone past the basics before she had been channeled into a technical specialty. But her mind had never been turned off. She studied people the way Sandy studied sensors and Ivan studied engines.

Now, sitting close, Mattim also caught the scent of her: lilac and woman. His nose didn't agree with what he saw. But what he saw was changing; her eyes deepened. Limpid, they drew him in past the locked and cocked guns that stood guard. It had been a long time since Mattim wondered what was real behind the face a woman presented to the world. The conflict and complexities that were Mary drew him in.

Mary let her fingers rove the man's arm. The massage had started her mind wondering. What would it be like to have soft, pliant flesh under her own fingers? It felt good just now.

Mattim clearly was a Navy type and an officer to boot, just like the puke she'd risked her neck to rescue. She might like Captain Anderson and Commander Umboto, but she had little use for the rest of them, supply officers who couldn't supply shit, ships captains who couldn't keep the damn colonials off her back.

She'd damn near KO'd the guy first time he moved in on her. She laughed at the memory. It would have felt good, but she'd have missed this conversation. She was talking, just talking to a guy. And he was listening. The CO's of B and C companies had listened to her, but their lives depended on what she said. This fellow was enjoying her just for what she had to say. It felt good in a way she hardly remembered.

When a fight finally broke out between her beasts and the weenies, it wasn't over nearly as quickly as she'd expected.

Of course, three other tables piled in to help. The bartender let them get their exercise, then brought out a stun rod and threatened to sticky-net the whole of them. The lights went up enough to show they were directly under said net. Even animals know when the fun's over. Mary offered to buy the next round.

Mattim said it was more like a tie; they both ordered a round. Mary had vented enough of her anger at the powers that be. As their drinks disappeared, she asked him to tell her about the places he'd been, the beauty he'd seen. Being stuck in the mines didn't mean she hadn't looked up, dreamed of what was out there.

The guy was quite a storyteller. He didn't just paint her a picture of this or that, but peopled the places. She found herself laughing at his misadventures among the locals as well as some of the strange things they did. When they left at midnight, she had an arm around him, and she actually enjoyed the feel of his arm around her. Rather than head anyplace, they just walked.

Wherever they walked was just a shabby base, hastily dug out of rock, but that was not what Mary saw. Mattim painted her pictures. She stood with him at the flowing lava falls of Kinsinka and glided through the perpetual clouds of Tristram. It was when he told her of the four dancing suns that she pulled away and almost slugged him.

"I may be a dumb miner, but I've heard of them. Nobody's been there. They're halfway across space. You liar. You've been shoving me a line. You probably haven't been anywhere you've said. What are you, some shit supply clerk?"

The man didn't back away from her, nor did he have the good sense to get ready to defend himself. He just stood there. "I guess I shouldn't have mentioned them."

"No shit, Sherlock." Mary's arms twitched; fists clenched without thought. All the anger, hate, and fear the last weeks had force-fed her wanted out. She wanted to reduce this liar to a bloody pulp the docs would have to sponge up.

He eyed her, defenseless as a newborn in a creche. Mad

as she was, it was still hard to smash someone so helpless. If only he'd run or fight, she could pound him. He took a quick breath. "Two weeks ago, my ship was lost and orbiting those stars." He spoke so softly, so matter-of-factly, she was slow to react. His words were like a rocket coming in low, under her sensors.

She studied him; his eyes were what drew her. They held the distant echoes of terror and triumph. No weenie could fake that. "Really!" she gasped. Her fists were hands again.

"Yeah. We saw some pretty spectacular places. None as lovely as this collection of junk when we found our way back."

"How?" she found herself whispering.

"We've been using one jump point to go one place. If you know how, you can go dozens, maybe hundreds of places."

Mary had a hard time breathing. Planets, asteroids, millions of them. Good places for people like her. "Shiiiit, the mine we could set up. Not some crappy passed-over claim, but a real goer." The joy took her; she twirled, arms high, dress spinning out. Again she faced the spacer. Without thinking, she found her arms around him, her lips on his. For a moment, he held back. She hadn't frightened him off with her fists. Just her luck; now he was afraid of her lips. Then he kissed back.

Oh, but this woman was wild. One second cold, then hot. One minute ready to take his head off, the next squeezing him in a bear hug just as life threatening, even if her intent was quite the opposite. For a moment, Mattim held himself on tight reins as a captain had to. Then he tossed himself to the wind. The woman wasn't asking for a twenty-year contract with right to offspring. He'd probably never see her again. And few women in the last twenty years had tugged at his heart like this Mary had.

When they came up for air, she danced around him. "You've changed the whole bloody galaxy! You've opened doors no one can close. You'll be up there with Neil Columbus, Chris Armstrong and Jon-Luc Jones of the *Challenger*.

You made it happen. The rest of us can hope again." Her eyes gleamed; her lips split in a grin, not the cynical one that had watched the other drinkers, but the wondrous smile of a child with her first butterfly.

Too worried about getting back, and too busy afterwards, Mattim had never permitted himself to *feel* what they'd done. Now he did, and he was lost in the joy and admiration of this woman's eyes.

It hit him. *He had! His* people and *his Maggie* had damn well opened a door, a door any ship could cruise through. It took six or eight jumps to reach some pretty inhospitable places. With just four jumps he had found a paradise planet. Four jumps . . . one paradise. Not a bad set of odds.

Now he did swing Mary off her feet—and kiss her.

"I got a room," she mumbled against his shoulder when they broke the next time.

"And a bed with clean sheets."

"Very clean." She chortled.

"The woman I met a few hours ago seemed pretty happy to have those clean sheets to herself."

"But the woman you're with now is too full of herself to fit in that bed alone." Arm in arm, and ignoring the rest of the universe, they made their way to Naomi's Place.

Next morning, Mattim came awake of 0515. Mary was still sleeping. He pulled on his clothes quietly and put his shoes on in the hall. Tonight, he'd be at the Dog Palace. If Mary was there and willing, so was he. Otherwise, he had one fine night.

Mary awoke to a soft knock at the door and an empty bed. She suspected it was late enough that a sailor not on leave had better be on the job—whatever that job was. The knock repeated itself. Mary wrapped the sheet around her nakedness and opened the door a crack. Naomi was in the hall, the credit machine held out to Mary. "Battalion called. Colonials are in-system. All leaves are canceled. They want you back."

Mary glanced at the machine; it charged her for one massage, and gave her back two nights lodging and two baths. "No time for even a bath." Mary heard her voice take on a whining twist.

"We civilians have one hour to report to the deep shelters." Naomi shrugged.

"Sounds a hell of a lot more sensible than reporting to the line," Mary snorted as she took the machine and signed.

"Here's your suit-liner."

Mary dropped her sheet and pulled it on. She still smelled of flowers and man. *Wonder how long that will last?* She double-timed to battalion. The armory had at least refreshed her suit. There was a truck headed for A company with supplies and six replacements. The kids looked terrified; she gathered the nuggets around her. "First, forget everything they told you at boot camp." Eyes grew wide behind helmets. Good.

"Second, do what your corporals and sergeants tell you. They want you alive as much as you want to stay alive. Third, you're going to be scared shitless. Well, let your suit take care of that. You got fifty rounds in your rifle. Once you've emptied that first magazine, you'll be over the hump. Now enough, crew. Rule four is sleep whenever you can. The colonials are headed our way, and you don't sleep when there's Collies around. Flake out and get some sleep."

They obeyed, as she would have expected of green kids. At least they stretched their bodies across the crates. Mary doubted many would sleep. She made herself comfortable. Her mind was a jumble, part going down the company's deployment, who would get this fresh meat. That was the lieutenant's job.

But the miner in her yelped with glee. *Wait until Cassie and Lek hear!* Maybe an entire solar system to themselves! All they had to do was stay alive.

Mary awoke to a start at Cassie's voice. "Mary, you made it back. Thank God. The colonials are rounding Elmo. We got thirty minutes before company arrives."

Mary sighed. She wasn't home, but she was back.

• • •

Trevor H. Crossinshield approached his patron. The man was feeding ducks! Trevor glanced around. In the trees ringing the pond, people moved, in pairs and singles. *How many are security guards?* Certainly a man of his patron's wealth did not risk himself in the open. Wasn't the virtual world enough for him?

"How goes my war, Mr. Crossinshield?"

"Very well, sir. The damage to New Canton is greatly exaggerated in both colonial bragging and Earth propaganda."

With a flick of his wrist, the patron dismissed the rape, pillage, and killing of fifty thousand—or five million, depending on which report you accepted. Even Trevor's sources varied from one hundred to five hundred thousand. "Not my investment. Now, my President Urm, is he well protected?"

"The best security guards and equipment money can buy, sir."

"And among them?" His patron smiled.

"A squad of people also in our pay who can turn him off like a light when you wish."

"Very good. It may be necessary to turn this war off rather suddenly. Six, maybe nine months more. I'll tell you when."

"Yes, sir."

"Is there anything else, Mr. Crossinshield?"

The proper answer to that was "No, sir." Today, Trevor paused before risking, "There is one other matter, sir."

Did an eyebrow twitch? "Yes."

"A cruiser, the *Sheffield*, has made a rather interesting voyage of accidental discovery." Quickly, Trevor filled in the essentials for his master. "It might be possible to visit every star in the galaxy with no more effort than it takes to go from Earth to LornaDo," he finished.

"Fascinating, but a tad too much change for my tastes. Hardly manageable. Who knows of this?"

"One of our men has it. It has yet to enter the normal Navy info stream. It appears that one outpost and a colonial planet have also accessed the information."

"Such insignificant places should not be hard to make disappear," his patron murmured. "Yes, Mr. Crossinshield, pay our man well and have him keep this away from Navy eyes. See what he can do to plug the leak, make them disappear."

Trevor nodded. "Yes, sir."

TWELVE

A WEEK LATER, Mr. Nuu asked Ray and Rita to accompany him to work. In the basement of an unused building, the spy master waited, identical briefcases in either hand. "I have been over both of these personally. Which one would you like to test?"

Ray pointed at the one in his left hand. There was an abandoned vault behind the spy. He entered it, exited a minute later, and secured the door. Ernest started walking for the other end of the basement. Rita, Ray, and the fat man followed.

"You have no detonator," Ray observed.

"I doubt any signal could penetrate the safe. It is on a timer." The spy glanced at his watch. "About now."

Thunder and sharp pings came from the safe. The spy headed back for the vault. Ray put out an arm to stop his bride from following. "If it worked, a few moments' delay means nothing. Until he says so, I do not intend to approach his explosives."

Ray, Rita, and her father waited.

Edging the safe's door open, the man peered in, then pushed it open wide. "Come see what this was meant to do."

What greeted Ray was promising. Driven into the steel of the door and vault were thin metal and plastic darts. The spacing was relatively even. Ray tried to pry a dart loose—and sliced his finger. The spy master offered a pair of pliers. On his fourth try, Ray levered one loose. A centimeter long, maybe two millimeters square, it was ugly and effective.

The spy opened the last briefcase. "The shell is a sandwich of metal and plastic. Both fragment into deadly flechettes. Between is an extremely powerful explosive coated to almost totally eliminate any outgassing. Sniffer dogs will find nothing. The most powerful sensors probably would also draw a blank. In your case, they will be overpowered by your meds."

"Very good." Ray nodded.

"And who, among your so secure staff"—Rita smiled through gritted teeth—"arranged for one to go off with only a pop?"

The spy master at least had the honesty to look uncomfortable. "A total surprise, but it is taken care of."

Rita took a breath, but before she could get a word out, Ray preempted her. "Not acceptable. If you trust us to send your fondest regards to the President, you trust us to know what we are up against. If you must keep me in the dark, I go nowhere."

That took Rita by surprise; Ray turned to her. "Being willing to do the job, love, does not mean I am willing to fail." He turned back to the spy master. "Someone knows these briefcases exist. That someone knows three are gone. That same someone I would not count among my friends. Who is he, and what have you done to eliminate or contain him?"

"Her," the spy corrected him. He rubbed his chin. "We have identified everyone connected with Unity and other governments. This woman is drawing her second paycheck through a very complex arrangement with Earth, but with no government involved." He glanced up. "I do hate contractors. They complicate personnel situations terribly. One does know who is working for whom."

"You've taken care of her?" Rita demanded.

"Young woman, her family is far too well connected for us to use a drastic approach. No, there are three briefcases where three should be. We will be careful what we let her know in the future, and of you, Major, she knows nothing."

"Thank you for that small favor," Ray drawled. "For the moment, we will assume surprise is on our side. I will need to maintain some flexibility. A man of my rank and condition should have an aide to carry my briefcase. Captain Santiago would be the logical choice. I understand he might be available."

The spy master nodded. "The new general of the Second Guards is not impressing him."

"So our task force is complete," Ray concluded.

"You forgot me," Rita said firmly. "I won't jiggle your elbow, but the daughter of a social climbing, early party member would surely go along to accompany you to the ball. There will be a ball, to celebrate the President and his hero," she said.

"Yes." The spy nodded. "But you need not be there."

"What conspirator would bring along his bride?"

The spy master rolled his eyes. "I can make reservations for two or three."

"Make them for three," Ray ordered. "You can always cancel one if I succeed in talking sense into this wonderful fool."

"Try," she challenged him.

He would, but he had no optimism he would succeed.

"So, Matt, did spending a day stuck to the bull's-eye help you think?" The admiral's brown eyes sparkled. The eighteen ship's captains in the room laughed.

"It did tend to concentrate my thinking. Up 'til then we didn't have much of an idea. I personally would like to thank the colonials for providing their demonstration." At that, even the admiral laughed. Actually, the chance to watch a battle from a single point had helped. At Miller's behest, he spent it at her sensor console. Now, she had passive sensors in high polar orbit above the gas giant. Even when the skunks were on the other side of the monster, she knew where they were. That started him thinking. Support didn't have to be all-inclusive. At the right second, an extra thumb on the scale could be all they needed. He outlined that help to the admiral.

As she listened, her head slowly began to nod. When he finished, she shook her head. "I'd hoped for something more, but I can't fault what you've done. Nobody on my staff has come up with anything better. We'll do it your way." She then summarized a set of drills and maneuvers she intended for the next two days. Several captains groaned behind their hands. Apparently, she had worked her squadron hard while he was gone.

It showed; the sortie went smartly. Ships backed out in an established order and were in battle line from the get-go. This admiral had no emotional attachment to the head of the line. Drills saw the ships forming multiple columns and cones with the flag in the best position to command, wherever that might be.

Mattim and Ding found themselves working hard in the new dance of warship with warship. While individual ships jinked around in their own space to avoid the laser bolts that were not here at the moment, coordinated maneuvers had to be perfect. This admiral knew how she wanted to use her ships, and her captains knew their parts well. Wise woman. Mattim found himself looking forward to the next encounter with the colonials, even if he was, once more, tag in charlie.

His wait was much briefer than expected.

They'd just pulled a pass by the gas giant near Beta Station, using its mass to slingshot the entire formation into higher acceleration, when comm called the bridge.

"Colonials are one jump out from ELM-0129. Task force will lay a course for Gamma jump and maintain two-gee acceleration. We go through the jump fast, but steady as a rock. This time we surprise the colonials. Admiral sends."

Mattim glanced around. He'd hoped for another week of practice drills. Sandy shook her head. "Should never have let that woman in on our secret." Then she laughed. "But if I got to go, I'd rather follow a gutsy gal like her into a fight."

Captain Horatio Whitebred studied the message he'd just decoded. *So, my employer is happy with my find.* He checked again the number of zeros behind the "1" that his employer was adding to his private and very secret account on Helvetica, adding very nicely to the tidy sum the Sommersby sisters had paid him for helping them run their ship of booze and broads into the 97th. He'd even known who in supply would make sure they got a welcome and not the boot. *Yes, this war was very profitable!*

With the fleet out, Horatio had time to remove references to the *Sheffield*'s message from the official logs. Navy computers were so old, it hardly took more than a tap with the tools he'd brought. Military secrets were a lot easier to crack than commercial ones. Then again, the Navy hadn't had a war in fifty years. Corporations were at war every minute. The Navy was smart to bring in professionals like himself when they got into a real war. Not smart enough to pay him what he was worth, but that just made it easier for him to do what he was doing now.

Quickly he released his search programs into the comm system. In five minutes, they had corrupted every message on the net about the jump point, and left a resident behind. Any restore from backups would find a garbled file when they opened it. *Sorry, all backups are corrupted, too.* He'd repeat this when the flag came back on net. If it came back.

Flagships had such a delightful tendency not to return. Horatio, of course, never spent any more time aboard the flag than he had to. *People got killed on those damn things.* There was no problem finding people on his staff only too eager to brief the admiral. Well, at least the first three admirals. The one out today was no volunteer; he'd made the mistake of beating Horatio at poker. Badly. If he returned, Horatio now had the money to pay up. If he didn't return . . . Well, he'd never spoil the boss's Friday night poker game again, now would he?

Life was arranging itself very satisfactorily. No slow climb up the corporate ladder for him like the one that had worn down his dad. No. Grab it quick. Grab it all. Then sit back and watch the others drop like rats. He put his feet up on the desk. Nice.

There was a knock at his door. Sitting up and dimming the obsolete screen that Naval Intelligence insisted its people use, Horatio said, "Enter." His number two-man did. Commander Stuart might be regular Navy, but he had the mind of a first-rate corporate weasel. Horatio had told him so, and made vague promises about postwar opportunities. This one wasn't dense like so many of the blue-suiters who missed his meaning. If he interrupted, he had good cause. "What you got, Stu?"

"What we've been looking for." The man grinned.

"We've been looking for a lot," Horatio reminded him.

"After the *Sheffield* thing I did a search on jump points. I thought you might like to know who was talking about them, both message traffic and real time." He held up a disk.

Damn! If this guy had a search log, it was already obsolete. And the backup he was waving was the only evidence Horatio had committed treason. Visions of splitting his fee with this enterprising fellow did not go down easy. *Maybe I've found my next briefing officer.*

"Most of the messages you'd expect," the commander went on, unaware of the problem he'd just become, "but there were verbals that intrigued me. A couple of tug skippers get together every night to bitch about the war and how it's costing them business. They checked out harmless, so we ignored them. Then I ran the jump search. They talked about jumps a lot."

"Is there an end to this story, Commander?"

"Elmo has a third jump point."

"Impossible. That system's been checked out thoroughly."

"Jump's not where you'd expect it. Deep in the gravity well, between the two stars."

"Can't be." Horatio didn't know much about jump points, but he knew they had to be well away from large gravitational bodies.

"I know. But this one is. Must have been trapped by the rogue when it entered the system. We hauled in one of them. Interrogated him. It's there, and it's a one-jump trip to Wardhaven, the colonials' biggest industrial powerhouse."

Also the only world the *Sheffield*'s information had leaked to. Horatio needed time to think. "Thank you, Commander. Get me a full report on the tug pilot's interrogation. I want to study this carefully. Used properly, this could significantly shorten the war. We don't want to throw this away, now, do we?"

"No, sir," the commander said, tossed him the floppy and a sloppy salute, and left immediately.

Horatio studied his fingers. He had ignored the paragraph of his message suggesting it would be appreciated if he could disappear the outpost and planet that knew of the new jump data. Until a moment ago, that option did not seem possible.

Now, if he commanded the squadron, who knows what might happen? Of course, a reserve captain being fleeted up to admiral was rare. Then, his employer had showed admirable initiative. There was the minor problem of the present admiral. But they had proven to be so temporary, hadn't they?

Two days later, Mattim threw himself in his bed, exhausted. It should have been a piece of cake. What went wrong?

They'd barreled into the system a good ten minutes ahead of the colonials. The skunks, all twelve of them, came through their jump point at even intervals, but slower.

"Destroyers on a resupply mission," Ding announced.

Shuttling between Thor and Sandy, Mattim quickly formed a picture of the coming battle. Their task force would get to the gas giant first and catch the tin cans as they did their swing around. Good. For once, the Navy could keep the grunts out of a pounding. The admiral kept them deployed in loose echelon. Any reflection on a ship from the drive ahead was on the side away from the enemy. The colonials were in for a surprise. A tight laser beam from the 97th corrected that assumption. They were jamming every radio wavelength, but the colonials had gotten off a similar tight laser communication warning the skunks. Still, nobody had lit off a radar. Blindman's buff again.

There was no more talk from the ground; apparently both sides were busy jamming the other. Mattim's plan required the free flow of data—this was not good. But with only a dozen destroyers on a resupply mission, they would not be using his plan. No use giving it away on a mouse; better to save it for the next time the elephants were in town. It didn't hurt his feelings to be chasing a batch of cans.

The squadron decelerated into orbit. Forming a loose cone, they went low and lit up a few radars, covering where the enemy cans should be in line with gas collectors out.

No enemy!

Every radar snapped on, reached high and low, hunting for the missing colonials. "High," Sandy screamed at the same moment every warning device started honking. "They're above us—and missiles are all over the place!"

Lasers swiveled. Sensors searched. Fire-control computers struggled to separate friend from foe and lay down fire that would miss the one and hit the other. All took time.

The enemy missiles were pure acceleration, with random jinks. The first shots missed. So did the seconds. Then the missiles were in the formation and ships were exploding. One cruiser went into a loop, its engines no longer balanced, shedding armor. A second missile slammed through where a chunk was missing. The ship came apart like an expanding snowflake. Another cruiser took a hit in engineering; in a flash it ceased to exist. Missiles stabbed into two other ships. Their skippers doused their fusion hearts and drifted helplessly ahead of the decelerating task force.

Then the missiles were gone, plunging into the gas giant to be lost in its massive coat. The *Sheffield*'s lights dimmed as its main battery took on the destroyers high above.

"Get 'em, Guns," Mattim shouted.

"'Till they're out of range, we will."

Other ships joined in. One, then another destroyer was blotted out, but the others were venting water and reaction mass, distorting the laser beams hunting for them and making firing solutions harder. Too soon they were out of range.

"Check fire, crew," Guns growled. "We'll be ready for them next pass."

"If there is a next pass," Mattim muttered as he headed for the helm. "They're high and fast. Can they dump supplies?"

"They can dump them, but the poor joes on the ground'll need a broom and dustpan to pick them up." Thor grinned. "And I wouldn't want to be any too close to where they land."

"So they'll head for the jump. Good. We'll give them some of what they gave us last time. Comm, anything from the flag?"

"Nothing, sir."

There was something else in the voice. The truth you expected, and a pregnancy. Mattim was about to mash his comm link and demand more when Sandy's whisper got his attention. "I don't think there will be anything." Her board showed the task force, ragged now with ships vanished, or struggling, or unpowered and pulling ahead. "There's no carrier wave from the *Magnificent*, Matt. She must have been one that blew."

Mattim had watched a bad admiral die, and now a good one. There was no logic to this crazy business called war. "Anyone announce they're taking over?" he asked comm.

"Captain Skobachev on the *Trustworthy* just assumed command. Undamaged ships form line three. Prepare for a head-on pass at the colonials." Ding pulled up the dead admiral's formations; line three was loose. Ding maneuvered them into their slot. Which left Mattim time to wonder.

"How'd they target us? They didn't search sweep us?"

"No, sir," Sandy assured him. "I suspect they found us the same way I found them the last time. Here we are all stealthy against the background of one of the most humongous emitters in known space. They just aimed for the holes."

"Shit" was all Mattim could say.

As they came around the gas giant, every radar was burning, searching high and low. Every gun was charged, rotated out to cover any angle, hungry for a target.

The skunks were high and accelerating out of orbit.

"Can we?" Mattim asked.

"No way, boss." Thor cut him off. "We got to do another half orbit before we can try to chase them."

"They don't have the fuel for this," the exec muttered.

"Better to coast home than be blown home," Sandy said.

Mattim settled back in his chair to see what the new fleet lead would do. Thirty minutes later, they were reaching the breakout point to either chase the colonials or head to Beta jump. "Comm, you got anything?" Mattim asked, his patience gone.

"Coming in now. We will stay in orbit to give cripples more time to mend ship. We will then proceed to Beta jump at one gee or less. Skobachev sends."

Around him flew softly whispered protests. Part of Mattim wanted to join them. The merchant in him checked the profit-and-loss sheet. The Navy's losses were far out of proportion to the damage they'd inflicted. Still, the colonial troops had not gotten supplied and the 97th had been saved another pasting. Looking at things from that perspective, honors were even.

Still, Mattim would dearly love to smash a few destroyers.

The *Sheffield* did a fuel scoop, then shared out part of the mix to the *Goben* once her tanks had been patched and she could hold reaction mass. The damage to the *Aurora*'s engines was too extensive. A week or more of uninterrupted towing might have brought her back to Pitt's Hope. A week of peace could not be counted on. Once her crew was off, they slowed her down. In a few hours she went flaming into the giant's atmosphere.

The task force stayed vigilant for surprise; Mattim only catnapped in the captain's chair. Only when they were halfway to Beta jump did he allow himself to collapse into bed. The admiral had done everything right. She'd drilled a squadron until it was ready. She deserved to have smashed a half dozen cans. Nothing about this war business made sense.

"How soon can it end?" Mattim asked any god listening. When he didn't get an answer, he shrugged and drifted off to sleep.

"In my sister's name, I thank you" was all Santiago said when Ray explained his plan. Ray showed him the briefcase. "One combination, and it's a briefcase. The other, and it's a very powerful bomb."

"What's the second combination?" Santiago asked.

"I am the assassin, Captain."

"And if you are shot dead and I can reach the briefcase, the mission will still fail. Major, we always allow for redundancy."

Ray gave Santiago the second combination.

The presidential invitation was hyped by the media as an honor for all of Wardhaven. Thus, the government's yacht *Oasis* was made available to them. Ray suspected the spy master's hand; the fat man beamed at the accusation. "The crew is Navy. I made sure they are neither on my side nor the other. Politically neutral. And we will give them nothing to suspect."

"Listening devices?"

The spy nodded. "Here is a complete set of my sniffers."

Getting the *Oasis* ready took a while. Usually, Ray liked time before an operation to plan, squeeze the data for plan A, B, C. The more the better. Here, there was no data—and the only plan left both him and the President dead. Intellectually, he accepted that with a soldier's shrug. His gut was another matter. They'd removed a couple of yards of intestine; he'd shrugged off their warning that he might have problems. Now, with the extra tension, he had problems. He stayed close to restrooms to avoid his incipient diarrhea embarrassing him.

The future lay heavy on Rita. Three times Ray found her quietly crying in private. The first time she shoved him away when he put his arms around her. The other times, she just cried on his shoulder, then dismissed herself to the ladies' room. Still, each night, she took him by storm. Ray had led desperate assaults. He recognized what Rita did for what it was.

Before departure, they fitted Ray with a walker. He'd still need canes for balance, but the powered braces made walking easier—and rubbed his skin raw. Ray was given an ointment for that. It took away some of the discomfort, would toughen his skin—and stank. The last was probably the real reason for the braces. Passing port security to board the *Oasis*, even without the briefcase, Ray set off the detectors. A quick examination of his walker and medicine mollified the guards.

Rita played the socialite basking in attention. She flitted about the ship, begged to pilot it, and pouted when she was denied. They adjourned to their suite. A check showed a microphone in the sitting room, but none in the bedroom or bath. Both of Santiago's rooms might as well have been a sound stage. "And you said I served no purpose," Rita whispered in his ear.

Once they were in space, lunch and dinner were taken with the ship's officers in the state dining room. The course of the war was studiously avoided. Still, battles were discussed and cussed, as much to delight warriors as to establish the pecking order of whose alternate strategies were right and less right. To Ray fell the duty of judging all.

The trip to Rostock required eight jumps.

Horatio Whitebred liked the orders he read; he was now an admiral. He'd been apprised by his other employer that there was a well-paid-for clerical error involved. In a week, ten days at the most, new orders would arrive correcting these and appointing another to the stars Commander Stuart was pinning on his collar. In a week, ten days, a lot could happen. The Navy might be congratulating a hero and glad of the mistake.

"Commander Stuart, I'll need a chief of staff. I can't think of anyone better than you. I'll have the paperwork cut on your promotion to captain, if you're ready to be my man."

"I'd be honored, Admiral."

Respect somehow was missing in the way his new rank rolled off Stuart's tongue. But Horatio had important things to do. Like making his new stars permanent. "Stu, the ships will be back soon. How long will they need to take on supplies?"

"Two days, one if you push them."

"Push them. Let me show you why." For the next fifteen minutes, Horatio ran through his plans for the Battle of Wardhaven. Here and there, the commander tied up a loose end.

"Which boat should we tap for my flagship?" Whitebred asked.

"Normally, the biggest," Stuart answered. "With what you have in mind, one of the converted cruisers might be better. In ninety days, a lot got left out of their skippers' training."

Horatio made an appearance of weighing the question. The *Sheffield* was one of the matters he had to make disappear. As his flagship, it would be easy to leave a little something behind in the computer for her next jump after he was safely off. "Lost in sour jump" should have been her epitaph—and would yet be. "*Sheffield*'s fresh from the yard and her captain has shown a certain willingness to adapt himself to a situation." Horatio smiled, then frowned. "As well as a tendency not to obey orders."

"In the old days," Stuart began slowly, "ships had marines aboard. Marines are a lot more willing to shoot sailors."

"And Elmo Four has a moon full of marines pissed at the colonials. Yes, Stu, we'll relieve the Ninety-seventh of a few good men—and women. Stu, you and I are going to go far. We think alike. I like that in a subordinate."

"Right, Admiral." This time Stuart pronounced the rank like he meant it. Yes, Horatio mused, things were looking good.

His comm beeped. Mattim mashed the button. "What is it?"

"No leaves authorized. Take on supplies and prepare for immediate sortie. Admiral Whitebred sends."

"Who the hell is he, or she?" he snapped, not at all happy to be rushing his ship and crew back into the buzzsaw they'd just escaped. Staff needed to do some serious thinking about how they'd gotten into that mess and how to avoid it next time.

"Uh, Captain." His exec cleared her throat. "You remember Whitebred. He was Chief of Intelligence. Took you to dinner."

Mattim remembered. Him! Ding didn't look any happier. Maybe she hadn't slept with the ass. "Thanks, comm."

"Sir, a second message." There was a pause. "Sir. We're the new flagship."

It took Mattim a moment to react. "Thank you, comm" was all he could think of. Rubbing his eyes, he asked the obvious question. "Ding, are we rigged to support a flag and staff?"

"No, sir. It usually takes a week in the yard to peel back armor, insert modules, rearrange things."

"And we're to be ready for space tomorrow." He sighed.

"Looks that way," she agreed.

"Commander, I'll be taking your stateroom." Mattim turned to survey the back of the bridge. "Have four full situation stations installed," he ordered. "God, I hate sharing a bridge."

"Yes, sir." Ding was all work again. She'd have to be; they had a rough day ahead, and a rougher cruise after that.

"Captain, this is Lieutenant Darjin on the quarterdeck. We've got a load out from the station armory that they want you to sign for personally."

"What is it?" Mattim snapped.

She told him.

It was worse than he thought.

THIRTEEN

THE ADMIRAL DISMISSED the reorganized bridge with a wave. "I'll spend any battle we may have in my day cabin. I'll need a secure communications lead direct to my office. I'm having to be my own intelligence officer."

"Yes, sir," Mattim said. At least the admiral's staff was small. He'd only had to roust out Guns to make way for the new chief of staff. "I'll move the stations in there." Ding quickly started the riggers tearing out what they'd just put in.

The sortie orders were given just as diffidently—a wave of the hand and a "Get us moving."

Mattim doubted that was the Navy way, but he was too new to know for sure. He glanced at the chief of staff. "Repeat Admiral Hennessy's orders," he said. "They worked fine." Mattim told comm to do so . . . and to keep the old message files with the last admiral's orders handy. He suspected they'd get a lot of use.

Once the *Sheffield* was on its course for Gamma jump, Mattim left the bridge to do a second set of inspections. He was especially uncomfortable about the last delivery from the armory. The *Sheffield* was not designed for that kind of load; he'd post a 24-hour watch on it. He never thought as a captain he'd be glad to be quit of his own bridge. Today he was.

Ding shrugged as the captain beat her to an excuse to get off the bridge. He didn't look any more comfortable sharing space with Admiral Whitebred than she was. She spent the time double-checking what she had already triple-checked. It was, after all, the Navy way and the best way she knew of to stay alive in space. Once the work crew reported the admiral's stations were on line, she checked them out and dismissed the chief and his party. She was about to follow them when the admiral cleared his throat. "Could you demonstrate this to me?"

The Navy joked that every kid reporting for boot camp knew how to operate an admiral's battle station; it looked just like a game station. Ding's dad had plopped her down before a standard Navy-issue station on her sixth birthday. It was nothing like a regular education or game station. She'd spent the last thirty years figuring out how to squeeze the last ounce of data from each modified and updated version. No way could she tell him in five minutes what she'd spent a lifetime learning.

So she showed him how to turn it on. As she toured him through the most obvious features, he stood behind her. When his hands began making circles on the back of her shoulders, she decided he'd seen enough, tapped the help symbol, and stood up. "That ought to take care of any questions you have."

"Doesn't look that different from my first information station at corporate, ten years ago." Ding would bet a month's pay he was wrong. She kept her mouth shut and headed for the door. *What did I think I saw in that empty bag of space?*

"Colin, could I have a moment to discuss our mission?"

She paused, wanting very much to be gone. But she'd learned at her father's knee that an admiral's request was an order. She turned; he was pacing back and forth at a comfortable distance.

"This may take a while. Why don't you sit down?" He

waved distractedly at the couch. So long as he kept his distance, the couch should be fine. She settled in.

"We've got a tough assignment ahead of us," he said, still pacing. "This war is gobbling up resources." He paused. "Financially, it's a disaster."

"And it's killing a lot of people, too," Ding added.

"Yes. Yes, of course. And it's only going to get worse. What we need is a strike that brings everyone to their senses. We can win this war in an afternoon if we cut through the crap."

Ding's study of military history told her such things sometimes happened. More often, a *coup de main* was full of surprises. Whitebred had stopped pacing and was suddenly on the couch beside her. His hand settled on her knee. In her black dress at the dinner party, that had been disconcerting. In her shipboard jumpsuit, it was damn distasteful.

"I need to know that when the time comes my orders will be followed to the letter. Will they?"

That hand was wandering her thigh. She tried to chuckle like her old man would have; it came out off-key. "We're not shopkeepers, Admiral. When you give an order, we obey," she quoted her dad. "Assuming, of course, the order is legal."

Now why had she added that? That orders were lawful was a bedrock assumption that went without saying.

"Of course, of course," Whitebred mumbled, "but if we pull off the endgame for this war, that will set us all up for life. We can write our own tickets." His other arm had slipped unnoticed over the back of the couch. Now it was very noticed as it slid down to rest on her shoulder. She didn't have much thigh left that the other hand hadn't covered. "There won't be anything you can't have, if you play along with me." While his hands held her like a toy, his eyes were focused far beyond her.

He wants my body, but will he even know it's me? A month ago, Whitebred had been magnetic. But in the last month, she'd followed a real captain to the end of the galaxy and back.

Horatio was offering her a door into his life. All it would cost was her soul. A month ago she'd never seen a ship fought, a crew led quite the way this strange merchant captain handled his command. A month ago, the unknown of Horatio's world had sounded pretty damn good against the known of her own.

But not now. Now she understood why her dad had toughed the Navy out for forty years. Now she knew what all the waiting and training was for. She'd fought and lived and opened up the galaxy. Damn, it had been terrifying— and fun! His hand was at the zipper of her jumpsuit. If she did nothing much longer—but there was no question what she would do. In one smooth motion, she fended his hand away from her neck and stood.

"Thanks for your thoughts, Admiral, but I've got a ship to run." She didn't look back, nor did she rush, striding calmly, an officer returning to her duty. At the door, she couldn't avoid a glance back. The man—and the emphasis was on the male part of the word—did indeed look frustrated. She left him.

Smoothly, she plugged herself back into the routine, moving from station to station, observing, checking. Only at Sandy's station did she pause. "Trouble?" the jump master asked, nodding in the general direction of the admiral's door.

"Nothing a big girl can't handle. But the young middies might bear watching."

"Even the one with a black belt?" Sandy's eyes sparkled.

"But think of all the paperwork if she busts his arm." Both women chuckled. But that did leave Ding with a problem. Did she tell the captain that Whitebred was out to win the war in an afternoon? How could she tell him that without also telling him the admiral had the morals of a tomcat and was on the prowl? While she liked the captain's style and wanted to see how he solved most problems, how he'd react to the new admiral sexually harassing his XO was not on her short list of ways to spend an evening before battle. She'd let this one slide unless something more came of it.

Mary got exactly twelve hours to mount out a platoon for ship duty. Half of that she lost waiting for battalion to ship someone over to hold her pass. She was not amused.

The corps had its own way of moving an armed mob from point A to point B. It was a part of the manual Mary had been a tad too busy to read. They sent her the lieutenant to help her out.

It was embarrassing to have him salute her first.

"Congratulations, Captain."

"I'm no captain." Mary tossed off his salute.

"You are now. Admiral who wanted you insisted we cut your promotion papers."

Interesting, but that didn't answer half her questions. "What do we take, fancy uniforms or antitank rockets?"

"Supply is doing a standard thirty-day package for you. Everyone takes their personal weapons and gear. The rest, brigade takes care of."

Four hours later, as she strapped herself into a troop module hooked to a tug, Mary was glad she hadn't had to do more. The air smelled of antiseptic; the tug had snuck in to take out casualties. Now it was taking her to a whole new kind of war.

As they sealed the hatches, Mary glanced at the troops of Company A, first platoon. Most of the old vets were already asleep. Even the replacements were headed in that direction. With a shrug for tomorrow, Mary leaned back and joined them.

"Damn, where did they get that bunch, off a chain gang?" Thor had put on the main screen and feed from the camera on the quarterdeck. The bridge watched as the marines came aboard.

"More like these are the rocks the chain gang couldn't crack," Sandy chuckled.

Mattim had to agree, they looked like pretty hard cases.

The armor was well worn and the personal weapons handled with casual, deadly familiarity. The exec had stopped her constant roving from station to station to watch the show from behind the captain's chair. "Interesting," she muttered.

"Yes?" Mattim asked.

"Not one marine rendered proper honors on boarding, saluting the flag painted on the aft bulkhead and the JOOD."

"They seemed kind of busy." Mattim smiled sourly.

"Yes sir, marines usually are, but the line beasts play a game with us. Just how sloppy a salute can they get away with? At least, the old hands do. I'd bet money not a single one of them is more than six months out of boot camp. Even the sergeants."

Before Mattim could add that to the muddle of his thoughts about a new admiral, a mission to nowhere, and the damn contents of his weapons magazine, the door to the admiral's quarters opened. "Captain," the chief of staff said with a grin, "the admiral would like to talk to you, your exec, and your jump navigator."

"Now we find out," Mattim muttered.

The admiral stood beside the work table in his quarters, its display zoomed to just the two suns. No sooner had they reached him than the admiral began. "Today we win the war."

Mattim had heard that enthusiasm before. "Today we make a mint" was usually followed by going bust. He didn't mind management losing money. He would mind very much this management hotshot losing lives. Especially those in his crew.

The admiral seemed disappointed that the three of them took the news with blank faces. "I can now tell you that I have uncovered the reason why the colonials have fought so hard for this worthless system." The slight tilt of the chief of staff's head suggested who had really made the discovery. The admiral didn't notice. Indeed, he no longer seemed to notice anything. Mattim knew this kind of "briefing." It wasn't to tell you anything; it was to let the speaker glory in the noise of his own voice. Today Mattim could not allow himself the luxury of zoning out; this man controlled a loaded and cocked battle squadron.

"Between these two suns is a jump point, trapped when the native caught the wanderer. That jump point will take us straight to Wardhaven, the most industrialized planet the rebels hold. In the next week, we will cut the heart out of colonial power. They will have to surrender unconditionally."

The admiral wasn't finished, but Sandy's eyes were locked on the table, studying the two suns, balancing their gravity, trying to figure out where they held their hostage jump point. She shook her head slowly. Mattim could hear her saying to herself, "It's gonna be a bitch."

Now Mattim knew why the *Maggie* was the flagship. There was no better jump navigator in explored space than Sandy. And the bombs in his magazines were for show only. He knew the rules the colonials fought by; he'd had to wait often enough while a planet negotiated its surrender with the fleet in orbit. To the colonials, checkmate was enough.

This admiral wasn't so dumb after all.

The admiral's speech was slowing down. Even he could see that his announcement had gotten their full attention. "So, Captain Abeeb, you will take the *Sheffield* through the jump point with the battle squadron right behind you. We'll have the colonials by the balls."

Mattim turned the order into a question and handed it to Sandy. "Can you find that jump point?"

She eyed the plot. "It's gonna be a bitch. We'll have to take it slow."

"We'll go as slow as you want," the admiral cut in before Mattim could answer. Well, rank has its privileges, and new rank usually takes a little extra. Mattim was in a very good mood. With luck, he'd be back to the Red Flag Line before New Year's. Trailed by more encouraging babble from the admiral, Mattim led his people back to the bridge. There was a general cheer when he passed the mission outline to the crew.

At Sandy's request the squadron spread out in echelon as

it began the dive toward the suns. Still, they were less than fifty million kilometers out before Sandy got the faintest hint of a gravity distortion near the center of gravity between the two suns. The fleet decelerated for another day. Most ships closed in on the flag, but Sandy asked and got the *Sendai* and *Jeanne d'arc* to hold station as the long arm of her gravity-anomaly detector. At ten million klicks, she shook her head. "Matt, I've got a good fix—rather, good *fixes*. That beggar jumps around like the proverbial Mexican jumping bean. It's the bitch of all bitches."

The door to the admiral's quarters snapped open. "You will lead the squadron through, Commander," the admiral demanded.

"We will make it." Mattim was out of his chair and moving to put himself between the admiral and his Jump Master."

"I hold you personally accountable for this, Captain."

"We'll get you where you can win the damn war," Sandy snapped. "I want out of this damn Navy." She really was having a bad day.

"The *Sheffield* hasn't met a jump point it couldn't handle," Mattim assured the admiral. Without another word, Whitebred turned on his heel and returned to his quarters.

Mattim turned back to Sandy. "Want to reactivate some of the science teams? Would it help to have a few of the middies?" That drew a glance between Sandy and the exec that said something to them, but nothing to Mattim.

"No," Sandy assured him. "I can handle this. You know me, I'm always looking on the downside of things."

Mattim gave her an encouraging smile and returned to his chair. There was something about this incident that didn't feel right. Slowly he replayed it. Nothing. Again he went through it. *How did the admiral know Sandy was having problems with the jump?* He glanced around the bridge. Like the quarterdeck, it had cameras. Just as they had watched the marines come aboard, the admiral apparently had been watching the bridge. He must not be very busy if he had time to watch over people's shoulders. Then again, a very paranoid person might feel that need.

Once again, Mattim ran through the situation he was charging into. There were too damn many unknowns or ambiguous values in this setup. And he wasn't likely to clear anything up today. This was no way to run a bargaining session. Not if you wanted to turn a profit.

Hours later, they crept toward the anomaly in space that could be the door to ending the war. "Two minutes," Sandy announced on a squadronwide hookup. "Keep your ships steady."

Mattim reminded himself to breathe.

"Damn," Sandy said a moment later. "It moved. Adjust course fifteen degrees to starboard, five degrees up azimuth." The fleet was in line astern of the *Sheffield*, intervals down to fifty klicks. Any closer and they'd boil the armor off the ship behind. Only the *Sendai* and *Jeanne d'arc* were out of line, two hundred klicks abreast to give Sandy a broad baseline. If worse came to worst, they'd break wide and come through later.

Over the next five minutes, Sandy made fine adjustments to her course, adjustments measured in nanodegrees. The other eighteen ships slaved their helms to her. The jump loomed ahead. Even the human eye could see the distortion it lent to light trying to pass through. Looking down an atmospheric tornado might be like this. Mattim squirmed in his seat, most uncaptainlike. He forced himself still, then forced himself to breathe.

"Ten seconds to jump," Sandy announced, but the mike caught her muttering. "Stay where you are just a little longer, sister, just a wee bit longer."

"Comm to captain." The call broke Mattim's concentration.

"Comm, we're busy up here at the moment. Wait one."

"Sorry, Captain, I can't. I've got the commander of the Ninety-seventh on live. He wants to talk to the admiral."

"Well, put him through," Mattim snapped.

"Admiral won't take it."

"Won't take it?" Mattim glanced around. The door to the admiral's quarters was shut.

"The captain wants to talk to you, sir."

"Put him on," Mattim snarled. At her station, Sandy gently played with the fine controls, edging the *Sheffield* toward the jump.

"Captain Mattim." Captain Anderson appeared in a window in the main screen. "I have a priority message from Beta Station."

"Got it," Sandy shouted.

The window went blank. The rest of the screen changed. The stars before Mattim were no longer the stars that had been. "Thor, where are we?"

"That's Ward Star out there. We're trailing Wardhaven by about a quarter of an orbit. Only seventeen ships got through."

"Damn jump jumped," Sandy growled.

It didn't stop Mattim from grinning. "Sandy, give me a full passive sweep. What's in this system? Thor, set a tom porary course for Wardhaven, two gecs. We'll wait for the admiral's orders to be more specific."

The door to the admiral's quarters opened. Chief of Staff Stuart joined them on the bridge. "Tell Skobachev to take the squadron to Wardhaven at three gees. The admiral would appreciate your presence and all your department heads as soon as possible in his day cabin."

Mattim nodded. He didn't know what the hell was going on here, but orders given were to be obeyed. "Quartermaster, order a department head meeting in the admiral's day cabin. Comm, advise Skobachev to lead the squadron to Wardhaven at three gees. Anything else?" he asked Stuart.

"Nothing for the moment."

The hatch to the bridge opened. Mattim turned, surprised that any of his department heads had made it so fast. Eight grim-faced marines marched in. The two officers wore sidearms, as did a pair of sergeants. All the enlisted personnel, sergeants included, carried assault rifles.

The officer leading the marines stopped, saluted in a direction that managed to include both Mattim and Stuart, and announced, "I have orders to report to the admiral's day cabin as soon as we completed our jump."

Stuart stepped aside. "The admiral's right this way." He waved his left hand and the marine captain led her troops across the bridge and through the door. Was there a hint of a smile on the chief of staff's lips as he followed them?

One thing was sure. The marine officer was Mary the miner.

Twelve days out from Wardhaven, *Oasis* docked at High Rostock, the station in orbit above the capital. Her captain came to assist the transfer to a shuttle for the trip down. Ray was just at the lock when a young junior officer rushed up.

"There's a major battle fleet in orbit over Wardhaven!" he shouted.

"Where's our fleet?" Ray shot back.

"What's left is in the yards," the captain snarled.

"Well, the yards are gone, and the ships in them," the messenger added.

"My father's people," Rita gasped.

"Terribly sorry, ma'am," the captain responded, but Ray didn't see much thought behind it. Both he and the ship's skipper were intent on one question. *Were the Earthies going to follow the rules?* The colonial worlds had been fighting among themselves for fifty years. The wars were wild affairs with each side doing whatever it took to beat the other into taking over their debt to Earth. One rule had never been violated. Once you lost control of the space above your planet, you surrendered.

Of course, under that rule, you did not destroy orbiting factories either. The Earthies had broken part of the rule. What did that mean for the rest?

It took Mattim five minutes to muster his department heads; the doc was last. He led them in single file. Armed marines lined the bulkhead across from his officers. He stepped forward, placing himself alone in front of the admiral, his body between his crew and the marines. Without orders, maybe following some ancient drill that had been skipped in his ninety-day intro to the Navy, the exec and Guns followed him, taking station a step behind him and to either side. They felt good there.

Mattim hadn't the foggiest notion what the drill was, but he doubted this admiral did either. Saluting, he reported, "All department heads present. We await your orders."

Admiral Whitebred beamed at the military honors, but the twist to his smile was pure evil. "In the next three days, I will win this war," he informed the officers. "While the rest of the squadron silences resistance around the planet, we will accelerate and, at the proper time, release relativity bombs. They will shatter all resistance on the planet, and the shock waves from them will travel the length and breadth of colonial space. All resistance will crumble, and this war will end."

"Good God" escaped lips. Mattim bit his tongue to keep silent. Now it all fell into place. The relativity bombs were never meant to intimidate; the stupid bastard meant to use them. Shock and numbness swept Mattim as he tumbled into the deepest pit of hell, a hell as real as the two-and-a-half-ton blocks of steel and stone his crew had so carefully stowed in the *Sheffield*'s magazine.

The admiral babbled on while Mattim struggled with his own demon. As if from a distance, Mattim heard gibberish about the need for the hard reality of war and death to be carried home. "Only when every man knows there is no place to hide will the killing stop." Mattim stifled a snort; Wardhaven held a billion people. Their raging ghosts would call up bloody war forever. Mattim started to say so, but found he couldn't. For twenty years he'd sat in business meetings, listened to stupidity and folly . . . and kept his mouth shut. For a second, practice held him quiet.

And that second gave him a moment to look around. One marine nodded. He fondled his gun, familiar with it and the death it dealt. Mattim eyed Mary, remembering their hours together. She focused on the admiral, but the heat of his stare drew her glance. But only a glance before she dismissed him and returned to the back of the admiral's head.

They knew! The marines had been briefed while he was collecting his officers. *What was in their briefing?*

"Excuse me, Admiral," Guns' soft rumble interrupted, "but no. I didn't joint the Navy forty years ago to commit genocide. And no man under my command will be a party to it either."

The admiral actually smiled at that interruption, that same blend of smug, confident evil. "I was afraid an old-school type like you might not see the need to reinvent war," the admiral said softly. He waved a hand, "Sergeant, I believe we have someone in need of counseling."

"Yessir," shouted a young sergeant. In five swift steps he was beside Guns, pistol pointed up under Guns' jaw.

"Commander," the admiral went on, "I suggest you reconsider your position. It has no future."

"I've studied war since before you were born, kid." Mattim cringed. Even with a gun in his face, Guns would not be tactful, much less retreat. "This idea stinks—morally and tactically. You'll get no quick peace. More likely a long war with no holds barred. You are wrong, and I will not besmirch the uniform I wear with the blood of a billion innocent people."

"Then we'll limit it to your own," the admiral quipped. "Sergeant, this man is guilty of disobeying an order and cowardism in the face of the enemy. We being at war, both crimes are capital. Execute him."

"That's not a legal order." Mattim didn't get the words out of his mouth before the gun exploded. Deafened, still Mattim could hear the roar of rage from behind him. The marines' assault rifles were coming off their shoulders even as he wheeled to find half his officers lunging forward, following the XO. His fist went out, slugging her in the gut.

"Back!" he ordered as Ding folded beside him and safeties clicked off behind him. One burst from those marines, and his ship would have no chain of command. "Back in place. Now."

They hovered for a split second, torn between obeying him and avenging Guns. The second passed, and they fell back.

"Very good, Captain," the admiral cooed. He had been very quick to get out of the line of fire. He stayed off to one side, a pistol in hand. "You'll go far."

"I won't have my officers massacred," Mattim answered through gritted teeth.

"No need for anyone else to get hurt," the admiral assured him, "except some colonials, and we're at war with them. Right, Captain Rodrigo?"

The marine Mattim knew as Mary took a deep breath. "Yessir," she whispered.

"Captain Abeeb. You have your orders."

"Yes," Mattim hissed and turned on his heels, no salute this time. And almost stumbled over Guns' body. "Doctor, please remove Commander Howard to the ship's mortuary."

"Immediately, sir."

Normally, the officers would have waited on Mattim. With a quick jerk of his head, he sent them out ahead of him. They left, but didn't go far. He found them milling about on the bridge. As he took his chair, Mattim's mind raced. Somehow he had to stop genocide and keep his crew from being shot by marines. For that, he had to get control of his people and his own rage. Ding limped to her chair, rubbing her stomach where he'd slugged her. The other officers gravitated silently toward the bridge hatch; what message would they take to the crew? Two marines came out of the admiral's cabin to take station on either side of the door. One of them was Guns' executioner—no, murderer. The safeties on both assault rifles were off.

"The briefing will not be discussed," Mattim told his officers, then glanced at the bridge cameras. "Carry on."

The officers filed out.

Mattim turned to Ding. "I need you, Commander," he

whispered. "I've already got one dead officer. We'll mourn him later. Right now, I and this ship need an exec."

Trembling—Mattim put it down to her own rage—Ding stared back at him. Slowly she nodded.

Before Mattim could say any more, the chief of staff entered, heading for the helmsman, no doubt willing to pass the admiral's orders direct to Thor. Mattim would not become a figurehead on a ship whose name would be linked with infamy for the next thousand years. He arrived at Thor's station the same second Stuart started talking. "We want a high-gee course. I suggest diving sunward, using it to accelerate the ship, then swing around."

"We'll have to swing by five or six planets to get us aimed at Wardhaven." Mattim pointed out the system map Thor had at his station. The helmsman looked on in growing puzzlement.

"I don't think so." Stuart was wearing that smug smile again. "A deflection around planet two, using four-gee lateral acceleration followed by three-gee acceleration for Wardhaven ought to do the trick. Don't you think?"

Mattim pursed his lips tightly to cover the impotency he felt. He was playing catch-up to a guy who had spent days planning this operation. Only the marines at his back kept Mattim from smashing the smug captain's head against the bulkhead. "Yes, that course will do it. It'll be rough on the crew, and the magazines might not take the load."

"You'll have a couple of days at two-gee acceleration. Captain, I suggest you order the course change." Mattim needed time, and they weren't giving him any. This was their hand. He'd lose money this round, but if he anted up, he'd be in and ready for the next—assuming there was time for another. He gave Thor his orders without mentioning relativity bombs. It didn't matter. About that time they brought Guns' body out on a gurney. Everyone swiveled to look, eyes growing wide. Ding looked, then turned away as tears slipped down her face.

Mattim had had all he could handle. "XO, you have the

conn. I'll be in my cabin." He left with as much haste as he could permit himself.

Alone, Mattim let his rage out in one long howl. Pacing his cabin, he slammed his palm into the bulkhead. What he wanted to pound was Whitebred, and Stuart, and the damn marines. Mary the miner had talked about after the war. Was that why she and her marines had bought into Whitebred's promises of wealth and power if they followed his every whim?

Grabbing control of himself, Mattim plopped on the edge of his bunk. Enough worthless emotions; he had a mission and orders he was damned if he'd carry out and a crew that he could not allow to be slaughtered. "Think, damn you, think."

He glanced around his cabin. Was Whitebred watching? The comm link did not face the bed. Whitebred had been on board for five days, but he had not asked for any work done by the ship's company. Still, any mikes and cameras on board were probably accessed, but no new ones added.

Maybe.

Mattim called up the load out the marines had brought. Most was standard issue. There was an exception. Lek what's his name, Mattim didn't even try to pronounce it, had several crates of uncatalogued electronic equipment and broken parts! Who was this guy? Mattim accessed the ship's personnel files. The marines had not been added. Okay, there was an electronic wizard on board, probably on the admiral's side. Coordinating anything was going to be a bitch.

Mattim settled into his bunk. What assets did he have? A crew that had followed him to the ends of the galaxy and back. They'd do whatever he asked. But he couldn't say what he wanted to without risking a bullet in the back. And he could not stand by and watch them be murdered.

He'd stopped at Wardhaven a dozen times. One industrialist had invited him home to enjoy an evening with his wife and daughter. While it hadn't slowed Mattim's haggling, now it gave him faces to match with the bombs.

Alarms went off. He drifted up from his bed. "Oh, shit."

His screen lit up—Whitebred. "Captain, you seem to have an engineering problem," he said softly. Then his face hardened. "If we are not back at two gees in five minutes, I'll have the marines fix it. Your way or my way, we *will* be back at speed in five minutes."

Launching himself from his bunk, Mattim was out the door and going hand over hand down the main passageway. "Make a hole," he hollered. "Captain coming through." People made space even if it meant drifting away from the emergency handholds. He passed two sets of marines. They watched him, but made no move to follow.

In engineering, Ivan and his watch hunched over stations. "Damn groundhog reactor hiccuped and sent a spike through the system. Damn near fried main power." He glanced up, a resigned scowl on his face. "I'll need thirty-six hours to straighten this out."

"You got two minutes," Mattim growled, "or they'll put a bullet in your brain like they did Guns. Sandy first, then you, then your team one by one until somebody cracks and turns back on what you turned off. Ivan, don't be stupid."

Marines clattered through the hatch. The sergeant who'd murdered Guns was leading.

"Back off," Mattim said in a harsh whisper. "Now, Ivan."

Ivan tapped his board several times. The normal hum returned to the engineering spaces.

"Very good, Captain." The admiral's unctuous voice issued from the speakers in engineering. "I knew you could make your man see the error of his ways. Sergeant Dumont, bring that officer to my quarters." And Mattim had to follow Ivan and his marine escort because he wasn't about to have another of his officers wheeled out of the admiral's quarters feet first. Meeting demands with counterdemands, screams with shouts, threats with veiled threats of his own, Mattim got Ivan back through the door alive. The admiral looked smug.

In his quarters, Mattim collapsed on his bunk, trembling. He'd been to zoos with poisonous reptiles and man-eating carnivores. He'd never been so up close and personal with one.

The comm beeped. Ivan was in tears. "They took her."

"Sandy?"

"Yes. While they had me, they took her to the brig."

"Let me take care of this."

"Please, Matt, she's my life."

"I'll get back to you." Mattim broke the connection. "XO, I need some help. Who has control of our brig?"

"We do," she answered.

"Maybe not anymore. Check with the chief master-at-arms."

"Wait one." Ding was back in only seconds. "The marines took charge of the brig about three minutes ago. Faced with assault rifles, our people bailed out fast. Hadn't had time to report. Damn it, he can't just take over sections of our ship!"

"He can and is." Mattim cut her off before she talked herself into the brig. "Okay, this is what we do. Sandy's in that brig. Ding, please call up the lead marine and offer her any assistance in making the brig secure and its occupants comfortable. Offer to have a couple of our people work under her people. Colin, I want our folks down there as witnesses to what happens in that brig. Sandy's only the first of us."

"Put our people under her marines?"

"Yes, Colin, our people. She's got to be shorthanded with this whole boat to patrol. If we put one or two nonthreatening old farts in there to be gofers and do the unarmed stuff, that's got to be a load off them. And I do mean old farts who know better than try to be heroes. No kids. Got that? No kids."

"Yes, sir. You are giving up the brig. We are to render full assistance to the marines in managing it." The XO said the words like they were poison.

Mattim didn't like it any better. "Yes, Colin. Anything to

get us through this without people dying." He hoped she noted his inclusive language. Not crew killed, but people.

There was a change in her voice when she said, "Understood."

Mattim made a quick and very unsatisfactory call to Ivan, then tried to settle back on his bunk. Sleep was impossible, but he had to get some rest. In the morning, he'd have to be sharp when he made a walk around. There had to be a way around Whitebred and his marines and his damn rocks.

Mary looked sharp as she made a walk-around of the guard posts before turning in. The crew was sullen as she passed them. There'd been no public announcement; still, you didn't keep the death of the gunnery officer a secret. Damn Dumont! He'd taken the admiral's bait, hook, line, and sinker. Stupid kid! And the admiral had played all of them like a damn piano. While she'd been trying to figure out how to react, he'd pushed Dumont over the edge. Pushed, hell. Dumont had jumped at the chance. And Mary couldn't let the sailors tear Dumont to pieces.

Now what? Her teams were stretched thin. The offer from the exec to keep a couple of hands around the brig was appreciated. Mary had rousted Cassie out of bed to take over the brig watch. She should be taking over soon.

"Captain." It was Cassie's voice.

"Yes, Lieutenant?"

"Brig is secure. Prisoner secure. For this you got me up?"

"You got two people from ship's company helping you?"

"Yeah, a middle-aged man and woman."

"Keep an eye on them."

Cassie snorted. "Hero types these two ain't, but understood."

"Rodrigo out."

Mary stepped carefully over the coaming of the bridge hatch. The bridge crew pointedly ignored her—only the XO nodded. Mary had assigned four marines to guard the admiral. The two male guards lounged in chairs outside the admiral's cabin, their guns at the ready. The two woman guards were nowhere to be seen.

The XO joined her. "Hope you don't mind us loaning your marines chairs. At two gees it gets a bit heavy on the feet."

Mary had glanced through the marine guard manual once. It was definite about *standing* guard duty. She hadn't noticed anything about high gees. "Thanks. I think."

The Navy type shrugged, then glanced around the bridge. "Tough situation. No need to make it any tougher on the poor working folks than necessary."

Obviously, this woman would never make it in management. "You know where my other two guards are?"

"Admiral said the women could stand their watch in his cabin." *More likely in his bed* hung unsaid.

Mary agreed; the admiral had been specific about two of his four guards being girls. "And the two helping out in the brig?"

"Captain suggested you could use a hand. We'll pick from the old and smart types. Captain doesn't want anybody killed."

"Thanks," Mary mumbled as she turned to go. So, Matt the merchant had no taste for blood. A virtue in a trader that had no place where they were, but Mary would use it.

Her last stop before hitting the rack was the brig. Cassie and two privates were monitoring the prisoner by video—a woman, an officer from the shoulder tabs.

"Why's she in?" Mary asked.

Cassie just raised her eyebrows. "One of Dumont's corporals marched her in. Don't know."

"She's the Jump Master," a middle-aged woman in blue Navy coveralls answered. "Wife of the chief engineer."

Mary stared at the ceiling for a moment, absorbing it all. Power loss. Chief engineer restores power; wife lands in the brig. That little admiral was playing hardball. Just how hard?

Mary checked her prisoner. The woman lay on the bunk, staring at the ceiling. "Cassie, enter into the brig log. I want to be called if there is any change in a prisoner's condition. All prisoners will be treated as guests and will leave here in as good a shape as they arrived. You got that?"

"You bet, boss. Loud and clear." Cassie grinned. "You hear that, guards? Pass that along verbally when you're relieved. You Navy types, too."

Mary took in a deep breath. She'd spent a night or three under hack. Mining company guards were picked for their heavy hands. She would have none of that on her watch. Mary yawned. Cassie quickly caught it.

"Girl, we're both too old for this shit," Mary said. "Get one of your sergeants to take over here. I'm headed for the rack. You too."

"Joyfully, Captain."

Mary was halfway to her quarters when something went thud in the mud her brain was turning into. *I said I didn't want any of the crew dead. The XO said* no people *dead. Was she quoting the captain? And did he mean that? No people! Well, Matt, does that include a billion enemy noncombatants?*

Mary undressed for bed, but kept her gear handy. It was already after midnight; she'd be back up at 0515. She needed some sleep. What she got was thoughts that wouldn't go away.

The admiral had told them quickly and bluntly what he wanted and the rewards they'd get in return. Just like at the mines, he'd say "frog jump" and they would. Mary rolled onto her side, tried to get comfortable at twice her normal weight—and rolled back over.

A billion people were going to die. She tried calling up the horrible visions of the hundreds she'd killed and imagined a million more for each one of them. Her mind balked. Since that first day, it had. Some part of her that cared about others had frozen over that day into icy stone. Marines she fought to keep alive. No one else mattered, any more than the waste runoff from the mines mattered.

Worker bees just did what they had to.

But I'm not a worker bee, Mary snapped at herself. *I'm an officer, just like Umboto.* She had sworn to defend humanity against all enemies, foreign and domestic. That had to mean something. The admiral said it meant a billion peaceful women and children dead. That couldn't be right.

Still, with Dumont in the admiral's pocket, could she stop him? Did Mattim really mean he wanted this thing ended with nobody dead? She had to talk to that guy. Maybe, just maybe, together they could figure out what was right and how to do it.

FOURTEEN

IMPECCABLY UNIFORMED, MAJOR Longknife, his bride, and his aide ate breakfast in the formal dinning room of the only grand hotel on Rostock. In the background, a live string quartet played softly. Despite the waiter's encouragement to try every pastry on the menu, they ordered plain food in small portions. As their meals arrived, a cheer went up from across the foyer.

"What is that?" Ray asked.

"I do not know, sir. There is a television in the coffee shop. I imagine further success on the war front has been announced. Should I find out?"

Captain Santiago lifted the briefcase from its place beside him, flipped it open, and called up the stored news feed. "I'll search on 'Wardhaven' first, sir." It was not a long search.

The President, in the red dress uniform of a field marshal, smiled confidently as he announced that Earth stooges were attempting to land on Wardhaven. "Our armies stand ready to show these cowards how real men fight. We will never surrender. We will crush their landings. We will collect the pathetic survivors and ship them to the outermost colonies where they can find out what real life is like. We will fight on to victory for us and our children. We fight for all humanity. We will be triumphant."

The watching crowd went wild cheering. Ray reached for the case and punched up the *Oasis*.

"Have you heard the news, Major?" her captain asked.

"One could not help but hear it. Captain, have the Earthie stooges formally asked for our surrender?" Ray used patriotic drivel to cover treason.

The captain coughed softly. "No, sir."

"Are their troopships moving into position to assault?"

The captain looked uncomfortable. "Our information is that they have no transports with them." Ray waited, calm as an officer must be when a subordinate is slow giving him the rest of an unpleasant message. "One ship, apparently the flag, has begun a dive toward the sun. It is picking up speed, sir. We do not know what course it will follow, or how long it will take it to acquire whatever energy it considers desirable."

Rita had been sipping from her water glass. It fell from her hands—shattering on the marble floor. "Thank you. I or my aide will talk with you after we brief the President."

"If you can possibly," the captain began slowly, "explain to the President the full military implications of the course of action the enemy is pursuing, sir."

"If the President affords me the opportunity"—Ray cut the naval officer off before one or both of them committed high treason for the records—"I will surely brief him to the fullest extent of my knowledge. Thank you, Captain. Out."

Ray sampled his oatmeal. At his leading, the others also nibbled at their meals while their waiter cleaned up the glass. Once alone, there was still nothing to say, nothing they could allow the inevitable mikes to hear. Meals were only half eaten when, by unspoken consent, they placed napkins on the table.

"The President awaits us," Ray said.

"Yes," both his wife and his aide agreed.

"Let's see what he takes from a tired old warrior's

words," Ray added as the two helped him from his chair. The hug Rita gave him as she settled him on his feet held love and loss, dedication and resolve in equal parts. He gave her a quick kiss; then, as he slowly marched to the elevator, he began the familiar process of turning flesh into cold, hard steel. He had done this many times before battle. The only difference today was the poor likelihood of the return to flesh and blood tomorrow.

Showered, shaved, and dressed, Mattim did a quick check of the bridge on his way to breakfast. The night had produced no more surprises. They would round the sun in another eighteen hours. If he didn't come up with something before three gees put everyone at high-gee stations and only able to talk on battle net, one billion women, children, and men would die.

As usual, Mattim took one meal a day with the crew. He chose breakfast today. The marines occupied a table in one corner of the mess. Ship's company were leaving it a wide berth. Mattim considered joining the marines, trying to build some sort of bridge. Sergeant Dumont, who'd pulled the trigger on Guns, sat at the head of the marine table.

Mattim headed for a table full of chiefs. They started to rise; he waved them down. "Relax, it's chow time."

"Kind of hard relaxing, sir," Chief Aso muttered as he sat. Mattim raised a questioning eyebrow to the chief who'd served for years on the *Maggie D* and now was a turret captain. "Don't like losing a good officer, Captain." Aso glanced around the table; all eyes were on Mattim, nodding agreement. "What we gonna do?"

Mattim's empty stomach lurched. *Why didn't I eat in the wardroom? No, in my cabin.* He took a deep breath. "Chief, you'll do what you've always done. Follow my orders."

For a long moment, Aso and the other chiefs, most of them regular Navy, stared back. Several of them sucked on their lips as if searching for words. Aso finally spoke.

"Yes, sir, I reckon we will. And you never gave us a bad one, not even when you was just a kid officer. I'll trust you, sir. Just don't forget to trust us." Mattim glanced at the camera in the corner of the mess deck; Aso did too. "Take care, sir. And put some chow in ya. You're getting puny."

That seemed to lighten things up. Mattim took a forkful of pancakes. As usual, they were great. Before he could say anything, laughter came from the marines' table. The sergeant Mattim had come to hate glanced around, measuring the eating sailors like a farmer might vats of growing protein. Their eyes locked. As the stare lengthened, a grin slowly spread across the marine's face. *I'm a killer. You want to be next?* it said.

I command, you obey was Mattim's response. But that bastard wasn't in his command. He did not have to obey the captain of the ship he rode. Mattim looked away, his appetite gone. He stood, mad at himself for flinching, unwilling to give the sergeant the pleasure of a second glance.

"Captain, I'll take care of your chow," Aso offered. With no backward glance, Mattim marched out of his own ship's mess. Inside anger raged. At the sergeant, and at himself for letting the anger loose again. Where was that damn Mary the miner who's really an iron-assed marine officer?

Mary slept straight through her alarm; it had been a long while since that happened. She quickly dressed and rushed for the wardroom. With luck, she'd find the captain at breakfast. There had to be somewhere the two of them could talk. Was he out to save his crew or get around their orders? She was none too sure how she'd handle the latter, but until she talked with him, there was no way of knowing. The captain was not in the wardroom, and the XO was just leaving. Mary stepped aside as the two passed. "Have you seen the captain?" she asked softly.

"No," the woman answered, "but he often does a morning

walk-around when we're not actually being shot at. He could be anywhere. Shall I mention you'd like to see him when I do?"

"No," Mary lied. "There's just something in the books about paying your respects when you report on board. I thought maybe I should, but this cruise doesn't look like it's normal."

"Yes," the exec agreed softly. "He's a good man; I hope you two meet." Which told Mary something—and nothing—all at the same time. Mary wolfed down breakfast and went hunting for Lek. Just how much privacy could she get in this fishbowl?

The hotel phone was blinking when Ray returned to their rooms. Rita quickly activated it. "I regret that the President's schedule has to be adjusted," a fresh-faced young colonel told them from a recorded message. "Your briefing has been delayed until tomorrow afternoon."

"Call him back," Ray ordered.

Rita messed with the comm unit. "It's not a flash message, and he left no return number."

"So we cool our heels," Santiago growled.

"Another day for us." His wife smiled at Ray.

"But how many days for . . . ?" Ray left the sentence hanging. In tears, Rita ran for the bathroom.

Mattim prowled his ship. His crew went about their duties, heads down, hands busy. No one looked up as he passed, no chief invited him over to share a word with his work party. Mattim could hardly believe this was the same bunch that had managed a smile and a laugh when home was on the other side of the galaxy. But then they'd known the mess they were in and had been pulling together to fix it. Now, he wasn't telling them anything and they all knew the mess. None of them knew how to get out.

But a few had to try. Returning to the bridge before noon to relieve the exec for lunch, Mattim had to stand aside as the chief master-at-arms led four away in handcuffs, includ-

ing the black belt Zappa who'd been critical to their jumping back home.

She looked him straight in the eye. "Well, somebody had
to do something," she snapped.

"Move along, miss." The chief gently urged her.

"What happened?" Mattim asked.

"Best talk to the exec, sir," suggested the second-class
coming up the rear. No marines were in sight.

"Captain on the bridge," the JOOD announced as Mattim
crossed the coaming.

"Commander, I'll take the conn and relieve you for
lunch."

"I stand relieved, Captain," Ding said, standing and heading for him.

He waited until she was close. "What was that all about?"

She shrugged. "A couple of the crew decided they could
talk the admiral into revising his strategy. They didn't get
much past the hatch, and our guards were able to take care
of them."

"Even the little middie, black belt and all?"

Ding shrugged. "She hadn't thought it through. They
couldn't go around me, and they"—a quick nod toward the
marines—"would have had to shoot me in the back. Brilliant
scientist, but I don't know what she was thinking with
today."

Mattim considered the fiasco. "Have the chief post security in the passageway so we can stop our problems before
they get here. Can't always trust the assault rifles to think
twice. Now go get some chow. Have a plate sent up here for
me."

The exec hesitated. "Ran into the commander of the marine detachment at breakfast. She wanted to know where
you were so she could pay her official visit. Told her to look
for you in your walk-around. Did you see her?"

"No."

Ding gnawed her lower lip for a second. "She seems like
good people to me."

What did Ding mean by that? With all the surveillance,

and nobody free to say what they meant, communications was going to hell. Working together, they'd beaten the odds and brought themselves back from nowhere. Now, locked in their own skulls, smart people like the middie were making stupid mistakes. *Damn!*

He checked to see that the four made it to the brig safely. Though a plate soon arrived from the wardroom, it was cold by the time he got to it. The admiral had found out. He wanted all four shot on live vid with all hands watching. Again, Mattim went through the cajoling and pleading, promising and bowing. If four lives hadn't depended on it, he would have told the admiral to go stuff himself. Mattim had the feeling the four didn't matter to the admiral. He just wanted to rub Mattim's face in how powerless he was. Mattim would have gladly stipulated to all of the above and got on with his day. Instead he turned in another stellar performance . . . and ate a cold lunch.

There was little to report to Ding after lunch. Course was steady for the sun. "You want to keep up your walks, sir?"

"I think better on my feet." *It hurts less on the prowl.*

"Had lunch with the commander of the marine detachment," the exec said casually.

Mattim stiffened in his chair, but tried to change nothing in his appearance. *Missed her again!* "Oh."

"Quite a woman. We swapped war stories. The last three months have been hell for them. It's a different kind of war on the ground. She seemed interested in that side trip we took. Kind of surprised she knew about it. Once things calm down, she wants to see my logs." Ding's voice was low, no inflections . . . and Mattim hardly breathed.

So Mary the miner hadn't forgotten. *If we just had ten minutes.* "What's she doing?"

"Making the rounds of her guard posts. Stopped by the bridge twice this morning," Ding said helpfully.

"And I'd better drop down to engineering, see how Ivan's taking things."

"I'll hold the fort. It's not as if we're going anyplace."

Mattim snorted. Life had reached a new low when diving

into a sun at two gees was going no place. Since a billion deaths waited at the other end, maybe they weren't.

He wanted to check the brig and engineering. He headed for Ivan first. Ivan could be depressing on his best days. It took Sandy's bubble to keep him smiling. There was no Sandy and no smile today. Mattim did his best to keep him at his job and out of mischief. Ivan took almost as much cajoling as the admiral. Mattim was an hour later getting to the brig.

"I guess we kind of blew it, sir." The young middie talked to her hands.

"You did that."

"But, sir . . ."

"No buts about it." Mattim was not going to say anything here in the brig that might land him in it. "You violated orders. You will spend the rest of this cruise here, and you will not cause either the security guards or the marines any trouble."

She glanced up, an innocent grin on her face, "I've offered to show them some of my best throws."

"Stay put. Behave."

"That's what the marine officer said, too."

"What marine officer?"

"The woman, two silver bars. Lieutenant?"

"Captain in the marines," Mattim corrected.

"Oh, right. She was in here an hour ago. Said behave and don't cause any more trouble." The middie reached over, tried to rattle very solid bars. "I guess we will."

"Good. I'll drop by to make sure." He turned to go.

"Captain, they're having ice cream tonight. Are we getting bread and water?"

Mattim glanced at the marines. An older marine corporal was in charge. She shrugged. "We got no orders."

A young man and a matronly woman had the Navy watch. "I've told the mess deck to make them trays," she said. "If you don't mind, I'll send Ahmadi to get it before the ice cream melts."

"Do it. When you marines due for relief?" Mattim asked.

"Not for a while, sir," the corporal answered.

"Ahmadi, bring enough ice cream for all of you. Tell Hassan I said so." The marines were smiling when he left. With luck, they'd find it harder to shoot sailors, prisoners or no.

Half an hour later, Mattim came across a different kind of marine. Bald except for a fringe of gray, the old fellow wore warrant bars. Alone, he stood on a ladder hanging a new camera to cover an arc of passageway. Now that the passageways were radials, not straight, it took four or five cameras to cover one corridor. That had to leave lots of dead space for the admiral's spying. *Damn! Why didn't I think of that sooner?*

Because conspiracy ain't part of my average day. "Old-timer, can I get a work party to help you?" Mattim asked.

"Thanks, sonny," the fellow said, grinning, "but I work best alone. Besides, the admiral wants us marines to do this." He squinted at Mattim's shoulder tabs and his eyes widened, "Captain, is it now?"

"Yeah," Mattim said. "I'm skipper of this lash-up."

"Sorry about the mess." The guy waved a hand, screwdriver still in it, at the walls. Mattim spotted another camera blending smoothly into the wall. Hardly a mess, unless he meant the general situation.

"They live yet?"

"Not 'til I activate 'em."

Mattim sidled around until he was in the visual dead space. "I been trying to say hi to your boss woman. She about?"

"Seen her twice today. Like you, she keeps moving on."

"If you see her, tell her I said hi."

"Will do that." The old guy saluted, screwdriver still in hand. Mattim headed for the magazine to check on his rocks.

Like a robot in a do loop, Mary made rounds, one post after another. She also kept missing Mattim the merchant. *Do I really want to talk to that dude?*

Truth was, she didn't know. There were three people in charge on this ship—the admiral, the captain, and her. Any two of them could cause or stop the death of a billion people. Mary was new to this officer business and didn't much care for the responsibility. But, so long as she missed the captain, the admiral stayed ahead on points. Mary walked slowly around an empty passageway. Lek had yet to put this one on camera. Out of sight of anyone, she stopped, leaned her forehead against the cool of the wall, and just stood there. Thoughts tumbled into her head. Like a trained gunner, she popped each one of them. *Don't think. Don't feel. Just be.*

She stood there for a good thirty seconds in peace.

"Oh, sorry, Mary. I'll come back later."

She turned to find Lek, his ladder and toolbox in hand. "Got a problem, old friend?" Why had she called him that?

He smiled, a sardonic one that wiggled all over his face. "You're standing where I need to put up a camera."

"Oh, sorry." She started to move off.

"Got a minute, Mary?"

"I guess." That wasn't the way a marine captain talked. But it was the way she'd talked to Lek since she was just a kid and he'd pulled her out of the way of a flood of acid that would have dissolved her down to her toenails.

"Boat's captain says hi. I think he'd like to talk to you."

"I imagine he would." She glanced around the corridor. "Is this dead space?"

"Dead as the crew of the *Flying Dutchman*. But it's a waste of my time covering them all. Any good observation program watches who goes into one and when they come out. They stay in too long, you got an anomaly. They stay in too many too long and you got yourself a real live skunk. It's a waste me doing this."

"Then why you doing it?" Mary asked.

" 'Cause there ain't nothing good I want to do for the bastard we're working for."

"The admiral."

"Yeah."

"Dumont likes him."

"Dumont's a kid and don't know better. Mary, how many times you been told things will be different this time, extra overtime for just a few more weeks and then . . . what do they promise us? Don't matter. Management don't deliver."

"You don't trust the admiral."

"Bad instruments don't give good data. The boy is bad. Nothing good's gonna come of him."

"Would you stop him?"

"How?" Lek shrugged.

Mary heaved a sigh. "That's the problem. How?"

"I don't know, Mary, but you're a good girl, smart too. Let me show you something." He handed her a disk not much bigger than a wrist comm unit. "Push that button, and cameras in line-of-sight go off-line for two, three minutes. I've used it a dozen times and the admiral hasn't bitched. Must put it down to cheap Navy shit."

She flipped it over; there was nothing to see. When she glanced up, Lek was studying a video display. "Captain just left the brig. If you're gonna talk to him, you better do it soon. We're an hour out from the sun doing its swing thing. Now, if you'll excuse me, I got a useless camera to install." Without looking back, he was gone.

Mary never remembered dropping down three decks, she just did. Even if they did bump into each other, he might have nothing to say. She didn't have to tell him about Lek's hole card. Even if she let him talk, she didn't have to agree. After all, the admiral was the admiral, and he did talk like he knew what he was doing. Mary swung down a ladder and picked up the pace. It wasn't fair to let a billion people die just because she didn't make a decision, didn't listen to the one man who might speak for them. A billion people deserved listening to—even if they were the enemy.

Ray smiled as Rita slipped naked into bed beside him. But the assault she began on him ended in tears. He held her close as she cried. When she went to wash away the tears, he was still awake. "Tomorrow, after I brief the President, things will be better for Wardhaven." There were mikes in the room. No video, but what they said was recorded.

Rita kicked the bathroom door closed. She was a long time coming back to bed.

Mattim sauntered slowly down the passageway. He'd bet everything on talking to Mary, and for seventeen hours he hadn't found her—*one* person on *his* ship. His weight tugged at him; the sun must be accelerating them up toward 2.5 gees. It was time to settle into high-gee couches. Even if he found her, there was no time left to negotiate. Sixty minutes wasn't enough for a gambit, proposal, cooling-off period, and closing. No time.

The marine CO marched around the curve, saluting as she approached. He came out of his depressing slouch to return her salute. "I understand you've been looking for me," she said.

"Uh, yeah, right," Mattim stuttered. "I wanted to welcome you aboard."

"Sorry about your officer. My sergeant was just following the admiral's orders." She came to a stop not a foot from him, face in his face.

"Yeah, I know. We're all just following orders. Makes for a good epitaph."

"It could end the war real quick. My people have had enough of being targets for these damn colonials."

Mattim rocked back on his heels at the sheer force she put into those words. *Have I ever felt that strong about anything?*

Yes, damn it. I want this war over, too. So we stand here and see who can shout "I want out of the war" the loudest. "How long you studied war?" he asked. That took her aback.

"Five, six months. And you?" she spat.

"Same six months. But Guns spent his entire life, forty years, studying it. My exec is a lifer too. Guns died saying this was no way to end a war. Ding—you had lunch with her—is just as sure. How long's the admiral studied war?"

"I cut the cameras and mikes out halfway through that spiel, before you got us shot." Mary held up a small plastic disk. "We got three minutes. Talk to me, Mattim the merchant. What are you selling? Admiral's offering a wide-open ticket for the rest of my life. What's in your bag?"

"A billion people who won't haunt your dreams."

"No good. Us marines already got more than we can sleep with, a billion more won't matter. Besides, they're enemy. To my folks, they're just targets waiting to die. You got to do better, Navy."

Time, Mattim needed time. But it was all gone. He rummaged in his brain for another argument. "They ain't after your blood yet. You massacre them, their ghosts'll be screaming for you to the day you die and beyond. You kill one planet, and ninety-nine others will come howling after you. You think this war has been bad, wait 'til the gloves come off. We've got a few like Guns and Ding who've studied war for twenty, forty years. The colonials got folks that have been fighting for fifty years."

"We got tech and industry. They ain't," Mary snapped.

"How long we gonna keep it when they start slipping ships through jump points at high speeds? It only takes a few minutes to launch relativity bombs. Sirius, Vega, Earth."

"That's suicide."

"Yes, and after we kill a billion people, you think everyone will stay rational." Mary didn't answer that one; Mattim pressed on. "You trust Whitebred to remember you if he makes it big?"

Mary gave him a curt head-shake. "Not five minutes unless we can make him."

"So for a promise from a guy you can't trust, you want to do something everyone who should know better says will only make things a hell of a lot worse. Mary, this is a no-brainer."

Now Mary's shake of the head was slow and sad. "Not for desperate people who want it to work. Matt, I got people behind me with loaded guns who came into this war with nothing. Whitebred may sound like an idiot to you, but to them, he's a golden skyhook. Those people have kept me alive, and I won't kill them just because you think they're wrong. No matter how this comes out, marine don't kill marine."

"Given," Mattim shot back. "Marines don't kill marines or Navy or the other way around. No matter what happens, we bring this crew out alive."

Mary chuckled. "I thought you wanted to save a billion."

"So I start small and work up." Mattim paused, to swallow his elation at getting this far and to figure out what his next step was. "You and I have an agreement. Now it looks to me like it's up to our crews. None of mine will fight for the admiral. Think you can work your marines around?"

"I'll have to talk to them."

"We don't have much time before we're in high gee beds. After that, we're all rigged for sound. Admiral is monitoring anything that goes over the net."

Mary laughed. "Admiral don't know Lek."

"The old guy?"

"Right. For years Lek's been getting us private channels the mine bosses didn't know about. Trust me, we can talk without being listened to."

"Deal, miner." Mattim offered his hand.

"Deal, merchant." She took it firmly and shook. Lek's gadget beeped. The cameras were back up.

Mary checked two guard posts, but her mind was elsewhere. No marines die. No more sailors die. It came down to trust. Whom did she trust, Whitebred or the man she'd shared drinks and a night with? She remembered Mattim talking about bringing his ship back from halfway across the galaxy. He knew how to lead people, help them pull together. He was no liar.

Whitebred was a lot of noise. Most managers were. Mary

would trust her instincts, and they said trust Mattim. Mary "happened into" Lek. "Dead space?"

"Still," he said.

"How's the net rigged for spare channels? We'll be in high-gee carts in an hour. Can the boss man listen in when you fart?"

Lek looked hurt. "Mary, you've always been kind enough not to notice. I'm hurt. We're covered."

"Got a spare line for some Navy types?"

"Figured you'd want them. Yep."

The shipwide address system crackled to life. "High gees in thirty minutes. Prepare for high-gee running in half an hour."

Lek yanked a half-installed camera from the wall. "Glad that's over. Now we do something for real." Mary hoped he was right. What if Dumont and his kids wouldn't get behind her? Would he run to the admiral, shoot her? She'd fought to save marines. Could she fight for navy and colonials, too?

"Captain, this is the admiral." The audio cut into her thoughts.

She jumped. "Yessir."

"This high-gee thing. I hope that doesn't mean you'll be closing down the guard posts. Sailors can still move about. I want your marines on alert for anything, anytime."

"Yessir," Mary answered, trying to figure out how to say no. She needed a face-to-face talk. With her marines scattered, that wasn't going to happen. Still, now was no time to tell the admiral no. "I'll keep guards at all posts. Anything else, sir?"

There was a pause. "Add another two men to my guard post." A longer pause. "And double the guard along the bomb accelerator." Mary waited. "Keep your eyes peeled. Don't trust anyone. And pull the marines out of the brig. They're getting too friendly with those damn sailors."

"Yessir."

"Good, Captain, good. You'll go far with me."

Mary hoped not too far.

• • •

Ward Star gave them a rough ride as it slung them toward the second planet of the system. The gee monitor on Mattim's chair bounced between three and six gees for the better part of an hour. Once the ship was steady on course at 3.8 gees, Mattim verified the damage was acceptable. Then he punched his mike.

"This is the captain. The *Sheffield*'s a good ship and you're a great crew. Let's call it a day. Set minimum watches and the rest, sleep if you can manage." He turned his gee cart to face Ding. "Exec, you have the conn. As soon as you can rustle up a replacement, hit the rack yourself. Tomorrow will be another busy day." Just how busy, Mary the marine would decide.

Ding answered with a "Will do, sir" that could fit most anything. Mattim motored off the bridge, his cart hardly slowing as it high-stepped over the hatch coaming. He had the passageway to himself . . . most of his crew would sleep at their posts.

His room was a shambles. The desk had sheared away from the wall. "Bet the bolts came from the lowest bidder." Mattim didn't laugh, not at three-point-something of his normal weight. His comm link lay scattered on the deck, still working, but monitor and camera facedown. "Off," he ordered. He'd hoped the room might provide some extra privacy. He hadn't expected this much. He activated his cart mike.

"Bridge, captain here. I'm in my cabin. My desk collapsed. We'll worry about it later. Call me on my cart if you need me." Mattim rigged the cart as a bed and settled in to see how well he'd sleep. Just as he got comfortable, the comm beeped.

"Merchant, do not reply." Mary's voice poured quickly into his ear. "When you want to talk freely, activate channel Lek twenty-three. My crew is staying at guard posts. We'll get no chance to talk. Any suggestions that could get all of us together in quarters would be gratefully appreciated. Out." Just what Mattim needed—another puzzle to unravel when he needed sleep. He stared at the overhead, trying to order the various parts of his problem. They kept cascading in upon themselves. He hadn't gotten much sleep when the comm buzzed six hours later.

FIFTEEN

NEXT MORNING, RAY ordered breakfast in their room; he would not talk to a recording today. Breakfast was half eaten when the room's comm link buzzed. It rang only once, then began recording a message. Ray interrupted the young colonel. "Another delay?"

"The President was up until very early this morning. His afternoon briefing is only for the most urgent, sir. As a field commander, you understand, sir. Now, if you will excuse me . . ."

"Colonel, I am from Wardhaven. Are there many issues on the President's plate as pressing as the situation at Wardhaven?"

The young man seemed surprised; he studied something out of sight. "Oh, you *are* from Wardhaven; an army type, though. I will advise my superiors. I must ring off now, sir." And he did.

"An *army* type." Santiago exploded from his chair and began storming around the room. "They are inviting the Earth to invade Wardhaven and have no time for an *army* type."

"Enough, Captain. Sit down." Actually, Ray would have loved the release of pacing. Deprived of it, it was mean of him to deny the captain that release. Still, he needed some semblance of tranquility to think. Santiago subsided into an easy chair. Rita began rubbing Ray's back. He found himself relaxing, almost against his will. "I suspect," he muttered, "that we will hear nothing more from that colonel today."

"The President must feel he has the situation well in hand," Rita mused without slowing her ministrations.

"So he's staying up to the small hours?" Santiago growled.

"You and I have been there. Check, double-check, and check again. We did it with our first platoon, and we did it with the brigade. What we checked was different, the long hours were not. Our President does a thorough job." Spoken loyally for the mikes.

"Ray, you are going swimming," Rita announced. "If necessary, I will drag you down to the hotel pool and throw you in. You need exercise."

Santiago jumped to his feet. "With willing help, Admiral."

"Pulling rank on me again, wife?" They laughed. It was a good day not to die.

Mattim wouldn't mind dying today, if he could just take that bastard with him. One glance at the changing of the guard outside the admiral's quarters showed what a waste any try would be. There were now five marines outside. Only the prettiest woman was invited in. Only she came in and out, and then only to get meals. Apparently even Whitebred and Stuart gave up their fun and games at three gees. No, Mattim could do something stupid like the middie, or he could wait for the right moment.

He rolled over to the helmswoman. The slingshot around Ward Two would be late tonight. A day or so after that and they'd be in place to start throwing rocks. *So, when do we stop the bastard?* Mattim was still looking.

"Helm, how close do we get in our pass?" Ding asked.

"Fifty kilometers, ma'am."

"Does it have an atmosphere?"

"Carbon dioxide," Mattim answered, "and lots of other crud. Lousy with storms last time I passed it. And I was a lot farther away than fifty klicks. Plan for another bumpy ride."

"Right, Captain. Our sun pass broke four carts loose. None were at battle station lock-downs. Two were marines. Captain, I recommend all personnel go into lock-down an hour before our close encounter with Ward Two."

"Please advise the marines." Mattim kept his voice even.

The admiral interrupted thirty seconds into the call. "I want all guard posts manned."

"Sir, I respectfully recommend against that." Ding stayed Navy formal. "Four carts failed. We got no chance to do maintenance. I expect a much higher failure rate this time."

"Sir," Mary cut in, "I have one marine in sick bay and another one who's just plain lucky. I only had fifty to start with, sir. I can't afford to lose any more."

"Sir," Mattim added, "everyone will be locked down at battle stations. We have cameras scattered about the ship. They can be put in surveillance mode." *As if you didn't know.* "Anybody moves off station, you'll know."

"You will keep the guards at my quarters."

Mattim knew he should grab the compromise and run, but bulldozing Whitebred felt too good. "Sir, there are no lock-downs outside your quarters. At three-plus gees, I can't have them installed. Here, on the bridge, we'll be juggling a very high-risk encounter. We can't have a cart go careening around."

Whitebred sputtered on net, apparently at a loss for words. Mary was gentle when she spoke. "You've had several marines in your quarters, sir. That looks like a pretty solid bulkhead between it and the bridge. I could move your guards inside."

"Do it. Admiral Whitebred out," he snapped.

Ding continued as if there had been no interruption. "Your bunk space has lock-downs, Captain Rodrigo. I'll have a work party help your troops lock their carts. Would you like them standing by in case anything comes loose?"

"That won't be necessary, Commander. I suspect my troops will sleep through the whole thing."

"I hope mine do too. Exec out."

"Glad that's over," Ding sighed. "Now, how much ice do we have left on this boat's snout? Damage control, exec here."

Mattim left her to her duties. Like a good captain, he motored from station to station, checking and double-checking. But his mind was elsewhere. *If the marines go with me, the bombing is off. And if they don't?* That was Mattim's nightmare. Mary sounded none too sure her marines would back her. If they didn't, Mattim wasn't done. Marines were marines; they rode in ships they didn't operate. If it came down to it, would any of them know whether a sailor was fixing a problem—or making one? Then again, a five-thousand-pound rock loose at three gees was not something captains wanted. How do you bust a ship so it can't throw rocks—and not kill anyone?

Mattim spent what spare time he had looking for just that spot as he prepared to sling shot around Ward Two. He'd studied everything and was going over the accelerator for the fourth time when it kicked him in the face. For the first time in a long while, he smiled.

For the first time since coming aboard this tub, Mary had most of her marines present. The six guarding the admiral were a mixed bag. Three were old miners who thought like her. The other three would follow Dumont through hell. The Navy work party was done and gone; her troops were locked down, some already nodding off. She glanced at Lek. "Now," she said.

Only one camera covered the room. With a soft pop it came off the wall, hanging by its cabling. In a few seconds, those wires gave way; the tiny spy shattered as it hit the deck.

"Listen up, folks," Mary announced. "We got a problem. In case you didn't catch it on the grapevine, let me fill you in on this mission, and what's in it for you." And she did.

Their reaction held no surprise. The billion deaths drew a shocked recoil from most of her miners. Dumont and crew shrugged it off. The promised reward got cheers from his crew—scowls from the miners. *Had any fighting team ever been so split?*

"So, why we talking, old lady?" Dumont hadn't used that crack in a while. "Pop a batch of colonials, end the war, and make a friend in high places. All fun and games by me!" It was to most of his youngsters.

Cassie almost came out of her gee-cart. "Didn't you hear her? Kill a billion people. A billion! God forgive us for even listening to the idea. We've got to stop him."

"Your God never done nothing for me," Dumont snorted. "If He's so all-fired against killing, where was he when Blacky or Amy or Har or any of us got popped? He got a special place in His heart for them colonials dirtside, He can play catch."

Cassie, the only religious one in the troop, turned pale. "Let me take this," Mary said softly. Slowly, she went over what she and Mattim had shared. The miners had no trouble agreeing that any promise from Whitebred wasn't worth the air he used to say it. The youngsters, however, bought his line.

"He forget us, we cut him up good" came from somewhere in the back. For the next minute, the youngsters competed coming up with nastier ways to remind a forgetful Whitebred of his old friends. Mary let it roll, then turned to Lek.

"What you think?"

"He wins this war by killing a billion people, there's gonna be a lot of eager folks that want his hide. Powers that be'll wrap him in a wall of security sunshine can't get through without a retina scan and strip-search. Take it from an old cracker and hacker. He don't want to see you again. He don't."

That quieted the kids.

"What worries me is whether this stunt will end the war," Mary said slowly. "I've been up to my eyeballs in war for six months. I don't want no more of it. You been there with me. Would this scare the shit and surrender out of you, or make you mad enough to never quit fighting?"

"Like we was when Blacky and Amy got popped" came a quiet voice from behind Dumont.

"I don't think this admiral's spent any more time in uniform than us. You think he really knows what them colonials will do?"

Dumont was uncomfortable with that one. "I don't know how long he's been Navy. Who knows how good he is? But he's got us here, and the colonials by the balls."

"Guy don't talk much about Navy stuff," one of the girls drawled. "He's all the time bragging. All of it's business."

"He talks when he's screwing you" came from the back.

"All you guys brag when you're screwing," she snapped back, "and you all a bunch of liars."

Mary couldn't afford to lose them to another catcalling contest. "Du, Whitebred's as green as we are. He's guessing. That old guy that went up against him. He was forty years Navy. Lek here's been in the mines for forty years. If he says it can be done, you can bet on it. If he says it's a bad idea, I want out of the way." A chorus of "Me too" and "You bet" backed her up.

"Well, Whitebred didn't exactly give me time to play five questions with the old fart. Boss man said joke him, I did the joke." Dumont was defending himself, no longer Whitebred.

Mary tried one more slice. "Dumont, there's a billion faceless people, and rocks are cheap, and people die real quick under them. Once we do it, who's gonna do it next? I left some friends behind on Pitt's Hope. How long before some crew with a ship full of rocks is looking down on them as a bunch of faceless enemies? You must have left some people you care about."

"Only person I care about is me" came from the back. This time nobody echoed him.

"Mary," Dumont said slowly, "the only folks I care about are right here. A mom or a dad are things other people got, not me. Mary, you could be right, but then again, you could be dead wrong. This is the one chance anybody's ever handed me in my life. I can't piss it away. Maybe Whitebred's like everybody else and can't be trusted. But maybe he can. I got to try." His voice went loud. "We got to try."

"Yes!" hissed from a dozen lips.

"You gonna turn me in to the admiral?" Mary asked. "Shoot me for him?"

"No! No way, Mary. You may be an old lady, but you're us. Gang don't turn in a sister. Marines don't shoot marines."

That got an enthusiastic response from Dumont's choir.

Mary weighed what Dumont had given her. Marines don't kill marines. Good start. But half the platoon wants done what the other half wants stopped! *How do I make everyone happy this time?* Guess this is what the corps calls a leadership challenge. *How do I lead troops in both directions?*

Mary spoke slowly. "Okay, Du, here's where you and your kids get to show us how good you are. The miners are going to try to stop the bombing. You catch one of them out of line, I take them off the duty roster and lock 'em down here. Admiral don't have to know why. Same for Navy types. Turn them in to me and I'll see they get put under hack."

Dumont looked around. There were a lot of smiles from his kids. "Mary, we been joking with the man's stuff on the streets for years and none of got caught. We'll spot you first try."

"I don't think you will, but we'll know tomorrow."

"Okay. Mary, this has got to be even up. Half the admiral's guards are from my side, and we shoot to keep him safe. I want most of the guards on the magazine and the launcher to be my people. Deal?"

"Deal," Mary said.

Her comm link beeped. Everyone in the room quit breathing. Mary let it ring. On the third, she slapped the key. "This better be fucking good," she growled sleepily, "'cause he was the best dream I've had in months."

There was a long pause. "Ah, Captain, the camera is out in your bunk room," the admiral said slowly. "I just wondered if anything was wrong."

"Damn thing fell off the wall a while back when we hit a bump. We were all half asleep. Damn near shot it to pieces. If you want, Admiral, I'll leave my mike open and you can listen to us snore," Mary added helpfully.

"No! Not necessary." Whitebred tumbled over his words. "Everything's okay. Go back to sleep." His line died.

"You want that for a friend," Lek observed dryly.

"Never had a suit for a friend. Don't know what they're good for," Dumont answered slowly.

"A billion dead people," Cassie snapped. Mary shot her a glance. *They can't hear you on that one, old girl. We got what we want. Don't push.*

"Captain"—Thor breathed a sigh of relief—"you ask me to do that again and I swear, I'll get out and walk home." The bridge crew laughed; they'd done good. *Sheffield*'s nose ice was down to millimeters. Engineering had red-lined the engines for the last hour, pushing them toward the planet they'd missed by a fraction of a heartbeat. Dozens of people could have ended the mission with one slip-up. No one was suicidal.

"We've done great, folks, so let's get some sleep. Tomorrow will be another busy day." *We kill a billion people, or we don't. No ties allowed.*

As he entered his quarters, his chair beeped. "Kids have not bought in. Consider all young marines hostile. However, the admiral is out of the loop. If one of your people is tagged, you must take her off the watch. Call me if you want more info."

So, no more people get killed. Some marines were friendly, some were not, and Mary hadn't had time to give him a program. For what he had in mind, he didn't need one. He used channel Lek 23 to call Chief Aso.

"Chief, we've got an oversight here. Bomb and loader were all designed for twelve gees—assuming a five hundred pound bomb. We got five *thousand* pounders, and at three gees we're in trouble. We reinforced the magazine, but I'm not satisfied with the work on the loader and the bomb thrower. You got a welder you can trust in some heavy work?"

"Dan from the *Maggie* signed over. What you got in mind, Skipper?"

Mattim told him. The chief beamed.

The phone in their room rang as Ray finished his oatmeal. Rita tapped the speaker phone. It was not the colonel. A major general beamed at them. "Major, you are included in today's briefing. It will begin at thirteen hundred hours. Be early. The president is very interested in what kind of fight the forces of Wardhaven will give the Earth invaders. Please include a full table of organization and deployment."

"Yessir," Ray snapped.

"See you then." The general switched off.

"Today," Rita breathed.

"Captain." Ray was all mission. "We have the required data?"

"Yessir."

"Let us redo our briefing," Ray sighed as if it mattered.

"Yes, sir."

Rita went to lay out his uniform . . . and hers.

Mattim called damage control first thing next morning using Lek 23. "We've reinforced the magazine, and it's taken the pounding. You've done some work on the loader and accelerator. I'd like to reinforce that. A two-and-a-half-ton rock loose is a hell of a lot of damage to control."

"Yes, sir," Commander Gandhi said. "I'll put a work chit in right away with your priority on it."

"I'd rather my name wasn't on the chit."

"No problem, sir." Tina didn't bat an eyelash. "I like a skipper who lets his people do their job."

"Thank you, Commander. One more thing. Chief Aso handled my toughest welding problems on the old *Maggie*. I don't think gunnery would mind you pulling him off for this."

"What with all the high gees and bouncing the *Sheffield*'s been taking, I can use all the help I can get. Will do." If the commander was part of a conspiracy, she hadn't showed it. Nor had she missed a line.

"Have at it, Commander."

Mary worked up the Order of the Day for her detachment with Dumont at her elbow. She would assign one, he would assign one.

"I get command at the rock slinger," Dumont said.

"We share that one." Mary finished the list. "Assignments are for all day. Chow will be catch as catch can."

"We're gonna stop you."

Mary pursed her lips. "We'll see."

Mattim did a morning walk-about. The crew was nervous.

"Is it true, sir, our armor ain't no thicker than frost on the freezer?" Hassan asked as he gave Mattim two pancakes.

"Never saw any frost on your reefer, you old belly robber." Mattim dodged the question. As he made his rounds, matters did not improve. The *Sheffield* showed the effect of high gees and close encounters. The crew went about their duties slowly, as the three gees required, tackling the worst of it. No one met his eyes. He almost skipped the launcher bay, but he always stopped there, and today could not be an exception. Mary's cart was parked in the center of the bay, the young sergeant who'd shot Guns at her elbow. Around the bay, six teams of marines traveled in pairs, one young, the other showing a touch of gray, the beginning of a paunch. *So that's the way it is.*

"Got everything under control, Captain Rodrigo?"

"Yessir." She saluted. So did the sergeant. His eyes were hard, measuring, as if he expected Mattim to produce a wrench and unbolt the launcher. Mattim ignored him and turned his cart in a slow circle, taking in the work crews scattered around the bay. "Lot of maintenance will need doing when this is over. We can't wait to fix this."

"Your crew better be fixing what they touch," the sergeant growled. "I got marines looking over every shoulder."

"Good." Mattim smiled. "Better job you marines do, the less the admiral will worry. And I don't like worried bosses." Still smiling, Mattim ended his circle facing the sergeant. *Let the poor bastard figure out what's coming down. I ain't paid to teach.* Turning to leave, he had to fight to keep the smile on his face. A bunch of Navy security guards escorted in a work team. The tiny middie rolled up the rear. *How'd she get out of the brig? What's she doing here?*

She glanced his way . . . and winked.

"Captain." Mattim's comm snapped in the admiral's voice. "I want you in my quarters. Immediately."

"Yessir."

At exactly 0945, Ray was uniformed, bemedalled, and shined. The batteries in his walker were fresh, and the brief-case waited in Santiago's hands. The official limousine arrived on the dot.

The sergeant driver opened the door . . . and then closed it. "My orders are for two officers. Who is she?" Ray could not tell if the driver's disapproval was for Rita, or the tight cut of her uniform. Ray opened his mouth, but Rita got there first.

"I am Senior Pilot Officer Mrs. Longknife. I will accompany my husband. And while I may have to wait in the car with you, Sergeant, I've just got to be there to hear everything he has to say after he meets the President." The stiff officer segued into a gushing girl that got a smile out of even the sergeant.

"Well, I guess it's okay."

"Thank you, Sergeant," Ray said.

As the limo moved off, Ray leaned back in the plush seat. He was prepared to meet the President—and any other god who took an interest in today's hard duty.

"Captain, despite what you may think of me, I am not totally lacking in human qualities. I just sent a message to the rebel forces on Wardhaven inviting them to surrender. I informed them if they do not, we will destroy all major cities on Wardhaven no sooner than twelve hours from now."

"They've already refused to surrender," Mattim risked.

"And their government will refuse this one. They don't think we have the guts. That will be the last miscalculation they ever make. But"—Whitebred shared another smile with Stuart that made Mattim's skin crawl—"it will be upon their heads. I offered them peace. They spurned it."

"Some colonials may not see it that way," Mattim risked.

"There're always some who can't get with the program. Dinosaurs die, Captain. Pity, but they die. Dismissed."

Mattim returned to the bridge. "Anything, Ding?"

"Nothing I can't handle, sir."

Mattim rolled up beside her. "You're making me feel unneeded, Exec."

"I never noticed that captains were all that needed. Ship's holding up, but we'll need some major yard time when we're done."

"We all will." Mattim glanced at a new clock; counting down, it changed—eleven hours, forty-one minutes.

The limo passed several outlying checkpoints before rolling up to a block of stone buildings fit to house the temples of many gods—or one very big one. The driver brought them to a halt in the courtyard. A security guard in a midnight black uniform opened the door. He was backed up by a dozen more in fixed positions and armored vehicles. Everything from assault rifles to laser cannon covered them as they dismounted. Ray had faced these withering shows of disapproval before; he tried to look bored . . . and prayed Rita would not crumble.

She helped him from the car, then clung to him. He noted every guard—all males—paid far more attention to her than him. She stood tall to kiss him on the cheek. "I wanted you to meet our President with a smile on your lips. My husband, I am pregnant," she crowed. From the guards there was a cheer.

Rita blushed, and Ray felt a warmth in his cheeks. Life and death twisted in his belly—and his gut knotted. When Rita stepped away, he faced the captain of the guard.

"Congratulations, Major. May all wounded war veterans be as successful in their recovery as you."

"And may their brides be more modest in announcing their accomplishments." Ray frowned at his wife, but her smile was contagious. One grew on his face, and others on most of the guard detail.

A guard technician cleared his throat. "We seem to have a problem, Captain."

The guard captain immediately turned to look over the technician's shoulder as the man pointed to an elevated line on his screen. "Ammonia," the tech whispered.

His heart pounding, Ray tapped the metal walkers under his uniform trousers. "They're hell on my skin. Need an ointment. Rita, did you bring it?" She produced a tube from her purse.

The guard captain passed it to the tech. Together they studied their machine. "Identical," the technician said.

The captain handed the tube back to Rita. "I will advise the other guard posts. However, Major, I must see the inside of your briefcase." Santiago opened it and spun up the computer. As he was about to close it, the comm unit beeped.

"Major, this is the *Oasis*'s captain. We are in receipt of a message from Wardhaven."

"Make it quick, Skipper. I'm passing through security for the President's briefing."

"Excuse me, sir. The enemy flagship has transmitted an ultimatum. If the planet does not surrender unconditionally in twelve hours, they will bombard all major cities."

"When was this given?" Ray asked.

"One hour ago. The flag has swung around the sun and Pico and is now on course to Wardhaven at point-oh-three of the speed of light."

"That sounds fairly slow." The guard captain tossed the statement off.

"A five-hundred-pound bomb"—Rita spoke through gritted teeth—"will hit with the power of a quarter million tons of explosive."

"Oh." The guard captain was impressed.

The Navy captain ended his message with a plea. "Please, Major, explain our situation to the President. We cannot defend against this attack."

"I will do what I can do, Captain. Longknife out."

"Only a coward fights like that," the guard captain snapped. "Honorable men face each other on the field of battle."

"With artillery and tanks," Santiago drawled.

Ray studied the guard officer. His tunic was full of ribbons, none of them for combat. "Let us hurry. Maybe the President can spare a moment before the briefing." Ray had eleven hours to swap a planet's rendezvous with death for his own.

"Captain, follow me," Whitebred shouted, bolting from his quarters. "I want that man shot." Mattim followed, not knowing where they were going or who was to be shot.

The admiral gunned his gee cart at full power. Mattim had put miles on his and had trouble keeping up. When he pulled into the launcher bay, Whitebred was already shouting, "Sergeant, shoot that man. He doesn't belong here."

"What man?" Mary and Sergeant Dumont echoed.

"That man." The admiral struggled to raise his arm. At

three gees, all he succeeded in doing was a wave that covered half the work parties in the bay.

"Who, sir?" the sergeant asked again.

"See down the launcher path. There's a chief near two welders. He doesn't belong here. I want you to execute him, now. I want everybody to watch this."

"Sir," the sergeant said with just a hint of derision, "at this acccleration, I can't draw my pistol, much less aim it."

"Helmsman, slow the ship down," the admiral snapped.

"Helm," Mattim quickly cut in, "belay that order."

Whitebred whipped his cart around to face Mattim. "Is this mutiny? Sergeant, if he says yes, shoot him."

Eyebrows raised in question, the sergeant wheeled to face Mary. "Can we slow down and figure out what's happening here?" she asked.

"He countermanded my order," the admiral shouted.

"You can't give the helm vague orders like that," Mattim said slowly. "Do you want to slow acceleration, or actually slow the ship? That would involve flipping the ship and staying at three gees or higher to actually reduce the ship's speed."

Whitebred glanced at his shadow. Stuart gave a tiny but quick nod of agreement. "Oh," the admiral said. "Take us to one gee."

"Helm, this is the captain, I have the conn. Maintain course and take us smartly to one-gee acceleration. Have the bosun advise the crew. Wait one." Mattim turned to the admiral. "Will we be at one gee long enough for the crew to get cleaned up?"

"No. Just long enough to execute that man in cart G61." This time the admiral did manage to communicate that he wanted Chief Aso. Two marines tooled off to collect him.

"What's going on here?" The damage control officer arrived. "Captain, is there a problem in my spaces?"

"That man is in the gunnery division," Whitebred snapped. "He doesn't belong here. I want him shot. Somebody get a vid hookup here. Sergeant, as soon as the captain can get us to one gee, shoot that man."

"Yes, sir," the sergeant said with a lot less enthusiasm than he'd had with Guns.

The damage control officer rolled his cart right up to Whitebred. "Admiral, that man belongs here. I asked for him and got him assigned to my work parties. He's a damn good ship maintainer and I need him, what with the way we've been hotdogging around space. With our armor down to icing, all the gunnery department can do is sit around on their duffs. I got real work to do and I want that man doing it."

Whitebred grew dangerously quiet.

"You got a work order to support that?" Stuart asked.

"Yessir. Let me call it up. Just a sec. Here it is. I'll transmit it to your unit."

Stuart and Whitebred gave it a sour stare. "Got the commander's chop," Stuart observed. "Looks okay."

"I want to see what he was doing," Whitebred demanded.

"Yes sir. Right this way." Gandhi led off, the admiral right behind her. It was quite a parade. The welders knocked off as the damage control officer explained. "This launcher is stressed for six gees using a five-hundred-pound round. That translates to just one-point-two gees for the round we've got now. We're doing three gees."

"But it's been worked on before," Stuart pointed out.

"Yes, sir, in stages to give us the safety margins I wanted. First we rebuilt the magazines up to three gees for those new two and a half ton bullets, then upped the launcher to two gees. Then we redid the magazine to six gees where I wanted it. Now's the loaders turn. I do what I need when I need it. And I keep this ship undamaged, which is the best damage control you can ask for."

The admiral and his chief of staff studied the welders' work. Mattim held his breath. Aso and his work party had done a terrible job. The actual welds were as solid as they came. But the welding torches had cut a broad swath, taking the temper off of the main girders. Here and there were nicks. The weld might hold, but the girders would twist and bend in the middle.

They'd done what Mattim had asked. Would they die for it?

"This looks like lousy workmanship," Whitebred groused.

"Never saw anything like these on any of my ships." Stuart backed him up.

Mattim wondered what Stuart had done aboard ship. He didn't look like the type to get his hands dirty. Commander Gandhi didn't retreat an inch. "Ever rip a sack, sir? You don't run a single strip of tape up the tear, you take a couple of strips and spread them out, to spread the pressure. Same with welding," she lied with a straight face. "Slap some paint on that and it'll look as fancy as any ship you ever rode, Captain."

Whitebred still looked like he wanted someone shot. Mattim went for the closing. "Admiral, if you want, I can put the chief in the brig. If anything he's worked on breaks when we launch, you can decide what to do then."

"I really need the help," Gandhi mooned.

"Not from gunnery," the admiral ordered. "Okay, we'll do it your way, Captain. But if my marines start shooting, you can bet they won't stop with chiefs." Whitebred stormed off, leaving Mattim staring at Mary and her sergeant. Neither one looked too happy with the admiral's claim on "his marines."

A fresh-faced colonel ushered the major into a hall half the size of the 2nd Guard's drill field. Officers, most of them generals, milled about. Ray and Santiago stood stiffly, waiting to be told where their place was. *Here begins a whole different kind of combat.* General Vondertrip excused himself from a group and hailed Ray. "So glad you could make it. What with the situation on Wardhaven, the President may ask you quite a few questions."

"The situation is reaching critical." Ray carefully skirted the boundaries of treason. *Assuming they hadn't moved again.*

"Yes, but do not forget the most important part, my young

friend." As the general approached, his voice lowered. Beside Ray, his voice was little more than a whisper. "The offensive is what matters to the President. Wars are not won on the defensive. 'Attack, attack, always attack.' "

Ray glanced around. Like the general, most of the people within earshot were whispering. "Is that why the Navy has not come to the aid of Wardhaven?" he asked.

"You will get nowhere attacking the Navy. The President is tired of interservice rivalries. And yes, the Navy is up to its ears supporting three offensives. Wardhaven has thirty million men under arms. If you can not stop the Earth stooges with that, you don't deserve to breathe." The general's voice took on the accent and cadence of the President as he recited the often-repeated phrase.

"No line of brave infantry can stop a relativity bomb."

"Oh, that. You have heard that bit of bragging. So they have the space above you. They can do nothing until they land and meet us face to face. They dare not use their bombs. They are the ones with the vast populations and crammed industry. If they start such folly, we will bake them in their own pudding. The President has announced that they are only bluffing. In ten hours, you will see."

"Where should I sit? The briefing begins at one."

"No need to rush; the President is never here before two. He does not like anyone new sitting near him. Despite all our loyal protests, and the endless guards we must pass, he fears bombs. You will sit at the end of the table, but I have arranged for you to be across from him. You will have a good view."

"Thank you, General. I have never met the President, and my wife will want to know everything he does."

"Yes, I understand you are in the family way."

"Does anything move faster than a woman's whispered word?"

"Not even light, my young friend."

"Could you show me to my seat? I have prepared a briefing, as your letter asked. It would be a shame if your computer could not interface with mine."

"We have the latest system, but be careful. The President has a short attention span for briefings. You must give him the highlights quickly. If he begins to speak, sit down. Never interrupt."

"As your note said."

"Here is your place. I have never understood these machines. My mother always said if God had meant for us to have computers, we would have been born with one."

"I thought that was what our brain was," Santiago quipped to the general's departing back.

"I doubt the general believes in them either," Ray answered softly. "Can you plug us in?"

"It requires a physical hookup! Ancient technology. But there are several cables in the briefcase. Let me see."

"You do this. I will find the restrooms. My stomach." Ray began a quick walk across the marbled floor, hoping he could control his roiling gut long enough to find the necessary room. Death would come easy. Keeping his dignity was a fight.

Mary sat in her high-grav cart—enjoying herself. Dumont and his teams rushed up and down the launcher, looking over the shoulders of every sailor working on the accelerator. Every ten or fifteen minutes they'd denounce some worker as a saboteur. Mary and the damage control officer would motor over to review the case. The chief of the work party would explain what they were doing, and the commander would assure them that it was part of the critical upgrade of the system. Dumont began to smell a skunk with Gandhi always going last, so he demanded she go first and the accused chief go second. Either they were telling the truth, or chiefs were just as good at whoppers as Gandhi was. Either way, Dumont was none the wiser.

Mary had spotted a few untruths so far. That one about welding arcs needing to heat up the surrounding area was one of them. She'd learned how to weld in a nonunion shop. You keep a good, tight bead—the smaller the better. Yep, there was a whole lot of lying going on.

Dumont turned back from the latest fracas. "Damn it, folks, you got just as much to gain from this as we do. You." He pointed at a youngster, two slashes on his uniform. Mary took him for a Navy corporal of some sort. "You think what they teaching you in the Navy'll get you a job when this war's over? If you don't got a friend in a very high place, you'll be back in the street with the rest of us again."

"Hey, man, they drafted me and sent me to school for two months. I know enough to carry the petty officer's toolbox. I can't tell you what he's doing," the Navy kid answered—in too-perfect English. Mattim had told her how kids fresh out of college had helped him get his ship back home. She wondered what this kid's degree was in . . . and told Dumont nothing.

That was it, really. The admiral had the power of authority. The marines had the power of the gun. But Mattim and his crew had the power of knowledge. She and her miners had played their part. Lek had taken away the admiral's stranglehold on their tongues. They had come together. What were they creating?

Mary glanced around the launch bay. Did anybody know who was doing what? Come launch time, this bay was gonna be damn dangerous. *Mattim, you didn't want any more dead. Can you get this place evacuated?* Mary suppressed a snicker. Was Dumont smart enough to be very far away from here in—she glanced at her chronometer—eight hours?

Ray stared at the ceiling and struggled to control his gut. Three hours ago, the President had marched into the room in his bright red space marshal's uniform and began to orate. Watching him on vids, Ray had been mesmerized. Now he saw him in person; no wonder human space trembled when he shook his fist.

The power of the man's eyes, voice, body held Ray. The President was father, mother, lover—all at once. If Ray hadn't faced the harsh reality of death, the President would have held him in the palm of his hand.

But Ray had watched rockets from the wrong end. Ray had made the hard choices of life and death. Ray had chosen life, and today he was choosing death. While other officers in the room hung on every word, Ray eyed the man with a dispassion he suspected was rare.

In the three-hour rambling monologue that had yet to pause, there hadn't been one reference to the present situation. Still, no general interrupted.

Ray kept his face a worshipful mask. Inside he roiled. This was theater, nothing more. They were the audience, he the center stage. Once, a general had become more involved; he'd been singled out for his department's failure to reequip troops as the President wanted for an offensive that failed. He received the President's full attention for an hour, struggling to answer questions in the brief moments when President Urm paused to catch his breath. It ended only when the general collapsed and was carried out on a stretcher. A trained lifesaver would have begun immediate heart massage; the guards did nothing.

As Ray watched his President in action, the disgust that had grown over the last two months boiled. Men were fighting and dying, struggling to make real this man's dreams. Here, the man who should have provided cohesion and direction strutted about like an actor—a world-class actor, but an actor no less. Only the guards kept Ray from reaching for his briefcase.

Guards were everywhere: by the doors, behind the President, even roving around the table, assault rifles ready. The table remained as broad—and empty—as the plain the 2nd Guard had attacked across. If Ray was not careful, his attack across this table might be as much a failure. The monologue ended abruptly as the President turned and strode toward the exit behind him. "Restroom break, at last," General Vondertrip muttered. "Did I warn you to go light on the coffee? Did you see the President glance your way before he quit? You will be next."

"My stomach." Ray struggled to stand.

Santiago came to his aid. "The war wound," he said. "Where is the nearest restroom?"

"Oh, yes. I forgot. The nearest will be mobbed." The general looked around. "Try that exit," he said, pointing. "Take the first corridor on your left. It should not be too far."

The exit looked miles away; Ray marched as fast as his stomach and braces allowed. Gladly he would have traded this for an advance into battle.

"Hell of a situation when the can looks like heaven," he snorted when he'd reached his goal.

"Yes, sir." Santiago let go of his arm and retreated, briefcase in hand, to stand beside a sink. Ray closed the door—no lock. *Security everywhere for the President and you can't even lock the bathroom door!*

"Captain, comm here. We've got a general announcement from the government of Wardhaven due in a minute or so."

"Helm, open a view on the main screen." It showed a room full of reporters. Before them, a man in a green uniform spoke. "People of Wardhaven, we will never surrender."

"That cuts it," Mattim sighed. Between the government of Wardhaven and Whitebred, there was no middle ground. The *Sheffield* could shoot around the system forever. Sooner or later, a relief fleet would show up to drive them away, and the *Sheffield* was in no shape for a fight. They'd won the bet, but the other side was just thumbing their nose at them.

Bomb us or bugger off.

That wasn't the way it's supposed to be!

The door to the admiral's quarters opened. Whitebred grinned from his cart. "Six hours. Six hours and we show that bastard who's got guts and who doesn't." The door closed behind him. Whitebred had no problem; bomb them. The problem was Mattim's; if he didn't bomb them, what was he going to do?

SIXTEEN

HIS STOMACH UNDER control, but no less a pain, Ray began to struggle to his feet.

"Let me help you, sir." Santiago was back, the door pushed aside.

"I can do it myself," Ray snapped.

"Not today, sir." Santiago reached down and deftly removed the power supply from Ray's walker.

Ray collapsed back onto the stool. "What?"

"Quiet. Please, sir. We don't want anyone alarmed." The young officer came to attention, briefcase hanging from his left arm. "Thank you, Major, for giving me this chance. Tell Rita this is my gift to her and the baby. Make the peace worth all we've paid for it."

Santiago saluted, did a smart about-face, and marched out of Ray's view. Ray tried to get to his feet. Now the walker fought him. He was still trying when the explosion came.

Santiago marched down the corridor. In only a moment, he entered the briefing room. Keeping his cadence perfect, he marched for the table where everyone was gathering.

He felt no fear. If anything, he was elated. Ever since the major had shared the second combination, he had known this moment would come. The fleet orbiting Ward-haven settled any question of necessity for him. Rita's announcement this morning settled who would open the briefcase.

Using the confusion of people finding their seats, Santiago paused across from the President. Two guards immediately turned toward him, guns at the ready. "My President, my Major is indisposed at the moment. His war wound is not healing as quickly as he would wish. He has done a very brief presentation with pictures of the defenders of Wardhaven preparing to destroy the invading Earth scum. May I run it for you?" Santiago rested the briefcase on the table. He'd put the combination in during the stop at the restroom.

"Yes, yes." The President beamed. "I love to—"

Santiago flipped the case open. The President didn't have time to say what he loved.

Mattim glanced at the clock. Four hours 'til launch. He gritted his teeth. If he survived this, he'd be buying a new set of caps. At his elbow, his comm link beeped. "Captain, we've intercepted a message. It's confusing, but it sounds like there's been a bombing on Rostock and the President may have been killed or injured."

"Give me the raw feed," Mattim snapped.

"Yessir. Sir, we've got a coded message here from the admiral. He wants it sent to someone on Wardhaven."

"Wardhaven?" Mattim exchanged a frown with Ding.

"That's right, sir. Someone on our target."

"If the admiral says send it, send it." Mattim sighed and began reading the first message. According to it, President Urm could be dead, wounded, or on vacation. Mattim remembered why he rarely bothered reading the general news.

"What do we do?" Ding asked.

"What do we do with this mess, sergeant?" Two soldiers looked down at Ray. His gut was suddenly cold steel. Like so many other heroes, Santiago had died for him. Now these guards were about to shoot him rather than look at him.

"Just part of the rest of the mess." The sergeant eyed Ray. "This one's the visitor. Didn't we hear his wife's waiting in his car? See if you can put a call through. She'll be glad to hear he missed the . . ." Both soldiers glanced in the general direction of the great hall.

"How'd someone get by us?" the private asked.

"Sure it wasn't us?"

"But wouldn't the general have gotten us all out?"

"Rats leave the ship, people start thinking it's sinking. Besides, Red and Titra weren't exactly the general's favorites. Hey, you." The sergeant nudged Ray with the toe of his boot. "Ain't you done yet?" Both snickered.

Maybe Ray wasn't done just yet.

"Isn't he a cripple, or something?" the private asked. "Didn't walk too well when he came in. Metal detectors didn't like him, but the screens only showed what he was supposed to be wearing. Think his braces were bombs?"

"Naw, he's still got them on. Okay, Mister Major, looks like we'll have to take care of you. Hope you don't need your butt wiped, 'cause you ain't getting it by us. Let's take him to the car park. That ought to keep us out of worse details."

They lifted Ray none too gently. He barely managed to get his pants belted. As they reached the main corridor, they had to pause as a gurney was wheeled by. Medics and guards surrounded it. The front top half of the body was a bleeding pulp, but there was no mistaking the President's space marshal uniform. Santiago had succeeded.

At the limo, they tossed Ray into the back seat.

"This one yours?" they asked the driver.

"Oh, Ray, when I heard the explosion, I thought . . . I was afraid . . ." Rita's tears covered his face.

"Get them out of here. We got bigger problems."

The driver slowly wound his way past other parked cars, moving security rigs, and arriving emergency vehicles.

They were the only one going out. They might not have made it, but Rita had been memorable on the way in that morning, and now her tears and Ray's condition opened gates that might otherwise have remained closed. Thirty minutes after the explosion, Ray was being settled onto his bed.

Rita reached for the phone. "Give me the captain of the *Oasis* in orbit."

"Ma'am, calls are restricted to national security issues."

"This *is* a national security issue. I am Senior Pilot Longknife and I must speak to the captain of my ship."

"Yes, ma'am."

"Captain Rose" came quickly.

"Captain, there has been an explosion at the Presidential palace."

"How is the President?"

"I do not know."

"The President is dead." Ray cut the words hard. "I saw his body. He is dead."

"The major says he saw the President's body. He is dead."

"I will send a shuttle for you and the major immediately."

"Thank you," Rita said as the line clicked. There were words Ray wanted to say, but they were not for the listening mikes. Rita held him close, painfully tight. Ray began to shake. Once more he and death had brushed elbows. Once more others had done the dying for him. The future had damn well better be worth the lives paid for it.

Mattim jumped as his comm unit beeped. "Captain, we've got another message intercepted from Wardhaven's Beta jump gate transmitter. It's in the clear and very explicit. Some major saw the President's body. He's dead." Mattim eyed the admiral's door. Three hours until launch; the door stayed closed. The marines sat their posts.

"Comm, pass the message to the admiral. Keep me informed of planetary intercepts." Whitebred might reserve to himself the power to decide what the messages meant to them, but Mattim was damned if he would let himself stay in the dark.

Sooner or later, he would have to make his own decision.

The car, the shuttle, and the yacht were all waiting for them. They broke orbit only minutes before a hold was put on all traffic. The captain scorned his orders back to dock. "My planet is about to fight for its life, and you want to keep me tied safely up at your pier. I'm headed for the fight."

"We'll shoot," they threatened.

They didn't.

"We'll never get there in time," Rita sighed.

"We already have," Captain Rose assured her.

Admiral Whitebred rolled onto the bridge as the clock went to zero. "My ultimatum having expired and the Wardhaven government not having surrendered, you may fire, Captain."

"With the death of the President, things may be a bit confused," Mattim observed.

"So you've picked up those rumors. That's all they are, rumors. Probably started by someone to buy time. They have no more time. Launch, Captain."

A billion people had run out of time, and so had Mattim. Slowly, he studied the bridge crew, the admiral, and his guards. Their guns were pointed out. The younger three looked all too ready to use them. Mattim had played for time, and it had run out. Well, maybe not all of it. *It's not over until it's over.*

"Bomb accelerator, this is the captain."

"Standing by, sir," said Commander Gandhi. "I have a bombardment pattern ready. Passing it through to you."

"Main screen," Ding ordered. A green globe appeared to the left of the screen, a single dot to the right. Red vector arrows departed the ship. The globe grew as the arrows approached. In a matter of seconds, they covered it with red splotches.

"Very good." The admiral grinned.

"Commander, begin autoloading bombs now."

"Say again, sir. Your message is breaking up."

"Autoload bombs now."

"Sir, I can't follow you. Static is breaking you up."

Mattim glanced at Ding. "Comm," she said, "we're getting a complaint from damage control of static on our line to them."

"You're coming through five by five to us. Wait one while we check with them." The pause was hardly long enough to take a breath. "They had no problem talking to us. Sir, I've never had static reported on an internal comm line."

"You have now. Ding, you have the conn." Mattim headed his cart for the hatch. Whitebred followed on his bumper.

"OOD, you have the conn." The exec passed it along and joined the parade. *Now it ends*, Mattim thought to himself. *Now it all ends—but will it be with a bang or a whimper?*

Mattim did not give the order to start as he crossed the coaming into the launch bay. He waited until his parade had arranged itself facing launch control.

"Commander Gandhi, you may begin when ready."

"Beginning autoloading now, sir," she said immediately. There was a brief pause. "Autoloader is not responding, sir."

"What?" Whitebred yelled. "What do you mean? It's testing as fully operational. I've reviewed every report. I've . . ."

"We've thrown a breaker on the main bus. I got my chief working on it. Just a moment."

Whitebred was fuming. "This woman is stalling. First she says she can't hear us. Now she says a fully tested and operational weapon system isn't working. She ought to be shot."

"Just a moment, Admiral." Mattim interrupted the first time Whitebred paused for breath. "Bridge. Give me a slow count."

"Yes, s . . . on . . . tw . . . th . . ."

"Thank you, bridge." Mattim turned to Whitebred. "There's something major wrong with the electronics in this bay."

"But only to the bridge?" Whitebred wasn't buying.

Behind him, Mary studied the ceiling. The sergeant beside her looked around, hunting for someone. Guess sailors weren't the only ones opposing this launch.

"A bit strange, sir," Mattim agreed, "but this launcher was installed our last yard period and never tested."

"Hundreds of people have crawled all over it. Maintaining it, you told me." Red was rising on Whitebred's cheeks.

"Yes, sir," Mattim agreed. "But without operating it, we can't be sure. This first launch is its test."

"Captain," Gandhi interrupted softly, "we've recycled the breaker. It will not hold. We are replacing it. We have a spare standing by, but at three gees it will be risky."

"Captain," Whitebred snapped, "get this ship to one gee." Mattim so ordered.

"Sir." Commander Gandhi frowned. "That'll change all my trajectories. Will we be going back to three gees?"

Mattim raised a questioning eyebrow to the admiral. "No," he snarled. "We will stay at one gee for the launch." Mattim wondered how many sabots had depended on three gees for the sabotage. At least they could get out of the damn high-gravity carts.

"Sir," Gandhi said as she stood up, "I'll need access to the ship's full network to redo my calculations."

Whitebred was distracted as he undid his harness; for once, Mattim was not interrupting. "Bridge, we need all computing power down here."

"Yes, sir." A moment later the PA system announced, "Knock off all nonessential net access. Stand by to load priority assignment in thirty seconds." A minute later, the computer was happily chewing on the new trajectories.

Five minutes later all lighting went off on the left side of the launch bay. "What?" Whitebred squawked.

"Engineering," Mattim said.

"Ivan here. We just cut power to number three main so

they could pull a breaker. Is that a problem?" he asked innocently.

"No problem," Mattim assured him. Whitebred relaxed.

"Bridge here," blared from the PA. "We have a problem."

"Captain here. Yes?" Mattim said as Whitebred turned to face him.

"We just lost power to a third of the distributed network," they informed Mattim and the entire crew. "That crashed the project we had running. We tried a restart, but it's corrupted. We're purging it and will restart as soon as we can."

"Thank you," Mattim answered evenly.

"What's going on? This is sabotage!" Whitebred yelled.

"Sir." Mattim spoke softly, trying to sound reasonable. "We are attempting a major project with no planning. With all the complex subactivities we've got going here, even the best team is bound to have a few social errors. They're a good team, and they're improvising the best they can," Mattim concluded. They were a *damn* good team and they *were* improvising as best they could—just not in the direction Whitebred wanted.

In the next five minutes, they restarted the trajectory problem, but using only one third of the net in case it was necessary to take down the second main that also supported the launcher. The new breaker box came on line—and immediately popped. That started a slow walk down of all the power cables in the bay.

"I watched carts go up and down those cables. What the hell were they doing?" Whitebred demanded.

"Just what we're doing now. Testing and looking for any trouble," Gandhi answered. "But from a cart, there is only so much you can see. Our problem is not something the tests show."

It took fifteen minutes to find a bum tester unit. Its replacement quickly isolated the frayed insulation that popped the breaker. The autoloader powered up and stayed powered.

"Finally," Whitebred breathed in exasperation.

"Load first round in test mode," Mattim ordered. For once

Whitebred did not second-guess him. Maybe the guy was trainable. Mattim hoped not. The first round rolled slowly down a conveyor, hit the bumper at the end of the chute—and kept rolling as the bumper bent and broke. Work crews scattered.

"That's impossible." There was awe in Gandhi's voice. "That unit is grown from a single crystal. It can't break."

"Hope it's under warranty," Mary drawled. "Sergeant, have a team look at that for sabotage."

"I look at it first," Whitebred shouted.

As a chief and work party set about corralling two and a half tons of stray steel, officers took a look. The shards were wickedly sharp. As Whitebred examined it, Mattim glanced around. Well back in the crowd was his tiny middie. Beside her stood a young fellow in coveralls carrying a tool kit. Mattim remembered him; the guy with the Ph.D. Guns said he had a lot to learn. Material properties probably wasn't among the lot.

Just how much of this contraption is sabotaged?

Having seen enough, Whitebred drew himself up to his full height. "Well, commander, it's broke. Fix it."

"Sir, we don't *have* a replacement. It's not supposed to break. And if it does, only a yard can clean it up."

The admiral and the damage control officer stared at each other. Mattim did not want to see what Whitebred's next move would be. The damn sergeant was edging toward the admiral.

"If I may have Chief Aso out of the brig, sir, I think we can solve this," Mattim intervened.

"Sergeant, release him," Whitebred snapped.

Five minutes later, Aso reported.

"Chief, fix that," the damage control officer said.

For a half a minute, Chief Aso studied the problem; then he started bawling orders. Fifteen minutes later, shoring beams buttressed a new brake, and sand had been added to the chute to slow down the slide of the rounds.

"Ought to take care of it for now," the chief muttered.

"Captain, launch those bombs," Whitebred demanded.

"Commander, let's bring one out slow."

"Sir, my firing solution needs recalculation. I'm way past the initial launch point."

"Launch it, damn you!" Whitebred yelled.

"Recalculate," Mattim said at the same time.

"Launch," Whitebred repeated.

"Admiral," Mattim spoke slowly, "the solution is blown. We could miss the planet, hit one of our ships. Who knows?"

"Recalculate." Whitebred capitulated. "And make sure there's nothing else wrong with this damn thing. Commander, I want maintenance people over every inch of it. Sergeant, I want marines looking over every shoulder."

"Yessir" echoed all around.

As personnel scattered over the launch bay, Mattim found himself next to Mary. "Where'll it be safe to stand when that thing goes off?" she asked.

"Good question." Mattim doubted the usual answers had any value. "The autoloader could take your hand off. The acceleration tube'll be loaded with energy." He glanced around. "I suspect there's a reason for the shiny new handholds." The bay and launch control were lined with railings at waist height.

"I hadn't noticed them. Strange what people miss." They exchanged a smile. There were five crises as young marines demanded explanations from sailors for what they were doing. Whitebred was into those rows in a flash. Mattim, Mary, and Sergeant Dumont were right behind. The list of people Whitebred wanted shot if this didn't go right grew longer and longer.

Fifteen minutes later, they had a firing solution. Without orders, most of the work crews arranged themselves along the wall, handholds in reach. Only Whitebred and his pet Sergeant Dumont stood in the middle of the bay. "Fire, commander, and you're a dead woman if you fail me again," the admiral growled.

Sergeant Dumont pointed his assault rifle around the room menacingly.

"I'm just doing my job the best I can," Gandhi answered. "Launch one."

A mechanical rammer shoved a round forward into a cage of cables and metal. For a second, the ugly slug just sat there—then it began to move. The naked eye could follow it for only a second as it shot down the launcher rail.

Then all hell broke loose.

Monitor reviews would later show the round departing the track at midpoint and tearing a wide gash in the port side of the *Maggie D*, exactly as Mattim and Chief Aso had planned it. At the moment it happened, Mattim was busy holding on to keep from being sucked out by the air rapidly evacuating the launch bay. Any space this large in a starship had to be designed with this in mind. Even as Mattim struggled to hold, the ship acted. Doors sliced shut along the launcher, sealing the damage and holding in the fleeing air.

Unfortunately, it also sealed Whitebred and his favorite sergeant in as well. Before Mattim could get a report on the *Muggle*'s situation, Whitebred was screaming at the top of his lungs, "Shoot them. All of them. Shoot them all."

While Dumont looked around, trying to catch his bearings and decide whom to shoot first, Mattim and Mary hustled to put themselves in the line of fire.

"Don't be stupid," Mattim snapped. "You can't start shooting people when we've got a damaged ship to handle."

"Shoot them!" was all the answer he got.

"We won fair and square," Mary said softly to her sergeant. "Marines don't shoot marines."

"Fair and square," Mattim and Whitebred both echoed.

"You had full rein to search. You didn't catch them," Mary continued slowly.

"We caught them. We just couldn't make it stick."

"It's the same thing, Du."

"Shoot them!" Whitebred screamed.

"Captain!" blared from the speakers in the launcher bay. "Comm here, I have a message for you from Captain Ramsey of the *Sendai*. He has orders for you."

"I'll take it in my quarters," Whitebred shouted.

"It's not for you. It's for the captain. Putting it on the screen down there." The wall across from the launcher control lit up. There was Buck Ramsey.

"Matt, this message is for you. Whitebred is released from command and rank immediately. All his orders are countermanded. Skobachev will assume command. I repeat, Whitebred is no admiral and he gives no orders. The orders promoting him are being looked at real close. I know nothing about that. What I do know is I have official orders from the military commander at Pitt's Hope to return him immediately. I will wait for your response. We would have been here sooner, but I don't know how Sandy found that point so fast. We've spent the last three days trying to pin it down. By the way, I think the war is over. I will await your answer. Ramsey out."

"Wait one, comm," Mattim said, then turned to Whitebred. "I don't know what this is about, but it's over."

Like so many things lately, Mattim had that one wrong too.

"You bastard. You lying bastard." Sergeant Dumont was so enraged he ignored his rifle and went for Whitebred's throat with his bare hands. As Whitebred fended him off with one hand, his other went for the assault weapon.

Even in defeat, Whitebred still wanted to "shoot them all."

Mattim hardly saw her coming. Kat the Zap came in fast and low. One moment the two men were struggling; the next second they lay ten feet apart and the middie stood between them not even breathing hard. Whitebred was screaming, clutching his knee. When this was all over, Mattim wanted to know two things: how his crew poleaxed up the launcher, and how one tiny young woman put two men twice her size down so fast.

"Mr. Crossinshield, you have a problem."

Trevor gulped; when his client knew he had a problem before Trevor did, something had gone terribly wrong. Today, his client met him at the edge of a pond in a pleasant park. The noise of the city was held at bay, whether by the trees or more exotic means Trevor did not need to know. The big man fed crumbs to white swans. To Trevor, he fed gall. "You have been out of touch with your man, the one who knows the door to the galaxy."

"Yes, sir. He is in the Navy and does sometimes go aboard ship. Communications through those channels are often strained."

"Yes, but do you know where he is? I am picking up strange rumors. I do not like rumors, Mr. Crossinshield. I like facts."

From across the pond, two ebony black swans knifed through the water to scatter the white ones. Trevor's client smiled and tossed them corn as their reward. Trevor glanced around. From the path through the trees, three men emerged and walked toward them. The one in the lead looked straight ahead. The two behind him signaled. People whom Trevor would have sworn were part of his client's security detail nodded and began to close in.

His client continued to feed the swans, both black and white. "Sir." Trevor was surprised to hear himself squeak.

"Speak up, boy."

"Sir, I believe you have company."

His client turned. And maybe for a split second Trevor saw surprise on his face. Then he calmly turned back to the pond. This time, however, he tossed nothing to the swans.

"Good afternoon, Henry." The man paused to smile down at Trevor's client. "I thought I'd find you here. There are things we must talk about. If you gentlemen will leave us alone." The guards turned at his command—all of them— and returned to their alert meanderings.

Trevor turned to go. "Not you. You will stay."

"Edward, is that any way to treat one of mine?"

Trevor had not recognized the man with his clothes on. Now he did. This was the other man, the man who had locked horns with his client in the sauna—and lost. He did not act like a loser now. "Henry, the question is, is anyone yours?"

Trevor's client made no reply. The new arrival settled comfortably on the other end of the bench. Then he reached over, took the small sack of grain from Trevor's client, and began feeding the swans. Behind the bench, Trevor wanted to run, but his legs were water. Unable to stand, he risked leaning his hands on the back of the bench. Surprise filled Trevor; despite the power shooting between the two men, he was not electrocuted.

After upending the sack, the man spoke. "Henry, the dogs of this war you released are chewing up some very unhappy legs. Your President Urm has met with an accident."

Henry's usual aplomb vanished. His head jerked around to spear Trevor with hard, obsidian eyes.

"I have had nothing but normal reports about President Urm, sir."

"When the general holding your security contract on Urm failed so miserably, Trevor," Edward said, "he came looking for a new employer. We reached an agreement very quickly."

Henry's glare was for Edward, but there was enough heat along its edge to burn Trevor down to cinder.

"I must thank you, Henry. Your man in Pitt's Hope has succeeded most admirably for me. By threatening all life on Wardhaven, he has driven the colonials to send emissaries, real emissaries with authority to negotiate. And by showing the planetary governments just how easy their own bureaucracy is turned against them, you have gotten their attention. Attention we do not want, Henry. None of us."

"Governments are nothing!" Henry huffed.

Edward cut him off with a smile. "So you have said many times. We give the politicos money to buy the votes they need, but they still think those votes give them power. They are ready to turn that power to a scrutiny of us and this unpleasantness."

"I can handle them."

"Yes. Yes, you can. And we have decided to let you. But you will need time." Edward sounded so solicitous. "With your many duties, you might have problems squeezing in the time you will need. So, Henry, we have decided that you should step down from most of your positions on boards of directors. If you do not, you will be voted out."

"You can't."

"You will find in the next week that we have. Not all, Henry. I have gone out of my way for you. Two boards you will stay on. Ones I direct. It will be a pleasure to see you sit through meetings quietly listening while others hold the reins. Watch you squirm when you can't get enough votes to even wipe your own ass. Yes, Henry, you will be an interesting diversion."

"You have not seen the last of me," Henry hissed, getting to his feet.

"Of that I am sure, Henry."

Trevor's ex-client stomped away. Only two guards departed with him—the two that had come with Edward.

"Would you like a seat, Mr. Crossinshield?"

Trevor stumbled his way around the bench and sat on its edge; it felt more like a collapse. He awaited his fate.

"I don't hold Urm's death against your general. Henry failed to see the pressure building. We don't have nearly the power he thinks we have. You, however, are interesting. Initially, you provided Henry with information my own sources overlooked. That was good." Trevor risked a faint smile.

"In the end, however, Mr. Crossinshield, you failed."

"Words spoken, sir, are not always heard." Trevor tried a gentle gambit.

The man sighed. "Yes, that is the problem. Whose words to believe, the ones you want to hear or the ones you need to hear? Damnably tough call." For a long minute the man stared at the swans. "I will take you on, Mr. Crossinshield. At a reduced rate, mind you. We will all have to trim our budgets thanks to Henry. Some of your people are worth keeping."

"Mr. Whitebred?" Trevor risked.

"Failed miserably," Trevor's new client snapped, then seemed to rethink himself. Was that a personal trait, or was today a day for second thoughts? Trevor would wait and see. "However, his heart was in the right place. Find a window office for him. Who knows, he may yet do us a service." Then his brow darkened. "Those others, the ones who stopped him."

"Yes, sir."

"We can not have people like that succeed, even in stopping Henry's blunders. Sets a bad example. Find a hole and make them disappear."

"Yes, sir." The meeting was turning out far better than he had any right to expect. He hastened up the hill. He had work to do. It would be good to impress his new client quickly.

The fleet was gone by the time Mattim brought the *Sheffield* into orbit around Wardhaven. Shedding energy had taken them on a grand tour of the system. Repairs would take longer. Orbit was a wreck; the squadron had really shot up the place on its first pass. Parts of stations and ships drifted everywhere, but shuttles were already back, bringing workers, parts—and a station manager.

"Earthie Navy ship, respond."

"Let me handle this one. I know Owen." Mattim switched on his comm. "Owe, it's me, Matt. *Maggie D* looks a bit different, but she's still the same old girl under all this extra gear."

"I don't care who you are. While you wear that uniform, you don't park there. Back off five hundred klicks. One of your boats is waiting for you."

"Boss, I've been meaning to talk to you about your bad breath," Ding laughed.

"Can't get no respect. Thor, what's five hundred klicks back?"

"Old tub, looks rigged for passengers, but just barely."

"Comm, can you raise a transport aft of us?"

"On the line already, Captain. Putting him through."

"Captain Abeeb, I am ordered to relieve you of Captain Whitebred and Commander Stuart. I am also to take off your draftees and give them a lift home."

"I figured we'd be going back to Pitt's Hope together."

"I don't believe so, sir. My orders just relate to your junior personnel. I'll transmit your orders, now, but the scuttlebutt is that the *Sheffield* is too banged up. She's being scrapped."

"Scrapped!" Sandy howled.

"You got to be wrong," Mattim assured him.

"Could be, sir. They're your orders. Read them."

Mattim did. "He's right. They're scrapping the old girl."

"Her engines are in great shape," Ivan roared as he came on the bridge. "Call 'em and tell 'em they're wrong."

Mattim tapped his board. "Comm, get me the port master."

"You got him."

"Owe, this is Matt, I need to send a message to Navy Command, Pitt's Hope."

"Who's paying?"

"Didn't the squadron set up an account at the armistice?"

"Yeah, and closed it when they left. You want to make a call, get me your charge code."

"You think they'd take a collect call?" Sandy asked.

Whitebred limped onto the bridge surrounded by three guards, including the tiny middie. "I want to get my personal effects. I understand there's a liner here to take me home." Mattim pointed to the transport on screen. "That? It's no bigger than an admiral's barge. Well, at least I'll have it to myself."

"You and three quarters of the crew."

"What? I will not be surrounded by a sea of . . . of . . ." Whitebred quit hunting for words.

Mattim grinned as he sputtered down. "You'll also go with only the brig suit you're wearing. I've got your gear under seal until a criminal investigator goes over it. Security, get this man off *my* bridge." They did, none too gently.

"Ding, pass the word to all hands. This may be the only ride home. Anyone wants on that transport, we will find space."

That led to a lot of griping, from Whitebred, from the transport's captain, and from the crew that got shoehorned into it. It took a day to load them all out. Zappa showed up halfway through the drill. "Sir, do we have to go?"

"May be the only ride for a while."

"Yes, sir, but we'd like some time to look over our raw data on that little excursion. We got the fixings for some great papers. If we could take the time now, while we're still together, to get everything in order, we could hit the journals like a ton of cement."

So the *Sheffield* or *Maggie D* or whatever she was today settled down in orbit. Without a station to swing her, there was no way to put gravity on the ship. What was usually only a momentary inconvenience became the norm. To the old hands, both Navy and merchant, it was something to adapt to. To the kids, it was fun. Part of the ship took on the look of a university, though one run by the students. The rest did what needed doing to keep the ship going. To some she might be scrap; to her crew, she was home. She'd taken care of them through some rough times; they wouldn't abandon her now.

SEVENTEEN

THE THIRD DAY, the port master called. "Hey, you squatter over there. We got orders to open that hulk to space and kill all the vermin. We're sending a couple of shuttles to lift you out. Be packed and ready. And pack lightly you hear."

"Owe, this is Matt. You've inspected the *Maggie D* a dozen times. You never found one bug. Hassan's baking up a batch of his focaccia bread. Come over for a loaf or two."

"Hassan's!"

"Yep. Even zero-gee baked, it tastes great."

"Damn it, Matt, I got my orders. You folks got to go."

"Can you give me an extra couple of days?"

"You really got some of Hassan's focaccia bread?"

"Three loaves are yours." Mattim rang off on that promise.

"What we gonna do, sir?" Ding asked.

"What's the Book say?" he asked.

"Nothing in the Book, sir, about being marooned on your own ship as it's going under the breaker's torch."

"Yeah." They'd won their battle and their war. They were alive and in one piece. So why didn't it feel so good?

That night, as had become their custom, all hands shared

supper on a single mess deck. With mostly officers and chiefs left aboard, and the middies falling somewhere in between, there seemed little reason to keep the crew divided along arbitrary lines. The eviction was news to no one as they settled in to their meal. They chewed Hassan's delicious rations and their future. The chow was good—the future lousy.

"We save the life of everyone on this planet and this is what we get?" seemed to say it for all. Finding a way home across half the galaxy was easy compared to finding a way through two bureaucracies bent on . . . what?

"What do they want?" Ding asked. "We're here. We've got no money for food or fuel. We can't call home. This is crazy. I always knew the ship I was on might be lost in battle, but lost in filing . . ."

"Matt, we got any credit on the Red Flag Line?" Sandy asked.

"Folks, Ding and I have tried everything, legal or no. We had some charge codes left over from our merchant days. Tried them. They're not valid. Tried our navy charge codes. All canceled. I even tried my own personal charge accounts. Funds are unavailable."

"I tried mine too," Ding added. "Same answer."

"We don't exist," Chief Aso said.

"You must have pissed a lot of people off—big time," Sergeant Dumont put in snidely.

"Can think of five or fifty, but all of them getting together to get me . . ." The miner/marine Lek shook his head.

"You and me both, friend." Mattim summed it up.

After supper, Mattim started an inspection walk; in zerogee it was more a drift. He soon found Mary beside him. "I thought your marines would have headed back on the transport," he said.

Mary laughed. "To what? Nobody wants us. Miners got no jobs. Dumont and his kids never had a decent one. Why go back? First day of shooting we were kind of hoping the colonials would ask us to surrender so we could get it over with quickly."

"Did they?"

"Nope. Killed a couple of us, and that didn't leave much room for talk. Listen, you were trying charge numbers. I got a couple with miner's money in them. Can we check them out?"

They did. Nothing.

Ray collapsed on the blanket under the trees. He'd spent an hour on the bars and walked all the way out here, just him and the damn canes. Of course, the braces helped. He was starting to like them.

Rita was wearing that sundress. Rather, one of them. He'd had to marry her to discover she had half her closet full of sundresses. He wondered how long the dress would stay on, and quietly prayed it would for a while. He was exhausted.

The dress was halfway off when a voice called, "Daughter, are you decent? I have someone to talk with you and Ray."

The dress came back on as Rita sat up cross-legged beside him. "We're over here, Father, and yes, we're decent."

Ernest appeared a minute later. He and the spy each carried a pair of lawn chairs. It took a moment for them to arrange themselves, Rita in a chair beside Ray, her hem pulled down demurely below her knees. The industrialist and the spy master were directly across from them. "Colonel, I want to thank you personally," the fat man began, "for saving all our lives. Earth would have pounded us, and Urm would have done nothing."

"Colonel?" Ray asked.

"A well-deserved promotion on your retirement," Ernest advised him.

Ray was familiar with "tombstone promotions": he winced. "Santiago earned the promotion. He's the one who saved us."

The spy shook his head. "You had the invitation. You got the bomb past the guards. If we had not had your war wound to hide behind, and you willing to walk in front, the bomb would still be sitting in what was left of my office."

Ray let that pass into silence. He still wasn't sure how he felt about it all. For a long minute nothing was said. Then the spy master went on. "The government is in shambles as we weed out the worst of the Unity thugs. Wardhaven is better off than many planets. We still have much of the previous government in place. Still, how do we come to terms with the nightmare of the last two years?" Ray had no idea; why did he have a suspicion he was about to learn? The fat man went on.

"You, Colonel Longknife, are something rare today. As a soldier, you fought for us. And, as a soldier, you fought against Unity. That makes you special."

"As a soldier, I lost my battle," Ray growled.

"And we lost the war. Still, you fought honorably and are much admired. We need men like you in the government."

Ray was shaking his head before the spy finished. "I'm a soldier. I fight an enemy. I'm not a politician. In case you don't remember, the one time I met one, I tried to kill him."

Ernest was grinning. "I told you he'd say that."

The spy nodded sourly. "Yes, you did. But your daughter said he had his price. We just have to offer him the right bribe."

"Wife," Ray said, turning on his bride. She was grinning from ear to ear. "What did you tell them?"

"Just that the job had to be one you could sink your teeth into. One that would make for a better tomorrow for our child." She played her ace, patting her not yet swelling belly. "One that would let you oversee the ships going out to explore the universe."

"Colonel Longknife," the spy began, "I have been asked by those who are forming the new government to ascertain if you would be willing to accept the post of Minister of Science and Technology."

"Science and Technology," Ray echoed. "Never heard of it."

"A new position," Ernest answered. "You can make of it what you want."

"Think of it, Ray." Rita was at his knees, hands playing along his thighs. Lately, he'd gotten feeling back there. "Science and Tech is our chance to get the rim worlds moving. No more waiting for Earth or someone else to come up with new ideas. Wardhaven is halving its defense budget. That money can go into R&D. Think of what we can do."

Ray had the distinct feeling that he might be wearing the minister's sash, but he knew who would be running his office.

"And we get ships," she finished. "The new Bureau of Scouting and Exploration will report to us." Her grin was so wide, the edges had disappeared around the back of her head.

"Think we can hire the ship that came back from the sour jump?" he asked her.

"Why not? It's in orbit above us and its crew, or the best part of it, is still aboard."

Long ago, Longknife had learned not to accept gift horses. He turned to the spy. "What's going on?" he growled.

The spy was a long time answering. He took out his sniffers and made a long show of confirming the area secure. "You recall the young woman who made your first briefcase go pop when it should have gone boom? Well, we have been looking into her employer very carefully. Especially since we intercepted a frantic call from a group of her comrades to the ship that was about to relativity bomb Wardhaven, asking to know where would be safe. Those who want money are frequently unwilling to die for an unspent bank account.

"We intercepted another hasty communication out of Rostock shortly after the President was pronounced dead. It seems that the head of his security detail was also double-dipping."

"Earth," Ray breathed.

"Not Earth government, or any other planetary government. Rather an association of likeminded power brokers."

"I've dealt with some of them," Ernest sighed. "Never knew it, but I was."

"Urm was their puppet!" Rita was incredulous.

"No." The spy shook his head firmly. "Urm created himself, and we cannot shirk our own responsibility for willingly selling our souls to him. We have no one to blame for this nightmare but ourselves. Let us say that Urm was greedy, and where greed rules, one is never sure who is leading and who is following.

"What matters to you is that the ship of exploration was to be the ship of our execution. And just as it refused to stay lost, it refused to slaughter us. Now, it is more lost, not in space but in a black hole of bureaucratic creation. Powerful men want it to stay lost. What do you say?"

"I say we've got a job for them." Rita and Ray spoke in unison.

"Not wise, but then, I myself am feeding the information from my investigation back to Earth. It will be interesting to see how their elected officials react to it. With luck, our mutual friends will be too busy to notice one ship escaping from their black hole."

They were halfway through breakfast when Zappa came flying into the mess deck, "I got e-mail from Mom," she squealed.

"Well, at least a mother's love can find us," Ding muttered.

As Mattim finished his tube of porridge, Zappa grabbed a handhold on his table. "I asked one of the kids going home to tell my folks I was all right. Mom's paid for a reply. What should I tell her?"

The speaker came alive. "Comm for the captain. We got message traffic from a ship that just jumped in-system."

THE FIRST CASUALTY · 321

"Things are looking up." Mattim grinned. "Put it on screen down here. No use making the troops wait for the rumor mill."

"Mat, this is Elie Miller. I've been mustered out, and I wanted to get back in touch with you. Had a lousy time finding you, but I remembered that girl from your ship, Zappa. Her folks told me she was still on Wardhaven. Andy is retiring and looking for new fields. I've still got six months of a sabbatical left, so I'm in no rush to get back. Thought we might team up. A couple of old tugboat captains at Pitt's Hope offered us a fast ride to Wardhaven. They look like pirates or smugglers to me, but we took them up on the offer. We're in-system. Do you still have all the kids with you? Over."

He glanced around the room. Every eye was on him, kids, marines, both Navy and merchant crew. "Right now we're having problems with our credit chits. People who get too close to us suddenly have their bank accounts unavailable and their credit numbers lost. The kids are still here. They've set up their own university. Over."

"Andy figured there was trouble when we couldn't find you anywhere on net. He and I bulletproofed our money before we took off. See you soon. Bye."

There were cheers among the middies, and back-pounding that led to some interesting twists in zero gravity. "Make enough friends," Sandy said with a grin, "somebody's bound to look you up."

"Comm here. We got a message from the port captain. There's a buyer that wants to look the ship over. Shuttle due here in thirty minutes."

Ding snorted. "Make enough enemies, and they're bound to hunt you down, too."

"This doesn't feel right," Ivan growled. "Selling a warship to the enemy. I mean, just been enemy . . . You know."

Ding shook her head. "Strange, but not unusual. Peace breaks out, wrecks get scrapped where they lay."

"The *Maggie*'s no wreck." Mattim gnawed his lower lip. "She's a crime scene and a working warship. I don't like this." He turned to Mary. "I'd like to prepare a reception for whoever it is who thinks they can buy a ship out from under me. You and yours game?"

Mary took in her marines. She liked what she saw. "Yeah."

Rita piloted the shuttle. Before docking with the *Sheffield,* she did a turn around her. Most of the ice was gone. One raw gash showed along the port side. Whatever had caused it had started inside. Ray had read the classified reports on the way up. He hated mutiny.

He hated genocide worse.

Things must have gotten lively aboard that boat.

Rita docked them with a gentle bump. Glad to leave his canes behind, Ray went hand over hand to the exit. He led, she followed. Rita's newly hired driver, an ex-corporal from the 2nd Guard, trailed them, his hand in his coat. So their fellow was armed.

Ray froze at the door. Drawn up along the back of the bay was a welcoming committee—damn near a platoon of marines in full battle gear. Left arms anchored them to a cable. Right arms held assault weapons at the ready.

Lines crisscrossed the bay. Out of the marines' line of fire to his left, a collection of naval officers drifted in formation. Ray squelched the automatic reaction to render honors as was appropriate when boarding ship; he was not in uniform. He pushed himself forward. "Mighty nice of you to meet us," he said.

Mattim wasn't quite sure what he expected. The show of force was just that, a show. If it came to a fight, he'd surrender before firing a shot. Still, he wouldn't give up the ship without a try at bluffing his way through. The *Maggie* was still a good merchant ship, dinged a bit, needed some work, but a quick and easy conversion back to what she'd been. She was also a very deadly warship.

The man who lead the "buyers" was military to the core, back ramrod straight even as he came aboard hand over hand. Mattim spotted the flickering start to rendering honors before it was aborted. The woman behind him was beautiful in a pilot's jumper, sporting military rank he did not recognize. Her he recognized. When last he'd seen her, she'd been a happy kid, showing him around her father's gardens. Hers had been one of the faces on the bombs he refused to deliver. The last man aboard screamed bodyguard both by his carriage and by the hand in his jacket pocket. Mattim moved to meet them; the three newcomers halted in place. With Ding and Mary at his back, Mattim quickly blocked their way.

"I am Captain Mattim Abeeb, licensed merchant officer and commissioned officer of the Society of Humanity Navy, presently commanding this ship, *Sheffield*." Okay, ape, let's pound our chests and see who runs.

"I am Ray Longknife, formerly of the Second Guard Brigade. This is my wife, Senior Pilot Officer Rita Longknife and her driver, also formerly of the Second. It seems I am to be offered Minister of Research and Technology in the next government for Wardhaven. My wife thinks we need a ship." The man didn't bat an eyelash as he laid his cards face up on the table. Not a bad hand, Mattim concluded.

"Seems like you need a yacht more than a beat-up light cruiser," Ding snapped.

Mattim pointed behind him. "This is my Executive Officer, Commander Colin Ding, and the commander of the marine detachment, Captain Mary Rodrigo, formerly of the Ninety-seventh Defense Brigade."

That brought raised eyebrows from the "buyers." "Were you at the pass the first day?" Longknife asked.

Mary nodded. "We did what we had to."

Longknife's eyes took on a distant smile. "I'd like to hear your story, Captain. Could I buy you a drink sometime?"

"Be glad to, but I'd much prefer you didn't buy this ship out from underneath me, sir," Mary quipped, and brought them to the heart of the matter.

"I don't know what you've heard about us." Mattim's

words were soft, but he poured as much power through them as Ivan pushed out his engines. "But we are not traitors. We may have drawn the line at bombing a billion civilians, but turning over an operational warship to Unity is not on the same side of the line. We've shown we know how to wreck a ship. We'll make sure it's nothing but scrap if we have to."

Rita looked around, almost lovingly. "I've lost one ship this war, I'd hate to cause the loss of another one. Especially one that's gone so far." That got Mattim's attention.

"Yes," Mr. Longknife said, "we intercepted your message to the Ninety-seventh about the sour jump, or rather my wife did. I've never seen her so excited. I have not let my wife talk me into a political post so others can use me for a figurehead. Once upon a time, I was a damn good soldier. And I promised a dead man I'd make the future worth all the lives that paid for it. I think opening up the universe would meet his specs."

"A billion stars just waiting for us." The woman smiled and patted her stomach. "What a present for our child."

Longknife held out his hand. "My friends call me Ray. The ship will have to haul cargo to keep us from going too far into the red. I need an experienced merchant skipper and crew."

Mattim looked at the hand. "If I'm going to be wandering the stars, never sure of what I may stick my nose into, I'll need more than the usual crew." He slipped aside and left the stranger facing Ding and Mary.

Longknife took the measure of the two of them. "I don't expect you to go looking for a fight, but good gunners and good troops can come in handy a lot of places. What do you say?"

Ding's answer was quick. "We're ready now, sir."

Mary glanced around at her marines. "It beats the last job we had. Sure is a damn sight more interesting."

Mattim reached for his new employer's hand. "My friends call me Matt."

"We get to go jump point hopping!" Zappa crowed from among the middies.

Sandy chuckled. "I wonder what we'll find out there? Or who?

STEVE PERRY

__THE TRINITY VECTOR
0-441-00350-8/$5.99

There were three of them...strange silver boxes, mysterious devices which individually could give you tomorrow's weather, or tomorrow's winning lottery number. Three people, each with a piece of the puzzle. Three people with nothing to lose. And everything to gain...

__THE DIGITAL EFFECT
0-441-00439-3/$5.99

Gil Sivart is helping a young lady whose boyfriend put his head in a stamping press. The Corporation calls it suicide. His lady friend calls it murder. And now Gil has to flush it out, level by level—before his discreet inquiries get him permanently spaced without a suit...

THE MATADOR SERIES
__THE ALBINO KNIFE	0-441-01391-0/$4.99
__BROTHER DEATH	0-441-54476-2/$4.99

Prices slightly higher in Canada